Wish You Were Here (Instead of Me)

Brawl of the Worlds 2

Frank Tayell

Reading Order & Copyright

Where we've been is never as important as where we're going.

Brawl of the Worlds 2: Wish You Were Here (Instead of Me)
Published by Frank Tayell
Copyright 2023
ISBN: 9798397387811
All rights reserved

All people, places, and events are entirely real, though some names have been changed to protect alien hermits currently hiding on Earth.

Science Fiction
Brawl of the Worlds 1: First Contact
Brawl of the Worlds 2: Wish You Were Here
Work. Rest. Repeat.

Strike a Match - A Post-Apocalyptic Detective Series
1. Serious Crimes, 2. Counterfeit Conspiracy
3. Endangered Nation, 4. Over By Christmas, 5: Thin Ice

Surviving The Evacuation / Here We Stand / Life Goes On
Book 1: London, Book 2: Wasteland, Zombies vs the Living Dead
Book 3: Family, Book 4: Unsafe Haven, Book 5: Reunion
Book 6: Harvest, Book 7: Home

Here We Stand 1: Infected, Here We Stand 2: Divided

Book 8: Anglesey, Book 9: Ireland, Book 10: The Last Candidate
Book 11: Search and Rescue, Book 12: Britain's End, Book 13: Future's Beginning
Book 14: Mort Vivant, Book 15: Where There's Hope
Book 16: Unwanted Visitors, Unwelcome Guests

Life Goes On 1: Outback Outbreak, 2: No More News
3: While the Lights Are On, 4: If Not Us, 5: No Turning Back

Book 17: There We Stood, Book 18: Rebuilt in a Day
Book 19: Welcome to the End of the Earth
Book 20: Small Cogs in the Survival Machine

For more information, visit:
www.FrankTayell.com
www.facebook.com/FrankTayell

First Contact So Far
20th August 2022, Four Days After First Contact

A man in a suit so deeply black it seemed to absorb the soft glare from the streetlights, and a woman in blue and green motorbike leathers, gloves, and a helmet whose visor was currently down, strolled along the terraced street of Harbour View, Cobh.

"Evening," the besuited man, Sean O'Malley, said to an elderly couple, then repeated it to the Gardaí officer sipping a mug of tea outside number five.

"No visitors unless you're expected," the police officer said.

"Over to you, dear," Sean said.

The woman slid the visor of her helmet up so the officer could see the grey skin beneath. "I'm Greta tol Hakon, chief of security for this solar system, and I'm pleased to meet you." She held out her hand, but the officer was too busy staring at her face to notice it.

"What's your name, lad?" Sean asked.

"T... T... Tony Cullen."

"I'm Sean O'Malley. She's here on official business, but we're trying to keep it a little quieter than on her first visit."

The officer finally managed a nod and stepped aside.

"Nice house, and with a bit of a sea view," Sean said. "You know, I think this used to be where old Mr Donovan lived."

"Can we reminisce later?" Greta said. "This motorbike helmet is pinching in all the wrong places."

Sean rang the bell. Heavy feet ominously clumped to the door. It was opened by a scowling man in sauce-stained chef whites who was brandishing a long knife.

"Why did you ring the bell?" the chef demanded as if no viler act had ever been committed.

"Hello, Padraig. I'm Sean O'Malley, and we're related."

"You might know me," Greta said, sliding her helmet's visor up again to reveal her grey face.

Padraig dropped the knife. It speared the carpet and thunked into the floor, vibrating almost in time with his opening and closing mouth.

"Can we come in?" Sean asked.

Padraig slowly nodded. He stepped back, regained his composure, and called for the cousin with whom he shared the house. "Niamh, there's people!"

"It's a nice home you have," Sean said as he stepped into the brightly painted hall.

"It's not mine," Padraig said. "It's Niamh's mother's, my aunt."

Greta pulled the knife from the floor so she could close the door. Thus, when Padraig's cousin, Niamh O'Keefe, came out of the living room and saw a knife-wielding motorcyclist, it was only natural that she screamed.

"Sorry, sorry, it's me," Greta said, putting the knife in the letter rack on the nearby table so she could remove her helmet and reveal her grey face and straw-yellow hair streaked with blue.

"You," Niamh managed.

"It's the alien," Padraig said unnecessarily.

"I can see that," Niamh said. "Hello. What's happened? Is something wrong?"

"We're here to offer you a job," Sean said. "Both of you. Perhaps we could sit down?"

"Of course. Come in," Niamh said and gestured towards the living room. Sean and Greta stepped into a room mostly furnished with stout. Pallets of canned beer were stacked against each wall, beneath the table, and in front of the armchair where, with a cushion on top, they were being used as a footstool.

"Are you planning a party?" Greta asked.

"It's crowded enough already in here," Padraig said, having retrieved his knife before following them in.

"Would you put that knife where it belongs?" Niamh said. "Every brewery in the land sent beer in case you were to visit again. Help yourself, please."

"As much as I'd love to, we're on the clock," Sean said.

"Sorry, who are you?"

"Sean O'Malley. I'm a distant cousin of yours. Of both of you," he added as Padraig returned, this time empty-handed.

"Is it tea, or is it coffee?" the chef asked in a tone that suggested there was a correct answer and an answer which would have him return with the knife.

"Tea, please," Greta said.

"D'you have tea in space?" Niamh asked.

"Of a sort. Most food is synthesised. Printed, in effect."

"D'ya have milk?" Padraig asked, each syllable laden with menace.

"Cows are unique to Earth," Greta said. "But there are plenty of other quadrupeds."

"In your tea! D'ya have milk in your tea?"

"Oh, no, thank you," Greta said.

"Sorry about Padraig," Niamh said as the chef stomped to the kitchen. "The part of his brain which processes manners is instead filled with recipes."

"He's not the first in our family like that," Sean said.

"How have things been for you since we last met?" Greta asked.

"Swings and roundabouts, and seesaws, too," Niamh said. "They've restricted the number of visitors to Cobh and have kicked out most of the press. I'm a teacher, and I had a lot of parents, and some colleagues, complain about the lesson me handing you a pint sends. I said that since it wasn't a lesson I was being paid for, it was none of their business, but that only made things worse. On a sunnier note, the bidding for my life's story has reached six figures."

"Don't accept anything less than eight," Sean said. "I think your story is about to get much more interesting. Are you still teaching?"

"I am. The children need the routine now that everything is so chaotic. So do I."

Padraig brought in a tray with a teapot, four cups, and a tray of freshly baked cakes.

"You'll eat these," he said with utter certainty.

"When we first met, you didn't speak," Niamh said. "Your accent is Irish, and the other... the other towani, the man who gave the television interviews, his is German."

"It's all to do with from whom we learned the language," Greta said. "I learned it from Sean. The ambassador, Johann, learned English and German from a German archaeologist."

"Johann's not an alien name," Padraig said.

"He took the name Johann soon after he settled here. He is Johann tol Davir. Tol means formerly known as. I am Greta tol Hakon. My brother is Gunther tol Dannan. Most Valley citizens who visit this system take an Earth name."

"The ambassador, in his interview, said you're descended from Neanderthals," Niamh said.

"We are. Fifty thousand years ago, five tribes of Neanderthals were enslaved. The legend, the scripture, says that they volunteered to leave so that the other members of the species would be spared annihilation. They were put aboard five ships controlled by monstrous beings who wore the vessels like they were armour. For a thousand years, our ancestors were bred as warrior slaves. Some think those captors might have genetically altered our DNA."

"And turned you grey?"

"Probably not. We think that occurred after our ancestors settled on Towan I. For a thousand years, they fought. We don't know who. We don't know why. But, eventually, they rebelled. Nowan, the first prophet, led the rebellion. After the battle, four of the ships were deliberately crashed on a habitable planet in that system, which they named Towan I in honour of the prophet. The fifth ship, captained by Nowan, left the system in search of our ancestral home."

"You mean here, Earth?" Niamh said.

"Did he find it?" Padraig asked.

"They. Nowan was non-binary. Many of our people were and are. Our ancestors developed very different social structures during their enslavement in deep space, where they could be moved from cell to cell or ship to ship, without warning. But no, Nowan was never heard from again. Some think they returned to their ancestral home, and searching Earth for evidence of the ancient ship will be a priority for our scientists. Those who crashed their ships on Towan I put everything they had into building new spacefaring vessels. They

4

had to develop mathematics, farming, metallurgy, computing, and so much more. What they didn't learn until it was too late was what environmental damage this rapid industrialisation would wreak. After a few hundred years, and we're not sure how many, they were able to return to the stars, but Towan I was, by then, uninhabitable."

"It still is," Sean added.

"They began looking for a new home," Greta said. "Instead of finding one new habitable planet, they found many, and some were occupied. Our ancestors hadn't forgotten their violent past, and so created a planet-spanning empire. They called their new homeworld Towan II. Empires rise, and empires fall, and so did theirs. Towan II was devastated by war. A different imperial family rose to power and selected a new planet as the new capital, Towan III, which remains the capital today."

"But it's not an empire anymore?" Niamh said. "Didn't the ambassador tell the reporters it was a federal democracy?"

"It is, though our politics is a little more complicated than that. Our federation is called the Valley and comprises two hundred and forty-seven inhabited star systems, many of which have many nations. There are many independent asteroids, moons, and space-stations, too, but democracy, in one form or another, is a pre-requisite for membership of the Valley."

"Then Earth won't be able to join," Niamh said.

"It will, in time," Sean said.

"A few thousand years ago, a terrible plague wiped out the entire imperial family and billions of others. Four of the most powerful families declared a regency. They created a council with five members. Each member represented one of the five tribes."

"You said four families. Four is never the same as five," Padraig said.

"Yes, because one seat on the council was reserved for the lost tribe, the descendants of Nowan. The council allowed any citizen who wished to propose a change in legislation to submit it. With only four on the council, two would always vote for a proposal, and two would vote against it. In the event of a tie, the status quo remained. Under the regents, nothing ever changed. Progress stalled. From spaceship design to taxation, unless it directly benefited the regents, very little happened. The regents were autocratic, tyrannical, and unjust. This sowed the seeds for the revolution."

"Yes, because the ambassador said that happened in 1888," Niamh said.

"Which is where and when I enter the story," Sean said.

"Who are ya?" Padraig asked.

"I'm your uncle."

"You're not," Niamh said.

"I was born in 1868."

"Get away!"

"I'm nearly two hundred," Greta said. "Johann, the ambassador, is over seven hundred, which is old, even for towani. Our ancestors cracked cellular rejuvenation technology millennia ago. We think it was developed on Towan I from equipment from those original starships."

"When I was still just a kid, I went to London to seek work," Sean said. "My older brother, Liam, was married to Maeve, and they had three children. Two girls and a boy. Liam died. Maeve remarried and took her new husband's name, and changed that of her children. Her second husband was Peter O'Keefe."

"You're the soldier!" Padraig said.

"I have been," Sean said. "On Earth and in space."

"I didn't say *a* soldier. I said *the* soldier," Padraig said testily. "Our grandfather told me a story he'd heard from his grandfather, about Pierre O'Keefe, the first baker. He said the first bakery was paid for by money sent home from a soldier named Sean, fighting in Africa against the British Empire."

"That's mostly true," Sean said. "Except the seed money came from selling the family's boat, I wasn't fighting the British Empire, and I wasn't in Africa. In 1888, I'd been working as a general assistant to the Earl of Lenham. I'd returned here, to Queenstown as it was then called, to bury my parents, but a storm delayed the ship, and I missed the funeral. I'd also come back to see if Maeve, a widow, needed support. But she needed no help from me and had no intention of leaving her bakery, which was already thriving. Feeling out of place in the town I once called home, I borrowed a boat and took it out onto the water, trying to rekindle some of my childhood memories. That's when Greta's spaceship fell out of the sky."

"He came to my aid," Greta said.

"Sailors always do. Johann picked both of us up in his ship. I was taken aboard, and while they bandaged a few cuts, they checked my DNA. It told them that I was a cousin and that the people of Earth were distant relatives."

"Why did your ship crash?" Niamh asked.

"Before he was officially a prophet, Johann was an advocate," Greta said. "The position combined the roles of a police officer and a judge, serving the outlying settlements. One day, he fined a man for speeding. In retaliation, this man murdered everyone in our family except for Johann, me, and my brother. This murderer was the great-nephew of a regent. The case was deliberately botched. The killer walked free. Johann, my brother, and I were exiled to a new colony on a barely habitable world. That was the trigger for Johann to begin planning the revolution."

"So the ambassador is your grandfather?" Niamh asked.

"You can add quite a few 'greats' to that, but he raised Gunther and me as a father, and that's how I think of him. Gunther infiltrated the military and rose to the rank of general. I became an advocate. We weren't the only victims of the regency's unjust rule, so we had no difficulty recruiting others to the cause. It took decades, but we were eventually ready to strike. We wanted the revolution to be triggered by a public demonstration of the corruption we wished to overthrow. We decided to arrest the murderer, take him to the capital, and demand justice we knew would be denied. The regents' order to release the killer would be the cue for the revolution to begin. We chased this murderer through many star systems, and eventually to Earth, but we arrived a few months after him. Our arrival triggered his attempt to escape. We fought in the skies, and he shot me down, but I was able to damage his ship so he couldn't flee."

7

"After they brought me aboard, they tasked me with finding him," Sean said.

"You were hunting an alien on Earth?" Niamh said.

"It *was* the first time, but it wasn't the last," Sean said. "The killer had been on Earth only a few months but had killed five women, leaving their bodies mutilated. The press had come to call him Jack the Ripper."

Padraig dropped his cup.

"Jack the Ripper was an alien?" Niamh asked as she helped Padraig mop up the spilt tea.

"He was. I tracked him to Whitechapel, and I killed him."

"We'd wanted him alive," Greta said. "But by then, it didn't matter. We'd found Earth, our ancestral home. We decided to reveal Sean as a way to start the revolution. We took the long route back to Towan III, presenting Sean to revolutionary leaders on outlying planets. Johann was always a very spiritual person, a true believer in Nowan's prophecy. Part of the prophecy states that a last prophet will arise when they discover the ancient homeworld. Johann had, and so he became the last prophet."

"Why not you?" Niamh asked.

"That's an interesting question. I've never really considered it. I suppose, to be a prophet, you have to know that you *are* one, and I know I'm not. When we reached Towan III, we revealed Sean, and he claimed the fifth and empty seat on the council. The revolution began."

"That was around the 19th February, 1889," Sean said. "Give or take. The revolution turned into a civil war that lasted until 1895. It didn't end with a peace treaty, but a truce. On our side was the Valley. On the other was the Voytay, the new name for the rump empire, by then solely ruled by Regent Volmar, the great-uncle of the Ripper."

"Wow."

"Are there others?" Padraig asked.

"Other who?" Greta asked.

"Federations? Planets?"

"Oh, sure. There are some independent planets and other empires and federations beyond the borders. The Towani Empire was the most powerful in the galaxy, and some of the worlds it subjugated were eager to emulate it after its collapse."

"And the Voytay are the ones who attacked Oxfordshire?" Niamh asked.

"They did, though they used mercenaries with no clear link to the enemy empire. Now, this comes into why I'm here. You see, Johann and I arranged an attack. Not *the* attack," he added quickly. "What we wanted was something much smaller in scale."

"That'll need a lot of explaining," Niamh said.

"I came back to Earth around Easter 1895. From then until about the year 2000, I tried many things to prepare Earth for first contact. Revolutions, the League of Nations, the U.N. Nothing worked. All I needed was for world leaders to stop declaring war on each other, but there's a type of politician who, on learning there's a good chance of living for hundreds of years, becomes a dictator. The Valley was getting impatient. There was a blockade of this star system, but visitors kept coming. Some were tourists or pilgrims. Others were smugglers or worse. It was getting increasingly difficult to cover up these incidents. We decided enough was enough."

"That was when you planned this?" Niamh asked.

"I began thinking about it after we adopted our kids," Sean said.

"Tempest and Serene," Greta said with a smile. "Did we say we're married?"

"You're married?" Niamh asked.

"It was love at first sight," Sean said.

"It was shock at first sight," Greta said. "By the time surprise subsided, we realised we were destined for one another."

"That's sweet," Niamh said. "And you have children?"

"We found our kids aboard a rusting cargo ship, floating off the coast of Somalia. They and forty-eight others were being sold to a smuggler and were to be sent off-world. The other forty-eight died."

"That's horrific!" Padraig said.

"It wasn't the only such group," Sean said. "Over in England, an alien had appeared to a sadist who set up a cult, recruiting young women to breed babies to sell. Even with the towani smuggler dead, the cult continued. There was only one survivor, Harold Godwin. His aunt rescued him when he was twelve. A few days later, before the authorities could liberate the cult, the other members died. Ultimately, it was deemed an accident, but it was probably murder-suicide. Harold's working for me now. He was there in Oxfordshire when the attack happened. He and his aunt run a bookshop in Woking. About a week ago, he wanted a holiday. He went camping and ended up at an old mansion called Lenham House. There he ran into our kids."

"You said you staged an attack," Padraig said.

"I'm getting to that," Sean said. "During the pandemic, our daughter, Serene, had been apprenticed to a towani archaeologist, and she'd stumbled onto a smuggling ring. Skulls and memorabilia were being sent off-world. She decided to investigate it. That investigation led her to Lenham House, where she and Tempest thought they would run into the sapiens smuggler."

"Sapiens?" Niamh asked

"Like us," Sean said. "We're *Homo sapiens*, Greta's *Homo neanderthalensis*. We're both human, but she's towani, and I'm sapiens. So are you."

"Got it. Go on. What happened?"

"What was *supposed* to happen was that three sooval mercenaries, who had landed in Lincolnshire and whom I'd driven to the house, would be discovered by Special Forces soldiers from twenty NATO countries who were training nearby. Greta and Johann would have come to their aid. The idea was to force the truth out into the open, and in such a way as to show everyone aboard this rock that the galaxy is a dangerous place, but that we have friends in people like Johann."

"That seems a highly dubious way of making friends," Niamh said.

"The plan was a bit more involved than that, but it doesn't matter because Tempest, Harold, and Serene were at the house. They fought the mercenaries, and killed all three."

"That's awful."

"They're handling it well," Sean said. "But Tempest was training to be an acolyte. That's like a warrior monk."

"Thankfully," Greta said.

"Ah, now, I was about their age when I killed the Ripper and went to war," Sean said.

"Let's continue that particular argument later," Greta said. "Where it went wrong is that the sapiens contact for the smugglers was the head of the UNCA in Britain. That's the part of the U.N. who arranged covering up the existence of extra-terrestrials."

"Alan Parker," Sean said. "He and his team were working with the smugglers and the Voytay. When he got wind of my plan, he turned it on its head. His ancestor was the butler to the earl I used to work for. Lenham House was built above an ancient chamber that Parker, and his ancestors, believed contained the Library of Alexandria. He offered to sell it to the Voytay. He says he was buying protection, a guarantee Earth would remain independent of both the Valley and the Voytay, but I think he's after a lot more than that."

"The Library of Alexandria's never real," Padraig said.

"The legend of the library is one of great knowledge that can bring greater power. The librarian was a nearly immortal being, of a species we call chroniclers. He'd been living on Earth for about fifty thousand years, studying how we evolved from hunter-gatherers to city-dwellers. This being had a data storage device, a data-core, containing all they had ever seen on this planet, and on others. It contained millions of years of societies and species, rising and falling. A little over two thousand years ago, the librarian was murdered. The data-core would have captured how. Learning how to kill a nearly immortal being is of obvious value to anyone, aside from the value of the other knowledge contained therein. The data-core also acts as a key to the chronicler's spaceship. Those are rumoured to be able to destroy a planet. The student's teacher, Celeste, came to Earth to investigate the crime and complete the student's work. She prevented ships from making contact with our species."

"Until 1888," Niamh said.

"Yes."

"Why did she change her mind?"

"Her motivations are hard to fathom, and that's when she explains them. Parker thought the data-core was beneath Lenham House. It wasn't. But he'd told the Voytay. He kidnapped our kids, thinking they would know how to access the secret chamber."

"You forgot to say that the kids think of Celeste as their mum, too," Greta said.

"I did, didn't I? After we rescued them, we moved to Carrigt-wohill. Celeste played the role of mother, because Greta couldn't be seen out and about."

"And because she wouldn't let us say she was their grandmother," Greta said. "She's touchy about her age."

"She looks human, then?" Niamh asked.

"Her appearance is a projection, so she can look like anyone, though she's usually kept the appearance of an African queen ever since we met. Anyway, Parker had sold the data-core without ever having got his hands on it. The Voytay sent that old battle-station. It was really just a shell, and was there to be the decoy while their spies claimed the data-core."

"Which wasn't there."

"Nope. I was, with the kids, and Harold, and his aunt. We held the line, a battle ensued, and the mercenaries were mostly killed, though we did take a few prisoners. They're now at a prison on an RAF base."

"So... Okay, that's a lot to take in. I've so many questions," Niamh said.

"Yes, tell us more about the first baker, Pierre O'Keefe," Padraig said.

"They really did break the mould with you," Niamh said. "You said you'd come here with a job offer."

"We had a plan for first contact, and despite everything we've got to get back on track," Sean said. "The galaxy is a dangerous place. The Voytay sent their agents to Earth. It's almost a declaration of war. Earth needs the Valley's protection. For that, we need to send a delegation to Towan III to formally accept an invitation to apply for membership. Actual membership will be decades away, but once the procedure begins, we can receive funding and other support."

"Where do we fit in?" Niamh asked.

"A conference is about to begin just outside Cork that will pick the delegation. Representatives from every nation in the world will be there, along with representatives from the Valley. Padraig, I'd like you to help with the catering. Niamh, I'd like you to attend, and, ultimately, both of you to be part of the official delegation to Towan III."

"Why us?"

"You're family," Sean said. "Besides, there's some nice symbolism in the first person to meet a towani also being the first sapiens to set foot on Towan III."

"But you've been there."

"Sure. But this is official," Sean said. "So, what do you say?"

Prologue - Caves, Tunnels, and Whales
30th March 2003, Ten Days After the Invasion of Iraq

"We're here," Sean O'Malley said as the Humvee rattled along the Iraqi highway.

"I can't see a cave," said U.S. Marine Corps Sergeant Leroy Burton, commander of the protection detail.

"There's a track a short walk behind us that'll take us up to the cave."

"No one gets out of the Humvee until I say," Burton said.

"It's a lovely day for a walk," Sean said.

"Sir, when my commander-in-chief personally tells me to keep you and your colleague alive, you better believe I'm not letting you even get out of breath."

"Fine, take a left, follow that track, but stop as soon as you see the cave," Sean said.

What Sean wanted to say was that there was a drone above them, and a satellite above that, with feeds going directly to the command post in the Valley embassy. There, a team of the galaxy's best military analysts were continually assessing the threat level. While there were many dangers in Iraq ten days after the U.S.-led invasion, there were none nearby. If any appeared, Gunther tol Dannan, scourge of the Voytay, general in command of all Valley forces in the solar system, and Sean's brother-in-law, was ready to deploy with a team of elite soldiers. Sure, if a flying saucer were to set down in the middle of Iraq, dealing with a few of Saddam's loyalists would only be the very start of his problems, but he'd pick problems over death any day.

But Sean couldn't say any of that because the three Marines in his escort detail, Burton, Washington, and Lopez, didn't know about the towani, the Valley, the Voytay, or the real reason the U.S.-led coalition had invaded Iraq ten days ago.

"This'll do," Burton said. "Washington, get on the fifty-cal and cover the road. Lopez, keep us ready to ex-fil. Sir, wait here."

Sergeant Burton, a ten-year veteran, exited first. Sean O'Malley, a hundred-and-ten-year veteran of more battles than he could remember, tried his best to be patient.

"How are you enjoying the trip so far, Alan?" he asked.

His companion, the twenty-five-year-old Alan Parker, was a direct descendent of a butler with whom Sean had worked before he'd flown to space in 1888. Trying not to repeat the mistakes of the past, Sean had offered Parker a job with the UNCA. With his initial training now complete, Sean had high hopes for the young man and thought him the ideal companion for this urgent mission.

"If I'd known we were coming to a war zone, I might have turned down the assignment," Parker said.

"Ah, we're perfectly safe," Sean said. "We've got friendly eyes in the skies, and the nearest potentially unfriendly ones belong to a goatherd about two kilometres due west."

"Did you say west?" Washington asked, swinging the machine gun in that direction.

"And keeping his head down because he wants no part of the trouble we bring."

"How d'you know that?" the Indiana-born private asked.

"Thanks to the aforementioned friendly eyes," Sean said.

Before the private could ask a follow-up, Burton opened the door. "It seems clear, but I have a bad feeling about this place."

Sean got out and adjusted his body-armour. It was, sadly, standard U.S. military issue, as was the desert camouflage. Back at the base, the general had thrown a fit at the idea of anyone going to war in a suit. It was a nice suit, too, high-breasted, with four buttons, and the very latest in kinetic-deflection technology that would easily stop an assault rifle's bullet without leaving even a crease in fabric or skin. Sean had tried to pull rank and had threatened to call the president. The general had called his bluff and contacted the president himself.

Of course, the president knew why Sean was really here in Iraq, but since the general knew no more about the extra-terrestrial presence on Earth than the sergeant, the president had deferred to the officer in the field. It was all Sean had been able to do to wrangle the escort down from an armoured column to a single vehicle.

"In and out, that's the plan," Burton said, clearly nervous. "If I say get down, you eat the dirt. If I say run, you sprint like it's barbecue night, and you heard they're running low on burgers."

"Oh, don't tempt me. My wife's vegan, and we're raising our kids that way. I don't think I've eaten meat this century. Don't forget the bag, Alan."

With Burton taking the lead, and Washington and Lopez watching the road, Sean led Parker up the well-trodden path to the Shanidar Cave.

This wasn't just *a* cave. It was *the* cave, the primordial cave imprinted on the soul of every human, towani and sapiens alike. A triangular void, surrounded by craggy rocks, marked an entrance twenty-six feet high and eighty-two feet wide. Any who dared brave the forbidding darkness radiating from the entrance would find themselves in a chamber one hundred and thirty feet deep. For uncounted millennia, it had been a refuge, a shelter, and a mausoleum to unknowable generations. More recently, it had become the focus of one of the galaxy's greatest mysteries. Parker, though, had turned around, taking in the grass-covered slopes of Bradost Mountain, dotted with Persian oaks and pistachio trees.

"I didn't think Iraq would be so green," Parker said.

"It was even greener the first time I was here," Sean said as he stepped into the cave's entrance.

"When was that, sir?" Burton asked.

"Oh, a few years ago now," Sean said.

It had been in 1956, just after the first set of Neanderthal remains had been discovered in the Shanidar Cave. Sean had come as an emissary of the Holy Johann tol Davir, ambassador to Earth and Last Prophet of the Five Tribes. Not that he'd said as much to the sapiens archaeologists. As far as they had been concerned, he represented a wealthy philanthropist keen to fund the dig. He'd returned a few times since, and not always on official business, though, in recent years, it had become impossible.

"There are no fortifications," Burton said. "It's too open to be a hidden refuge, but I don't like all those posts and cords."

"They're from a recent excavation," Sean said. "Do you see how the soil has been disturbed?"

"Perfect spot to plant a mine," Burton said.

"We'll be careful," Sean said. "If you keep watch outside, we'll take our readings, make our recordings, and we can hurry back in time for those burgers you promised."

"I didn't… ah, fine." Burton didn't look happy, but few people in this embattled country did.

As the sergeant returned to the cave's entrance, Sean bent down and removed what looked like a bulky video camera from the bag. "Here you are, Alan. Press the blue button to record. You can see what's in frame on the screen. Oh, hang on, it's switched to radiation detection." He tinkered with the controls. "There. And let's turn the microphone off. We'll be giving a copy of this to the White House, and we don't want them to learn more than they need."

"Sir, how certain are you there are no mines here?"

"Seventy-three percent," Sean said.

"Really? How did you work that out?"

"I guessed. What answer do you want me to give? My scans show nothing. The drone that visited the place this morning showed nothing. Here." He took the camera back and tinkered with the screen. "Now it's performing a chemical analysis, and it tells us there's nothing explosive any nearer than Sergeant Burton's webbing. But there are no certainties in life, and this *is* a war zone, even if we're a good distance from the fighting."

"That's not at all reassuring."

"Which is why it's sometimes best not to ask questions," Sean said. "Start here, with these new excavations. They look hurried, don't they?"

"I'm not sure. Sir, why are we here? Or is that another question I shouldn't ask?"

"You were taught about the towani during orientation?"

"Yes, sir. You introduced me to your wife."

"Of course, yes," Sean said. "So you know, fifty thousand years ago, five family clans of what came to be called Neanderthals were abducted from Earth. The historical record of what happened next is spotty. It relies primarily on the holy scriptures written by the prophet Nowan about a thousand years after they led a successful rebellion against their captors. The towani went on to found three successive empires which ruled a large swathe of the galaxy. Jump forward to 1888, and when my wife crashed on Earth."

"You were abducted."

"I don't like to use that word, but yes. News of Earth's existence was taken back to the heart of the Towani Empire. Now, we know that the Neanderthals' captors genetically altered their captives. We don't know how much they were altered. How primitive were they when they were taken from Earth? How much of whom they became was because of the medical experiments made by their captors? Or, to put it another way, to what extent were these captors, who are considered demons by the faithful, actually their creators?"

"What's the answer?" Parker asked.

"We still don't know," Sean said. "Towani science might be millennia more advanced than ours, but it still requires research material, and only a few hundred sets of Neanderthal remains have been discovered on Earth to date. For nearly forty years, it was thought that one of the ancestors here was buried with flowers, suggesting ritual, and so religion, imagination, and culture. He was found... over there, I think. But the recent consensus is that a bird introduced the flowers into the grave later on. That doesn't mean the Neanderthals didn't have religion and the complex social structures that go with it, but we don't have proof."

"But why are we here rather than continuing our search with the weapons inspectors?" Parker asked.

"Ah, because the drone we sent in showed recent excavations. I wanted to see them for myself. Now, start recording, but remember that this is sacred ground."

Sean stepped out of earshot, letting Parker work as he called Greta tol Hakon, head of security for the Valley embassy, and his wife of over a hundred years.

"*Kal*, my love, what have you found?" she asked, her face and torso projected onto his lenses so it appeared as if she was hovering, legless, in front of him. Behind her, and less distinct, was the front room of their little house in Ireland.

"Only confirmation of what the drones recorded," Sean said. "The excavations are recent, certainly within the last year. The freshest look hurried, as if they were scooping out the soil with shovels."

"That suggests desperation," Greta said. "The most likely hypothesis is that the dictator wanted remains he could sell on the black market."

"Do we know whether that market was on Earth?" Sean asked.

"My team have found no proof," Greta said. "We finished examining the wreckage of the ship that tried to play chicken with the moon. They were just rich kids with more money than navigational skills."

"Sure. I imagine not slamming into a moon is one of the first lessons they teach you in pilot school. Were they Valley or Voytay?"

"Valley, but their ship had a new form of shielding that made them invisible to our monitoring satellites. That technology must have been developed by the Voytay and sold in one of the black markets in the borderlands."

"That sounds like the next problem to solve."

"My next problem is lunch," Greta said, bending out of shot to pick up one of their children. "Say hello to your da, Tempest."

The toddler waved.

"I hope you're being a good boy for your ma, Tempi," Sean said. "So you're saying that while that ship on the moon isn't linked to our problem with Saddam, any number of other ships could have

19

purchased that cloaking technology. We could have smugglers regularly visiting Earth, and with us unawares."

"The sensors are being upgraded, so we'll regain the advantage, at least until their technicians invent another new type of shielding. For now, I'll assume that the Neanderthal remains were sold off-world. That might be sacrilege to the faithful, but they would be worth a fortune to a collector, and there are far too many of those."

"If Saddam was selling remains off-world, he would have taken weaponry as payment, and there's been no sign of it on the battle-field."

"Not yet," Greta said. "The invasion only began ten days ago. No, Serene, put that down!"

The image cut out. A second later, the audio returned, though not the video. "I've got to go," Greta said. "Celeste was supposed to be here half an hour ago to take the kids for a walk. There is one lead. My team reviewed the intel the weapons inspectors gathered. About a year ago, a lot of archaeology tools and equipment were taken from the museum and university in Mosul."

"That's after the other ship crashed," Sean said. "It might be something. Where did they go?"

"An old gold mine near Mosul," Greta said. "Something had obviously been found, but neither the museum nor the university ever received any samples from the digs. When the weapons inspectors visited, they found no new excavations at the mine and no indication of radioactive ores. They assumed the tools had been stolen and sold, and so moved on. But there's a compound nearby. Satellite imagery shows frequent visits from a Fedayeen convoy before the invasion. It's the same vehicles each time, and it was conjectured Saddam might have been a passenger on two occasions. The convoy last arrived a month ago, and the compound now appears deserted."

"Send the address to me, and send it via the general. My escort won't drive us there unless the orders come through official channels. Be good for your mum, kids. I'll be home soon." He ended the call.

It was three years since he'd rescued his two infant children from a ship off the coast of Somalia. He'd arrived too late to save the other forty-eight children aboard. When he'd learned those children were to be sold off-world, he'd officially retired. Since then, he'd been living in Ireland, where Celeste pretended to be the children's mother and with Greta visiting as often as it was safe.

Though he occasionally undertook liaison work for the Valley embassy, like this mission to Iraq, he had stopped meddling in how the world was run. He'd tried war; he'd tried revolution; he'd tried the U.N. Since they'd all failed, he'd decided to try doing nothing and let the planet sort itself out. He was starting to think he'd made another mistake.

An alert flashed yellow. Four kilometres away, an armed group was gathering. Here, in the Kurdish region of Iraq, they might not be hostile, but it wasn't a risk worth taking.

"That'll do, Alan," he called out. "Time for us to head back."

"Any traffic?" Burton asked when they returned to the Humvee.

"Only civilians, and they sped up when they saw us," Lopez said.

As they got back in, Burton called the base. "Change of orders, sir," the sergeant said. "We've got another lead. The general said it came from your wife."

"She's in intelligence," Sean said. "Just don't ask which agency."

"Ah, got it," Burton said, his shroud of suspicion fading a little. "There's an old gold mine ten klicks from Mosul that became the focus of an archaeological dig. We're to inspect a compound nearby."

"That's not too far from the base. I can almost hear the burgers sizzling," Sean said.

As they left the remote cave behind, the sounds and sights of war returned. Crackling gunfire came from every direction. Plumes of smoke, more numerous than the clouds, rose like pillars supporting the sky. Sundered tanks slumped by the roadside alongside burned wrecks barely recognisable as having once been cars.

Sean opened his equipment bag and took out a hardened laptop. Burton looked on with interest as Sean brought up a satellite feed of their new target.

"Is that real-time?" Burton asked.

"It is."

"It's more detailed than I'm used to," Burton said.

"It's experimental. This compound looks abandoned." He handed the laptop to Burton.

"No vehicles and no signs of life," Burton said.

"But we might find a clue as to where they've gone," Sean said. "Can I have the laptop back? Thanks. I'll switch to thermal. There. Nothing. It's not a guarantee, but I think the compound is deserted."

"Sir, what's this about?" Burton asked. "Sergeants don't usually get direct orders from the commander-in-chief to work as an escort to mines and ancient graves."

"Believe me, there are some questions you don't want answered."

The Humvee stopped outside a large concrete-walled compound on an otherwise undeveloped track. A large metal gate sealed the vehicle entrance, though a smaller pedestrian door was ten metres to the left.

"Grab the bag, Alan," Sean said as he got out.

"We should wait for reinforcements," Burton said. "And then you should wait until we've cleared the interior."

Sean drew his sidearm. "The longer we linger, the greater the chance we're spotted and have a real battle on our hands. If no one is here, we'll be in and out in five minutes, but if you like, I'll take point."

"Not a chance, sir," Burton said.

"Then after you," Sean said.

"Washington, take point. Lopez, crew the turret," Burton said and headed for the door. Washington covered his flank with Sean, and a reluctant Parker, strolling along at the rear. Using a breaching charge, Washington blew the door's lock. Before the explosion's echo had faded, Burton entered, sweeping right. Washington swept left.

"Clear," Burton said.

"I believe that's our invitation," Sean said and stepped inside.

Facing the door was a long desk, behind which was a single wooden door. The ubiquitous photograph of Saddam took centre stage on the wall to the left. On the other wall, facing the glowering dictator, was a photo-style painting of an ancient Assyrian palace and a framed mock-up of an ambitious spaceport.

"I thought this place was part of a gold mine," Washington said.

"An old mine, perhaps put to a new purpose," Sean said.

Parker walked to the door behind the desk at the same time as Sean tapped on thermal imaging. A red and yellow glow marked two figures on the far side of the door. Sean dragged Parker down even as the door swung inward. A burst of automatic rifle fire came from the shadows beyond. Burton and Washington opened fire, spraying bullets into the far room, but thermal imaging told Sean the enemy had taken cover behind an overly thick wall.

Sean raised his pistol. It might have looked like a Beretta M9, but it was loaded with self-propelled projectiles designed to pierce the body-armour of a Voytay breach-team. The Iraqis stood no chance. The bullets tore through the concrete, and then the two enemy soldiers.

"Clear," Sean said, getting to his feet. He helped Parker up.

"We should have waited for the army," Parker said.

"We're Marines, son," Burton said. "The army waits for us."

"Let's see who we've found," Sean said. He entered the dark, windowless room and switched his glasses to low-light vision. "Black uniforms. It's the Fedayeen Saddam. Very loyal, but not well trained. The thermal scan showed that this place was clear before we entered. Those soldiers had to come from somewhere, and it's probably below ground. Shall we see if we can find the hidey-hole?"

Burton insisted he and Washington took the lead as they moved from the windowless room to a corridor with barred windows overlooking the interior courtyard. On the other side of the corridor were cells with solid metal doors. Burton opened the hatch of each in turn.

"Empty, but recently occupied," he whispered. "There's a bed, a bucket, and some books. Must have been keeping prisoners here."

"Probably sapiens," Sean said.

"Who, sir?" Burton asked.

"I'll explain later. Let's keep moving," Sean said.

Beyond the cells, the corridor turned ninety degrees and ended in an open door leading into a large room, big enough to be called a warehouse. In the centre of the room was a ragged but nearly rectangular hole, about twenty metres long and ten wide. What looked like a dismantled crane's winch was now attached to a small elevator, precariously dangling over the hole.

"I can't see the bottom," Sean said, peering down. "I'd say that's a good sign. You should wait here, Sergeant."

"No way are you going down alone," Burton said.

"No, I'm taking Alan. It's why we're here."

"Where you go, we go," Burton said.

"You'll regret it," Sean said. "What you'll see could well change your life."

"War changes everyone," Burton said. He stepped outside to open the compound's metal gate.

"There was a drawing of a spaceport in the entrance area," Parker said, keeping his voice low so Washington couldn't overhear.

"There was," Sean said.

"Is this shaft big enough to fit a spaceship?"

"A small one."

"Have we found the ship?"

"We've found something," Sean said. "You went through weapons training?"

"I did."

"Grand, so the first thing you should do is draw your gun, but if it comes to a fire-fight, take cover and wait. Help won't be long in coming."

"From the Valley?"

"From me. Relax, Alan, I've done this kind of thing more times than I can remember, and I haven't died yet. Ah, Sergeant, Privates. For what you are about to see, may I apologise in advance."

The elevator pendulously swung as it descended into the dark. Twenty metres below the compound, the shaft met a much larger and much more ancient tunnel. This was about ten metres in diameter and was perfectly circular, though the packed earth on the floor created a nearly level surface. Everywhere else, the tunnel was covered in baked terracotta, which had been carved and painted into elaborate scenes.

"What is all this?" Lopez asked, shining his light on the mural.

"A tunnel," Sean said, shining his light along the packed earth floor. "Most of the footprints head this way, towards Mosul."

"This is… it's…" Lopez stammered.

"It's hostile territory," Burton said. "Lopez, you've got our six. Washington, on me."

Slowly, they followed the sergeant down the dry and stifling tunnel, their lights occasionally illuminating an identifiable part of the mural. Burton was brought to a halt when they came to the carved depiction of a fish-tailed monster that curved above their heads.

"Ah, now I understand," Sean said. "This tunnel isn't leading to Mosul, but to Nineveh, the ruins of which are now found in that city. Before it was sacked in 612 BCE, Nineveh was the big power in this part of the world. I'd say this tunnel is a few decades younger than that. The entrance is probably blocked, and in a well-populated area, so they created a shortcut in that compound. This section retells the story of Jonah and the whale. Look, there's a person trapped inside, do you see?"

"That's no whale; it's got claws," Burton said.

"Perhaps the witnesses had no better word to describe it," Sean said.

"Do you really think this tunnel is two and a half thousand years old?" Burton asked.

"A bit older, but yes," Sean said.

"How did they dig it?"

"Let's save that question for later," Sean said.

"This predates the Library of Alexandria," Alan said.

"It does," Sean said. "Shh." His lenses had flashed yellow. The microphone had picked up voices still too distant to be heard by ear alone. "We've got company ahead. Two people, speaking Arabic, asking when they might leave."

"How do you know?" Burton asked.

"That's another question for later," Sean said. "However strange things get from now on, remember your training."

They crept up the tunnel with their lights off, using low-light goggles. The guards' light came into view first. An electric lantern stood on the floor between two black-uniformed guards. Just as both turned to look down the tunnel, Burton and Washington fired. The bodies fell to the floor faster than the gunshots' echo faded.

"We could have done that a bit quieter," Sean said. "Quick now."

Beyond the now-dead Fedayeen, the tunnel opened onto a stone staircase that led down into a large, square chamber dotted with lanterns that barely illuminated the faded mural adorning the walls. At the base of the stairs were a dozen stacks of coffin-sized wooden crates piled at least five high. Against the walls were long tables covered in trays and tools, with more trays beneath, filled with soil. But in the centre of the chamber was a sleek green and white dart, about fifteen metres long and four wide, with a window at the front, narrow fins at the side, and an engine at the back. The craft stood on skids and was positioned so it was pointing towards the tunnel, almost as if it was ready to take off.

"What's that?" Burton whispered.

"You could call it a spaceship, but I'd call it a promotion," Sean said as he began to descend the stairs.

"A spaceship?" Burton repeated.

"An alien spaceship," Sean said. "It crashed here about a year ago. Saddam refused—"

A grey-faced demon in an armoured red spacesuit leapt up from behind a set of stacked crates, and opened fire with a twin-barrelled handgun as he ran towards the ship. The safe-for-space bolts were designed to shred flesh without penetrating a bulkhead, but they chipped chunks out of the stone staircase even as Sean jumped down the last of them. Sean took cover behind a stack of the coffin-shaped crates and raised his gun, but the alien had gone to ground.

"What was that?" Burton asked, having pulled Parker to the dubious cover of a neighbouring stack of crates. Washington and Lopez had held position at the top of the stairs.

"A genuine enemy alien," Sean said, switching to thermal. He found his target, twenty metres away. To take the shot would require firing through the stacked crates, but if they contained what he thought they did, that would be sacrilege.

Sean stood and stepped sideways, trying to get a clear shot. As he did, a black-uniformed soldier appeared from cover to the left. Sean dived for cover as the uniformed man opened fire, spraying the crates with a fully automatic burst. Two of the crates shattered, spilling loose bones on top of Sean, and confirming his hunch about their contents. His assailant's attack was cut short as Lopez opened fire from above.

"Hold your fire!" Sean said, switching magazines, and language, speaking in Mid-Tow, the common tongue of both the Voytay and the Valley. "You're cornered. That ship won't leave this tunnel. Surrender, and there's a good deal to be made."

The towani smuggler, now wearing a full-face helmet, stood, and opened fire, targeting Sean. He ducked low as the bolts shredded the crates, raining down more bones. The Marines returned fire, but their bullets bounced off the alien's heavy-duty armour. The smuggler began walking backwards towards the ship, still firing at Sean. If disturbing the bones of the dead was sacrilege to the towani, he'd atone for it later. He fired two armour-piercing rounds through the remains of the crate, but neither penetrated the enemy's spacesuit.

"What kind of armour is that?" he muttered, firing again.

The smuggler had reached the ship and was already on the ramp. With regrets about not coming better armed and armoured, Sean was about to call for a retreat. Before he could, a fist-sized hole burned through the alien's chest.

"Cease fire!" Sean called, even as the towani collapsed.

"Please!" a woman called from inside the starship. "Please help."

"Step outside, slowly," Sean said, fully standing up.

A woman in her early twenties, wearing a dirt-flecked white dress, emerged from the ship with her hands raised. She staggered down the ramp.

"Alan, help her. Sergeant, check the chamber for any more Fedayeen. Washington, can you run back up the tunnel? Make sure no one else comes down here. Washington?"

The Marine didn't answer, but merely stared at the ship, mouth open.

"What the Sam Hill is all this?" Burton asked.

Careful not to step on any spilled bones, Sean walked over to the dead towani and undid the clasps holding the helmet in place. He removed it and pointed at the grey face beneath.

"This is a towani. That's the species. Look at the face. Does it remind you of anything?"

"My uncle Charlie, except he's not grey," Burton said.

"Really? Well, this species is descended from Neanderthals."

"Neanderthals?"

"Five tribes were abducted from Earth fifty thousand years ago. They defeated their captors and formed an empire, and created a religion. Their principal faith is centred around returning to their ancestral home. Earth. About a hundred and ten years ago, they rediscovered Earth. That triggered a revolution that turned into a civil war, which ended with a truce. The good guys are the Valley. The bad guys are the Voytay."

"Which side is he on?"

"He's probably just an opportunistic smuggler. Bones are worth a lot. Neanderthal bones are worth even more. A few years ago, a spaceship crashed here in Iraq, near Mosul. Aboard was an utter eccentric who was convinced that the secret to reincarnation was to die on their ancestral homeworld. She died during the crash. Saddam handed over her body, but he kept the ship. This ship. From the look of it, Saddam was selling Neanderthal bones to that smuggler. In return, the smuggler must have pretended he'd fix up the spaceship."

"Was this the WMDs that we were looking for?" Burton asked.

"In a manner of speaking." Sean tapped the side panel. "Crashed ships, or any non-terrestrial technology, are supposed to be shipped over to Area-51. Some of it is stored there, and anything dangerous is sent off-world for disposal. When Saddam kept refusing to return the ship, your president grew concerned about what he might do with it. But this ship crashed. The repairs have been made with steel and house paint. One way or another, turning the engines on would certainly create a lot of destruction. The towani must have known this, but maybe he just hoped to blast his way out of the tunnel."

"You're like Agent Mulder?"

"Something like that. Alan and I work at the U.N. in a special department covering up incidents like this. A department to which, Sergeant, I believe you are soon to be transferred. Now, I need you to secure the tunnel and this chamber. I'm going to secure the ship."

Before he did that, he picked up the tool the woman had used to blow a hole in the towani. It wasn't a weapon, but a thermic drill. Originally, it was designed for mining, but this one had been modified for a much shorter range. It was a favourite trick of hijackers who wanted to cut through the armoured hull plating of an unsuspecting spacecraft.

The inside of the spaceship looked like a prop from a movie, and was just as space-worthy. The four passenger-seats had come from a fighter jet, crudely welded to the floor. The pilot's chair looked original, though roughly re-upholstered in green leather. The control panel looked impressive, with buttons and levers, back-lit in red, set below a digital readout which, if it was to be believed, said this ship was currently flying a zig-zag route through an asteroid field. He scanned for a power source and found it behind a panel to the left. It was a portable unit, of a type usually used to recharge a ground vehicle. It certainly wouldn't power the engines. But if this ship was little more than a model, why had the smuggler tried to get back aboard?

He found the answer in a cabinet behind the passenger seats. There were three suitcases containing women's clothing. Next to them was a deactivated navigation beacon that could be used by an inbound starship traversing skip-space to guide them as to where to land. While the chamber was large enough to accommodate another ship, skipping into such a confined space would be perilous. The suddenly displaced air would create a shockwave liable to bring down the roof.

Next to that was an ancient flight recorder, about the size of a brick, whose protective orange surface was tarnished and faded. According to a readout displayed on his glasses, it was of a kind not used for two and a half thousand years. He tried to access any data stored inside, but it was inoperative.

He stepped back outside and approached Parker and the young woman, both sitting on one of the long crates.

"Her name's Dr Awat Masadi," Parker said.

"You're a medic?" Sean asked.

"I'm an archaeologist," she said. "I was brought here a year ago to investigate the tunnel. More recently, I've been cleaning bones. There were more of us here, but they were murdered." She looked over at the coffin-shaped crates and then lowered her eyes.

"Has Alan explained who we are?"

"You work for the U.N. and have been looking for this ship," she said without looking up.

"We have. Are all the bones Neanderthal?" Sean asked.

"Most are human. Some are ancient. Some are fresh."

"Have any been shipped out?"

"Twice. The second time, that thing arrived." She pointed at the dead towani. "He began repairing the ship. Saddam was going to travel to space to prove his superiority to all other world leaders. But then the invasion happened."

"There are suitcases inside. Whose are they?"

"Mine. Saddam was due to arrive any day. When he did, the ship would leave. He was offered sanctuary on some alien world. I was to go with him."

"And the smuggler?"

"It was going to be collected, along with all those bones."

"Well, no one was going anywhere in that ship unless it was to a grave," Sean said. "All of these bones would be worth a fortune, and so worth taking such a great risk. We'll talk again, but I should speak with the president."

It was an interesting find. They'd stopped a smuggling operation dead in its tracks and found an ancient tunnel that could shine a bright light on sapiens' history. The bad news was that a smuggler had visited Earth twice without being detected. This was the sixth major incursion in the last three years, counting the one where he'd rescued his two children as the first. Minor incursions, in which non-violent tourists or pilgrims were stopped from setting foot on the planet or who had no physical contact with any sapiens, occurred at least once a week. It was getting harder to protect Earth and harder to keep the truth from people. First contact couldn't be delayed for much longer.

Part 1
RAF Space Command

England
16th - 19th October
Two Months After First Contact

Chapter 1 - No Tips for the Tour Guide

Harold Godwin checked his blue and green tie in the mirror before giving his shoes a quick shine on the back of his leg.

"If the air marshal saw you doing that, she'd have you polishing the barracks, inside and out," Flight Sergeant Theresa Linton said.

"Why do you think I'm giving them a shine?" Harold said. "I left my top button undone last Friday, and she tried to make me run laps of the runway."

"Just imagine what she'd have done if you were in her chain of command," Linton said. "Ah, the minibus is here. Our guests have arrived."

Harold took one last swig of tea. "Has everyone placed their bets on what the tickets will cost today?"

"Oh, yes." Linton patted her pocket.

"Then let's get this over with."

As Linton went into the hangar to alert her team that dignitaries were inbound, Harold left by the other door, stepping out onto the airbase where, under the watchful eye of two RAF police officers, an assorted cluster of business leaders and senior military figures impatiently waited.

"Good morning. I'm Harold Godwin, and I'll be your tour guide today."

"Are you an alien?" asked a man in a shiny suit with an equally shiny face. On the inside of Harold's AR glasses, a tag identified him as Trent Woodsman, the billionaire founder of a cat-sharing app.

"I'm human," Harold said. "The towani soldiers guarding the prison and our planet are also human. They are *Homo neanderthalensis*. I, like you, am *Homo sapiens*."

"I paid two million for an alien guide," the brusque billionaire said.

"I suggest you take that up with whomever you gave the money to, because it wasn't me."

33

"Mind your tone, airman, or I'll have you written up," the billionaire said.

"You mind yours. I'm not in the RAF. I'm the official Valley liaison for the Oxfordshire clean-up, and I report directly to the Holy Johann tol Davir, Last Prophet and ambassador to Earth. The ambassador asked me to provide an orientation class for sapiens specialists who are about to join the clean-up effort. You're who showed up today, so if you can gather round, I'll begin."

For the last eight weeks, Harold had been providing a daily orientation tour for new staff. For the last seven, the government had been selling tickets.

"As you and the rest of the planet knows, it's two months since first contact took place in Cobh, and one day less since an ancient battle-station appeared in the skies over Oxfordshire. After that battle-station crashed, a ten-kilometre exclusion zone was established from Didcot in the west to the River Thames in the north and again in the east after the river takes a misguided southerly turn towards London. Here, at RAF Benson, we're just east of the river and so outside the exclusion zone. This base has been re-designated as RAF Space Command and is the hub for the clean-up operation. The British government didn't want to introduce another lockdown or travel restrictions, so, as I'm sure you know, Berkshire and Oxfordshire have been flooded with tourists hoping to collect a piece of extra-terrestrial scrap."

"I bought some online," Woodsman said, pulling a necklace from beneath his shirt. Hanging from the chain was an imperfect star-shaped piece of grey metal set in silver. "It came from the captain's chair in the control room. Cost me a million, but it's worth it."

Harold frowned, mainly to stop himself from laughing. "I hope you had it tested."

"Tested for what?"

"Radiation and toxicity," Harold said. "This is why we've set up testing centres. While some teams are combing the countryside for hazardous materials, there just aren't enough of them." He left the cause of their understaffing dangling as he led them into the hangar.

There, a small team of RAF specialists were sorting through today's first assignment of crates.

Harold stopped at an empty workstation and picked up a palm-sized device, grey in colour, flat on one side, and curved like a shell on the other. "We can use this scanner to identify the constituent chemicals and impurities in the object and so pinpoint where it's from and whether it's dangerous. May I?" He held out his hand.

Woodsman's eyes narrowed with suspicion. "What are you going to do with that?"

"I'm going to make sure it won't burn a hole through your skin before dusk."

Distrust never leaving his face, the billionaire removed the necklace.

Harold held the device close to the necklace and pointed to the screen above the workstation. "If you look at the screen, you'll see that it's steel and terrestrial in origin. You were scammed, Mr Woodsman. That you were told it was from a captain's chair should have been the first clue. How would some litter-picking tourist know which chair belonged to whom?"

Woodsman tore the necklace off and made to throw it down before changing his mind and pocketing it.

"How many people have become sick?" asked a tall woman whose roaming stare seemed to be memorising everything in sight. A tag on the inside of Harold's glasses identified her as Wana Shoneyin, a Nigerian airline magnate.

"Twelve people were hospitalised, and over a hundred received minor chemical burns," Harold said. "Immediately after the crash, the Valley deployed drones to scan for contamination, and we think the most dangerous areas have been sealed off, but it's wise to be cautious. This is why the ambassador, the Holy Johann tol Davir, has offered a reward for any scrap handed in. Anyone who finds something can take it to a collection centre in exchange for a bounty paid in twil, the principal currency used across the Valley."

"What's the exchange rate?" asked a bony woman with a beak-like nose. His glasses identified her as Ingrid Hermann, deputy chief of the IMF.

"There isn't one yet," Harold said. "I imagine working one out will be your next job."

"How does that scanner work?" Shoneyin asked.

"I've no clue," Harold said. "Which might be why I'm giving this part of the tour. The scanners used out in the field have a screen attached, but people from the Valley would get the read-out via an ocular implant or on the visor of their helmet. *Please* take the scanner out from underneath your jacket, Mr Woodsman. These devices are on loan from the Valley. If you steal one, they *will* come to reclaim it."

Woodsman reluctantly put it back on the table.

"The field teams check everything before it's sent here," Harold said. "Anything dangerous is sealed, but everything will get sent to Groom Lake."

"You mean to Area-51, in the United States?" Shoneyin asked.

"Yes."

"Why is it sent there?"

"Because that's where wreckage is always sent," Harold said. "Or, to put it the other way around, it's why Area-51 was built. When there's enough to fill a space-freighter, a ship lands to transport it off-world for disposal. Due to the sheer volume of wreckage from the crash, the ambassador has sent for specialist recycling equipment."

"And why was this facility built in America in the first place?" Shoneyin asked.

"In the 1950s, it was the least worst option," Harold said, giving the scripted answer.

"That's right because they've been living here for years," Shoneyin said.

"Non-terrestrials have been visiting Earth for millennia," Harold said, again sticking to the script. "Indeed, it was on one such visit that the ancestral towani were abducted. That was about fifty thousand years ago."

"They were Neanderthals?" Hermann asked.

"Yes. For around a thousand years, they were held as slaves and bred as warriors. Finally, they rebelled, killing their abductors. If you can all look at the screens, I'll bring up the footage."

A figure in a kilt, covered in swirling red tattoos, stood in a cavernous, ill-lit chamber. Grey tentacles, dripping with dark, viscous fluid, hung from the ceiling. In the left-hand corner, a woman in a simple white shift, and holding a very complicated axe, was trying to catch her breath.

"Who's that?"

"The woman with the axe is the high priest, Jallin. The figure in the kilt is the Holy Nowan, the foundational prophet of the Valley's major religion. The tentacles belong to their captors. This footage shows the moment of victory when the enslaved ancestors defeated their captors. There were five ships. Four were deliberately crashed on the planet they were orbiting. Those freed slaves called the planet Towan and built a society whose primary goal was to return to the stars. Unfortunately, they had to learn about environmental damage the hard way and completely wrecked the planet. They *did* return to the stars, though, and began to create the first empire. That fifth ship, captained by the Holy Nowan, disappeared in search of Earth. If you'd like to follow me outside, we'll look at the ships they use now. Mr Woodsman put the scanner down!"

Shaking his head in irritation, Harold led his group outside.

"When the ambassador gave his television interview, he said he'd first arrived in 1900," said Admiral Bruce Smith of the Australian Navy.

"Around then, yes," Harold said. "The ambassador's ship crashed off the coast of Ireland, near what's now called Cobh. A local fisherman came to their aid and was taken aboard. He'd been injured, and during his medical examination, it was discovered that this sailor shared some of the same DNA as the towani. The ambassador, Davir, had discovered the ancestral homeworld, thus fulfilling the Holy Nowan's last prophecy. So the ambassador became the Last Prophet, so now he is addressed as the Holy Johann tol Davir. Tol means formerly known as."

"He's old, then?" Hermann asked.

"Over seven hundred, I think, but I was taught it's impolite to ask."

"How is that possible?" Shoneyin asked.

"Again, I don't know the specifics," Harold said. "But they will make their medical science available to us. We're not so genetically similar that we can receive the same treatment, so there'll have to be medical trials first, but yes, the diseases that plagued us will be cured. The cellular regeneration technology will give us longer lives."

"Where do we sign up for that, because my knees are pure murder in the cold weather?" Admiral Smith said.

"I think the first trials will be for AIDS patients in South African townships and the refugee camps in Kenya. But we'll need to ramp up the planet's energy output for a global roll-out."

"And are they going to help with that?" Hermann asked.

"Yes. We'll start with fusion because it's what our scientists and engineers will be almost familiar with. Even with some parts shipped in from the Valley, building enough power plants and upgrading the electrical grid will still take years."

"And will this help be for everyone, everywhere?" Shoneyin asked.

"Absolutely, just as the ambassador said in his last interview. The Valley has a policy of non-interference in local politics, except where not intervening would lead to a greater disaster. The key thing to remember, I suppose, is that they're interested in the planet, not in us. They'll help, up to a point, after which we're on our own."

Until last month, RAF Benson had been a base for helicopter operations. Situated on the eastern bank of the serpentine River Thames, halfway between Oxford and Reading, and due east of the main crash site, it now bustled. A cargo plane sulked on the recently extended runway, utterly ignored by everyone who'd found an excuse to get through security. The visitors were only interested in the two spaceships, a V-shaped flying wing and a flying saucer barely bigger than the twin-rotor Chinook crouching beside it.

"They actually zip about in flying saucers?" the admiral asked.

"This is a very old design," Harold said. "The old empire was change-averse. That was one of the reasons for the revolution that began when the Holy Johann tol Davir returned to Towan III with news that he'd found the ancestral home. At the time of the revolution, the empire was ruled by a Committee of Regents, all of whom were towani, but there were many other species in the empire, and that was a source of discontent. After the revolution, came the civil war. On one side were the Voytay, led by the former regents. On the other was the Valley, led by a council representing all the planets and species. The civil war lasted nearly seven years and ended in a cease-fire, not peace. Both sides were bankrupt, so the Valley kept producing ships like this as it was cheaper than retooling the factories."

"In the footage of people being rescued from the floods in Pakistan, they seemed much larger," Shoneyin said.

"Those ships were Type-17 transports. This is a Type-21 fighter."

"Can we see inside?"

"No. It's a working ship and belongs to the towani guarding the prison. Because it was easy to discredit the idea of a saucer-shaped ship, they were used here on Earth, but they'll slowly be replaced." He led them over to the neighbouring ship, a V-shaped vessel. "This is a Ree-Bee flying wing. As soon as we've trained the pilots, a thousand of these will be given to Earth so we can defend ourselves." He tapped his finger and thumb together. On his glasses, a menu appeared. He selected the recipient. "Hi, Melly, can you open the ship? *Lok.*"

The ramp slowly descended. "The controls are remotely locked, but if anyone wants to look inside, be my guest."

Woodsman nearly knocked over the admiral in his eagerness to run up the ramp. Not everyone went aboard, however.

"How will the pilots be chosen?" Shoneyin asked.

"That's above my pay grade," Harold said. "But I guess the world leaders will have to get together and figure it out, just like with this conference in Ireland where they're supposed to pick a delegation to visit Towan III."

"What *is* your pay grade?" Shoneyin asked. "How is it you came to be working here?"

"I was out camping and ran into a mercenary advance guard," Harold said. "I was rescued by citizens of the Valley. A couple of days later, we had the Oxfordshire incident. Since the UNCA was disbanded, and since some of their members were involved in luring the Voytay here, the ambassador wasn't sure whom he could trust. Since I'm no one, he thought he could trust me."

His answer wasn't the whole truth, but it was well-practised. He was asked that question during every tour and by every visiting politician. He often asked it of himself.

"Can we see the prison now?" Hermann asked.

"That would be a breach of the Geneva Convention," Harold said. A heavy drop of rain fell onto the runway. He decided to use that as an excuse to cut the tour short. "If any of you did want to begin work as a scanning technician, you should return to the hangar for training, but I'm guessing you were promised a tour of the crash site, for which you should head over to the Chinook helicopter."

Woodsman sidled over to Harold. "I'll give you two million for one of those scanners."

"They're not mine to sell," Harold said.

"Five million."

"The helicopter's waiting."

"Decide on a price. I'll be in touch."

Harold just shook his head. In the nearly two months he'd been doing this, there'd been at least one attempted bribe on every tour. He sent a message to the towani soldier to reseal the ship, and went to work.

Chapter 2 - Through a Scanner Brightly

Being a Man in Black wasn't like Harold had expected, nor was first contact. There were no rooftop chases, no cover-ups, and no shootouts in which the fate of the universe was at stake. For once, reality was far better than fiction. He returned to the hangar where Sergeant Linton lingered in the corner they used as a break room.

"Perfect timing, sir," Linton said. "I just made a brew."

Inwardly, Harold winced. To the RAF personnel, there was nothing unusual about someone his age being in a position of authority. Since this was the *Royal* Air Force, they were also used to young people occupying an undefined, yet stratospheric, position in the hierarchy. Of all the daily surprises that first contact had brought, Harold found receiving professional deference one of the most challenging concepts to accept.

"Cheers," Harold said, taking the offered mug.

"How much were the tickets?" Linton asked, getting to the real reason she'd been waiting.

"One guy paid two million."

"That's double yesterday," Linton said. She stuck her head around the door. "Oy, Blake! You won. They're charging two mil now." That produced a cheer edged with shocked disbelief from the workers in the hangar.

"They're just going to keep raising their prices, aren't they?" Harold said.

"*This* government? Of course."

Chief Technician Blake, the walking definition of why some military personnel were described as grizzled, entered the hastily built chamber. Despite being twice Harold's age, he was still taut-chested and straight-backed, with an impossibly tapered waist. If he'd been put on a recruitment poster, everyone would think he was an actor. In reality, he was a spy. So were half of the team. British spies, but spies nonetheless. Harold's position at the base was tenuous. His presence was tolerated as much because the government wanted to turn him, and his direct line to the ambassador, into a source, if not an agent, as because cooperation with the technologically superior Valley was obviously in everyone's best interests. They didn't know he knew, so he was happy to play dumb.

"I've come to claim my prize, sir," Blake said.

"Sure," Harold said. "What do you want to ask?"

"Was Elvis an alien who faked his death so he could go on an intergalactic tour, and is he about to launch a comeback gig on Earth?"

"That's what you want me to ask?" Harold said.

"Absolutely. I read it on the news this morning," Blake said.

Harold shrugged. He tapped his thumb and forefinger together. A keyboard appeared on the inside of his lenses as if it was hovering beneath his hand. He typed out the question and sent it to Sean.

"I've sent it to the embassy. Oh, and I've got a reply already. It says Elvis was an Earther."

"Ah, but it doesn't say he's dead?"

"It doesn't say that, no," Harold said.

"I knew he was on an intergalactic tour." Happily vindicated, Blake returned to the hangar.

"When will we get some of those smart glasses?" Linton asked.

"I'll ask the ambassador's office, but I don't think it'll be soon. For the towani, these are very old technology. Most use implants. Some use visors, but their cranial structure is too different for their helmets and glasses to fit comfortably."

"Can't they just print them like they print their food?" Linton asked.

"I don't know," Harold said. "Maybe that could be tomorrow's question."

"Or you could ask now, to satisfy your own curiosity and then tell us."

"I do know the pilots of the spaceships will get them," Harold said. "I suppose the ground crew will get them, too."

"Then I'll just have to get onto that training programme," Linton said. "Speaking of printing things, can I get your opinion on something?"

"Sure," Harold said and followed her into the hangar.

The county had been inundated with tourists since the battle above Oxfordshire and the battle-station's crash. Despite the increasingly inflated prices, planes, trains, and hotels were booked for a year in advance. The queue for the Calais to Dover ferry now began in Paris. Every spy, scientist, and treasure hunter from across the world, and who had canyon-deep pockets, had come to the Home Counties, and so had the natives.

Of all the things Harold would have expected to happen after first contact, curiosity wasn't at the top of the list. Sure, there'd been some light rioting, frantic stockpiling, quick coups, and political resignations, but no more so than during the pandemic. The Covid lockdowns were still fresh in the global consciousness. People wanted to do something, anything, but most were too broke to do more than watch the news. But anyone in Britain willing to brave the national gridlock could walk through countryside famed in history and fiction and perhaps stumble across a piece of singed alien scrap.

Woodsman's million-pound necklace was an outlier. Even so, a single bolt was currently fetching low five figures online, and the prices were only rising. Attempts to curtail this scavenging proved logistically difficult, and became politically impossible when three ex-prime ministers were photographed among the treasure hunters.

Linton stopped at a pair of trolleys, each containing eight of the standard storage crates.

"These sixteen boxes came from the collection point at the library in Didcot," Linton said. "The documentation says they were all collected by the same scout troop. There's nothing dangerous about them, but they all look identical."

Harold opened the lid of the first box and found it full of screw-thread bolts about ten centimetres long and plain white in colour.

43

Harold let his glasses scan one. "It looks like the kind of bolt used to hold the… well, I've no idea what the words mean, but it's part of the engine mounting."

"It's plastic, isn't it?" Linton asked.

With a wave of his fingers, Harold opened the other app and then picked up a portable scanner. "Yes, it's plastic from Earth, the kind used in 3D printers."

"That's what I thought," Linton said. "There's over two hundred in here, and those other boxes contain the same. What is it they get paid?"

"Fifty twil per item, straight into a Valley bank account set up in their name."

"It's a scam," Linton said.

"Or it's initiative," Harold said.

"You're going to let them get away with it?" Linton asked.

Harold weighed it up. He wasn't sure it was his problem. On the other hand, if it wasn't his, whose was it? "Whose name is on the receipt?"

"There are seventeen names, and going by the handwriting, I'd say they're kids."

"I'll note down the names, and make sure they know we don't want this to happen again," Harold said. "But if it's a one-off, where's the harm?"

"The kids don't bother me, but someone in Didcot signed off on this," Linton said.

"Ah. Good point. I suppose I should go and have a word with them, too."

"Send the RAF police. That's what we have them for. Shall I arrange it?"

"I suppose so."

"Yes, sir."

Harold sat at his desk and grimaced at the size of his in-tray. Every crate arrived with paperwork listing what had been found and who had found it. He picked up the first page so the camera on his

44

smart-glasses could scan it, and add it to the embassy's database, then picked up the next.

While most of his work was data entry, officially he was a liaison, and his main job was to be helpful. The only Valley citizens on the base were the squad of soldiers, all towani, guarding the prison, and they didn't speak much English. Those who *could* speak English were at the crash site or assisting with the ever-present natural disasters, like the flooding in Pakistan, in a hearts and minds mission to show that the Valley was different to the Voytay.

They should have had the members of the British branch of the UNCA to assist in the task, but five had been jailed, and the rest were under observation. Alan Parker and his team had been working with the Voytay, helping coordinate the Oxfordshire incursion. With Sean O'Malley busy running the investigation into Parker, the ambassador had asked Harold to act as the local liaison. That Harold knew barely more than any observant tourist was considered a boon. He was a filter, fielding questions from RAF technicians, the spies, the air marshal, and even the politicians, all so the ambassador and his team could stay focused on the next stage of first contact.

When given a question he couldn't answer, he'd send it to Greta or Sean, or sometimes straight to the ambassador himself. It was a strange job, and he definitely preferred being a bookseller, but this line of work had one clear advantage: it paid. He'd gone from working three shifts in a pub to break even to earning fifty thousand a year, plus a further fifty thousand twil, in *advance*. The notion of paying someone in arrears was baffling to the towani. If an employer didn't trust an employee to turn up, why hire them in the first place?

He'd frittered away his first month's pay on food and overdue bills. The rest, though, and for the next two years, would be carefully hoarded so he could put down a deposit on a bookshop of his own.

Linton came over with the next batch of forms. "This brings us up to date, so I'd say that's lunchtime," she said.

Dining options on the base were limited, and all came with the certainty of uncomfortable questions. Most of the base's personnel treated him with wary suspicion. Visiting dignitaries were worse. So many refused to accept that he really was human that he assumed there must be a note in some official file. After the first week, he'd taken to eating sandwiches at his workstation. Turning one corner of the hangar into a cheery and distinctly un-martial break-room had been Linton's idea. The installation of a food-printer had been a gift from Johann, another friendly gesture from the Valley. It used more electricity than the rest of the base combined, so after the second brownout, they'd limited its use to lunchtime. The only oversight was that the screen's interface was entirely in Mid-Tow, the common tongue of the towani, which Harold had to translate using his glasses.

The printers required cartridges, and these were programmed back in the Valley. The menu was inspired by Earth dishes but tinkered with by chefs who had never left Towan III. The steak tasted like curry, while the curry was served inside a purple wrap. He punched in the code for the technicians' orders one by one.

When he got to Air Specialist Hamza Demir, the airman held out a sealed plastic box filled with salad. "Can you test this?"

"Did you get that at the supermarket?" Linton asked.

"This all comes from my mother-in-law's greenhouse. There's some rocket, spinach, red peppers, radish, celery, and red cabbage. No dressing, and no croutons. Does anyone want to bet it *doesn't* say it's dangerous?"

This produced a thoughtful pause.

"Does she use pesticides or fertilisers?" Linton asked.

"Not a one," Demir said.

"Any takers?" Harold asked.

"I'll bite," said Blake, an inveterate gambler who'd once tried to place a bet on the length of a rainbow.

"What are the stakes?" Demir asked.

"Whoever loses does clean-up for the winner at the end of the day," Linton said.

Harold took the salad, transferred it to one of the printer-safe bowls, and opened the hatch at the machine's side.

Only some of the worlds in the Valley, or the empire before, were so urbanised that printed food was the only option. There were many agricultural planets, but many more partially geo-engineered worlds where agriculture was a daily struggle. Greta, Gunther, and Johann had been exiled to one of those by the regents, and they were far from unique. Transportation and exile to a barren world was a favoured punishment of the old regime. On a dust-bowl planet, where a day's farming might only grow blisters, hunting and foraging were often the difference between a meal and misery. To ensure that the exile's punishment wasn't brought to a premature end by food poisoning, the food printers could scan a sample, provide a complete chemical analysis, and identify whether it was deadly, dangerous, or edible.

"And the result is... dangerous," Harold said. "I told you, the machines are built by corporations who profit from the sale of cartridges. It's not in their interests for people to find an alternative food source."

"Double or nothing on what your mother-in-law will say when you tell her," Blake said.

"I'm going to tell her it came up edible, and maybe she'll lay off asking when we'll give her another grandkid."

Harold finished printing the remaining orders. For himself, he selected his usual: macaroni and cheese. The pasta was sweet and star-shaped, while the purple sauce tasted like barbecued bacon. He loved it.

"That BBC Valley podcast is putting out a live episode in a few minutes," Linton said. "Mind if I put it on?"

"Live? Has something happened?" Harold asked.

"A budget," Linton said as she synced her phone to a set of small speakers.

"*Welcome to a special edition of Towani-Cast,*" the impossibly cheerful Welsh host began. "*I'm Gracie Davies, in the studio with a very special guest. My father, Evan. Say Hi, Dad.*"

"*Hi, Dad,*" the father said.

"Longtime listeners will know that won't be the last dad joke today, and you'll also know he's our resident economic expert. We recorded an episode this morning, which will be available to download later, where we spoke to the Vice Chancellor of Warwick University. They are pausing teaching in all physics classes until the curriculum can be updated. Other universities may follow suit, raising the question of what this means for students who are currently enrolled. In the second half of the episode, we talked with Ahmad Amjad and Parveen Iqbal, two filmmakers from Pakistan who were rescued from a rooftop during the floods by a towani ship and taken up to the peace platform where they filmed a documentary that will be released next week. It's an amazing interview and an amazing documentary, so keep an eye on your podcast feed. The reason why you're not listening to it now, and why we're live, is because, for the first time in two months, today's big story is something that happened in Westminster, and to explain, I'm going to hand over to my father."

"Thanks, pet. At nine o'clock this morning, the chancellor began delivering the much-trailed mini-budget to deal with the changing circumstances. He finished speaking at a quarter to ten. By eleven o'clock, the stock market had fallen by ten percent and is still dropping."

"And what did he say?" Gracie asked.

"It was a brief budget. There'll be across-the-board tax cuts, funding to retrain the military, and a rebuilding fund for Oxfordshire."

"Why did this trigger such market turmoil?"

"Firstly, because of what was missing. The NHS rescue plan, and the Education Reform Act, both of which received much press during the pandemic, are on pause at least until the spring, to give ministers more time to assess what impact Valley technology will have on health and education."

"Okay, listeners, no one is allowed to get sick between now and then, promise?" Gracie said.

"To encourage us to stay at home, all road and rail infrastructure projects have been indefinitely paused," Evan said. "To quote the chancellor, as the future of travel will be through the air, we don't want to ruin any more beautiful countryside with tarmac and steel. He went on to say that the government was committing to phase out all road vehicles by 2040."

"In favour of what?"

"He didn't say, but this raises huge questions for those in the automotive industries, and it's their shares which have fallen the most."

"So is the pause in spending how he's funding the tax cuts?"

"Not entirely. He's proposed a pilgrimage tax targeting towani believers who wish to visit holy sites in the United Kingdom."

"I think I can guess the answer, but is it legal to introduce a tax specifically targeting people of one particular faith?" Gracie asked.

"Every lawyer with a social media account has posted no. The only potentially workable solution would be to call it a tourism tax and target everyone."

"Let's say it was implemented. How much revenue would it generate?"

"He said an additional trillion pounds a year, but the real answer is that there's no way to know. We asked the Valley embassy for comment, and they referred us to their previous statement on pilgrims visiting Earth. To summarise, while billions of believers would wish to visit their ancestral home, there is still concern over Covid, general safety, capacity, and potential damage to the holy sites. For a decade, or perhaps longer, visitors will be limited to clerics with archaeological training and the military personnel protecting our solar system. In economic terms, while we might one day expect more tourists than we can handle, it won't be soon."

"But in the long term, is it a viable plan? Are there many potential pilgrimage sites here in the UK?"

"That's a great question."

"I know, it's almost as if we pre-planned me asking it."

"The key word is potential. This is a religion about which we still know very little. We don't know which places would be considered holy. There are three archaeological sites where Neanderthal remains have been found in the UK: Pontnewydd Cave, Swanscombe, and La Cotte de St Brelade in Jersey. There's also Gibraltar, where, in addition to some remains, ten caves have been found that were once inhabited by Neanderthals. We've got a guest who can discuss the significance of these finds. Professor Alice Brunhelm from the University of Surrey is here to talk through the archaeological record of Neanderthals in Britain and beyond."

"Sir, do you think we'll all be zipping about in the skies in twenty years?" Linton asked.

"I'm not sure, but I'll ask," Harold said, tapping out a quick message before he resumed his lunch. He'd nearly finished when Sean O'Malley walked through the door with the answer.

"It'll be at least fifty years before you need to pack a parachute for your commute to work," Sean said. "Upgrading the planet's power grid will take five to ten years. When that's done, we can start building a space dock to use as a hub for mining the asteroid belt to get the materials needed to feed the factories. But none of that can happen until we have a legitimate international decision-making body that can decide who gets which asteroids and what the new rules for air travel will be. The first stage is that conference in Ireland."

"How's that going?" Linton asked.

"Imagine wrangling a pack of cats on a chicken farm. Harold, are you busy? I'd like a second set of eyes on something."

Chapter 3 - A Waiting Watchdog

"How's your aunt?" Sean asked as they left the hangar and headed for the car park.

"In imminent need of a dentist," Harold said, buttoning his jacket. The brief rain shower had ceased, but had been replaced by a chill wind. "She's signed up for another three chocolate-by-post sub-scriptions. We really appreciate you giving me this job, even if it's a bit random at times. Do you know what they're charging to go on my tours now? Two million."

"I told them they were choosing short-term profit over long-term gain, but they didn't want to listen. Politicians rarely do. The Valley's decontamination team should arrive within the next two weeks to begin dismantling the battle-station and clearing out the hangars in Area-51. If we can resolve the issue of those sooval prisoners, we can reduce our presence here, and I can send you to Germany to help coordinate the resumption of archaeological digs."

"Wow. Cool. But I don't know anything about archaeology."

"That's why you'll be working with archaeologists. It's a liaison position between the bone brushers and the Valley priests. Any site where we find a Neanderthal's remains is considered sacred, so the excavations will have to be conducted in accordance with the traditional rituals."

"I don't know anything about those, either."

"But Tempest does. You'll be working with them and Serene, assuming this conference in Ireland ever manages to pick a delegation. Too many countries are still playing politics, so it's probably time to change the rules. Johann has recruited a few of the flood victims from Pakistan to act as guides to the peace platform. In a week or two, he will start offering tours."

"How much will those tickets cost?"

"Nothing. They'll be allocated at random. Locals need to know aliens are friendly, not face-sucking chest-bursters. Not all of them, anyway. Hopefully, that'll light a fire beneath the diplomats at the conference."

"If it doesn't, you could send Serene a box of matches."

"Don't tempt me. I always knew first contact would be hectic, but I assumed I'd have the UNCA to lean on. Now that's been disbanded because of Parker's betrayal, understaffed doesn't begin to describe the situation."

"Have you caught any more conspirators?"

"We've found no one yet, but that's not to say they don't exist. I was expecting the U.N. to collapse when people learned it had failed in its original purpose of preparing the planet for first contact. Still, I thought the selection of a delegation to Towan III would swiftly provide us with the framework for its replacement. From there, we could quickly establish a military rapid-reaction force to whom I could have handed out the battle rifles, and they could have been sent on today's little trip. Instead, it'll be you and me."

"Rifles?" Harold said, his heart sinking. "How dangerous is this trip?"

"Probably not at all," Sean said. He stopped by his tank-like SUV. "Last night, the air marshal's daughter was stargazing behind their house with a few friends. They spotted a drone. It probably belongs to some media organisation, or a creepier member of the civilian population, but the air marshal's house is on the edge of the exclusion zone. She's worried it might have been one of the drones used by the mercenaries and Voytay during the attack. If it is, whoever goes hunting for it must be armed with modern weapons. An armed Valley soldier traipsing around Berkshire will generate curious bystanders who could too easily become collateral damage. That leaves you and me. Fancy driving?"

"I still don't have a licence."

"I thought I gave you one."

"I mean, I've not had any lessons. What kind of message would it send if I reversed into a helicopter? Most of the personnel on the base already think I'm a spy. I don't want them to think I'm a saboteur, too."

"Suit yourself," Sean said and took the driver's seat.

Harold took the passenger side. The car began to move without either pedal or button being pressed. Harold briefly closed his eyes but found it didn't help. There were times he missed the reliable tedium of selling books.

"Really, though, how dangerous will this trip be?" Harold asked.

"Not at all," Sean said. "If it wasn't the air marshal who was asking, I'd have left it to the local police. But as it's her, we'll take a look to keep things friendly."

"But it could be another attack," Harold said. "Don't those mercenaries never give up on a job once they accept it?"

"Broadly," Sean said. "Now that we don't need to hide our presence from Earth, we've launched a much more comprehensive monitoring grid. If a ship skips into the system, we'll pick it up within minutes. No, if this is an imperial watchdog, it was left behind during the battle. But if that's the case, why didn't it attack the stargazers last night or anyone else during the previous two months? If this is anything, it is just as likely to be a ruse by the British military to lever a few of my rifles out of the stores."

"You don't want to give arms to Britain?"

"I don't want to give them to Russia. But if we start issuing the rifles to the British, what reason would I have to tell Russia they couldn't have some?"

"I can think of a few," Harold said.

"And what's to stop Moscow from asking the Voytay for arms? If Russia gets them first, we can step in and confiscate them. If other countries have them first, it becomes harder to intervene. Once we've rounded up any last associates of Parker's, the risk will be reduced."

"Until the Voytay send an agent disguised as a pilgrim or something," Harold said.

"Oh, exactly. We'll solve one problem but create a new one. Still, on balance, first contact is going far better than I expected."

"Yeah, I was expecting civil wars. Or at least some religious wars."

"So was I, and I think some might come, but not until people better understand, or misunderstand, the Valley."

The air marshal's home was ten miles north, in Great Haseley. Despite their flashing lights, navigating the heavy traffic displaced by the exclusion zone turned what should have been a twenty-minute drive into a frustrating fifty. Along the way, they saw some fields where farmers had erected signs, fences, and barbed wire to dissuade scrap hunters. Others were selling tickets.

The air marshal's house, on Rectory Road, was detached, but far from the mansion Harold expected a senior military figure to have. Only the RAF Police officer outside marked it as anything but another semi-rural home.

Sean parked behind the RAF police car. As their identity was checked, the front door opened. A woman in her late teens, dressed in a linen suit covered in badges and buttons, dragged out a suitcase.

"Are you the alien cops?" she asked.

"I'm Sean O'Malley, and I'm very human. Are you Tabitha Melchett?"

"I am, and I can't stop. I've got to get back to uni."

"Oh? What are you studying?"

"Astrophysics. But it *was* business. I've just switched and have tonnes to catch up on."

"Then we won't keep you. Last night you saw a drone in your garden."

She checked her phone. "You have me until my ride arrives. I'll show you where."

She led them to a side gate with a mechanical keypad and monitored by a discreet camera. "You're really not an alien?"

"I'm just from Woking," Harold said.

"Oh, sorry," she said.

Beyond a tennis court whose fence had been removed and onto which a bright H had recently been painted, the garden gave way to an increasingly dense shrubbery before it ended in trees. "There," she said. "It was above the laurel. It flew in, stopped, hung there just long enough for me to get a clip, and then flew away."

"In which direction?" Sean asked.

"West," she said. "Have a look." She took out her phone and played a short clip. There was little to see besides three small points of light. The phone buzzed. "And that's my ride. Good luck." With that, she dashed off.

"Oh, we didn't get a copy," Harold said.

"I did," Sean said, his hand moving as he typed on a screen only he could see. "And I've sent it to the platform for analysis. It was too indistinct for me to say what it was, but imperial watchdogs were designed to attack anyone who strayed into, or out of, a set perimeter. Prisoners sentenced to hard labour were dumped on asteroids and moons and told to start digging. A finite air supply kept them from straying too far from the work site, while the drones attacked anyone who tried to go beyond it to a waiting rescue ship. The Voytay modified them during the civil war, leaving them aboard derelict spaceships broadcasting a mayday, ready to ambush anyone who came to investigate. There's no reason they couldn't be modified again. But what for?"

"To spy on the air marshal. She'd resigned just before first contact, but is now running Britain's most important military branch."

"She'd resigned? I didn't know that."

"She had a job offer with an aerospace firm until she was given this job. That firm went bust last week. She got the news as I was giving a tour to the President of France. How hard would it be to build a fake casing for a sapiens drone?"

"Not too hard. There's plenty of footage online of the drones used in the battle above Oxfordshire."

"Maybe this is the work of a foreign government, trying to get some kompromat to blackmail her."

"I think you read too many thrillers, which isn't to say you're wrong," Sean said. "Since the drone is gone, there's not much more we can do here."

"There's a path behind those trees," Harold said. "The daughter said the drone came from the west. We could see if we could find where it was piloted from."

"A grand idea. You take a stroll, and I'll have a word with that police officer."

A walk in the countryside, even on a squally day, was better than spending it inside the hangar, but it didn't take Harold long to re-alise there'd be nothing to find. A drone would have been flown in from some distance away, probably from the back of a van, and, most likely by some journalist.

"Killer! Killer!" The word was shouted and came from ahead, where the path led into a narrow strip of woodland. It didn't sound like a warning, or a declaration of intent. He guessed it came from a woman and had that confirmed when she stepped out of the trees and onto the path. She was grey-haired, dressed in hiking gear bear-ing the Norwegian flag, and incredibly flustered.

"Killer! Killer— oh. Hello," she said. "You haven't seen a dog, have you?"

"Sorry, no. Does it answer to Killer?"

"Sadly, yes. My grandsons named her. I tried to get her to answer to Petunia, but she took that to be an instruction to dig up the flowerbed."

"What does she look like?"

"Oh, she's a black and white labradoodle. Hang on." She fished out her phone and showed Harold a photograph. "That's her with my eldest grandson. He plays the flute. And this is with my daugh-ter. She's in finance. This is my husband's birthday. We went to Nor-way. Killer's not in that picture."

"How long has she been missing?" Harold asked, interrupting before she dragged him too far down memory lane.

"Since last night. I put her out for some air at around eleven. When I went to call her in, she wasn't to be found. Wasn't to be heard, either, and that's more worrying. She's not fond of the out-doors."

"May I ask where you live, ma'am?"

"Just over there," she said.

Harold turned. "Not far from the air marshal's house?"

"You work for Lucinda?"

"Yes, ma'am," Harold said. It was a lot simpler than trying to explain. "Do any of the other houses here have dogs?"

"This is more of a cat neighbourhood," she said. "I'm sure it's given Killer a complex."

"Let me call my boss," Harold said. He raised a finger to his ear and spoke into his sleeve. It was unnecessary since the mic and speaker were on the glasses, but he didn't want the trouble that would come with an explanation. "Sir, there's a woman here looking for her dog. It went missing from her garden last night at around eleven, and her house is a hundred metres from the air marshal's."

"I'm on my way," Sean said.

Five minutes later, while the dog owner made tea, they examined her back garden. Near the fence, the dirt had been disturbed.

"There's blood on this ivy." Sean bent down and used a stick to clear away some flattened leaves. He then used the stick to trace the edge of something lodged in the dirt. "Well, it seems like the air marshal's daughter was correct. There *was* a drone. That's the same calibre of bolt a watchdog fires." Gingerly, he picked up the thumb-length bolt. "Interesting. Usually, the bullets are tipped with an acid cartridge so it can eat through a hull or wiring, but the cartridge has been removed."

"The drone killed a dog, and someone removed the body?" Harold asked.

"Probably," Sean said, leaving the shrubbery to check the edge of the lawn. "If the dog was injured but still mobile, it would head to the house. No, I think you're right. They came to collect the dog, probably thinking the bolt was lodged inside. They wanted to hide the evidence."

"Serene told me how, when she and Tempest went up to that artist's house in Lincoln, they found a drone there. Parker left it in the lake, right?"

"Probably, though he hasn't confessed to it. He's not confessed to anything yet, not even a preference for what he gets for breakfast."

"So if he's got an accomplice, they could have some of these drones?"

"Sure, it's possible."

"Then I bet this was an assassination attempt. They shot the dog to keep it quiet, then went onto the air marshal's house, but she wasn't in the garden."

"Why would anyone want to assassinate her?" Sean asked. "Sure, I can think of the obvious reasons, but I only get to Benson once or twice a week. Have you heard or seen something specific?"

"No, but what else could it be?"

"A kidnapping that was called off because there were too many witnesses. It could be that they want to bargain for Parker's freedom. It's safe to assume the assailant didn't know the area well, so used the path for navigation. After the drone flew over this house, the dog began barking, so it was killed. The drone continued to the air marshal's home, but too many stargazers were in the garden, so it returned to base. The drone might have been equipped to lift and carry, so either it or the operator came here to fetch the dog, thus removing the evidence. Agreed?"

"I think so."

"And what do you think we should do now?" Sean asked.

"I dunno. I suppose we continue following the path west. Find somewhere someone could park a van. Then I guess we could check for traffic cameras. Maybe we'll get lucky."

"Maybe we will."

The path followed the edge of the woodland and was marked by a frequently broken fence. Once they were beyond the trees, the fence grew sturdier and was topped with a strand of electrified wire. Since the field was full of cabbages, the electric wire was probably there to keep people out of the old barn at the field's edge. The stone walls still bore the marks of a fire, and two-thirds of the roof had been removed. Sean clearly saw something amiss, as he drew two pistols with a barrel below the grip as well as above. He handed one to Harold, who reluctantly took it.

"Hello in there," Sean called. "I'm with military intelligence. Would you mind stepping outside for a moment?"

"What is it?" Harold asked, keeping his voice nearly as low as the gun barrel.

"Thermal imaging picked up a void—" Sean began, but stopped as a shiny, black diamond-shaped drone rose from inside the ruin. A metre long and nearly as wide, it hovered above the tumbledown barn. With oft-practised fluidity, Sean levelled his gun. Long bolts flew from both barrels, but the drone merely cut its engines, letting gravity assist as it dodged the shots. It rose again, firing a shot of its own that slammed into Harold's chest. As he flew backwards, Sean pulled a short tube from his pocket and hurled it towards the drone. As the tube began to arc downwards, a burst of flame erupted from the rear. The miniature missile curved upwards. Again, the drone dodged, but the small missile had a lock on its target, punching a hole through the left wing. As smoke plumed from inside the machine, the now spinning drone crashed onto the field.

Thankfully, Harold's life hadn't flashed in front of his eyes. There was a pain in his chest, but a far bigger one in the small of his back that, as he gingerly sat up, turned out to be caused by a rock he'd been lying on. There was no blood on the ground, and none on his side. The drone's bolt might not have punctured his skin, but it had surely bruised his ribs.

"Up you get," Sean said. "Your vitals look fine. You're going to be okay."

"It shot me," Harold said.

"Consider that a practical lesson in the importance of a good suit. Yours is made of the same material as the latest military body armour. It disperses the force. Of course, if that drone had been firing acid-tipped rounds, it'd be a very different story. Maybe you should pick up your gun."

"Right. Yes. What was that you threw it at?"

"Essentially a small guided missile," Sean said. "They're designed for fighting in zero-g, but they can work under gravity within a short range. Stay behind me but to the right. If someone comes out of the barn running, they'll make for the trees. Try not to shoot me in the back."

The downed drone had split a fence post, making it easy to clamber over. Harold kept his eye on the missing roof as they neared the barn, but no other drones rose into the air.

After the fire that had destroyed the barn, the farmer had boarded up the windows and doors, but though there was a padlock on the door, it only took one shot to break it.

"Hands up, we're coming in," Sean said.

But the drone's operator wouldn't have understood the instruction. For one thing, they were unconscious. For another, it was a sooval.

Chapter 4 - Dr Griffin

"Now, here's something you don't find every day," Sean said, walking around the reptilian non-terrestrial. Its left arm was splinted with tree branches. "Harold, keep watch outside for curious locals."

"Are we in danger?" Harold asked.

"No, it's unarmed, unconscious, and unlikely to live much longer," Sean said.

Harold was glad to get back outside until he saw the irate farmer sprinting across the field. Along the path adjacent to the field, the dog-walking grandmother was speed-walking towards them.

"Gerroff my land!" the farmer roared.

"I'm here on official business with RAF Space Command. Please keep back."

"What are you doing in my barn?" the farmer bellowed.

Harold weighed his options, but one of his conditions for working for the ambassador, and for Sean O'Malley, was that there'd be no more cover-ups. That didn't mean he'd tell the whole truth, but he would tell some of it. "One of the alien drones left over from the space battle was lurking in that barn. It attacked. We destroyed it. This is now a crime scene."

"What about my dog? Did you find Killer?" the grandmother asked.

"Not yet, ma'am." His glasses flashed yellow, with a five-letter warning in Mid-Tow that he didn't recognise, but as his eyes followed the arrow pointing upwards, he saw a flying saucer making its descent. "Watch out!"

With a spray of soil and a fountain of cabbages, the saucer set down. Two armoured towani were first off the craft, and utterly ignored the grandmother, Harold, and the now-apoplectic farmer as they entered the barn. Dr Griffin was next, followed by two more Valley soldiers.

"Keep these people back, Godwin," Dr Griffin said, the words a near growl.

"What's that?" the farmer whispered hoarsely.

"That's Dr Griffin," Harold said. "He's the chief medic for the Valley in this system. And he's a paxley."

"Looks like a rabbit without the ears," the grandmother said.

Though the doctor had long legs in proportion to his body, he had short arms. He wasn't as tall as Harold, but his air of professional superiority was bigger than most planets. On his face, and lending to the rabbity look, was dense, latte-coloured fur-like hair, which was clipped short except at the chin, where it had been grown longer and dyed black. Of course, Dr Griffin claimed that was natural, in the same way he denied he was going bald on top.

"He's really great at his job," Harold said, "but he has a temper like an alligator in a paddling pool. It really would be best if we gave them room."

"Why's it here?" the farmer asked.

"He, not it, and because there's an injured person inside."

"Was he hurt by the drone?"

"It, not he, and we don't know," Harold said and was saved from further extemporisation by a shout from Dr Griffin.

"Godwin, be useful! Get the stabiliser."

Harold ran to the saucer and up the ramp. He'd been given a short first aid course as part of his training. *Very* short, mainly consisting of instructions on how to call for help, but he'd also been shown where, on the fighter craft parked in Benson, the emergency medical equipment was held. That included what he thought of as a stretcher, which was stored upright with a flat base that merged with the wall. As Harold detached it from the alcove, it swung down, and he grabbed the handles at the side. The entire panel was the size of a door, but a foot deep, and seemingly solid. It certainly weighed a ton as he hauled it down the ramp and over to the barn.

"This is no time for weight training," Griffin said as he entered.

"Turn on the repulsors," Sean said.

"The what?"

"Here," Sean said, pressing a blue button beside the handle.

Harold was almost knocked off his feet as the stretcher flipped, hovering in the air at waist height. Sean pushed it down and alongside the injured sooval.

The top of the stretcher slid out and under the unconscious mercenary, turning the device into a shallow box. The lid retracted, dragging the sooval inside the alcove.

"What's the prognosis, Doc?" Sean asked.

"Blood loss. Blood poisoning. Dehydration," Griffin said, each word punctuated by his cutting at the sooval's battered flight suit, revealing the yellow skin beneath. "Starvation, and food poisoning, on top of multiple infections around at least four contusions." Griffin removed the splint on the sooval's arm. A pyramidal mask swung out from the top of the stretcher. The doctor placed it over the mercenary's mouth, then stepped back as six metal arms appeared, three on each side of the stretcher, pressing against the sooval's skin.

Though the doctor was standing above the patient, his gaze was focused on the middle distance as he examined the read-out on his optical implant. "Good. It will live, but we need to take it to the prison for further treatment, and possibly up to the platform."

"When will you know?"

"Just before I tell you," Griffin said, pushing the stretcher out the door.

"I think he's mellowing," Sean said. "It must be all the fresh air he's getting."

"How does the stretcher work?"

"Stabiliser," Sean said. "It's the same principle as the rejuvenation technology, but in a much higher dose. Organic nano-bots will repair the damaged tissue."

Outside, quite a crowd had gathered, all with their phones out, recording the saucer.

"Can you all step back? There's a downdraft when the—" Sean began, but couldn't finish before the saucer took off, creating a cabbage-laden tornado that knocked two spectators down.

"That's half my crop gone," the farmer said.

"For which you'll be compensated," Sean said. "My associate will take your details in a moment. Harold, with me."

Harold followed Sean back into the barn.

"Want to guess how it got food poisoning?" Sean asked as he headed to a small fire pit near the rear wall.

"It was eating the dog, wasn't it?"

"And a few foxes, and maybe a cat or three," Sean said. "There's a stack of skulls over in the corner. The drone must have been killing and bringing back the animals, which is fascinating. I've not seen programming quite like that before."

"Has that sooval been here for eight weeks?"

"Probably, though not in this barn, or that dog would have vanished long ago. When you speak with the farmer, find out how often anyone comes out here. Then try to stop them from stealing the drone. I'm going to have a word with the air marshal, and then I'll have to give the bad news to the dog's owner."

Chapter 5 - Prisoners of War

Benson was fifty miles from Woking. Travelling by train and bus would take three hours, if the trains were running. Instead, Harold took a cab to work. The eternal congestion didn't make the journey much faster, but at least he could catch up on the news.

For once, the main story wasn't about first contact, or at least not immediately, but was focused on the fallout from the chancellor's statement, and the economic crash it had precipitated. Not wanting to be tarnished by association, most of the cabinet had gone into hiding, leaving it to the Minister for Culture and Sport to announce that no, the prime minister had not fled the planet. As the pundits frothed over how low the pound might sink, Harold had a reminder of how the world had been before first contact, and a hint at how little had really changed.

From how the morning tour was full of more suits than uniforms, the crisis gripping Westminster wasn't affecting ticket sales. After the group had flown to the crash site, Harold went to the hangar and found Sean in a heated argument with Blake, much to the amusement of Linton and the other NCOs.

"Nessie *is* real!" Blake said.

"It was just a cover story that got out of hand," Sean said. "A ship tried to land in the loch, but it's too deep. The ship sank. Retrieving it safely would have required too much large equipment, so it was left there."

"Nine years ago, I went up there and saw her myself, clear as day," Blake said.

"After the battle-station has been dismantled, cleaning up Loch Ness will be the next priority for the decontamination crew. I'll make sure you're part of that team, and you can see for yourself."

"Ho, hang about," Sergeant Linton said, playing peacemaker. "Didn't you say there's a sentient aquatic species?"

"There's a few," Sean said. "The only ones living on Earth are fi-randa."

"Well, maybe that's what you saw," she said.

"Someone once told me that all things are possible," Sean said. "But if you'll excuse me, I need to borrow Harold."

"What's up?" Harold asked.

"The prison's newest guest is awake."

To the north of the runway, and utterly out of bounds to any sightseers, no matter how much they'd paid, was the prison. The outer fence was guarded by the SAS, who made a show of checking their I.D. before letting them through. The inner fence was guarded by armoured towani, who saluted Sean. Inside lay a guard post where Sean handed over his weapons. It took him a while.

"Nessie is supposed to be a plesiosaur," Harold said. "And the fi-randa are humanoid."

"Humanoid-ish," Sean said. "The small tribe on Earth are the origin for the legends of mermaids."

"How would you confuse the two?"

"You wouldn't. The photograph of the creature with snake-like humps was a telescopic arm belonging to a submersible that broke."

"Why didn't you tell Blake that?"

"Some people choose to believe, but there are others who need to," Sean said, adding a knuckle duster to the pile of knives, guns, and miniature missiles. "I think that's it." He stepped through the Valley-made body-scanner. It pinged. "What did I forget? Ah, of course." He took out his wallet and removed a credit card. "It's a breaching explosive."

This time, the scanner made no sound as he walked through.

"Do you really need all those weapons?" Harold asked. "More importantly, will I?"

"Each time I've escaped imprisonment, I ask myself afterwards what would I have needed to extricate myself sooner."

Harold recalled his own imprisonment by Parker. Perhaps it was a stratagem worthy of some more thought.

66

Beyond the security station was the surveillance room. Four towani were bent over consoles, monitoring the prisoners in the main compound. Above the consoles were screens, showing camera views of the corridors and the exercise yard. Those screens weren't for the benefit of the towani, but for the visitors in the twelve-seat gallery.

While tourists weren't allowed to gawp at the inmates, this prison was in Britain, and so subject to inspection by the Home Office and the increasingly misnamed human rights lawyers. Currently, there were six, all wearing an expression of deep bewilderment that was the current fashion across the world.

There were many sooval in the Valley, and some among the Voytay, just as there were towani, paxley, jajan, firanda, and most other species. The sooval who'd taken part in the attack on Earth were mercenaries, part of a criminal gang with over five thousand members, and infamous for their raids on remote monasteries in the borderlands. Seventeen had been captured alive.

As usual, the sooval were fighting. Today's bout seemed to be six on six, with the remaining five chanting behind the brawling group.

"That song's a classic. It's won the championship at least a dozen times," Sean said.

"They really call this a sport?"

"Sure, each team has to stop the other from singing. Lose the beat, and you lose the game."

"But it's so violent."

"It's not much different to wrestling."

"Wrestling is staged."

"That's just a myth," Sean said. "Come on."

They went through another checkpoint, and into the small clinic where the prisoners were treated for cuts and bruises after their daily exercise. Currently, there was only one patient, attended by a towani orderly, and watched by a soldier. Dr Griffin was seated by the door, slowly pecking at a sapiens laptop, on which he appeared to be creating slides for a lecture.

"When are we upgrading this planet's technology?" the doctor said by way of greeting.

"As soon as we can," Sean said. "How's the patient?"

"Recovering. It can be transferred to the main facility tomorrow. It wants to speak with you."

The humanoid was only six feet tall, smaller than was usual for its species. Its long limbs and barrel body were covered in yellow-green scales tipped with red on its face.

As they neared the bed, the sooval began speaking. Harold had been expecting a sibilant hiss, but the tone was surprisingly sonorous and in the Mid-Tow language common throughout the galaxy. After a sentence, auto-translate kicked in, and an English translation was played through the speakers in the arms of his glasses.

"Take me to your leader," the sooval said.

"I'm Sean O'Malley, and I speak for the Valley, and Earth. You'll get no one more senior."

The sooval gave Harold a soul-piercing glare with its golden eyes. "And what is this?"

"My assistant," Sean said.

"It was with you yesterday?" the sooval asked.

"Yes," Sean said. "We found you and brought you here for treatment. You'd have died without it. When did you arrive in this system?"

"I am Larneth Fee Hurnot," the sooval said, and it clearly meant something to Sean. The sooval reached beneath its sapiens-made hospital gown and pulled out a medal hanging on a chain around its neck.

"It's a long time since I last met a larneth," Sean said. "Did you arrive with the battle-station?"

"I did."

"And since then?"

"I have been hiding."

"In that stone barn?" Sean asked.

"I moved around."

"You sent your drone off to hunt small animals."

"I re-programmed it, yes."

"And took the acid tips off the end of its darts," Sean said. "Why didn't you attack any people?"

"Because I seek sanctuary."

"Why?"

"Because I am a larneth."

"Then how did you end up here?"

"My trainer got into debt. I was given to the stable to pay it off. Now I seek sanctuary."

"Who ordered the attack on this planet?"

"The Voytay."

"But who among the Voytay?"

"I do not know."

"A while back, I placed a contract with your stable, requesting you come to Earth to collect a data-core. Three sooval came. They died. It was a trap."

"We know. The Voytay contracted us to spring the trap, and to then be a distraction while their agents stole the data-core."

"It was never there," Sean said. "The Voytay agents who came with you all died. We almost took one towani prisoner, but she killed herself before she could be captured. We've taken seventeen sooval prisoners and recovered the bodies of ninety more. There are five thousand in your stable. Why have the others not attacked?"

"I am not with them. How can I know?"

"If you want sanctuary, why didn't you reveal yourself before now?"

"Now I am caught, I ask for sanctuary. Before, I was waiting for rescue."

"Who was going to rescue you?"

"The Voytay. In our contract, within sixty days, any sooval captured during the attack would be rescued. Sixty days have now passed. No rescue is coming. The contract has been breached. Will you grant me sanctuary?"

"I'll have to speak to a few people," Sean said.

"You said you spoke for Earth."

"I do, but not alone," Sean said. He turned to the orderly. "Keep this one apart from the others. I'll be back soon."

"Now that's a turn-up for the books," Sean said, after they had stepped outside the clinic.

"Do those books come with a translation?" Harold asked.

"A larneth is a lead singer, like a striker or quarterback, but with perfect pitch. You only get the title if you've *won* a championship. That's what the medal indicates. It's a big deal. It sounds like it was essentially sold to pay off a debt."

"Why bring a singer to a battle?"

"A song can be great for morale. Sanctuary won't be a problem, though we'll move it away from Earth. More interesting is that the Voytay promised to stage a rescue, and it hasn't come. If it was promised within sixty days and has yet to occur, then this is a breach of contract. Of course, it depends on how they're measuring the length of a day. Each planet has its own local time, and there's an interstellar time system for the depths of space."

"We should increase security just in case."

"Definitely. Honour and prestige are as important to the mercenaries as they are to criminal gangs here on Earth. Once a contract is accepted, the entire stable vows to complete it. It could be that there've been no more attacks because the rest of its pals are waiting on this bunch to be rescued."

"So no rescue means no more attacks?" Harold said.

"And maybe ever, at least by this stable. They take their contracts that seriously. The reason we set a trap for this particular stable is that they've been a plague on the borderland monasteries. There are plenty of other gangs, and I'm sure another will fill the void, but we'll buy ourselves a bit of time. If you squint, that can look a fair bit like peace. I'll have to speak to Johann, and with Greta, and then I suppose I better call the British government. Would you mind filling in the air marshal on what was just said?"

"All of it?" Harold asked.

"All of it," Sean said.

Harold marked off each sealed crate of waste from the crash site as they were loaded onto the cargo-plane, while thinking of stable doors and bolting sooval. The air marshal had been horrified at the idea of a prison break. It was understandable, of course, but her response had been a tripling of the guard, with attack helicopters on standby and fighter jets overhead. If it came to a battle, they wouldn't stand a chance. Then again, what else was she supposed to do? Perhaps this was why she had been brought out of retirement, to take the blame if a second attack led to a massacre.

The smell of French fries preceded Sean O'Malley's return. He'd brought enough arch-decorated brown bags that he needed a trolley.

"One's for us, and the rest are for the sooval," Sean said. "I just wanted the ketchup, but those wretched self-service machines don't have a button to sell sauce separately."

"You're giving them a treat?"

"Sure. It's always good to do the unexpected, and it might encourage them to talk. Johann is ready to send them home."

"What, they're going to be freed?"

"If a rescue were to come late, they might view the contract as being honoured, and so their comrades might launch another attack on Earth. But if we send them home, we can guarantee the contract *was* breached."

"That's sneaky. Did the government go along with it?"

"I couldn't get through to the prime minister. How long until the plane's full?"

"About half an hour."

"I'm going to hitch a ride over to Area-51. I thought this might be a good time for you to take a look at the place."

"In America?" Harold asked.

"There's a great little diner near the facility. Does fantastic shakes. We can do a taste comparison with these."

"And?" Harold asked. "What's the bit you aren't telling me?"

"I want you to have a word with Alan Parker," Sean said. "He's said nothing to me so far, but he seemed happy preaching to you after he abducted your aunt. Let's see how he reacts to the news the larneth told us."

Chapter 6 - It's Usually Stalin

Harold spent the first two minutes of the flight inhaling tepid fast food, and the next hour updating Serene, Tempest, and Aunt Jess on his day at work. The update from Serene and Tempest only took five minutes. Jess's daily recap took even less.

"I had four people come in today asking if we had a towani phrase book," Jess said.

"There's an idea," Serene said. "We could write one."

"Everyone will be using translators soon," Tempest said.

"Until then, we could make a fortune," Serene said.

"Oh, I've got to go," Jess said. "Samir's at the door. Call me when you land, Harry. Wait, no, don't do that because it'll be the middle of the night. Call me in the morning."

"Call us all in the morning," Serene said. "We've got to go, too. The President of Ireland is coming for dinner again."

One by one, their faces disappeared from his immediate field of view. Harold removed the small camera from the seat in front of him and looked around for something to do. While it was a large plane, it had a small passenger cabin with only ten seats. Sean was the only other passenger, and he was engrossed in a biography of Saddam Hussein. Not having a book of his own, Harold accessed the Valley encyclopaedia, bringing up its entry on Area-51, but it was surprisingly sparse. He rubbed his eyes, feeling an eyestrain headache coming on.

The glasses were amazing, but they did turn every waking minute into screen-time. On their own, they allowed thermal, low-light, and magnification, not to mention correcting his vision. When linked to the phone-like computer the Valley called a *jeed*, which he wore on his wrist, they could provide an augmented reality view of the world, and a virtual reality view of many thousands of others. He wore a ring on each thumb that the lenses tagged and used when he needed precise motor control, but even without them, he could type, operate a scanner, or lose to Tempest at any of a million towani games. They truly were marvellous, but he'd drawn the line at switching on remote charging. No matter what Serene said, electricity zipping through the ether to a device bookending his brain surely wasn't safe.

"Sir, can I ask you a question?" he asked.

"Sean, please. And if it's whether it's safe to fly a quarter way around the world in a plane filled with toxic waste, I say no, but imagine how happy we'll feel when we land safely."

"I'd not thought of that," Harold said. "Why didn't we take your spaceship?"

"I didn't want to draw attention to the place. If we land a ship there, people will begin asking questions about Area-51, when I want them asking why their politicians can't even pick a handful of representatives to send to Towan III."

"Oh, fair enough. Actually, my question *is* about Area-51. Today, on the tour, I was asked why the facility is in America."

"What did you say?"

"I stuck to the script, but the answer is very vague. Was it really the best option in the 1950s?"

"Stalin," Sean said. "I set up the United Nations as the Second World War was grinding to an end, so the explanation for most of the mistakes I made is Stalin. Some is the lingering stench of Hitler. And a few are explained by my exhaustion after too many years of fighting. If the UN ran the storage facility, Stalin would have had a right to send his representatives there, so it had to be run by a local, national government. If it wasn't protected by a superpower, Stalin would have invaded. The Nevada desert seemed the best option. It had the Hoover Dam for power, the desert to keep away most of the idly curious, and it was remote enough we could land a space-freighter when we needed to ship the more toxic wreckage off-world."

"But why didn't the Americans reverse-engineer all that technology?"

"They did," Sean said. "Mercury, Apollo, Pong, you name it, it all came from the stars."

"Then can I ask that question the other way around? Why did you *allow* them to reverse-engineer it?"

"Because I didn't want to be a dictator. All governments are secretive, and no side wanted too many people knowing extra-terrestrials existed, so the number of scientists granted access was limited."

"But why were the governments secretive at all?" Harold asked.

"Because first contact requires two. I told them that any unilateral announcement would have caused the towani, and all other non-sapiens, to quietly leave Earth. Any leader who'd said aliens were real would be thought mad. It was a bluff, designed to get them talking. It kept the peace, but was otherwise a failure."

"So the world leaders know about the Valley?"

"Oh, they knew. What they didn't know was how many people the others were allowing access to extra-terrestrial technology. It was in the interests of all sides to pretend any invention and every advance was the work of pure sapiens genius. If Chuck Yeager broke the speed of sound in 1947 in an aircraft designed *without* any Valley technology, just imagine what could be achieved if they opened Area-51 to every university's engineering class. If Sputnik 1 was a purely Soviet design, imagine what could be launched if the communist empire included a tour of their Star City vault in every science program. They had to limit knowledge, but pretend they'd limited it even more. Remember that the speed of sound was *only* broken in 1947. Sputnik 1 was *only* launched in 1957. That was with their lead engineers having access to extra-terrestrial technology. They knew we were so far behind the Valley that it would take centuries to break the speed of light."

"So Stalin had ships? I thought crashed ships were supposed to be handed over to Area-51. Wasn't that part of the deal when the U.N. was set up?"

"It was, but you must have read a biography or three on Stalin. He handed over enough to make it seem like he was handing over everything. I knew what he was up to, but thought allowing him to conduct some research of his own would help him realise just how impossible it would be for him to build an interstellar engine, and so hasten first contact. It was just one more of my many mistakes. I don't like remembering those years. Ask me something else."

"How many prisoners are held at Area-51?"

"Fifty-six."

"And they've had no trial?"

"They have, but according to towani military law. A panel of five judges heard their case, and their ruling was then put before a jury for confirmation or rejection. The sentencing was adapted to reflect our shorter life span. These are bad people, Harold. Parker's not the worst of them. After an encounter, most people didn't understand what they'd seen and were willing to buy into the cover-up. The few that didn't were offered a job or a pay-off. Some took the money and then tried to go public. Those, we discredited. A few more went mad. There's only ever been a handful we had to detain."

"What happens when their sentence is finished?"

"House arrest in northern Quebec," Sean said. "There are only five currently alive up there. It's not ideal, but it is better than an execution."

Harold leaned back in his seat. He knew he was privileged to be at the very heart of first contact. He had no special skills and had been given the job because Sean, Greta, and Johann felt guilty over his childhood. Soon, the embassy would start recruiting scientists and experts. If he was to keep his job, he needed to learn as much as he could, and be as useful as possible. He knew that, but right now, he was starting to miss his ignorance.

Chapter 7 - Area-51

After ten hours, they finally landed, but thanks to the inconsiderate nature of time zones, it was still the middle of the night. They had to wait for the plane to be towed into a hangar before they disembarked. As a work crew came to unload the crated wreckage, a man came to meet them. He was about fifty years old, greying at the temples, firm-jawed, and wearing a government dress-code suit that didn't entirely hide his shoulder holster.

"Leroy! I didn't expect to see you here," Sean said. "Harold, this is Leroy Burton. Leroy, this is Harold Godwin, my new assistant."

"Pleasure," Burton said, extending a hand. "Just remember what happened to his *last* assistant."

"Why? What did happen?" Harold asked.

"He means Alan Parker," Sean said.

"And the reason I'm here," Burton said. "I was reassigned yesterday, but only after nearly two months of interrogation. It's Special Agent Burton, now. FBI, A-Files division."

"A-Files? You're joking," Sean said.

"I wish I was," Burton said. "We're replacing the UNCA here in America."

"Leroy was part of the UNCA team here in the United States," Sean said.

"The deputy *director*," Burton said. "Can't say that this new role feels like anything but a demotion."

"Now we've got first contact out of the way, the Valley embassy will begin hiring soon. There's a place for you there if you want it," Sean said.

"In Germany? Madeleine's only got two years of high school left. She wouldn't appreciate being uprooted."

"Then I'll keep the position open for a few years," Sean said. "She's sixteen already?"

"Fifteen, but yes."

"Time does fly," Sean said. He turned to Harold. "Leroy was part of my protection detail in Iraq, just after the invasion in 2003. That was Parker's first assignment with me, too."

"And where Parker met his wife," Burton said. "I'd like to interview her."

"I suppose that will have to be arranged through the British Home Office now," Sean said. "She's being watched, but hasn't been charged. Not yet. I've spoken to her a few times, but she's had less to say than her husband."

Burton turned to Harold. "Harold Godwin? Parker abducted your aunt as leverage, yes?"

"How do you know?"

"It's in the file, sorry," Burton said.

"Thanks," Harold said, uncertain whether the apology was for the abduction, or for the existence of a file that would undoubtedly contain details of his childhood.

"Let's talk and walk," Sean said. "I assume there's no problem with us interviewing Parker?"

"As an emissary of the Valley, no," Burton said as he and Sean began walking towards what appeared to be a windowless office in the corner of the hangar. "I should tell you that one of my responsibilities is to draw up a plan to shut down the prison before the next election."

"Ah, and you were given the task because you have a direct line to me?" Sean said. "Well, I can't say I didn't know this day was coming, but one problem at a time."

Harold followed Sean and Burton to a windowless room in the corner of the hangar that concealed a security station. Two uniformed military police NCOs stood behind a Valley walk-through scanner identical to the one at the sooval prison at RAF Benson. Once again, Sean began divesting himself of his personal arsenal.

"Expecting trouble?" Burton asked as the tray began to fill up.

"It's the unexpected kind that troubles me more," Sean said. Once he'd finished, his overloaded tray and Burton's sidearm, were

78

each placed in a separate locker. Only then did the door at the rear of the room slide open, revealing an elevator with no buttons.

After a stomach-lurching descent, the elevator opened into a grey-walled checkpoint illuminated by light-panels in the ceiling. Behind a desk covered in monitors, three half-drunk cups of coffee, an empty donut box, and a bookmarked paperback sat a solitary uniformed guard. The sergeant, a man in his forties with more of a gut than was usual in the military, had clearly been expecting them.

"Raymond! Good to see you again," Sean said.

"Welcome back, Mr O'Malley," the sergeant said. With the press of a button, a door in the wall opposite the elevator slid open.

"They interrogated him, too," Burton said as they walked along a grey-painted corridor wide enough for a jeep.

"Raymond Washington is another veteran of Iraq," Sean said.

"There were three of us in the detail," Burton said. "Lopez didn't make it out. Car bomb."

"Oh, I'm sorry," Harold said.

"Wasn't the first, wasn't the last," Burton said. "Washington stayed in the military and was transferred here about nineteen years ago."

The door at the end of the corridor led into the surveillance centre, a circular chamber with more screens than a newsroom. Four military police warders were on duty, but though they looked alert now, there didn't appear to be much for them to do. Some screens showed empty corridors, but fifty-five showed a ghoulish green and white low-light view of a sleeping prisoner. A fifty-sixth showed a well-lit room in which a woman was knitting.

"There he is, lucky number thirteen," Burton said. "Do you want me to wake him?"

"It's the least he deserves," Sean said. "And we'll speak with Olawayo, Afiz, Ricard, and Penn while we're here. But bring Parker first, and bring him to the exercise yard. Let's keep him wrong-footed. I'll take Harold via the junkyard."

"That's a cell?" Harold asked, captivated by the screen showing the lit room.

"It is."

"It's huge. It's basically a studio apartment."

The exact size was hard to judge, but there was room for a bed, a small table, an armchair, and a semi-private area for the toilet and shower.

"The prisoners were tried according to the towani military code, so they've been imprisoned according to the same regulations. Confinement is the punishment, and the goal is rehabilitation."

"Does she control her own light?"

"A light switch is a privilege," Sean said. "She's suffering from chronic back pain, but her beliefs won't allow her to take medication. Sleep's hard for her, so she sits and knits."

"Wow," Harold said. "It's miles better than any cell I ever had. What did she do?"

"That's Heidi Morganthal. She's the sole survivor of a plot to blow up the embassy and is ten years into a twenty-year sentence. If she were a towani, with the longer life span, she'd be doing a full century."

"Twenty years for plotting?"

"For murder," Sean said. "Four sapiens were killed in an explosion as she tried to evade arrest. One was a UNCA agent. The other three were members of a family living in the apartment below her."

"Oh. *Only* twenty years?"

"It's complicated," Sean said. "The old empire punished people through labour camps, forced colonisation, exile, and with execution. When the Valley created its penal code, it wanted to do things differently. Some say the pendulum swung too far the other way."

"What'll happen to them if the prison is shut down?"

"We'll build a new prison somewhere else, and they will continue to serve their sentences, or they can opt for a new trial under local laws. Since that is almost guaranteed to produce a much longer sentence in much worse conditions, I doubt many will avail themselves of that option."

"Have Parker and his team been tried, then?"

"No. How and where that takes place is still being debated. Let me show you the junkyard."

A nondescript door led onto the top level of a gantry at one edge of a vast underground hangar. Below, and against each wall, were glass-fronted display cases. In front of those, illuminated by spotlights, were seventeen spaceships in various states of decrepitude. In the chamber's centre, curved benches formed five concentric circles around a two-metre-wide dome.

"It's like a museum," Harold said. "I thought you said this was a junkyard."

"It *is* a junkyard," Sean said. "But it's also a museum. Eisenhower went a bit overboard when he had the place built. There was far more space than was needed, so JFK turned this hall into a museum. The toxic waste and scrap are stored next door. Now that recycling equipment is coming, we won't need to ship it off-world. We'll process the rest of the waste in Oxfordshire, and set up a training course so all future waste can be processed here."

"I'm not sure I'd like to do that."

"There's good money to be made in planetary decontamination. It's a dangerous job, so not many people in the Valley want to do it, but that means plenty of vacancies. Right now, there aren't many jobs a sapiens would easily be able to qualify for. Some are *more* dangerous, like soldiering, but for anything else, it'll take decades to bring Earth's education up to what most employers would consider the bare minimum. Even a basic decontamination qualification will take a year, but the exams are all in Mid-Tow, and no translators are allowed, so people will have to learn the language first. That'll give us time to update the medical databases."

"So we're stuck on Earth until then?"

"With a few necessary exceptions, like the official trip to Towan III. Sapiens are similar to towani, but we're not identical. Sure, sealing a wound is straightforward, but any towani medication, transfusions, or transplants could prove lethal. Dr Griffin has been studying sapiens anatomy for years, but a study needs subjects, and they need to give consent. Now that we've had first contact, he can start recruiting for formal trials. That'll enable him to update the medical databases and recruit some doctors for retraining. Come on, there's a ship I want to show you." He began descending the stairs.

"Do any of these ships work?" Harold asked.

"The engines were dismantled. It would be too dangerous to leave them here without maintenance. Even if we hadn't, Parker doesn't know how to fly one, if that's what you're worried about."

"A bit. What's in the display cases?"

"Some of the more interesting artefacts we seized over the years." They'd reached the bottom of the stairs. Sean headed to a small glass case. "Read the plaque."

"Valley communicator captured by Nazis in Italy, 1943."

"Actually, it was captured from me," Sean said. "Keep reading."

"Part of the artefacts taken from Hitler's bunker in 1945."

"Taken *by* me before Stalin could his grubby mitts on it," Sean said. "Hitler was obsessed with *außerirdische waffen*. Most of the cases in this section are linked to World War Two. That shallow dome in the centre of the hangar is a holographic projector they were gifted a few years ago. It shows the story of each of the crashed ships. You can have a look later. Do you see that rectangle with wings?"

It was the size of a bus and looked to have a similar structure, with rows of seats inside, but no floor.

"Is it some kind of troop carrier?" Harold asked.

"It's a sightseeing bus," Sean said. "There was an eejit of an entrepreneur who thought the prohibition against setting foot on Earth could be taken literally. This was in 1960, I think." He checked the plaque. "1961. Alaska. He charged eight pilgrims a modest fortune to bring them to Earth for an aerial tour. Once they neared the planet, they transferred the paying customers to this ship, while his associate on the mother-ship distracted the Valley patrol. He'd not considered that a fighter pilot might think this vessel was a giant Russki doodlebug. The American pilot opened fire, the towani tour guide panicked, and the ship crashed. The tourists all died. Now, this is the one I wanted you to see."

He pointed to a sleek green and white dart-shaped ship, about fifteen metres long, and four wide, with a window at the front, narrow fins at the side, and an empty engine mounting at the back.

"Is that writing on the side in Arabic?" Harold asked.

"It is. This ship crashed in Iraq in 2001. Aboard was a religious zealot who thought dying on the ancestral homeworld was the key to resurrection. Saddam Hussein handed over the body, but not the ship. The U.S. president grew increasingly, and unnecessarily, worried what Saddam might do with the ship, and eventually launched the invasion."

"This was the WMDs they never found?"

"Essentially, yes. Unbeknownst to us, the dead zealot wasn't the pilot, but just a passenger. The pilot was an agent working for the Voytay who wanted to set up a smuggling ring. He struck a deal with Saddam to buy bones to sell on the black market. Sapiens bones were, sadly, easy for a dictator to get his hands on. Neanderthal bones presented more of a problem, but there are several famous archaeological sites in Iraq where they had been found, including the Shanidar Cave."

"Is that what this is?" Harold asked, pointing at a case containing photographs of a circular tunnel whose walls were lined with carved and painted tiles.

"No, that's where we found the ship. Starting beneath the ruins of the ancient city of Nineveh, in what is now Mosul, is a tunnel, a little over ten miles long, dug by Celeste's student at least two thousand and seven hundred years ago."

"The Librarian of Alexandria?"

"The same. This tunnel predates Alexandria."

"Oh. Why did he dig it?"

"You see this square chamber here? That's where the student once lived. The tunnel was probably to facilitate the launch of a ship, though when I asked Celeste, she said he just liked digging tunnels."

"But that was a joke?" Harold asked.

"I'm not sure. We don't know precisely how old the tunnel is, but for a long, long time, there wasn't much happening on Earth. We do know the locals added these tiles and painted the mural, somewhere around 650 BCE. They're a visual depiction of local legends, which, in that part of the world, include biblical stories. That one there is part of the story of Jonah and the whale."

Harold peered at the photograph of a two-dimensional monster, painted in faded reds and blues, but it was difficult to make out the details. Next to the photograph was a much clearer pencil sketch of the painted carving. Hooded eyes were set up above a greedily open shark-toothed mouth. The body curved downwards, and did contain a crude figure, but there was only faded shading where the tail should be. From the body, instead of fins, snaked curling tentacles that ended in claws, one of which was wrapped around a second figure, this one surrounded by what looked like three small birds.

"That's supposed to be a whale? It's got claws."

"That's what I thought. A towani archaeologist, who's now Serene's tutor, Abi tol Demener, thinks they're tentacles. Abi's retired to Towan III, but not before publishing a theory. Can you guess what it is?"

"Not a clue."

"Then I'll give you one. This photograph shows where some carved tiles had fallen away, revealing what was beneath."

Angular symbols had been carved into the tunnel's wall in a pattern that looked almost familiar. "Is that writing?" he asked.

"It is, and in characters similar to the machine code the towani use. Similar, but not identical. And the machine code is the most ancient towani written language. Now tell me what that whale with clawed tentacles might look like."

"Wait, it's the monster that kidnapped the ancestral towani? Like in that video clip of the Holy Nowan?"

"Possibly. That's Abi's theory. Celeste said that her student arrived here after the abduction. Once here, the librarian stayed in touch with Celeste, and the wider galaxy so he could have heard of the rise of the towani empires and their religion. The mural could have been created by locals who'd heard the story from the librarian, but that doesn't explain the writing hidden beneath the tiles."

"What does it say?"

"No one knows," Sean said. "The characters are similar, but the language isn't. Only small sections of the original tunnel wall were visible, and not enough to begin decoding what we could see. This is a major find, but the region became too unstable and dangerous for Abi to remain there."

"They actually went to Iraq?"

"For about three months. The concern was that the local insurgents would wonder why there was such a large military presence at a place with zero strategic significance, and it might lead to the tunnel's discovery and destruction. Instead, the tunnel was sealed, and its exploration was put on hold. This is one of the first sites we want to reopen."

"Wow. But it's only two and a half thousand years old."

"The terracotta tiles are about two thousand seven hundred years old. The tunnel might date from around then. Some think it might be a lot older. There are a few who think Nowan returned to Earth and wrote that inscription on the tunnel themselves."

"Did you ask Celeste?"

"Of course, and so did Johann, and Abi, but Celeste merely said there are some answers which must be earned, not given. When it comes to religious figures, she's often tight-lipped. We'll probably begin excavations there next year and start getting answers soon after. For now, let's go back to 2003. Saddam had created a new entrance to the tunnel and built an anonymous compound over it. Underground, not far from the entrance, was the big chamber where the spaceship had been moved. This picture was taken a few days after the discovery."

The photograph captured a moment in time. Glaring spotlights filled the chamber, illuminating carvings on the walls as well as the ship. A much younger Burton and Washington, and a third soldier who must be Lopez, stood by the base of a stone staircase, an expression of confused disbelief on their faces. Beyond them, a sapiens woman and an elderly towani appeared to be collecting bones that had been scattered about the floor. Next to them was another towani, this one in a cleric's robes, who held her hands across her chest in prayer.

"That's a lot of bones."

"Mostly sapiens. Mostly recently used. Saddam thought he could use the ship to escape, but he'd been conned. That ship wasn't space-worthy or flight-capable. When we arrived, and the shooting began, the smuggler made his way back onto the ship. Our bullets did nothing, not even mine. He was wearing a new type of armour. We think he was trying to retrieve a navigational beacon, and that orange brick, and walk back through the tunnel knowing we couldn't stop him. He'd have hoped to get top-side, use the beacon to summon his ship, and then escape. We'd just discovered that a new type of masking technology had been developed to hide a ship from our sensors. Later, we learned that a ship had landed twice to collect bones as a down payment."

"What is the orange brick?" Harold asked, moving to the next cabinet where it was displayed. The artefact was a little larger than a brick, and the orange colour was some form of plastic-like coating that was cracked at the top, and singed in the bottom-left corner.

"A flight recorder as old as the tunnel's terracotta tiles. The data is mostly corrupted, but it contains some seemingly banal conversations between a pilot and the librarian. The pilot was a collector of sorts who'd occasionally visit the librarian. According to Celeste, they were friends."

"Why is it here and not in the embassy, or sent back to Towan III?"

"Because it belongs to Earth. Besides, the Valley doesn't want to appear too eager to investigate Celeste's people for fear of gaining their wrath. If you look at that photograph where the bones are being cleared from the chamber floor, you can see a sapiens woman helping Abi. That woman is Dr Awat Masadi, an Iraqi archaeologist who'd been surveying the tunnel before she was retasked with preparing the bones to be shipped off-world. There had been other archaeologists, but they were murdered before we arrived. She was supposed to accompany Saddam into space. Instead, she killed the towani smuggler using a mining laser that was aboard the ship. A year later, she married Parker. Until a few months ago, I assumed Awat was an innocent victim. A prisoner of Saddam's. What if she wasn't? What if she killed the towani smuggler to stop him from talking?"

"From saying what?"

"From telling us how the smuggler communicated with the Iraqis? How did the smuggler first come to trade with Saddam? Did someone at the embassy broker a deal? When was the tunnel discovered? And by whom? Back then, Dr Masadi said she didn't know, and I had no reason to disbelieve her. All the other scientists working there had been murdered. When he was caught, Saddam refused to say anything except for that one brief outburst during his trial where he revealed the embassy's location."

"He did?"

"The trial wasn't broadcast live, and that was edited out of the record. I'm now wondering how far I can trust anything Dr Masadi told us. Was the death of the smuggler simply to cover up that she wasn't a prisoner, but running the operation there?"

"You said the ship crashed in 2001. That's not long after they tried to abduct lots of babies like me, and Serene, and Tempest."

"It's a big galaxy, but yes, it could all be linked. Now that you're up to speed, let's have a word with Parker, and see if we can get more than a word from him."

Chapter 8 - One Deal on the Table

The exercise yard was an indoor garden whose ceiling was currently patterned with stars. A short running track ringed the perimeter. One corner held some free weights; another had a basketball hoop, but everywhere between was dotted with lush grass, neat flowerbeds, and low bushes shaped like animals.

"It's beautiful," Harold said. "I almost feel like I'm outside."

"Indoor gardens are a big deal on Towan III, and on the larger ships. We can thank the jajan for that."

"Weren't they the first species the towani met after abandoning Towan I?"

"They were. The towani outsourced agricultural production to the jajan. You know what they look like?"

"They're tall. About three metres high with thin limbs, but a big head that protrudes at the back."

"They're too tall to move freely aboard a towani ship, so they didn't make great recruits for the crew. When they were press-ganged, they usually found themselves allocated a task that didn't require them to run back and forth along the corridors. To make their workspace a little less oppressive, they'd grow a few plants. At some point between the third and sixth generation of ships, the empire began putting a garden onto every spacecraft they made. As they urbanised, and when they created giant mega-cities like Towan III, the techniques for growing in space were used planet-side to build green spaces inside buildings."

A path led between the flower beds to a cluster of picnic tables where Parker, wearing a tubular white tunic and trousers, sat in a day-bright cone cast by a spotlight above. Burton stood behind him, with a warder in front, both just beyond the circle of light.

Parker looked smaller than when Harold had last seen him. His hair was unkempt, his beard was raggedly trimmed, and his shoulders sagged with a deep weariness, undoubtedly caused by more than just being woken in the middle of the night. But when he saw them approach, his back stiffened, his eyes narrowed, and his lip curled with disdain.

"Harold Godwin. Let me guess, he thinks I'm more likely to speak to you than I am with him."

"Pretty much," Harold said.

"I'm not inclined to speak to anyone in the middle of the night," Parker said. "Has he recruited you?"

"He gave me a job," Harold said.

"Of course he did. How do you think first contact is going?"

"It'd have been better without a million tonnes of spaceship creating a dent in England."

"Worse will come," Parker said. "It didn't have to be this way, but now Earth is a piece on the board. My advice to you is to go back to your bookshop, dig a bunker beneath it, and have nothing more to do with O'Malley."

"The sooval were expecting a rescue," Sean said. "It didn't come. That's a breach of contract. Those mercenaries will never work for the Voytay again."

"As I understand it, there are plenty of other mercenaries."

"Tell me about the skulls we found in the embassy," Sean said.

"I've never been further inside than the lobby," Parker said.

"They were professionally cleaned," Sean said. "There aren't many professions where they teach you how to do that, but archaeology is one."

Parker bit his lower lip and flexed his hands. When he next spoke, the weary disdain had been replaced with anger. "My wife has nothing to do with any of this."

"You'll understand why I'm not inclined to believe you," Sean said.

"If you won't believe me, why ask any questions?"

"If Awat goes into custody, what'll happen to your son?"

"I wondered when we'd reach the threats."

"Maybe we'd never have reached here at all if you'd said more than a few words to me. You could take responsibility for any part your wife had in this. She'll remain free, and your son would remain out of care."

Parker took his time before answering. "If you want my confession, I want to serve my time in England, at the closest prison to my family. Harold, I'll ask you because I don't trust him. Speak to my wife. Make sure she knows I'm alive. Warder, we're done."

"*Are* you done?" Burton asked.

"Take him back to his cell," Sean said. "And bring us Afiz. Let's see if anyone else wants to cut a deal."

"They have a son?" Harold asked as they waited for the next of the imprisoned conspirators.

"He's twelve, I think. Parker wasn't my assistant, not as such. I did hope he might become my replacement, to act as a liaison between Earth and the Valley, but after his son was born, he settled into family life in Britain. There was a vacancy at the top of the U.K. office, and my recommendation sealed his position. I thought I was doing him a favour."

"Who hired the other four?"

"He did. There were twenty active in the U.K. The other fifteen have, so far, been found to have no link to the conspiracy. Penn, Ricard, Afiz, and Olawayo all joined the agency after Parker's promotion. They seemed like good people. Well, they seemed competent."

Nadia Afiz sauntered into the exercise garden as fresh as one of the many daisies in the nearby flowerbed. "Any change in routine is welcome, but it is a little early for visitors," she said. She smiled. "Harold, isn't it? Yes, I remember you. How are you?"

"Better now you're not pointing a gun at me."

"Such are the risks in this line of work. What is so urgent that it couldn't wait for morning?"

"I'm here to offer you a deal," Sean said.

"Oh, how delightful. What type of deal?"

"The towani sentencing guidelines would allow your time to be halved."

"Except I haven't been sentenced yet," she said. "What do you want in return?"

"A full confession. Every name and detail."

"Is that all? I'm not against it in theory, but I would still be serving my time here, associating with my colleagues whom I would have betrayed. That wouldn't be a wise survival strategy. I'll take my time and medical treatment, and still have centuries of life to enjoy when I leave. Was there anything else?"

"Take her away," Sean said.

Olawayo was brought in next. He barely glanced at Harold before dismissing him. He turned to Sean. "What do you want?"

"There's five people in custody, and one deal on the table," Sean said.

"You would have spoken with Parker first, then Afiz. Maybe I'm third, maybe I'm last, but I wasn't first. You've been turned down at least twice. Logic dictates I do the same."

"Logic would suggest you speak while you can."

"What authority do you have to make a deal? Get me something in writing, and I might consider it. Now, please, I wish to sleep."

Penn's response was little better. She didn't even sit down.

"You came here in the middle of the night. You're getting desperate. Like I said last time, I want my lawyer."

"This is a limited-time deal," Sean said. "The value of any information you have decreases with each day you're in here."

"I want my lawyer," she said.

Ricard was last. He'd had a superhero physique before he'd been arrested, but had spent the last two months turning it into that of a supervillain. He'd removed the sleeves from his shirt to show off his bulging muscles and near-bursting veins.

"What?" Ricard said.

"How would you like to cut a deal?"

Ricard laughed. "Just as soon as the world learns about this secret prison, we'll all be set free."

As the warder took Ricard away, Burton walked over to the table. "That went as well as I expected. Do you know when the trial will be?"

"No, the Brits are undecided if they want the trial to be held there, according to their own laws for terrorism, or if they should be charged by the ICC with war crimes. It's not helping that they're on their third home secretary in four months. Either way, it'd be a life sentence."

"What would they get if they were tried by a Valley military tribunal?" Harold asked.

"Maybe twenty-five years for Parker, ten for the others."

"If they haven't been charged yet, I think they're hoping a lot of the evidence will be disallowed," Harold said.

"Perhaps. Or it's as Afiz said. They knew they'd be caught. They plan to do their time, take advantage of the longevity treatment, and then retire. Not on Earth, but on a planet in Voytay space."

"Parker seemed willing to talk," Burton said.

"He did. He has the most to lose, and he'll know the most. I'll speak to the British government, and see if they'll agree to his request. Now, Harold, how about we see if we can get ourselves that milkshake I promised? Leroy, why don't you come with us? You can tell Harold about Nineveh."

Chapter 9 - Spilled Coffee

Harold was woken by the sound of peckish indecision. In the small kitchen on the other side of the wall a cupboard opened, was closed, and another was opened.

Between the time zones and the flight hours, he wasn't sure what day it was, but judging by how the sun had yet to reach the diplodocus's tail, it was still early. He picked up his glasses. As he put them on, the faded dinosaurs swam into focus. Aunt Jess had painted them onto the walls when she'd first taken on the lease for the property. He'd been twelve at the time, and she'd thought he'd be released into her care within weeks. It had taken five years. Jess hadn't painted over them out of superstition. She'd refused to believe anything other than he'd be coming home any day. In the five years since he'd been set free, he'd repainted the room twice, but couldn't bring himself to paint over the dinosaurs. They gave him a hint at the happy childhood he'd almost had.

He got up and padded into the kitchen where Aunt Jess was still vacillating over breakfast.

"Sorry, did I wake you?" she asked. "I can't decide whether to be sensible and have muesli, or fill my stomach with sugar."

"Isn't today when you do yoga with Celeste, or was that yesterday?"

"Today. You're right, I'll need to fuel up," she said, picking up the chocolate-coated flakes that contained as much sugar as wheat. "You'd better hurry, or you'll be late for work."

Over the drizzle from their low-power shower, he heard the jangle of the shop bell. When he was clean and dressed, he entered the shop and found it wasn't an up-early reader, but his boss.

"What are you doing here, sir?"

"I told you, call me Sean, and I'm also telling you that you're not going to Oxfordshire today. Greta's orders. There's a chance an attempt to rescue the sooval might still be made, so the tours are cancelled, and all non-essential personnel have been told to take a few days off."

"A holiday sounds nice," Harold said. "I might head to London. It was so disappointing when we went there with Serene and Tempest right after first contact and found all the museums were closed."

"Bad news, then, because I've categorised you as very essential. We're going to have a word with Mrs Parker. You can pass on Alan's message. Then you can fly back to Nevada, and pass on whatever she says."

"If a rescue attempt is likely, why not ship the prisoners somewhere else?" Jess asked.

"We'd like to," Sean said. "Ideally, we'd arrange for their travel home so we can guarantee their contract with the Voytay is breached and this stable cuts off all ties with the Voytay. But the prime minister is ducking my calls."

"And the press," Jess said. "No one's seen her since the budget. The press is predicting she'll quit."

"The timing's not ideal," Sean said. "I suppose I could land a spaceship in Buckingham Palace and crash her chat with the king, but it's not the impression the Valley wants to create. Still, that's a problem for later. We better be off."

"Give me a minute," Harold said. "If I've got another ten-hour fight ahead of me, I want to pack a couple of books."

"We'll swing by here on the way back," Sean said. "You'll have time to pack a bag, too."

Outside, the SUV had gained the attention of a traffic warden. Sean flashed a badge. "Official police business," he said. The traffic warden scowled at being thwarted, but stopped writing the ticket.

"I suppose I should stop pulling that trick," Sean said after he and Harold had got into the car.

"Why not get diplomatic plates for the car?" Harold said as they began an automotive attempt to escape Woking's gravitational pull.

"It would be a more conspicuous way of travelling, but maybe it's the right thing to do," Sean said. "The shelves in your shop were looking a bit bare."

"Tell me about it," Harold said. "The big publishers have pulled most of the new releases so they can be rewritten with an extra-terrestrial angle. Biographies are about the only thing they're throwing our way."

"What are people reading?"

"I don't know that they are, but it's not biographies. A lot of readers want old sci-fi, but those are getting harder to source. Historical romance and cosy mysteries are doing as well as ever, but it's not enough to pay the rent, so I'm grateful for the job."

"I sense there's a but," Sean said.

"Is it always going to be so varied?"

"Now, that's a fine way of describing it. Yes. Or no. Perhaps. You know, I've no idea. First contact's never happened before, so I've no clue what'll happen next except it won't be like what I did before. Then again, one day was never much like the last, so that's not a helpful comparison. All I can say is that the job will be peacekeeping in its most literal sense, and that's always a hectic life. I've given you access to the files."

"Which files?"

"All of them," Sean said. "Greta calls it gossipedia, but it's every record the UNCA ever made. There are some fascinating files from the old League of Nations days, and some even older than that. If you want a hoot, start with the invention of the foxtrot, but first look up Dr Awat Masadi."

Harold opened the interface. A notification said he'd been granted access to tier-three information. Wondering what was in tiers one and two, he clicked on the stone-tablet-shaped app, and opened the database.

"Born in 1979, in Baghdad. So she was twenty-four when you met her. It says she was ordered to study archaeology by Saddam and started training at sixteen. When did Saddam find out about the Valley?"

"I learned he knew in 1992. There was a general assumption the Soviet collapse would mean first contact was imminent, and he sent an emissary to the embassy itself to ask for money to build a space-port in Iraq."

"If he recruited someone to train as an archaeologist in 1995, was that when he started selling Neanderthal bones off-world?"

"I don't think so, but it might have been when he first thought it was possible. Awat wasn't the only archaeologist he had trained, but she was the only survivor."

Harold brought up a three-dimensional rendering of the tunnel. "It's amazing that was just sitting there, lost for two and a half thousand years."

"Lost, yes. But was it forgotten? That there was a chamber be-neath Lenham House was a family secret for Alan Parker. Perhaps those tunnels were a secret known to the Masadi family. Up until two months ago, I assumed she was another innocent caught up in a dictator's pursuit of power. Now I'm rethinking everything I know about her, and Alan. He offered to talk after I suggested he could take the blame for his wife's involvement. The implication is that there was some blame to be taken."

"Her family's all dead," Harold said. "That's amazing. Not that they're dead, but all the detail this database has. After you saved her, it says she stayed in the tunnel. Why?"

"To finish cataloguing it," Sean said. "Burton, Lopez, and Wash-ington stayed as guards. Alan stayed, too, as the official liaison. But the country was increasingly unstable. We had to seal up the tunnel. Alan and Awat married and moved to England."

"Do you trust Burton?"

"Good question. Right now, as far as sapiens go, and as a direct consequence of Parker's betrayal, I trust my kids, your aunt, and you. But Greta found no link between Burton and Parker. Nor did the FBI. He's never visited Britain, and worked as the presidential li-aison from 2007 until 2017. One of Parker's avowed goals was to force first contact. If that's true, and if Burton was working with him, the time to do it would have been when Burton could leverage the

White House. It's unlikely he's involved, but we won't assume anything."

Harold turned back to the file. "Now Dr Masadi is a history professor at Southampton University. She specialises in the ancient Mesopotamian kingdoms. I suppose that makes sense. Their son is Yūnus, and he's twelve."

"It's the Arabic version of Jonah."

Harold clicked on another link and found himself looking at the painted carvings adorning the tunnel wall. "Parker knew about the chamber beneath Lenham House. He must have told his wife about it."

"Probably. But what else did he tell her? And what did she tell him?"

The Parkers had a secluded house in Toothill just north of the sprawling metropolis of Southampton, and more immediately north of an observatory. Shielded by a screen of towering pine trees, the turning was almost invisible, but they left the road, joining a track that curved through carefully trimmed woodland until it widened into a driveway outside a thatched cottage currently playing host to a parked police car.

"Something's wrong," Sean said, as he stopped the car.

"Do you think the police came here to arrest her?"

"No, the police are watching her because her husband committed treason. I mean something's wrong about that car. Wait here." He drew a gun before opening the door.

Harold watched as Sean approached the police car. He paused by the driver-side window, and looked back, past Harold. The car doors clicked as Sean remotely locked them before he headed towards the house. The front door swung open with a nudge from Sean's foot. His gun raised, Sean disappeared inside.

Harold waited. And waited. Suppressing a growing sense of trepidation, his gaze went back to the police car, but he couldn't see whatever it was that had spooked Sean. He looked around, taking in the dense laurel hedgerow ahead, the patio with the wooden table, and the scuffed lawn with a football net, but couldn't see anything unusual. When he caught movement in the corner of his eye, it was from the house as Sean came back outside. With a click, the car doors unlocked. Harold got out.

"What is it?"

"The two police officers are dead," Sean said. "They were shot. In both cases, it was a head shot."

"No! What about Dr Masadi and her son?"

"She's missing. I called the school. Yūnus is in class."

"She was kidnapped?"

"I think this was a rescue," Sean said. "I've called the local police, and they'll be here soon. Those two last did a radio check-in two hours ago. There are a couple of coffee mugs in the footwell. As best I can tell, she brought them coffee. While the officers were distracted, the two shooters stepped out from behind the hedge and fired. I think I got it wrong. Alan Parker isn't the mastermind behind all this. It's his wife."

Part 2
International Disagreement

The Hop Island Hotel, Cork
19th October 2022

Chapter 10 - Diplomacy for Dummies

The squeak of the breakfast trolley had Serene jumping out of bed before her eyes were open; after eight weeks in the hotel, she had developed a Pavlovian response to the audible approach of pastries. Yawning, she tugged on a gown and had her room's door open before the wonky-wheeled trolley clanged to a stop.

"Do you want your food?" Padraig O'Keefe asked, each syllable dripping with menace.

"Absolutely! You're a brick, thanks." She took the tray. Padraig bared his teeth, which Serene had learned was his attempt at a smile, and wheeled his trolley towards the Chinese security team guarding the room next door. Serene smiled at them, and in the interests of diplomatic neutrality turned so she could offer the same smile to the Americans guarding the room on the other side of her, before retreating into her sanctum.

Her room in the hotel was an architectural oversight caused by a brown sauce stain on the plans being misinterpreted as a load-bearing wall. Subsequently, on a floor that was otherwise filled with multi-room suites, she had a simple en-suite. It was smaller than her rooms in the embassy, and a lot smaller than her mum's luxury apartment in London, but it had a view, came with someone who made the bed, and had the craziest bathroom she'd ever stepped into. The shower had been an eye-opener. Literally. She'd not been expecting horizontal nozzles all the way up the wall. Puzzling over why anyone would need to power-hose their knees had kept her entertained during the droning dullness of the circular debates she had to listen to each morning.

She took her breakfast tray to the table by the window and opened the curtains. Outside, despite the morning rain, her sibling, Tempest, and the towani cleric, Dorn-Tru, were performing their morning exercises. According to scripture, these were a covert martial art, developed by the first prophet, the Holy Nowan, while the

ancestral towani were still enslaved. According to more recent historians, they were the invention of the eighth empress, who was keen
on callisthenics.

Serene preferred to start her morning with croissants. Today's
were shaped like flying saucers. She grinned. Padraig O'Keefe had a
way with flour that he completely lacked with words. Niamh
O'Keefe, the first cousin of Padraig's who shared a house with him,
had been the one to make official first contact with Greta down in
Cobh. Both Sean and the Irish government had invited Niamh to attend the conference. Padraig's invite had come from Sean alone,
with a request to take over baking duties. Six weeks ago, after two
weeks of diplomatic gridlock, Niamh had opted to return to the
comparative calm of her classroom. There was no such escape for
Serene.

Two hundred and six representatives of nations and states had
been invited to attend a conference to select a delegation to travel to
Towan III. There, they would be formally invited to apply for membership in the multi-planetary federation that was the Valley. This
delegation was purely ceremonial, and membership talks would be
as long and tedious as for joining the EU, but it would make Earth
eligible for the technological aid it so sorely needed in the interim.
All they had to do was select someone who could smile and say
thank you. How hard could that be? Two months in, the answer
turned out to be impossible.

The ambassador had used a very broad definition of what consti-
tuted a nation when the invitations were sent out. Naturally, the first
argument had been over who had been invited. Afghanistan objected to the Vatican having a representative, while the U.S. objected
to Afghanistan being represented by the Taliban. China had walked
out when they saw Taiwan was present, but the Communist Party
official had walked back in when Dorn-Tru had announced that attendance was optional, and the conference would continue regard-
less.

The death of Queen Elizabeth II had brought a new delay as Dorn-Tru, the second most senior towani cleric in the system, had attended the funeral with the ambassador. Instead of this reminder of everyone's mortality ushering in a spirit of cooperation, it had merely given the diplomats a chance to plot.

Theoretically, there was no head at a square table, but there was a host, Tadgh O'Connell, Ireland's new Minister for Intergalactic Affairs. Who got to sit next to him, and who sat opposite, became the next bun fight, creating a real mess for the hotel staff to clean up.

China argued that the Security Council members should get precedence. But the U.N. Security Council, like the U.N. itself, was effectively moribund. Russia demanded that the nuclear powers should be given priority, and as the holder of the most warheads, he should get to sit first. Dorn-Tru had said any use of atomic weapons on Earth would be deemed a threat to the towani holy sites, and so would be strongly ill-advised. America said, as the host of Area-51, it should get priority. Brazil demanded clarification on *why* the United States was host to alien technology. And so it went on. And on.

Finally, nearly two months after Greta and Niamh had supped a pint of the black stuff in Cobh, they'd solved the seating conundrum by agreeing places would be on a first-come, first-served basis, but the host would sit last.

Serene took her seat at the desk by the door, waiting for the tedium to begin. Travelling in their cliques, like the world's most internationally diverse high school, the diplomats arrived. Most headed for the buffet table against the far wall, since it was a good half hour since they'd had breakfast. On the other side of the room, the German and British diplomats nearly came to blows over whether a towel could be used to reserve a seat. The Russian delegate annexed the pastry basket, but made the mistake of putting it back down so he could pour coffee, allowing its liberation by a Ukrainian-led coalition. Before the conflict escalated, Tadgh O'Connell walked through the doors.

"Good morning, everyone. Can we take our seats?" the Irish politician asked.

One by one, and with some pushing, shoving, and muttered promises that the pastry war would resume at lunch, the delegates sat.

"Thank you," O'Connell said, taking the last remaining seat, between Tuvalu and Barbados. "Before we begin, let's just recap the task before us. We need to select a delegation to travel to Towan III for an official ceremony. This delegation is entirely ceremonial and will conduct no negotiations, yes?" The query was directed at Serene.

"Yes," Serene said, reading the official answer given to her by Johann. "The key event is the invitation ceremony where Earth will be invited to apply for membership in the Valley. There'll be a parade and a religious service, but the only critical part is accepting the invitation from the leader of the council."

"And this invitation doesn't mean we *have* to join," O'Connell said.

"We'd be mad not to," Serene said, before remembering what Johann, Greta, and even her father had reminded her about being diplomatic. "But no, Earth doesn't have to join if the planet decides it doesn't want to."

"And whether we join or not, we'll still get the technology package?" O'Connell said.

"Yep," Serene said. "Cheap electricity, better medicine, up-to-date communications technology, the works, but only if we accept the invitation."

"Then we should send a mailman," the representative from Brazil said.

"Better than sending a politician," said Father Maguire, the local parish priest who was representing the Vatican, though currently from the buffet table.

"And better than sending a religious figure," the British ambassador said.

"Can I finish?" Serene asked. "The *Holy* Johann tol Davir suggests twenty would be a nice number because it'll fill an entire bench in the cathedral, and twenty is an auspicious number to the towani."

"Twenty people," O'Connell said. "By the end of today, I'd like us to have established a framework for choosing them."

"Let's make it simple," the U.S. delegate said. "We'll send seven people, one per continent."

"Are you proposing we send a penguin?" O'Connell asked.

"China vetoes that suggestion, unless we receive our own delegate, recognising our greater proportion of the planet's citizens."

"In which case, India must have a separate delegate, too."

"So Asia will have three representatives, and Africa will have only one?" Mali asked.

"Central America has none," Panama said.

"Fine," the U.S. delegate said. "You said twenty delegates? We'll pick the twenty most populous nations. Each sends one."

There was a brief pause as phones and tablets were checked so people could see where on that list they lay. The hum of objections rose to a roar, but Barbados's voice rose above the others.

"Smaller nations are forever being overlooked," she said. "Big nations would pick delegates who represent their special interests, disregarding the needs of the rest, but we will no longer be ignored."

"Why must it be geographic?" Iraq asked. "We should send archaeologists and historians. My country has some of the most important Neanderthal sites in existence. Surely these are what the aliens would wish to discuss, and so an expert is someone who will make the greatest positive impression."

"We could agree to the principle of that," Belgium said.

"Of course you'd say that. The earliest Neanderthal remains were found in Belgium in 1829," the Congolese representative said. Like all the diplomats, and most of the planet, since first contact, everyone had become an armchair expert in the history of archaeology.

"And they were misidentified as human," the Malaysian delegate said.

"Neanderthals *were* human," Mongolia said.

"We have taken the most damage during the recent invasion," Britain said. "Since Oxford was attacked, a representative from the university would be symbolic."

"Symbolic of decadence," Russia said. "As the largest nation on Earth, we shall send five representatives. That is our final offer."

"Friends, please," O'Connell said. "We'll get nowhere if we keep at it like this. Could I propose something different? Could we agree on the one person who should be part of this expedition? Niamh O'Keefe, the woman who met the towani in Cobh."

"Afghanistan cannot agree to women being part of this mission."

"Now we're going backwards," O'Connell said.

Chapter 11 - Front Row Seats to a Sermon

Midday couldn't come soon enough. As the diplomats disappeared to report to their capitals on the morning's bickering, Serene went to the office provided to the Valley delegation. After eight weeks of stalemate, that was now just Serene, Tempest, and the cleric Dorn-Tru. Currently, only Tempest was in the office, patiently sorting through questions from the query box.

Serene fell into her chair. "I am a worm's-width away from sealing the politicians into that room and telling them they can't come out until they've reached consensus."

"They'd starve," Tempest said. "Or eat each other. Did you see the message from Harold?"

"No. I've not checked. The politicos get super-snarky if I'm not paying attention. What did he say?"

"There's been a murder."

"A what?" she said, even as she pulled up the message. "The two cops watching Mrs Parker were shot. Oh, and now he's not answering."

"He said he and Da had to give a statement to the local police," Tempest said.

"You spoke to him? What else did he say?"

"Not much more than is in his message. Mrs Parker is missing, the two cops are dead, and Da's convinced it was a rescue rather than a kidnapping. Harold said he'd call when he'd finished giving his statement."

"It's all go over there," Serene said. "The most exciting thing that happened in my morning was when the New Zealand representative sneezed so hard, she fell off her chair. Will these murders affect us?"

"I can't see how," Tempest said. "Even if it did, the delegation must still be selected."

"What questions have we been asked today?"

106

"More of the same," Tempest said. "How faster than light travel works, what kind of weapons the ships have, that kind of thing."

"So nothing to do with the delegation?"

"Of course not," Tempest said.

"I better check in with Dorn-Tru," she said.

"And I'll start with the questions from Father Maguire," Tempest said. "At least those are about religion."

Originally, the Valley delegation had been much larger, with fifty experts ready to brief the actual delegates on the social norms and customs they would find on Towan III. As the conference stuttered and stalled, those experts were reassigned to assist with the clean-up in Oxfordshire and the rescue efforts following the autumn's annual catastrophic natural disasters. One towani had remained behind, Dorn-Tru, personal assistant to Johann tol Davir. At only three hundred years old, she was young to have attained such a high rank in the faith.

Serene followed the sound of hammering to a freshly built pentagonal wooden cabin hidden among the trees behind the hotel.

To the faithful, Earth was a sacred place. The planet had changed, and the stars had moved since the ancestral towani had been enslaved, but the same types of insects buzzed between the same varieties of towering trees. Simply to be outside was to experience an echo of the ancestors' life. Since Dorn-Tru, like many towani, had only lived in cities, spaceships, and then in the bunker beneath the Neander Valley, she had eschewed a room indoors in favour of a partially enclosed wooden cabin with a dirt floor. First, of course, she'd had to build it.

The cleric's shaved head bore the swirling red tattoos of the most devout, though she had currently swapped her vestments for overalls, and the ceremonial boots for sandals. In one hand was a hammer, in the other was a chisel with which she was carving the pattern of her tattoos into the walls.

"From your scowl, I sense this morning's meeting was no more productive than yesterday's," she said.

"No, Your Grace," Serene said, being formal and polite as Greta reminded her at least once a day. Dorn-Tru wasn't a relative, after all. "I think they're deliberately trying to tank the talks."

"And who are they?"

"All of them. I bet they each think whoever remains stubborn to the end can ask for a bribe to say yes."

"Patience is the fuel which helps us find peace," the cleric said. "The empire wasn't overthrown in a day."

"Oh, don't say there'll be seven years of this," Serene said.

"Tasks which appear simple are often a mask for complexity," Dorn-Tru said. "And sometimes the most complex decisions have a straightforward solution. But the solution to this decision is not ours to find, so we will continue to answer their questions, offering what guidance we can. Perhaps I shall make that the centrepiece of to-day's sermon."

"We got a message from Harold, our friend in England. There have been two murders."

"The Holy Johann informed me an hour ago," she said.

"Oh. Do you think it will change anything?"

"Everything changes everything, but by how much is difficult to predict."

"Then I better get the room set up for this afternoon."

Where the mornings were allocated to arguing, the afternoons contained a lecture. At first, these had been pre-prepared holographic spectaculars covering the varied cultures and different species in the Valley. In what Serene considered an unforgivable oversight for a prophet, Johann had only prepared ten. They'd run them twice. Now, Dorn-Tru spent the afternoons giving a sermon. It was due to begin at two. By ten past, there were only twelve attendees, including three hotel employees who evidently didn't plan to be changing sheets for the rest of their lives.

At a quarter past, and having run out of polite chitchat, Tadgh O'Connell announced, "Let's begin. It might teach the latecomers a lesson in punctuality."

108

One consequence of there being so few attendees was that Serene couldn't sneak out. She sat near the front and tried to appear attentive as Dorn-Tru launched into a sermon on how the 19th Precept could be applied to simplify decision-making. For two hours.

"There are fewer each day," Dorn-Tru said after she and Serene had returned to the office.

"You had two hotel employees listening yesterday. Today there were three. They're clearly smart enough to realise the value in new information."

"This is not something I am suited to. I am used to addressing the faithful who know the precepts, the prophecies, and our faith's history. I am failing."

"If you're failing, then so are we," Serene said. "So how do we un-fail?"

"I think you mean succeed," Tempest said.

"After eight weeks, I'm not setting my sights that high."

"First, success must be defined," Dorn-Tru said. "In this case, success would be the selection of a delegation. Let us not forget that this is only the first step on a long journey towards Earth becoming a full member of the Valley."

"Maybe we should tell them that the membership requirements include ending war and tyranny," Tempest said.

"The Holy Johann tol Davir has said we should not. He feared that would lead to the inaction we have sadly seen."

"They liked the 3D shows," Tempest said. "We could make some more."

"That would take months," Serene said. "Since the diplomats are skipping these afternoon sessions, why don't we do the same?"

"I would prefer not," Dorn-Tru said. "The afternoon talks are supposed to enthral the audience, to bring them together and make them see the value in compromise."

"What if we put on a towani documentary?" Serene asked.

"They don't have an English narration," Tempest said. "I suppose we could use auto-translate, but that's always a bit dry."

"We'll use auto-translate to create a script, edit it, and get an actor to record a new narration. The question is, which movie megastar do I most want to meet?"

"It is a good idea, but it will take days of work for one afternoon's instruction," Dorn-Tru said. "In the meantime, the conference is beginning to drift. We need to focus their minds, and force them to make a decision."

"You'd think a crashed battle-station would do that," Tempest said.

"Maybe we just need a bit of variety," Serene said. "Let's find some other speakers to take over a session or two."

"Gramps would be the obvious choice," Tempest said.

"If the Holy Johann arrives, the presidents and prime ministers will follow, and we will get even less done," the cleric said.

"We've tried explaining the benefits of joining the Valley," Serene said. "Maybe what we need is someone who can scare them. If Gunther wasn't out-of-system, he could tell them some war stories. Greta's busy with the investigation. Who else speaks English?"

"What about Dr Griffin?" Tempest asked.

"We don't want to scare them that much," Serene said.

"Those who can speak English are busy in Oxfordshire," Dorn-Tru said. "There are some at the embassy who can speak German, of course, but how many diplomats know that language? However, yes, I think you are correct, Serene. We have been trying to win hearts and minds with good deeds. Perhaps it is time they learned who the Voytay really are. It had been intended to end this conference with a lecture from Clee. We could bring it forward."

"The hermit?" Tempest asked.

"The spy?" Serene said.

"She is both and has been living in exile on Earth since the end of her sentence. Her first-hand experience of the Voytay would surely convince them there truly is no time for delay."

"Perfect," Serene said. "Where is she?"

"Only your father knows," Dorn-Tru said. "I will consult with him and see if he agrees to this change."

"I'll do it. He always answers when I call," Serene said.

This time, Sean didn't, sending a brief text-only message that he was currently being questioned by the home secretary, and would call soon.

"Okay, so while we wait, back to the important question, which actor should we get to narrate some of the documentaries?"

They'd drawn up a shortlist of over a hundred names before Sean called.

"Everything okay?" he asked.

"There were only twelve attendees at this afternoon's talk," Dorn-Tru said. "We need to change our approach. I understand Clee has requested to give a talk at the end of the conference. I thought we could invite her to give the speech now."

"She's prepared a speech, yes," Sean said. "Have you seen any of her speeches from the speaking tour she went on after the war?"

"Only the highlights," Serene admitted.

"I have," Tempest said. "They're quite something."

"They are sublime," Dorn-Tru said.

"You've watched them?" Sean asked.

"Of course," Dorn-Tru said. "They helped me truly understand my faith."

"Tempi, what do you think?" Sean asked.

"I agree with Dorn-Tru. I think most nations are ready to reach an agreement, but no one is motivated to compromise first."

"Let's give it a try," Sean said. "You'll need to pick Clee up, but do it first thing in the morning. She won't want to sleep in a hotel."

"Where is she?" Serene asked.

"Clee lives on Church Island, in the middle of Lough Currane."

"Where's that?" Serene asked.

"Almost in the Atlantic. She has no communication system at all, not even a phone, so you'll have to visit her in person. Don't fly there. Drive. There's a boatyard on the north of the lake. I'll call ahead and book you my usual boat. After she finishes her speech, she'll want to return there, so we don't want anyone to know there's a paxley hermit living on the lake. Clee requested that this speech be

111

recorded for broadcast across Earth, throughout the Valley, and even to the Voytay. Dorn-Tru, you'll need to organise a camera crew, and ask Mr O'Connell to arrange a local TV crew as well."

"It sounds like she's going to say something important," Tempest said.

"She is. She's planned this for years. When I took her supplies, she would often run through a draft."

"What's she going to say?" Serene asked.

"I don't want to spoil the surprise," Sean said.

"Okay, but why will it be broadcast across the galaxy? Who is she?"

"Maybe the best way to explain is to tell you about the first time I met her," Sean said.

"I'm familiar with the story," Dorn-Tru said. "If you'll excuse me, I'll arrange the camera crews."

Part 3
The Turning Point in the Civil War

Deep Space
March 1893

Chapter 12 - Fishing for Mines

"It's a pity there's nothing you can fish for in space," Sean said. Beyond the narrow window in the interstellar freighter's control room, there was nothing to see except the swirling red patterns of subspace. Inside, there wasn't much more except the blinking blue lights confirming that all was well in the cargo hold. There were only two people in the control room, himself and his beloved, Hakon, whom he had first met after she'd crashed into the freezing waters of the Atlantic, off the coast of Queenstown, four and a half years ago.

"Some animals can survive in the cold, airless vacuum of space, but they don't *live* in it. What would they eat? Why is that thought bouncing around your brain?"

"I was thinking about my father," Sean said. "He'd never agree to captain a ship if he couldn't throw out a net."

"Your father caught aquatic animals for food, yes?"

"Aye, until he sold the boat to open that bakery just before he and Mam died. He'd fish in a river, or a lake, but he had salt water in his veins."

"You've been talking of your family a lot lately. Do you want to go home?"

"Of course, but it's not an option."

"For you, it could be. We promised Celeste you would be returned."

"This is my war, too," Sean said. "For better or worse, it's Earth's war as well. I'll not let others do my fighting for me. It's not that I miss my old life, but I regret how it ended so quickly."

"What is that saying of your mother's? Cherish the past, but don't cling to it."

It was over four years since Sean's arrival on Towan III triggered the revolution. The rebels had fought street-by-street, ship-to-ship, and planet-by-planet. At first, the Valley's victory had seemed as-

114

sured, but the tide had turned after Regent Volmar had escaped, and taken nearly a quarter of the fleet with him. The planet Ellowin, home of the imperial shipyard and a hundred commercial starship factories, had become the regent's new capital, and many of the rich and powerful had flocked to his banner.

While the Valley couldn't produce enough starships to replace their losses, Volmar, and his new empire he called the Voytay, had built so many that he could sell the excess to the old empire's former enemies. Now, the Towani Empire's former territory was unequally divided between the Valley, the Voytay, and the non-aligned planets who were sick of them both.

The Valley was losing. Ships, equipment, and people were increasingly hard to replace. Where at first, Sean had toured different worlds as living proof that the towani's ancestral home had been found, he was increasingly on the front line, or, as now, deep behind it.

"We're almost there. Seal your suit," Hakon said.

Sean pressed the button on the screen on his forearm. The seals on his helmet and gloves gently clicked into place. "Suit's sealed. Our cargo has been informed. Internal comms are now disabled."

"In three," Hakon said.

The swirling red pattern was replaced by the blackness of infinity, dotted with a few faint stars and a distant gas giant, but immediately ahead was a small dark-grey planet.

"If you had that net, you could fish for mines," Hakon said, as their sensors alerted them to the minefield surrounding the planet. Before she'd finished speaking, another alert flashed on his lenses, and the screen above his workstation. They were being hailed from the interstellar navigation beacon that was also host to a formidable missile battery.

"This is a restricted area. State your business, or you will be destroyed."

"We're transmitting the authorisation codes now," Hakon replied.

Like many worlds on both sides of the conflict, Drameer was now ringed with an orbital minefield to prevent ships from jumping close to the planet, bombarding the surface, and escaping before defences could be mobilised. The missile batteries outside the minefield would obliterate any approaching ship without the correct codes.

"Now we'll see if Clee can be trusted," Sean said.

"She hasn't let us down yet," Hakon said.

"I'd feel more confident trusting her if someone knew who she was, or if she would communicate with someone other than your brother."

"Secrecy is often the best protection," Hakon said.

A message came from the missile platform. "Access granted. Welcome home, *Starfinder*. Prepare to hand over control of your systems to a remote pilot."

"There, see? We *can* trust her," Hakon said and surrendered control of the ship to the enemy.

"What's our cargo supposed to be used for?" Sean asked.

"Two hundred thousand tons of beryllium? It's essential for their missiles. This shipment is supposedly stolen from the Valley by their spies."

Guided by a remote Voytay pilot, their ship moved through the minefield, following the only safe path. There was no point memorising the route since the mines would regularly be moved. Their destination was a small planet with an atmosphere too thin to support life. Beneath the surface was a research station where imperial scientists had been investigating how to increase the strength of the rock's magnetic field so it was better able to hold onto an atmosphere. According to the Voytay's official records, that was what it was still doing. According to their spy, beneath the surface was the Voytay's newest munitions factory.

"I'm detecting over a hundred ships in orbit," Sean said. "I can't tell their type without turning on the scanners."

"Don't just yet. We're just delivery agents. We've no reason to wonder how heavily armed they are."

116

Slowly, the ships came within visual range. Sean relaxed. "Most of them look like freighters. I count only two warships."

"They'll have ground-based fighters, too," Hakon said.

The remote pilot shut down their engines. "*Starfinder*, prepare to be boarded for inspection," came the call from the enemy pilot.

"Clee was right about that, too," Hakon said. "Honestly, it's so transparent. What is there to inspect in here? Our bunks?"

"Ah, I don't mind. Bribing a customs official reminds me of home," Sean said. "When do we make our move?"

"We've still got forward momentum. We want to get as close as we can."

On his screen, a small skiff was approaching from the planet. Sean watched the blip get nearer.

"Now?" he asked.

"Not yet."

The skiff drew nearer still.

"It's about to dock," Sean said.

"I know, but the closer we are, the greater the chance of success," Hakon said.

"Then let them dock, and let's see if we can get ourselves a prisoner or two," Sean said. He released his harness. The original designers of the ship cared more about the cargo than the pilots, and so hadn't installed a costly artificial gravity system. With a push, Sean floated towards the airlock. The freighter juddered as the skiff made contact. The lights above the airlock flashed yellow to show it was in use. Yellow turned to a steady blue as the inner door opened, revealing three soldiers in armoured red space suits that still bore an old imperial sigil, the five-pointed star of a military prison detachment.

"This is a standard inspection," said one who bore the four spots of a squad leader.

"And with fines for non-compliance, I understand," Sean said.

Sean's opaque visor was down. They couldn't see his face, but his unfamiliar accent got a quizzical tilt of the head from the squad leader. As it usually did, greed won over caution.

"A shared understanding is always beneficial," the squad leader said, quoting one of Regent Kudon's preferred sayings.

"Isn't it just," Sean said. Hakon had left her chair and had pushed herself towards the airlock, but kept a position behind and to his left. On his display, the leader gained a blue outline, while the other two guards turned yellow as they were claimed by Hakon.

"Remove the helmet. Let me see your face," the squad leader said.

"Ah, now. What you want to see is in my hand," Sean replied, holding it out.

"Your hand is empty," the leader said, now sounding confused.

"Let's call it the hand of friendship." Sean bent a knee, and then kicked at the edge of the railing below him, propelling himself forward. Sean clenched his fist while engaging the electrical contacts in his glove. Hakon fired, launching two self-propelled missiles at the bodyguards. The thrice-hardened bullet-shaped warheads pierced the two guards' armour at the neck joint. Only then did they explode into flesh-shredding shrapnel that pulverised their torsos.

The squad leader opened fire, launching three bolts before the electrical points in Sean's glove made contact with his suit. The soldier went rigid, then limp, as the electrical charge surged through his body.

The ship shuddered with the small detonation of the explosive bolts holding the walls of the cargo hold in place. As the deck plates fell away, the breaching pods concealed inside were launched.

"Phase one is away," Hakon said. "Is he dead?"

"Sorry, yes, I think the charge was too high," Sean said, drawing his sidearm.

"The portable missiles worked," Hakon said. "That was a good idea of yours."

"How goes our hijack?"

Hakon returned to the control console. "I have a hundred freighters in-system, just as Clee said. The breaching pods have each locked onto a target. I don't know if we were close enough for them all to reach. The two warships are approaching. Yes! They're targeting us, not the pods."

The ship shuddered.

"Were we hit?"

"It's the skiff. Someone's still aboard and trying to rock themselves free."

"Well, we can't be having that," Sean said, taking a breaching round from his harness. With another kick at the deck, he launched himself into the airlock, slamming the breaching round onto the skiff's closed door. The reinforced casing forced the explosion into the enemy ship. As the casing fell away, he threw his two portable missiles into the skiff before, with another kick, launching himself back into their ship. He closed the airlock and released the clamps holding the two ships together.

"The warships are inbound," Hakon said.

"The skiff's free, but it's about to explode. Prepare for shrapnel."

Before they were beyond range, he ignited the two missiles. While Hakon monitored the breaching pods' attack on the freighters, and the approach of the warship, Sean focused on the skiff. The sensors and cameras created a side-on rendering of the immediate battle-space, showing their freighter, and the skiff. Most of the blast from his missiles had been contained inside the skiff, but the small ship had begun to spin and was clearly out of control.

"The skiff shouldn't be a problem," he said. His lenses flashed danger-yellow as their cockpit depressurised. "Were we hit?"

"Yes. The warships are already in range."

"That's fast."

"They're a new design. I'm collecting as much data as possible, but our shields won't last long. I've ordered the fighters to launch."

"They're not using any ground-based missiles," Sean said.

"They don't want to hit the remaining freighters," Hakon said. "Fifty-two have skipped away, but I don't know whether our crews were in command. They've launched fighters. We need to deploy phase-three."

Phase-one had been the breaching pods. Each contained a five-soldier squad who would, all being well, force entry into the cargo freighters, seize control, and then skip away. Phase-two were the saucer-shaped fighters whose presence would make it seem they were launching a ground attack on the facility itself. In reality, they were a distraction while the final piece of the freighter's cargo was deployed: one hundred ground-penetrating warheads. But there was a problem.

"Those soldiers are guards from a military prison detachment," Sean said.

"I know. It can't be helped."

The freighter shuddered from an explosion just aft of the control room. Jagged shrapnel pierced the hull, and nearly pierced Hakon as it smashed through the console in front of her.

"That's it, we've lost shields. I've given the retreat order," she said.

They hurried to an inner airlock that led into the unpressurised cargo hold in which their strike team had been hidden. Only one ship remained, a battered fighter that had barely survived too many battles to remember. They hurried aboard and, even as more explosions shook the freighter, they skipped out of the system.

Chapter 13 - No Time for a Holiday

Sean jogged along the wide outer corridor of the Valley warship, trying to clear his mind. They'd captured forty cargo-haulers and had definitely destroyed another ten. The rest of the Voytay freighters had escaped. Rather, they hadn't made it to the rendezvous, so it must be assumed the breaching teams had failed, and the Voytay crew had taken the ships to safety. The missile barrage would have caused some damage to the factory, though they had no idea how badly, or how easily it might be repaired. Where they caused damage, they would also have killed workers, and it was a near certainty that some would have been prisoners of war.

No doubt the enemy would increase security on its production sites, and on its convoys. For a time, that might reduce the number of starships available for an attack, but the Voytay could build ships much faster than the Valley.

They'd lost eighty-eight soldiers, either dead, missing, or captured. Mathematically, it was a victory, but he couldn't help but question whether it was worth it. He increasingly found himself asking that same question about the revolution itself.

A flashing blue light on his eyeglasses alerted him to an urgent message from his beloved, requesting him in the information centre. He turned around and picked up his pace.

The secure room at the heart of the ship had only one occupant, Hakon.

"If it's just us, we could have chatted in our room," Sean said.

"We just received a message from Dannan," Hakon said.

"What new world has your brother conquered now?"

"This isn't good news," she said.

A small green and blue planet appeared to hover above the table. "This is the star system of Haxar, and the planet Restore."

"It's not really called that," Sean said, thinking he'd misheard.

"Two thousand years ago, it was a lifeless planetoid," Hakon said. "The Marninni Corporation geo-engineered it to support life. It became a holiday planet."

Sean frowned. "A what?"

"It's just what it sounds. Let me show you an advertisement from before the war."

The three-dimensional planet was replaced with a moving image of a towani couple jumping from a cliff top. As they fell, iridescent wings deployed from small packs on their backs. Jets slowed their descent so they landed gracefully in the back of an open-topped wheel-less carriage, hovering thirty yards above the ground. Once aboard, the couple were driven across a grassland plain just above the heads of a stampeding herd of long-necked, purple-feathered quadrupeds. The machine rose higher into the air, docking atop a stilt house with a glass-bottomed swimming pool. The couple removed their suits and, naked, entered the pool. From the house, a small robot appeared, bringing them drinks.

"Ah, so it's a pleasure planet for the toffs," Sean said.

"The rich and powerful had their own resorts. These planets were built for the everyday folk. It's common, every century, to take at least half a year to recharge and relax. This place was built for workers like me, or even writers like yourself, Sean."

"I don't know if I'd like to wash in a glass-bottomed bath with all those animals below staring up at me," he said as he shook his head, trying to clear it of the general befuddlement that visited him whenever he was confronted with the economic reality of the empire they'd just overthrown. Yes, it had been riddled with corruption and inequality, but not even Queen Victoria had access to the luxuries afforded to the lowliest of constables such as Hakon had once been.

"Did you ever visit?" he asked.

"No, but only because we were on Volmar's watch-list." Hakon spread her hands; the planet replaced the couple in the pool.

A speck above the planet grew larger, becoming a wheel-shaped space station, in a geostationary orbit. A large central ring was attached to a central pylon by thousands of small spokes. Above and below the pylon were two smaller rings. As Hakon kept zooming in, and some of the docked ships finally became clear, he realised those rings weren't so small after all.

"This is the harbour," she said. "Ferry-ships would bring the guests to the harbour, hundreds or thousands at a time. They would dock at the upper ring, and be shuttled to their accommodation on the planet below. Privately owned ships could dock inside the larger ring, then travel to the central pylon for transport."

"They couldn't just fly down to the planet itself?"

"By the time of the revolution, no privately owned craft could. It was a way of making more profit. The Marninni Corporation, and so the planet and harbour, is owned by Regent Volmar's family. The system has no defences, no weapons, and the harbour has no engines. Fearing the negative symbolism that would have accompanied our capturing the system, when the revolution began, he shut the operation down and conscripted the staff. Without proper maintenance, most of the livestock and plants on the planet died, but the harbour was occupied by smugglers, and has now become a haven for deserters."

"From which side?"

"Both, as long as they can pay. One from our side, Dello tol Savin, worked in data analysis. Her personal life was fraught. She was about to lose her job, meaning she'd have been pushed into military service. Instead, she stole our records on known Voytay agents and sympathisers within the Valley. She sought refuge in the harbour, and made contact with the Voytay, intending to trade the information for a new life. Fortunately, the Voytay agent she made contact with was Clee. She will guarantee the deserter doesn't leave the harbour, but she wants us to send agents to extract her."

"It sounds like she's going to be there."

"If she is, you'll get a chance to meet her. Since we're closest, you and I are going in. We'll extract the deserter, secure the missing data, and slip out before she tries to sell it to someone else. If there's time, maybe we'll see if we can find one of those glass-bottomed pools."

They left the battleship behind, travelling aboard an orbital passenger transporter. The lightly armoured machine lumbered and creaked, but other than the recently captured cargo ships, it was the only non-military vessel in their ramshackle flotilla.

As no one else among their increasingly depleted crew had the security clearance to know that Clee even existed, the two of them travelled alone. With a pleasure-planet as their destination, Sean couldn't help but think of it as a holiday, even if he did spend half the voyage clearing up a water leak from a broken recycler.

Hours became days, even if he couldn't figure out the date. The first towani calendar, still used by the church, was based on the rotational cycle of Towan I, the first place the ancestral towani had settled. When the environmental damage forced them to abandon the planet in favour of the sunless interstellar void, they had adopted a new calendar of ten-day weeks, five-week months, and a ten-month year. When they settled on Towan III, the emperor declared a new calendar based on that planet's rotation.

It was maddeningly confusing. Even more so as the Valley's new ruling council had decreed they should add a fourth official calendar, that of their ancestral home. Until he could pop back to Earth and ask someone the time, he had to trust the towani's thinking machines when they told him it was 1893.

They worked. They trained. They loved. But all holidays, even working ones, come to an end. As the one-hour countdown began, they took up position in the control room, with Hakon in the pilot's seat, and Sean at the sensors.

"I think it's somewhere around Easter," Sean said.

"What is?" Hakon asked.

"The date. I think it's Easter, 1893."

"Easter is your winter holy day?"

"No, it's in spring, with fasting beforehand. The rations we've been on lately certainly remind me of Lent."

"Ah, yes, it's your celebration of reincarnation."

"Resurrection," Sean said.

"You've been thinking about Earth a lot lately," she said.

"Half the time I worry I'll never see home again. The other half, I worry we'll get there only to find the Voytay have already arrived."

"There are many faithful among the Voytay. They might not accept Davir as a prophet, but they can't deny that Earth is the ancestral home of all towani. Volmar is too cunning to take the war to Earth. If he does, our sentries will alert us, but Celeste will protect the planet."

"And I shall protect you," he said.

She snorted with laughter. "Isn't it almost always the other way around?"

With a disconcerting clatter and a sudden feeling of weightlessness, they returned to normal space.

"Gravity's dropped to half what it should be," Sean said, checking the instruments. "While we're here, we should see if there's a mechanic we can pay to examine the ship."

"There's no one here," Hakon said. "No one at all. I'm picking up an automated signal from the harbour. It's an order to evacuate issued two days ago."

"It came too late," Sean said. "Have you seen how many wrecked ships are here?"

"Is the deserter's ship among them?"

He began scanning the wreckage for the discus-shaped Type-9 fighter the deserter had stolen. "I can't see it. The identifiable wrecks are all civilian models, and they're all battle-damaged. Did the Voytay attack?"

"The evacuation message says a rogue faction attempted to seize control of the harbour. A ship exploded while in the dock. It says that they're running on emergency power, but they are leaking air. Everyone should leave while they can. Then the message repeats."

"I'm checking the encrypted channels, but there's no message from Clee," Sean said. "I *am* picking up a few emergency beacons. Two from ships, and a few dozen from spacesuits. No life signs, though. That's out here. There's even more coming from inside the harbour. A lot of people didn't make it. Maybe our deserter is one of them."

"We'll go aboard, and look for her ship. If it's gone, we'll know she's escaped, and probably to Voytay space."

Sean switched the focus of his scans to the upper ring, where four large ships were docked. They looked once to have been cargo freighters to which extra armour and weaponry, cannibalised from ships of both warring fleets, had been added. They didn't appear damaged, and weren't broadcasting a distress call, but nor could he detect any life signs aboard. The lower ring had been shattered in three places and now looked more like a semi-circle than a wheel. The larger central ring was less damaged, though it had still been breached in many places. His instruments couldn't penetrate far into the shielded berths, but there appeared to be more ships left than the number of emergency beacons he was picking up.

"It must have been a massacre. How big is this place?" he asked as they drew nearer, and the harbour grew larger.

"They claimed they could process a million guests a day," she said.

"A million?"

"If you believe anything Volmar said."

Theirs was no speedy fighter craft, but a lumbering transporter, slow to turn, and slower to accelerate. Yellow warnings flashed on every sensor as they ploughed through the debris field from the recent battle. With their shields swiftly diminishing, there was no time to hunt for a dock with atmosphere, so Hakon piloted them to the nearest breach in the main ring large enough for their ship. Inside were forty jetties in four rows of ten, one above the other, each with an extendable airlock. Only two shattered wrecks remained, both blocky freight-haulers that were cheap to run, but hard to maintain. Both appeared to have sustained missile damage to their engines.

Hakon manoeuvred them to a jetty furthest from the debris.

"The remote docking systems are inactive," she said. "We'll have to swim."

"Ah, it's not swimming if you don't get wet," Sean said, detaching his harness. "If the harbour's systems are inoperative, its orbit will decay, and it'll crash to the planet below."

"Within a few weeks, yes."

"I was reminded of one of Davir's prophecies. Didn't he have one about a space-station crashing to the ground?"

"That the answers beneath leave many questions, but could bring peace. That's one of Nowan's prophecies, not Davir's."

"Ah. I wonder if it means we should search the planet."

"If the deserter has left, she'll go to Voytay space, not the world below. Deserters wouldn't use implants, so we want a portable terminal belonging to a member of the dock-crew. They must have kept records of who was docked where. I'm switching off our gravity field."

They swam into the airlock. Without power, the harbour's artificial gravity systems were as dead as the crew. In better times, an umbilical airlock would have extended, and connected to their ship. Fragments of that lifesaving tunnel now hung in the vacuum along with a body. Hakon grabbed hold of the frozen boot, pulling the corpse close enough that she could check for a data storage device, but where it should be was a jagged triangle of shrapnel.

"It's too damaged to use," she said. "It's sooval anyway, so can't be the deserter we're looking for."

"Not that we'd get so lucky," Sean said. "There's an emergency exit over there. It's open."

It was only half open, but they were able to squeeze inside and into what should have been an airlock. The inner door was firmly closed. The control panel had been opened, exposing the circuitry. Hakon diverted power from her suit to the panel, and the door juddered ajar, but there was no outrushing of air.

One advantage of the harbour being part of a tourist-focused destination was that the internal layout was in the public record. Sean brought up the map that Dannan had sent with the mission briefing. "Where are we heading?"

"The dock chief's office for this quay. It should be ahead and to the right. When this was a hotel, there was a data-storage room behind it that would keep records of arrivals and departures. If the deserters maintained any records, they'll have used the old system."

The server room behind the dock chief's office had been professionally destroyed. So had the dock chief. Two large wounds pierced her chest, leaving a floating trail of blood in the air that marked the projectiles' onward flight into the bulkhead. On her wrist beneath her suit, was a slim tablet that, like Sean's own personal thinking machine, would link to the helmet's visor. The tablet was encoded to the dock chief, but it was an old device, with old encryption they knew how to break.

"A Type-9 saucer was here at the time of the collapse," Hakon said. "The pilot was allocated a cabin next to the berth."

"Maybe our luck's changing," Sean said. "Where are we heading?"

"To the luxury side of the harbour, the place where small ships would come. Rooms were provided for the crew who weren't going to get a paid vacation below. It's not far."

They made their way through the service corridors until they reached an airlock that gave them access to the customer-facing side of the harbour-hotel. The deserters had paid less attention to cleanliness than their hotelier predecessors, but even topped with grime, the luxury was evident. The corridors were wider and taller, and more brightly decorated with ornate fitments. On the walls and floors were screens that would once have advertised the pleasures to be had on the planet below. Small rectangular betting chips floated in the doorway of a casino, mingling with broken glass from the neighbouring bar.

"How much did sanctuary here cost?" Sean asked.

"I'm not sure, but it would be a lot."

"What happened to the deserters who ran out of cash?"

"If they were lucky, I suppose they were recruited as crew."

"And why did we let the place keep on existing?"

"There was no strategic value in capturing it, only the embarrassment it caused Volmar. We hoped he might waste some of his resources trying to take it."

"Perhaps he did," Sean said as a corpse floated out of an open doorway. It was a paxley, and only half dressed, with obvious small-arms wounds on the torso.

"Blue light ahead," Hakon said, pointing to an airlock. "That means they've got air, and so power. There might be survivors."

"It might be our deserter," Sean said.

"It might not," Hakon said, raising her side-arm before entering the airlock. As with the other airlocks, the control panel had been hacked, but this time, there was a gentle pressure from above as air entered from a ceiling vent. Even when the air reached normal levels, they kept their helmets on.

The corridor beyond was illuminated by emergency lighting, which shone through a broad viewing window to illuminate the Type-9 fighter berthed outside. The other four berths in this section were empty.

On the other side of the corridor were five cabin doors. The door opposite the berthed starship slid open. A towani in a spacesuit, but without a helmet, floated through, hands already raised.

"You're Dello tol Savin, the deserter," Hakon said, keeping her gun aimed at the woman. "You're under arrest. We've come to take you home."

"No," she said. The terror in her voice was as clear to hear as it was to see on her face. "If you don't drop your weapons, I'll blow up." She pointed to an explosive belt strapped to her waist.

"You'd rather die than go to jail?" Hakon asked. "We're not the old empire. You won't be executed or tortured. You'll even receive treatment for your addiction. Just remove the bomb, and come with us."

"I can't. I want to, but I can't. The bomb has a remote trigger."

"Who's controlling it?" Hakon asked.

The answer came from a speaker in the wall. "Discard your weapons, and then you'll find out."

129

Hakon let go of her sidearm, and with a flick, pushed it behind her. Sean did the same. Those were far from their only weapons, but he would only relinquish the others if explicitly asked.

The cabin door opened again. Two figures floated through. Both wore armoured red space suits of the old imperial type issued to the regents' elite bodyguards, and carried short-barrelled carbines. Their visors were opaque, but from the long limbs of the one on the left, he'd guess that was a sooval.

The figure to come through next had removed her visor, revealing that she was a paxley. This one had shaved the fur-like hair from her face to better display the swirling pattern of red tattoos on her skin. Hanging from the suit's shoulders, and with the ends pinned to her waist, were four strips of red cloth. She was one of the feared red-robes, the nickname given to the regents' religious enforcers.

"This was a trap," Hakon said.

"Yes," the red-robe said, before raising her hands, pointing one each at the back of the heads of her bodyguards. From each wrist, a bolt was launched, exploding on impact, killing the Voytay soldiers. "But the trap was not set for you. Remove your helmets. I would like to see who you are."

Hakon removed her helmet. "Who are you?"

"I am Clee, but you are the prophet's adopted daughter. It was dangerous for you to come here yourself."

"Evidently," Hakon said.

Sean pulled off his helmet.

Clee stepped back in astonishment. "Impossible."

"Sean O'Malley, pleased to meet you," Sean said, offering his hand.

Clee didn't take it. "You can't be here."

"I'm sure I am," Sean said. "Why don't you tell us what's going on?"

"I had a vision of the future, and you were in it," Clee said. "I saw myself standing over you. If I killed you, I saw the entire galaxy consumed with flames. If I let you live, peace would come to the galaxy. And I *was* going to kill you both while you were still aboard your ship. I wanted no witnesses. No survivors. Yet something stayed my hand and I gave the order to let your ship dock. It is miraculous."

"You came here because of a vision?" Sean asked.

"No, I came here to trigger this trap. I was sent here to capture this deserter and the agents sent to fetch her. It was thought those agents would know the identity of the spy known as Clee. The two I killed are both Volmar's personal bodyguards. Between them, they have access to all the information I have provided. I always intended to kill them and frame them as the spies. That Clee was more than one person would explain why catching this spy has been so difficult. I was going to claim that they killed the deserter and the Valley agents sent to recapture her. Instead, my hand was stayed, and I let you live. We must hurry. There are more of the enemy aboard a ship docked at the other side of this harbour. You must leave. Do you want to take the deserter with you?"

"We will."

"If she lives, she can't reveal my identity."

"I'll install her in a monastery," Hakon said.

"Very good. Remove the explosive belt. It won't detonate. Not yet. Take the bodies with you. It will be better if it is thought they escaped with you. When the explosion comes, use it to cover your escape. One last thing." She placed her hand against the bulkhead. "I need an injury to show I fought. Remove my hand."

"You're joking," Sean said.

"It was in my vision, too."

Part 4
The Intergalactic Anchorite

Church Island, County Kerry
20th October

Chapter 14 - Living Saints

With rain spoiling her view, Serene nibbled on a croissant while reading the news from the Valley. It was weeks old, travelling no faster than a message-pod's hop engine, but the story it told hadn't changed much in the last year. The big news still focused on the raids on the new colonies near the galactic hub. The official reports now stated the Voytay were not behind the attacks. As the government couldn't identify who was, a lot of people didn't believe those reports. This had led to calls for more military spending, but also to a discussion over whether some, if not all, of those colonies should be abandoned.

She skipped to the sports pages, and the latest results in the sooval singing league. This year's theme was bountiful harvests, and her team had lost. Again. And despite performing so hard that five of the best players were now too injured to compete for the rest of the season. She skimmed the rest of the bulletin, but it was just the usual mix of disgraced politicians, strident celebrities, and unpreventable tragedies. The only mention of Earth was lingering concern over Covid.

Local news wasn't much different. RTE led with the skyrocketing cost of property in County Cork, especially on Great Island, home to the town of Cobh. A new curriculum was being developed, with xenobiology and astrophysics becoming compulsory for all ages, just as soon as lesson planning had caught up with enthusiasm. Internationally, there was rioting in Saudi Arabia, an uprising in Myanmar, and the ongoing war in Ukraine, but those had little to do with first contact. That wasn't preventing commentators on both sides from asking why the Valley didn't step in to help.

Serene crammed the last of the croissant into her mouth, and made her way down to the office where Tempest was waiting.

"Where's Dorn-Tru?" she asked.

"Waiting for the camera crew from the peace platform to land. Are you ready?"

"Let me just grab some pastries from the kitchen."

Hop Island, on which the hotel had been built, was southeast of the city, on Lough Mahon, and was closer to the town of Cobh than to the centre of Cork, just as long as you had a boat. With only one road to the mainland, keeping away the uninvited only required a small checkpoint and a very tall fence. For the first few weeks, every boat owner in the county had made a small fortune piloting journalists as near to the shore as the police patrols would allow. Now, the journalists were gone, and so were the curious citizens. Only a few protestors remained, relegated to a low-fenced camp in the corner of a mainland car park. Their signs were beginning to sag, and so were they.

"Do you think Da really shot off Clee's hand?" Serene asked as she drove them west.

"I suppose we'll find out when we meet her," Tempest said.

"It's a shame Da got that summons from the British police. I'd have liked to have heard what happened to the deserter."

"Dello tol Savin? You don't know?"

"Which is why I said I'd like to find out," she said.

"I mean that you don't know Dorn-Tru is Dorn-Tru *tol Dello tol Savin*."

"No. Really? So what happened to her next?"

"I only know she went to a monastery, and that Gramps gave her the job of assistant when he, and Da and Greta, came back to Earth after the war finished."

"She didn't serve time?"

"I don't think there was even a trial. She would have qualified for the amnesty after the war. We had that citizen-swap agreement with the Voytay. If she wanted, she could have gone there, but she stayed."

"I don't know how I feel about that. I mean, I like her. She's a bit stern, and a lot religious, but she can be fun in a Sunday-evening kinda way. But she was about to sell out the Valley. There should have been punishment."

"Isn't it better that she repents through good work?" Tempest said.

"I suppose. Have you read any of Clee's sermons?"

"Some. I read some more last night. They're mostly about repentance."

"Where do you stand on her role in the faith?"

"The original teachings of the Holy Nowan spoke of messengers as well as prophets. She never thought of herself as either, but there are some who do. Her teachings are very popular, more so now than when she was in prison. She could have had a comfortable life. Instead, she chose exile and the life of a hermit. That level of dedication is impressive."

"If she believes that strongly, I've got to wonder why she'd give up her hermitage just to speak to a few politicians."

"Do you remember when we were ten, we went to the lake when Da tried to teach us how to fish?" Tempest asked.

"I remember trying not to throw up when he gutted that trout to cook on the campfire. It's the same island?"

"It is. I don't remember seeing her. Do you?"

"I only remember the look of glum surprise on that poor fish's face."

It was pleasant driving through the Irish countryside, and doubly so with Tempest as her companion. They'd spent their first five years living in Carrigtwohill, to the north of Cobh and Great Island. After they'd relocated to the embassy in Germany, they had returned to Ireland for an occasional holiday, but they couldn't risk going anywhere Greta might be seen. Remote cottages meant no chance of playmates, so it had just been the two of them, running nearly wild up hills and along rivers, as their father had done, and much like Greta had done, though on an alien world. Looking back, she wished there'd been more days like that. She sighed.

"What's up?" Tempest asked.

"Life goes by too fast," she said. "I think we're nearly there."

"And I think I've worked out why she picked this spot," Tempest said. "She's not the first hermit to live on the lake. Church Island was home to St Fionán Cam in the 7th century. It says he was a prophet when he was a kid."

"Cool, but do we go left or right?"

"Straight ahead," Tempest said, pointing at the wind-whipped lake now waiting directly in front of them. "Church Island is in the middle."

"Great. Let me just engage the car's wings. Dad said we want the boat hire place in the north."

"Then you want to go right."

Despite having only two boat-houses and a small shop, there seemed to be no end to the services the owner offered on the army of sandwich boards by the edge of the car park. From lake tours to sailing lessons, and from bait to coffee, if it had anything to do with water, the owner offered it. Nearly obscured by a nailed-on addition of 'boat recycling' was the name Brian Finnegan. The man himself was sitting at a picnic table, coiling a rope.

"Now, would you be the O'Malleys?" he called out as they pulled in.

"That's us."

"Your father called, and ordered you a boat. I suppose you've come to visit your ancestor buried on Church Island."

"That's it," Serene said, eagerly grasping the cover story.

"Your father often visits," Finnegan said. "Strange days, these. It's wise to reconnect with the past. It might help us prepare for the future. Are you happy with boats, then?"

"I've got my pilot's licence," Tempest said.

"Grand, then I'll leave you to it. Oh, and be mindful of the bees."

"Bees?"

"There's a few hives on the island. There's some as say they were installed by the ghost of an old anchorite nun who sealed herself in a chamber beneath the church a thousand years ago. There are others as say it was Mrs Cortez who moved here from Spain at the turn of the century. I'll let you decide for yourselves which to believe." He returned to his ropes.

As soon as they were away from shore, Serene released the sisters. The small drones rose from the dock on her forearm. Macha and Badb circled above them. Nemain attached itself to the stern and propelled them onward faster than a speedboat. They were nearly airborne when they reached the island, and it needed the other two sisters to bring them to a teeth-jarring and wave-drenching halt.

The drones didn't have faces. Nevertheless, Nemain looked sheepish as it dripped its way out of the water. Serene waved the drone away. "You nearly killed us. For that, you can stand watch."

The island was only four acres in size, barely large enough for a well, a small graveyard, a few wind-bowed trees and storm-lashed bushes, a trio of beehives, and the ruined, roofless church whose stones were held together with prayer rather than mortar. What was missing was anywhere an alien hermit might call their home.

"Where do you think she lives?"

"It must be underground," Tempest said. "I bet tourists come here, and local fisherfolk, not to mention the beekeeper. Clee must only come out at night, or she'd long ago have been discovered."

"Fair point, so where's the door?" Serene asked.

"Da didn't tell you?"

"No. You?"

"Not yet. I'll call him."

"No, wait a bit. Let's try to solve the puzzle first," she said.

Slowly walking between the moss-covered stones, she looked for footprints.

"It wouldn't be inside the church," Tempest said. "That would be sacrilegious, and Clee's very devout."

"What about hiding an entrance in one of the graves?"

"That'd be worse," Tempest said. "What about the well?"

The well appeared to be as old as the church, with pebbles filling the interior and thick moss draped over the sides.

"I don't think it's as old as it looks," Tempest said. They pushed at a stone at the top. It didn't budge. "These stones are mortared together. Wait, here, on the inside, there's a stone carved into a pentagon. And, look here beneath the moss, that's a camera." Tempest pushed at the pentagonal stone, and the entire floor of the well, pebbles and all, swung inward, revealing a shaft with a ladder.

"Oh great light, I summon thee!" Serene declared. "Ladies, that was your cue."

Badb and Macha slowly descended, shining lights down the vertical tunnel.

"About twenty metres deep," Serene said as the lights came to a halt.

"It's not a very well-concealed entrance," Tempest said. "Any tourist could have pushed that stone."

"I bet she saw us on the camera and unlocked it. Nemain, keep watch. If people come, let us know." Serene swung herself over the side of the well, and began to climb down.

The shaft was made of a grey composite that put her in mind of the embassy tunnel in the Neander Valley. At the bottom, other than a drain in the floor and a lingering smell of damp, was a solitary door. The door had no lock and was already partially retracted into the tunnel's wall. Serene pushed it open. She sniffed. "That's not damp."

"I think it is," Tempest said.

"I mean, it's not *just* damp."

The entrance led into a hallway with two doors on either side and a fifth at the far end. The first door almost led outside. The room had no floor, just bare rock. It had walls, and those were covered in paintings: Leaping salmon, a setting sun, angry bees, burning spaceships, towering cities, and open plains. The pictures told a story, but she didn't know where to begin. Whatever the tale, it appeared to be unfinished. There were three gaps, each the size of a dinner plate, near the door.

"Serene!" Tempest called out, having continued along the corridor. "You better see this. Actually, no. You better not."

"What?" Serene asked, stepping back out into the corridor. Tempest was walking back from the door at the corridor's far end.

"I found Clee," Tempest said. "She's dead. You don't want to see."

Serene ignored her sibling, and pushed past them. The former spy lay on the floor of the large living chamber. She had been disembowelled, with her organs arrayed between her splayed legs. Serene backed up, gagging.

"Greta, it's me," Tempest said, already placing the call. "We found Clee. She's been murdered, and it looks just like the work of Jack the Ripper."

Chapter 15 - Jack's Return

The sisters flew them upwards, out of the shaft, and back into glorious sunshine. There, with the drones protectively circling, they waited for Greta, too shocked to discuss the horror below.

Shattering the tranquillity of centuries, a spaceship dropped from the sky, hovered, and set down on the northern side of the island. Before the mud and grass had settled, Greta ran down the still-descending ramp.

"Are you two okay?" she asked.

"Not really," Serene said. "She was gutted just like the poor victims of Jack the Ripper. It was... well, I'm trying to forget what it looked like, but I don't think I'll ever forget the blood."

"The smell," Tempest said.

"Look at me and focus," Greta said. "Did you see anyone when you arrived?"

"No. And there were no boats," Tempest said. "The sisters would have told us if there was anyone here."

"I hope they would," Serene said, "But they've been acting stroppy for weeks."

"How did you get inside?" Greta asked.

"There's a pentagonal stone inside the well. I just pushed it," Serene said.

"Do you mean the door was unlocked?" Greta asked. "Okay, wait here."

"She was missing a hand," Tempest said.

"She was? I didn't notice."

"And she'd let her fur grow back on her face."

"Are you okay, Tempi?" Serene asked, catching the distant tone in her sibling's voice.

"All she did was preach peace and redemption, and she hasn't even done that for decades. I was looking forward to meeting her. Few people have. Or *did*. Imagine what wisdom she could have imparted. Her death is a loss for the entire galaxy, but no one should be treated like that."

"It's like Gramps says, antiquity has no monopoly on barbarism," Serene said.

"But it should." Tempest crossed their arms and began to pray.

Serene paced, stopped, sat on a pile of stones, and then stood and paced some more. Since she couldn't shake the image of what she'd seen, she tried to dilute it by bringing up the footage the sisters had gathered while down in the tunnel. She didn't look at the corpse, but at the large chamber in which the body had been found. It was sparsely furnished, but not uncomfortable, and thoroughly clean. There were a few terrestrial books on a shelf, wilting flowers in a vase on the table, a blanket on the armchair, and an easel in the corner. The only screen was a dusty monitor for the well's security camera. There was no computer, or TV, unless it was hidden behind one of the doors they hadn't opened, but there was a battered Bakelite radio as old as the hermit's self-imposed exile.

One of her drones buzzed low, flying a tight circle in front of her face.

"What is it, Nemain?" she asked. The drone flew back towards the shore. She followed until she saw the boat ploughing through the lake towards them. She opened comms. "Tempi, Greta, we've got company."

She jogged over to the jetty to meet the newcomers. Even as it still approached, she had her glasses zoom in. Brian Finnegan, the owner of the boatyard, was piloting the green-painted vessel, but its passengers were two uniformed Gardaí.

"Is that your spaceship, ma'am?" the police sergeant asked as she got out of the boat.

"Sadly, no," Serene said. She heard footsteps behind her. "It's hers."

"Officers," Greta said, hurrying to meet them.

The young constable's mouth fell open in shock at the sight of a towani. In Serene's opinion, the surprise was unwarranted. Who else would be piloting a spaceship? The sergeant, hardened by years of crime scenes where grey was a common colour for skin, handled it far better.

"You can't park your ship there," the sergeant said. "Park on the mainland, and use a boat."

"I'm Greta tol Hakon, head of security for this star system."

"And I'm Sinead Plunkett, the police officer for right here. Move your ship, or I'll write you a ticket."

"I'm investigating a murder," Greta said. "The victim was not a sapiens."

"A murder?" the sergeant asked.

"The victim is a cleric. A hermit. She's been living in a chamber beneath this ruin for the last sixty years."

"You're saying the anchorite was no ghost?" the boatman asked.

The sergeant waved him into silence. "Could you explain why someone was living beneath this old church?"

"She was considered a living saint by some in our faith," Greta said. "Your saint, who built this church, was said to have the gift of prophecy. So did she. That is why she requested this as the location to make her final home."

"And this was sixty years ago?" the sergeant asked.

"Modern medicine is wonderful," Greta said. "She received continual, if irregular, treatment so she could extend the length of her suffering."

"I have an aunt like that," the boatman said.

"You said she was murdered?" the sergeant asked, latching onto the most familiar detail. "You better show me the body."

"It's not a pleasant sight," Greta said.

"It never is," the sergeant said. "Constable, remain up here. Your assistants can remain here, too."

"Call the ambassador, Serene. Call Dorn-Tru, and tell her to inform Mr O'Connell. And call your father."

In the morning, the lake had rippled with glorious promise. By sunset, it had settled into orderly sadness. The sapiens forensics team had been and gone, at least for today and so had Greta, taking

Clee's body to the peace platform for an autopsy. Glaring lights marked a large police presence at the boatyard. Other lights flashed and shimmered along the shoreline as officers maintained a loose cordon around the lake. Serene and Tempest were alone on the island, except for the sleeping bees and wary ghosts, until a light on the lake grew brighter, marking the approach of another vessel.

"Gawpers inbound," Serene said. The sisters rose, shining their beams on the approaching boat before buzzing an excited circle overhead.

"Why are they doing that?" Tempest asked.

"Who knows why they do anything?"

They found out when the boat docked, and a familiarly familial face jumped onto the jetty.

"Evening, kids. Are you both okay?" Sean said as he secured the boat.

"Hey, Da. Harold, hi! Why are you here?" Tempest asked.

"We brought dinner," Sean said. "Help Harold with the gear. I want to take a look at the crime scene."

"These look sapiens," Tempest said, taking a chair passed up by Harold.

"They are," Harold said. "We picked them up in Kenmare an hour ago. Here's a stove."

"A stove?"

"To cook tea," Harold said. "I said we should grab some pizzas, but your dad thought this would be better. Was the hermit really laid out to look like one of the Ripper's victims?"

"She was," Tempest said.

"Yep, and I'm officially done with horror films for good," Serene said.

"Your father thinks it must be linked to the murder of the two police officers and the disappearance of Dr Masadi."

"Who?" Serene asked.

"Mrs Parker. I think Celeste's worried, too. While your dad was buying all this gear, Jess called to say that Celeste had arrived at the bookshop and insisted she pack a bag and go with her. For safety."

143

"She must think your aunt is a target again," Tempest said.

"If she is, then so are we," Serene said. "And Da's solution appears to be that we should go camping."

"We've got police on shore, the sisters overhead, and satellites above those. I say we're safe," Tempest said.

"Well, *don't* say it, or you'll jinx it," Serene said. "Are there any leads in the police officer shootings?"

"I don't think there are even any clues," Harold said. "I've been stuck in one interrogation room after another ever since we found the bodies. I can understand why, but the more I explained how little I knew, the angrier the cops became. And then they looked up my record. Let's just say I'm glad to be out of Britain. What about here?"

"The entrance has a lock on the inside," Serene said. "Clee could lock herself in, but not lock herself out. The lock was disengaged, but not broken, so either Clee let the visitors in, or she was surface-side when they arrived."

"That's what my money is on," Tempest said. "There's only one camera, and that's in the well, but there's no bell or light, so unless she was expecting a visitor, you'd have a long wait. I bet she slept during the day and went topside at night to fish, walk, and think. No one's missing a boat, and no boat on the lake has any indication it was used last night without permission. There were no helicopters or spacecraft detected nearby. Greta thinks the killers drove here, towing a boat of their own, and sailed across the lake."

"If they drove, they're sapiens," Harold said. "So maybe it's the same two who shot the cops. Sean's sure that they were professionals."

"Professionals seems right," Serene said. "Before she was a hermit, Clee was a professional torturer for the regents. She knew how to fight."

"But that was a hundred years ago, and there's no sign of a struggle," Tempest said.

"Maybe she was stunned first," Serene said. "We'll have to wait for Dr Griffin to finish the autopsy. How does this stove work?"

"I think it helps if you light the match," Harold said. "I thought you went on a camping holiday during the pandemic in your mum's camper van."

"Which came with an electric cooker," Tempest said.

"And a credit card," Serene said. "We bought most of our food."

As the kettle began to boil, Sean returned. "Perfect timing. We're sitting watch tonight. At the first sunset after Dr Griffin releases the body, Clee will be interred in the room with no floor. The door will then be sealed, and remain shut for five hundred years."

"You mean she built her own tomb?" Serene asked.

"She wanted to spend eternity like her spiritual ancestors."

"But she's paxley," Serene said.

"And a believer in the Holy Nowan," Sean said.

"Is that a common funeral custom in the Valley?" Harold asked.

"During the clean-up operation on Towan I, they've so far discovered around a hundred sealed tombs," Sean said. "Radiation is still too high to search for more, but the theory is that it was common among some of the earliest and most senior monks. It became more popular during the second empire, but after the relocation to Towan III, it was a practice adopted by the emperors. As the cities merged into one, and space became scarce, the emperors decided this practice would be reserved entirely for them. After the Red Plague and the rise of the regents, the practice fell out of favour. But since the revolution, on planets where space allows, and especially on some of the new homestead colonies, it has risen in popularity."

"Some say the practice stretches back to the days of enslavement," Tempest said. "When someone died, their story would be painted on the wall, so they would never be forgotten."

"What happened to the bodies?" Harold asked.

"It's taboo to discuss it," Tempest said.

"They were probably recycled, broken down to be used as raw ingredients in the food-printers," Serene said.

"Sis! We *don't* discuss it!" Tempest said.

"And now Harold knows why," Serene said.

"The discovery of Neanderthal cave art on Earth suggests the ritual's roots might be even older," Sean said. "One of the traditions is to leave a few gaps to be finished after you die, thus showing that your story continues even after death. She wanted Greta, Johann, and me to add a little something. She also asked that on the night after her death, I would sit outside and remember her to the stars. That's a paxley custom. Ideally, we'd have an open fire, but that would only have some of the Gardaí pop over to check we weren't burning evidence. A stove will have to do."

"If she left instructions, it sounds like she was expecting to die," Serene said.

"She was," Sean said. "Harold, do the honours and make some tea. She'd already decided to stop receiving medical care once first contact occurred. She'd probably have lived for another two decades or so, but I think she was ready to die. Not like this, of course."

"Who was she?" Harold asked.

"Before the revolution, she was a red-robe," Sean said. "In Mid-Tow, the specific word used for red is an archaic one that also means blood. Red-robes were religious zealots, and enforcers and torturers for the regents. But she was also a revolutionary, and the author of many anonymous tracts, all on the theme of peace and equality. This was in the days of the regents. No one knew who she was, except that she published her tracts under the name Clee. They were critical in ensuring that everyone in the empire knew they were sharing the same injustices. Because Johann didn't know who she was, she wasn't part of the revolution, but she made contact with Gunther after the civil war began. She was with Volmar when he fled Towan III, and though she had a junior rank at first, she would often find a way of implicating her superiors in any data breach, and then be promoted when they were arrested."

"How could you be a torturer by day, and advocate of peace at night?" Harold asked.

"The nature of her day job was the cause of her switching sides," Sean said. "If you want a rational explanation of her visions, they could be the result of the horrors she inflicted while pursuing the greater good."

"Tell Harold how you met her," Serene said.

"Greta and I walked into a trap. We were hunting a deserter who had approached a Voytay agent, offering intel in exchange for asylum. Fortunately, this fell across Clee's desk. At the same time, the Voytay were increasingly aware there was a high-level spy in their ranks. She told us where the deserter would be, then met the deserter at an abandoned space station, but then waited for us to arrive. That's where it gets interesting."

"She killed her two bodyguards," Serene said.

"Yes, but they were two of Regent Volmar's personal bodyguards. She returned the deserter to us, and framed the two dead soldiers as both being our agents. She made it seem as if there wasn't just one spy, but an entire spy ring. That led to a purge at the top of Volmar's inner circle, and to the promotion of a lot of inexperienced officers. Clee was also promoted, and the value of her intel improved dramatically, and I chose that word deliberately. She got us the algorithm that the Voytay were using to move the defensive minefields on their remote bases. We were able to launch a simultaneous attack on their shipyards and their training bases. In one week, we took away their manufacturing advantage. Before I met her, we were losing. Thanks to her, we were able to claw back enough territory we could sue for a relatively equal peace."

"But then she was tried for war crimes," Serene said.

"At her own insistence," Sean said. "She provided the evidence against herself. It was all very detailed. Initially, she was sentenced to twenty years. She appealed on the grounds that it wasn't long enough. It was extended to fifty years. Afterwards, she went into voluntary exile, choosing life as a hermit."

"Why on Earth?" Tempest asked.

"Partly for her own safety," Sean said. "Because there was a trial, her identity became known. She is a hated figure to the Voytay. Maybe even more hated than Johann or Gunther, because her actions lost them that war. Many would want her dead. But in the Valley, her anonymous pre-revolutionary writings had led to her being considered a great spiritual thinker. She kept writing during her imprisonment. I won't say she created a cult, but her followers number in the millions, and would want nothing more than to hear her speak in person. When she was released from prison, she went on tour. She was electrifying, but it didn't bring her inner peace, especially since there were three assassination attempts during the tour. Hence her going into exile."

"Why in Ireland?" Harold asked.

"Only I, Celeste, and Greta knew where she was," Sean said. "And only Celeste and I would visit her. Clee liked the idea of anchorites, the nuns who would seal themselves in a chamber below a church. There was one, living here, many centuries ago."

"Was she really going to speak to the conference?" Serene asked.

"That was part of our agreement. After first contact, she wanted a final chance to speak to the galaxy. Her last act of repentance was to have been a call for peace so skilfully framed that her words might make dreams a reality. So she hoped. But instead, she was murdered."

"Do you have any idea why, and why now?" Tempest asked.

"I have a theory that the murder was commissioned by the Voytay. Don't forget, the Ripper was the great-nephew of Regent Volmar. Now, Volmar is no longer in charge of the Voytay, but he's still an influential figure. Having their most hated traitor murdered in a way that echoes his nephew could be on Volmar's orders, or to gain favour with him. To explain why, I need to go back a bit, to the year the civil war ended."

Part 5
The Revolutionary Returns Home

The British Empire
May 1895

Chapter 16 - Promises Kept

Sean O'Malley watched the sun rise over the cultivated kelp beds in Dillith's Shallow Sea. Though it stretched for hundreds of miles, separating three of the planet's many island continents, it was never more than two people deep, as long as those people were the long-limbed jajan. Different varieties of the underwater plant had been cultivated to have different colours and lengths, and then planted in meticulous curls and vivid sweeps. When low tide coincided with the sunrise, the pattern was said to depict the story of creation itself.

"It's beautiful," he said.

"I'm sorry it's just a recording," Hakon said.

"That's real enough for me," Sean said.

"One day soon, we'll go there together," Hakon said. "We'll go everywhere. We'll see everything."

"One day," he said, taking her hand. "But if we don't, it wouldn't matter. The war is over, we are alive, and we're together. There is truly nothing more I need."

"But it's only a ceasefire. It's not even a proper truce. There are far too many systems whose ownership is disputed. It would only take one uprising in the borderlands for the war to resume. Volmar will probably wait until after the exchange of prisoners, and of citizens who want to leave, but only so he can plant more spies in our ranks."

"Are you saying we won't do the same?" Sean asked.

"No, I suppose we will. It's just that I can see war returning, and the next time, we won't have Clee to pass on the enemy's secrets."

"For now, we have peace. For however long it lasts, I'll be sincerely grateful. Is that a fella in a canoe?"

A long yellow canoe rocked back and forth as a green-skinned jajan paddled across the sea. With each stroke, they would twist their body, lowering their head nearly as low as the water before twisting their body to the other side. They stopped, balanced the paddle on the canoe, and picked up a long pole with a hooked blade. With much-practised skill, they lowered the pole into the water to prune a rebellious plant.

"That's one of the curators," Hakon said. "It's a prized job."

"I wouldn't mind work like that," Sean said.

"Perhaps in the summer," Hakon said. "In the winter, the sea can freeze. They have to polish the ice so it can be seen through. Let me see if we have footage of that. Oh, wait. I've just had a message from Dorn-Tru."

"Hmm."

"That's the noise you make when our customs butt up against your upbringing. Life is nothing but constant change, so it requires constant self-evaluation. If the person we are isn't the person we were, we all have the right to define who we've become."

"I don't object to her changing her name," Sean said. "In fact, I completely understand why she'd want to, since when we first met her she was trying to desert to the Voytay. But changing names doesn't change the past, and our past informs who we are in the present. It's only two years ago that she betrayed us all."

"The past might be part of us, but it doesn't have to define us," she said. "That is the fifth precept, and often considered the most important. The Holy Nowan declared that who the ancestors were as warrior-slaves was not who they always had to be."

"Hmm."

"You did it again. Doesn't your holy book teach of redemption and repentance?"

"Yes, but stuck between whole chapters on punishment."

"You don't have to trust her, but Davir is certain her faith is sincere and her desire to atone is strong, or he wouldn't have brought her along as an assistant. Anyway, she says we're nearing Earth and are needed on the bridge."

The warship had once belonged to the corpulent Regent Kudon, and was by far the most luxurious in the Valley's fleet. The now-dead regent had used it as a base for simultaneous oppression and gluttony during the twilight years of the empire. The ruling council had gifted the vessel to Davir so that he could make a ceremonial visit to Earth. Aside from being overly armed and overly decorated, the front of the ship featured a transparent-walled viewing room in which the regent could feast while watching planets being bombarded.

The bulkheads still bore the scars from the battle in which the ship had been captured. The carpets and drapes had long since been removed, along with the decorative wall paintings of the regent ascending to glory, but the viewing window was still intact.

Kudon was known to be a tempestuous tyrant, so while the chamber had been designed for a hundred, it was rare for anyone other than his food tasters to share the space with him. Now, it was full. At the front stood the last prophet. Though the diminutive preacher was half the height of even the shortest of his followers, he commanded the room. As at the beginning of the revolution, he wore a ceremonial kilt, and his skin had been painted in swirling red patterns that matched those worn by the Holy Nowan during the slave uprising. Beyond the transparent wall, a similar pattern of curling red lines could be seen, though these moved and danced as the ship travelled outside the normal bounds of space.

Beside Davir stood the Bishop of Towan, traditionally the leader of their faith, except when a prophet was recognised. Other clerics were arrayed behind, with the former deserter, now called Dorn-Tru, at the very back, looking small and lost in her new clerical vestments. Sean almost felt sorry for her. Almost.

He and Hakon made their way through the crew lucky enough to have won a ticket for this moment, to take their places next to Davir.

"Welcome, Sean, Hakon," Davir said, his voice easily carrying across the room. "We return to where it began. Where an act of kindness set in motion events that led to our freedom. But we are also returning to where *we* began, to where our ancestors were forced into exile and slavery. We return as free people. Free from slavery, free from the tyranny of the empire, and free from the oppression of the regents. We return home."

With what was surely well-practised timing, the swirling red patterns were replaced with blackness, at the centre of which was a blue marble. There was a gasp from some, an ecstatic cry from a few, and tears from many others.

"Our home," Davir said. "Our ancestral home, and our future home. Let us enjoy this moment."

The Bishop of Towan began to sing a hymn, one of the oldest in the faith, a song of loss and longing, and of the hope of one day finding their homeworld again. Now that they had, the last line, roughly translating as '*what glories will the future hold?*' had gained a poignant urgency.

With the hymn finished, the bishop began a prayer while Davir led Sean and Hakon from the chamber. A head-bowed Dorn-Tru scurried along behind, ready to record any accidental teachings that Davir might impart.

"You may wait outside," Davir said to Dorn-Tru when they reached the prophet's quarters.

The new cleric sagged even further, clearly trying to make herself look invisible as she took up a position to the left of the door.

Sean followed Hakon and Davir into a chamber that had been stripped of its opulence. The dining table and torture rack had been replaced with five simple chairs. The prophet had simple tastes, but it wouldn't have been seemly for the largest suite to be given to anyone else.

"How are you finding Dorn-Tru?" Hakon asked, pointing at the now-closed door.

"She has yet to find herself," Davir said. "The trick, of course, is to cease searching and let ourselves find us. Now, we must get to business. Sean, Celeste promised that if you went with us, it would change the galaxy. It did. I promised her that I would bring you home. Now we have both kept our promises, but she must be shown that we have. You must speak with her."

"How do I find her?"

"I imagine she will find you," Davir said.

"Then I'd like to see my family," Sean said. "I'd like to see my old home."

"Of course," Davir said. "Hakon will fly you down at night, though her ship will not land, and she will not step foot on the planet."

"I know, there's a ritual to be followed," she said, in a tone that made her sound a century younger. "But I have set foot on Earth before."

"Ritual is important," Davir said. "The discovery of our home is inextricably linked with the revolution. We must portray this expedition as a victory, or people will question what it is we won during so many years of war."

"So I'll pop down to the planet and chat with Celeste. Then what?"

"Then I will speak with her before I take up permanent residence."

"I thought you were going to live on Towan III?" Hakon said.

"After much reflection, I have changed my mind. If I am in the capital, my opinions will be sought. Whatever I say carries the weight of prophecy. It would be inevitable that I would become a new emperor, and that is not the outcome for which so many have died. I will stay here and help guide the people of Earth after first contact. Of course, first contact with your people must be planned. Remember what we discussed. It will take time."

"I think I've learned a bit of patience."

Hakon laughed. "You? Patient? The man who scalds his mouth every time he eats? I think not."

"You will wish to prepare," Davir said. "We will reach orbit in two hours."

Sean and Hakon returned to their more modest cabin to change. Sean removed his flight suit and donned the trousers, shirt, waistcoat, and jacket modelled on the funeral suit he'd been wearing when he'd first met Hakon.

"It's a grand suit," he said. "Though perhaps too grand. People will notice me."

"Good. You're not a servant anymore. You're a general."

"Not anymore. I'm just a former soldier."

"You are still a leader," she said, smoothing his collar. "You're a hero and one of the most known and respected figures in our new federation. Don't forget it. The fabric will protect you from the kinetic weapons used on your world, but there's nothing to protect your face." She raised a hand to his newly shaved chin. "Be careful."

"Aren't I always?"

"No more so than you are patient," she said.

Chapter 17 - Opened Letters

As soon as Sean stepped off the ramp, the flying saucer, hovering inches above the soil, rose back into the sky. He looked up, but between the rain and the darkness, there was soon nothing to see. He breathed deeply. The mud, the manure, the hint of new growth; it certainly smelled like home, and like spring. Beyond that, and that it was probably 1895, he had no idea when he was. Where was easier, because he'd picked the landing spot from orbit. He was north of the village of Carrigtwohill, which made it a six-mile walk to Queenstown, via the Belvelly Bridge.

On the inside of his spectacles, an arrow showed him the way to go. He adjusted his hat and began to walk. Slowly, the mist of memory cleared, and the horrors of over six years of violence receded. The years of civil war were over. He was home, and in a land at peace.

By the time he reached Queenstown, he found himself out of breath. The gravity on Earth was a good deal higher than he'd grown used to. The air was colder, and the sky was darker, but the birds had begun their morning chorus, so sunrise couldn't be far away. Smoke was already rising from the bakery's chimney, with flickering firelight creeping around the window.

At the door, he hesitated, uncertain whether to knock, uncertain what to say, uncertain what he expected to hear. Then it came to him. A memory so vivid he could almost taste it. He opened the door.

"Any chance of a cup of tea?" he asked.

Four flour-dappled bakers looked up, irate at the distraction, and were clearly willing to turn their fists from pounding dough to pounding an intruder.

"Who are you?" asked one.

"I'm Sean O'Malley. I've come to see Maeve O'Malley, and my nieces and nephews."

"It's Maeve O'Keefe now," a voice said. Sean turned. There she was. Her youthful beauty was now bracketed by wisdom, but unmarred by the many sorrows visited upon her harrowing life. "I knew you'd come back."

"Maeve!" The learned habit of his years away took over, and he stepped forward, intending to hug her, before remembering the social restraint of his place of birth.

"Have you grown taller?" Maeve asked. "Either you have or I've shrunk. You'll tell me everything, but you'll do it after we work. Take off that coat and scrub your hands. We've a ship due to depart at ten, and all must be ready by eight."

With ten minutes to spare, the fresh loaves, and the delicate pastries for the first-class passengers, were loaded onto a cart, and Sean was finally able to speak to Maeve alone.

"This wasn't the homecoming I was expecting. Business is good?" he asked.

"It is, and thanks to you, better than I'd ever dreamed it would be," she said.

"Me? How so?"

"The African queen you're working for has been sending us money."

It took Sean a moment to decipher that comment. "Celeste has been paying you?"

"She said that was what you'd asked. Sir John has been sending us money, too, though not as much and not as often. You were fighting, yes?"

"I was. For nearly seven years, I think."

"I haven't been counting the days, but it's six years and five months since you disappeared. War's changed you. I can see it in your face. But you weren't fighting for the British?"

"No," he said, truthfully.

"As long as the money still came, I knew you were alive. When the newspapers printed accounts of the wars in Africa, I tried to work out which you might be involved in. Is Sir John funding the resistance against the empire?"

"I've no idea," Sean said.

"We assumed that's how you got caught up in soldiering."

"Not exactly." He was at a loss for what to say. As much and as often as he'd thought of coming home, he'd given little thought to what would happen next. He'd merely wanted to reassure himself that Maeve was alive, and to reacquaint himself with the town whose memory had sustained him during the darkest times. For now, he decided to lie. "I was approached by Celeste to write a few stories. Things escalated."

"And you lost?"

"We didn't always win, but we held our ground," Sean said. "I'll tell you about it soon, but it's not something I want to think about now."

"Are you here to stay?"

"Eventually," Sean said. "I have a few things to attend to, but after that, yes, I think I'll be here for good."

"You'll be wanting the letters, then. Your African queen left one for you. Sir John left another."

"He did?"

She took down a metal box from behind a shelf and took out two envelopes.

"You opened them," he said.

"Of course. Getting money from queens and earls is not a common occurrence in these parts."

The envelope from Celeste contained a visiting card, not from a person, but from a London spice merchant. The letter from Sir John was more to the point, simply reading: *Visit me when you return.*

"Did Sir John know where you'd gone?" Maeve asked.

"Not in so many words," Sean said.

"Then be careful," Maeve said.

That evening, it was a thoughtful Sean O'Malley who walked back to where he'd been dropped off. The flying saucer ascended as swiftly as it had set down, leaving him clinging to the safety bar in the airlock until the ship reached an altitude where it wouldn't be seen. There, it hovered. Sean released his grip, and joined Hakon in the control room.

"How was it?" she asked.

"You weren't watching through the glasses?"

"I didn't want to pry."

"Well, it wasn't what I was expecting," Sean said. "Maeve is well, as are her children. She married Peter O'Keefe. He's the baker who trained in France. They seem happy."

"You were expecting they would be unhappy?"

"No. I was dreading they might be dead, and I'm glad they're well. Celeste has been sending them money. They think it's my salary for being part of some band of revolutionaries fighting against the British Empire in Africa."

"It's not too far from the truth."

"It's half a *galaxy* from the truth," Sean said. "Celeste left a calling card for a spice merchant in London, so I expect that's where we'll find her. But now we get to the unexpected part. Sir John sent Maeve money, too, and left a note of his own, asking for me to call on him when I return. I think he guessed I'd left the planet. I can't settle back in Ireland without squaring accounts with him. He'll want something."

"Perhaps he can help navigate the complexities of first contact. You said he was influential, and not a bad man."

"Perhaps," Sean said. "But it's unsettling that he involved Maeve. I feel like there's an unspoken threat in the money he sent her."

"Sending money doesn't sound very threatening," she said.

"I suppose not. It's just... well, for so long, it seemed so unlikely I'd ever return that I didn't give much thought to what would happen next."

"What would you like to happen?"

"I'd like Earth to join the Valley. It's the only way to guarantee the planet is safe from the Voytay."

"But what do *you* want?"

159

"To show you where I grew up. Then I'd like us to visit some of the grand sights I've only ever read about, like the pyramids, or the temple in Timbuktu. And then I'd like us to go to Dillith and all the other worlds. Maybe even to a pleasure planet if any of those ever open again."

"That sounds expensive."

"We've earned it."

"We have, though we might have to earn a bit more to afford it, but that's what we'll do. After first contact."

"I don't think the planet's ready to learn that there are worlds beyond this one. If you and I were to walk the streets of Queenstown, they'd run screaming."

"So we must prepare the ground," Hakon said. "The first step will be to make contact with Celeste. Are we heading to London?"

"To the sandpit in Woking where you landed after the Ripper died. The ship wasn't spotted there before."

"I'll set our course. A message-pod arrived with news from our spies among the Voytay."

"Does the truce still hold?"

"It does. Volmar's been inaugurated as the Voytay's sole leader. During the ceremony, his granddaughter stood behind him. Traditionally, during imperial coronations, that was the place the heir would take."

"Ah, well, it was always clear what title he wanted. Was it a religious ceremony?"

"No, but there were blessings before and a service afterwards which he attended. He was never a believer, and his granddaughter, his heir, was accompanied by a nun from Dillith. They may be seeking to encourage the dominance of a different faith."

"What about the red-robes?"

"There were none in attendance. It looks as if they really have been disbanded. Another gift from Clee. She must have known that, once news of her impending trial, and so her unmasking, reached Volmar, he'd grow suspicious of all the religious enforcers. Perhaps

160

he'll be distrustful of others in his inner circle, and until they're re-placed, the peace will hold."

"We didn't have to put her on trial to reveal her name. Dorn-Tru, and so many others, didn't face justice."

"Clee requested the trial. After all she did for us, it is the least we can do for her."

"The least we could do was let her live a quiet and anonymous life."

"Her belief runs deep. She thinks that her actions as a torturer undermined her faith, and thus must be atoned for. She had a vision that through public repentance, she can erase the sins of others. You said there were many deeply spiritual people in Ireland who shared a similar form of belief."

"There's even one or two in London," Sean said. "But the only person I've known to have visions was old Mrs Doherty, and those came to her after she was kicked in the head by her own donkey. She used to say there'd be a time when words would fly through the air faster than people."

"We can send messages at the speed of light, or faster if we use a message-pod," she said.

"But Mrs Doherty also said she could see the words. Sometimes, she'd read them aloud."

"Then you won't like the last part of the message," Hakon said. "Clee had another vision involving you."

"Oh?"

"We are in space. You, me, and Gunther, the last members of the prophet's clan. Behind us is Davir. Behind him, stretching back to the beginning of time, are all the members of the clan who have ever been. Before us, are our children. Beneath us are two worlds, repre-senting the possible futures for both us and the Voytay. One world is green and lush, the other is barren and desolate. We can have peace for both, or destruction for all. The decision will be made not by the prophet, but one of the clan's children."

"So we're to have children after all?"

"Is that all you take away from her message?"

"She's saying that the fate of the galaxy rests in either mine, yours, or Gunther's hands? It wouldn't be the first time that's been the case, and it's not much different to what Celeste said to me before I left Earth. How long until we reach Woking?"

"About half an hour."

"Then there's just time for you to enjoy a cup of tea and a freshly made cake."

Chapter 18 - Herbert and the Retired Horse Watchers

Reluctantly, Sean put the packet of tea into a locker. In his enthusiasm to share his beloved beverage with his beloved bride, he'd overlooked the obvious. "I'll pick up a teapot and a kettle when I'm in London. We can use the welding laser to heat the water in the kettle."

"You won't. I didn't survive all those years of war to die from your attempt to make tea ending in an explosion of super-heated steam frying the ship's life support system."

"For tea, it's worth the risk," Sean said.

"The cake was delightful, though," she said. "We're beginning our descent."

The ship didn't set down, but hovered just above the ground. Sean jumped out, and into a swirling sandstorm as Hakon took her vessel back up into the night sky. Sean jogged away from the still-settling sand and into the woodland. He'd just gathered his wits when he heard a shout from further in the trees.

"Hoy! Hallo! Did you see it?"

"What's that?" Sean asked, slipping his hand into his pocket. He'd been so focused on the risks of war, he'd utterly forgotten the everyday dangers of life in England. Approaching him was a moustachioed man of about his own age, smartly dressed, carrying a stick in one hand and a lantern in the other.

"Those lights," the man said. "That's why you're here, isn't it? I read that piece about the lights in the sky seen here seven years ago, and came to see if I might spy them for myself. I've been out on ten nights this month, and was about to call it a fool's errand, but I saw something. You saw it, too."

"All I saw was something falling. I thought it might be a meteor."

"No, I distinctly saw it rising again. There were strange lights beneath."

The man pointed back towards the sandpit.

"Sean O'Malley. I'm with the army." Sean hoped the martial lie might dissuade a potential thief.

"Wells. H.G. Wells." An expectant pride took over the young man's face, though it faded as it became clear Sean wasn't familiar with the name. "The author of *The Time Machine*?"

"You're a writer?" Sean asked, finally taking his hand out of his pocket. The pen might be mightier than the sword, but the young man had yet to draw either.

"I am." Wells walked past Sean and into the sandpit. "Ah, come here and look. This must be where it stood. See the three indentations? It must be some three-legged machine."

It wasn't. The indentations in the sand were caused by the downdraft of the engines, but Sean kept that to himself.

"Do you think it came from the moon or Mars?" Wells asked.

"The chances of that are a million to one," Sean said. "I suppose you'll write this up for the morning papers."

"Who would believe me? I'd lose all credibility, and it's been hard-won. I know what I saw, and the knowledge will have to suffice. Ah, but it's late. Good evening to you."

"Good evening."

Wells walked off. Sean lingered, until he got a call from his wife.

"Trouble?" Hakon asked, her words transmitted through the arm of his glasses.

"No, but I think, last time you set down here, the ship was seen."

"We'll need to identify a new landing site," she said. "Who was the man?"

"A local writer, but I don't think he'll be any trouble."

It was a short walk to, and so a long wait at, the railway station for the morning's first train. The stench of civilisation, of which there had been a bud in Queenstown and a bouquet in Woking, blossomed, died, and swiftly turned to decay as the train reached London. The smoke was so thick he wanted to ask for a pick-axe, while the sound was so loud it drowned out his thoughts. It reminded him

164

less of his life before leaving Earth than it did of the worst days of the war. Battling his way through the crowds, he found a cab to take him to Celeste's shop.

The Celestial Spice and Tea Emporium on Bond Street was a balm to the senses. The moment the door shut behind him, the world seemed to slow down. Cinnamon and mace filled his nostrils. Smokeless oil lamps produced a crystal-clear light that glittered off the jars filling the walls, and glinted off the mahogany counter, polished to a mirror-shine. The only sound was the creak of the laden shelves until it was joined by a greeting from a shopkeeper.

"Wotcha, guv. What'll you have?"

Behind the counter stood a man unlikely to have reached his eighteenth year. His tie was blue, as were his waistcoat's side panels, and far too rich for his voice.

Sean laid the visiting card on the counter. "My name's Sean O'Malley."

"Here, Charlie!" the assistant called out. "There's a cove out 'ere saying he's Sean O'Malley."

Another young man entered from the backroom, a teacup in hand. "Nah. O'Malley was taller."

"He was shorter," said a third young man, coming out with a teapot.

"So even it out, and I'd say that makes me spot on," Sean said. "Is Celeste here?"

"Hold your horses, because we don't have to do that no more," Charlie said. "Ollie, get him the box."

The first young man ducked into the backroom. He returned with an empty cup, and a rectangular black box, about the length of Sean's arm and as wide as his palm.

"What's this?"

"It's a box," Ollie said.

"I can see it's a box," Sean said. "What do you want me to do with it?"

"If you're Sean O'Malley, you can open it," Ollie said. "Pour us a cup, Pip."

As tea sloshed into the cup, Sean picked up the box. It was far heavier than it looked, weighing at least four pounds. The sides were smooth and cold, but felt more like stone than metal. Slowly, he turned it over in his hands. There were no latches, keyholes, or seams on the sides or top.

"It's a puzzle box," Sean said.

"Evidently," Charlie said.

Sean hated puzzles. His brother-in-law adored them. There was nothing the grizzled warrior liked more than relaxing after battle with a brainteaser. Sean preferred to stand under scalding hot water, trying to steam his brain clean.

"See, I told you it weren't him," Pip said.

"There are other ways of seeing," Sean said. With a flick of his fingers, he switched his eyeglasses to thermal imaging. Not only was the box not radiating heat, it seemed to be absorbing it. However, on one face, and darker than the rest of the surface, the number 45,213 appeared with each digit in a different square. The number meant nothing to him, but perhaps that was the point. He pressed 1, 2, 3, 4, and then 5. The end of the box seemed to melt away. Inside was a pocket watch.

"Welcome home, Mr O'Malley," Charlie said. "Please step this way." He gestured to the doorway behind the counter.

"I'm looking for Celeste. Who are you?"

"I'm not surprised you don't remember us. We looked after her ladyship's horse and carriage that day you killed the towani Ripper."

Sean stretched his mind back. "You were the three urchins in Whitechapel?"

"That's it. Her ladyship told us to wait here until you returned. Now you have. Please." Again he pointed at the door.

Sean stepped through, and into a cosy office with four armchairs, one far less worn than the other three, but otherwise identical. The walls were panelled with wood. A spiral staircase led up to a landing with two doors. At ground level, another door led to the back. In the other wall was a roaring fireplace whose flames emitted no smoke.

"You work for Celeste?"

"Only on the days that end in a 'y'."

"What do you do for her?"

"Mostly, we sell spices. Would you like some tea?"

"Absolutely, but where is she?"

"Somewhere in the Ottoman Empire, but now you're back, I'm sure she'll return."

"How will she know?"

"Not a clue, but her ladyship always knows." Charlie crossed to the fire. With a flick of his hand, the flames vanished. The interior of the fireplace was as soot-free as if it were freshly built. With another wave of his hand, the bricks at the back vanished, revealing a neat stack of leather valises. He removed the top one. "Her ladyship said you'd want to know about this first. I'll get your tea." Charlie slipped through the door at the back.

Sean undid the blue ribbon holding the case closed, opened it, and found a piece from the society pages announcing Sir John had purchased land in Oxfordshire on which he planned to build a new house. The next stated that he'd bought land in Hornchurch. Beneath that, cut from one of Sir John's magazines, was a request for stories about people living on the moon. A third was a copy of a private letter to the Royal Academy where Sir John had asked for a list of the empire's leading astronomers.

"What's he up to?" Sean asked when Charlie returned with a cup.

"The Ripper didn't fly here on wings," Charlie said. "After you flapped off to space, Sir John returned to the tannery where the Ripper had died. You took the body, but not the pieces of its flying mechanical attack dog. Sir John collected them, and every other bit of scrap that he thought might belong to the Ripper. After that, he went hunting for the Ripper's starship."

"Did he find it?"

"Oh, yes. He's a smart man, that earl. Smart enough to know to hire people what are even smarter."

"He's got a starship?"

"He bought the land where he found it. It's still there. He's got guards watching it. As far as we can tell, he's only told a few people."

"Celeste let him?"

"She said Sir John was a friend of yours. I told her it was unlikely you was actually friends, but she didn't want to interfere."

"So what does she want me to do about it?"

"Don't know, sir. I'd say that's another puzzle for you to crack. But her ladyship said that everything we do is like a brick dropped in a pond, setting off ripples that spread far before they inevitably fade."

"Ripples, indeed. I'd better see whether Sir John is at home."

Chapter 19 - The Toff and the General

It wasn't far from Bond Street to Sir John's house in Mayfair so Sean decided to walk, and regretted it almost immediately. Aboard the starship, and on Towan III, and especially among the poorer classes who made up the bulk of the rebel army, space was so scarce it often had to be imagined. In elevators, on troop carriers, or crammed onto benches in a warship's small garden, even when literally rubbing shoulders with a general, one pretended one wasn't. He'd forgotten how Londoners barged through this more affluent quarter of the imperial capital. He'd not forgotten how often pockets were picked, though, and saw off two potential thieves before he reached Sir John's home.

The door was opened by a boy too young to shave. Too young to be at work, too, if he'd been living in the Valley.

"Young Parker, isn't it?" Sean said. "Is the earl at home?"

The boy sniffed at Sean's accent before adding up the apparent wealth of his clothing and came to a positive answer. "If you would come inside, sir."

Sean stepped into the hallway.

"And wait here, sir," young Parker said, and scurried off inside.

The house seemed a little smaller, but otherwise hadn't changed. The hallway was still lined with portraits of the earl's paternal ancestors, all dressed in martial finery. There was no portrait of Sir John, as his withered arm had prevented him from serving. Instead, that gap on the wall was occupied by a painting of a printing press. As he looked around, memories returned, and by and large, they were happy ones. Compared to the tannery, the work hadn't been arduous. He'd travelled. He'd had time to write. He'd been well-fed every day and slept in the warm every night. Sir John wasn't a friend. He was an employer, but they had enjoyed a friendly relationship. Yes, they had been good days.

"O'Malley! Heavens descended, and so have you!" Sir John called out from the top of the wide stairs. While he might not be a tall man, the earl had a towering voice, and the confident presence that could command any room. The last six and a half years hadn't been kind to him, though. His face was lined, and his hair was in retreat, while his stomach was on the advance.

"It's good to be back," Sean said.

"Parker, bring tea to the library!"

The library had always been more of a reference room where rival publications were dissected rather than a place in which books were collected. While there were still shelves filled with bound periodicals, in front of them were easels on which were sketches of battleships and airships, all flying the British ensign.

"Where have you been? What have you seen?" Sir John asked, bee-lining for a decanter.

"Everywhere and everything."

"But in space?"

"Yes."

"And you returned here in a starship?"

"I did."

"Well, start at the beginning. Do you want a whisky?"

"It's a little early for me," Sean said.

"Do they have whisky in space?"

"They have intoxicants, yes."

"And?"

Sean sat in one of the leather chairs. "I suppose I should begin at the beginning, but it began fifty thousand years ago…"

"That is quite a tale," Sir John said when Sean had finished his account. "You're a general?"

"The war's over, so as long as it doesn't restart, I'm just an ordinary citizen."

"Don't shy away from the rank. An officer is a gentleman. Your friends are religious revolutionaries, but these regents, they were usurpers?"

"That's it," Sean said, picking his words with care. "The regents were tyrants. Under their regime, society stagnated. People lived in fear."

"And this Valley, this federation you're aligned with, they're run by this prophet?"

"No, the Valley is governed by a council," Sean said. "Individual communities, or nations, within the federation each have their own system of local government, chosen by one system of direct election or another. The council oversees trade and defence."

"Ah. So it's similar to parliament?"

"Very much so," Sean said because it was easier than explaining that the complexities of governance were still being worked out. The Valley had pledged direct elections for all localities, but many were still run under the same martial law, and by the same military governors, as during the emergency of the civil war. But he understood why Sir John considered these questions a priority. Sir John's withered arm had prevented him from joining the army, but like his forefathers, he was a pillar of the British Empire. While an ancestor had been Cromwell's leading butcher in Ireland, another had become a staunch defender of King Charles II. Since then, they had never been far from the throne of what was currently Earth's largest empire.

"What are their intentions?" Sir John asked.

"They consider our planet a holy place. Many will want to visit. Some will want to live here. And because it is considered holy, they are prepared to protect the planet."

"Fascinating. And you say there are local governments on individual planets?"

"There are, yes."

"Good. Interesting. Are we to go to the palace and inform Her Majesty?"

"Victoria is still alive?"

"Oh, indeed," Sir John said. "She'll outlive us all."

"I need to speak with Celeste before we begin any discussions," Sean said. He leaned back in his chair while Sir John walked over to his decanter, both men lost in very different thoughts of what the future might hold.

"You said you were married to one of these... ah, these towani?"

"I am. Their customs are different, of course, but we are both committed to one another."

"Do you have children?"

"Not yet," Sean said.

"I have a son," Sir John said. "He's five."

"Congratulations. And your wife, is she at home?"

Sir John's countenance darkened. "She died shortly after the birth. I don't think she ever truly believed me when I told her of the Ripper. Especially not since there were more murders afterwards."

"There were more?"

"Six more, stretching into 1891. I thought it might be more starfolk, but my investigations were no more fruitful than Scotland Yard's."

"The Ripper was a high-ranking member of one of the regency families. He'd been murdering for so long, and with such impunity, evading the constables had become a game to him. I think he enjoyed the chase as much as seeing the fear in his victims' eyes as he killed them, but he was acting alone."

"Then the nature of the murders must have been chosen to obscure the real motive. But we are unlikely to find the killer now." He returned to his chair. "I gathered what I could from what the Ripper left behind. That mechanical guard dog of his, and a few other accessories and accoutrements. I showed them to Elizabeth. My wife. She just saw them as mechanical junk. Even the starship wasn't believed."

"Celeste knows you found the starship," Sean said. "She left a message for me to that effect."

"Does she want it for herself?"

"If she did, she could have taken it. Where is it?"

"Where I found it, in the parish of Hornchurch. The damn thing's too heavy to move, and not even the sharpest saw could penetrate its hull."

"How did you find it?"

Sir John waved a hand at the shelves of periodicals. "I looked for reports of lights in the sky and other strange occurrences prior to the Ripper's first murder. After that, it was simply a case of identifying somewhere it could be hidden. It was concealed in a shallow lake. I bought the land, drained the lake, and hired a few scientists to assist in deciphering its secrets."

"How many people did you tell about the Ripper, and show the starship?"

"A mere handful. Gads, I didn't want to be thought a lunatic."

"You didn't go to the government?"

"At first, I hoped to reap the benefits of what had been found. I approached many scientists, asking them to venture an opinion of the fragments of that flying guard dog. Very few had anything useful to say, but I selected the best. It didn't take long to realise that the vessel is a millstone. Every empire would wish to claim it and prevent any other from holding it. Ownership brings the threat of sabotage, or even invasion. We might even see the rest of the world unite against us to stop us from unlocking its secrets. No, it had to be concealed as it was studied, but after all this time, we have learned precious little. We've been unable even to open the doors. I hoped we might have better fortune with the vessel you said crashed near Queenstown. I reasoned it might have cracked open in the crash. To that end, I've been funding research into submersibles, but perhaps that's now unnecessary."

"And airships and battleships, too," Sean said, pointing at the easels with their sketches and plans.

"Our research hasn't been entirely fruitless. Our failure to do more than scratch the vessel's hide has led to some advances in metallurgy that the Royal Navy has found particularly useful. I've been trying to persuade them that the future of warfare will be in the air, but they are reluctant to forgo the waves. They'll turn puce with envy when they see your warship. Imagine the good we can do with that vessel. We can unify the planet! There might need to be a little pruning at the top, but we can unite the European kingdoms. Amer-

173

ica, Japan, and the other upstart empires will either comply or be conquered."

"And what then?" Sean asked. "Would you rule the world?"

"Not I, no. A parliament of parliaments will, like in this Valley of yours. Britain, Germany, France, Russia, Belgium, all the empires will have a seat at the table, thus everyone on the planet will be represented. Now, where should we begin? It would probably be best to keep news of this to a small circle until we're sure we can avoid panic. How can we convince the prime minister without a ship landing in Downing Street?"

"I'll give it some thought. I'm due to report to my starship. Let me contact them, and I'll return here and we can make plans."

Sean could have made the call from the house, but he needed room to think. The meeting with Sir John had not gone as expected. In many ways, it had been worse.

The emporium had a customer when Sean returned. By the look of the man, he was a servant from a grand house.

"Why not try the cardamom? It's the freshest in London," Charlie said.

"Just the tea," the servant said.

"Have you tried putting cardamom *in* the tea?" Charlie suggested.

The servant looked aghast. "Who would do such a thing?"

"I'll have Pip deliver your order to the palace within the hour," Charlie said.

With a nod to Sean, the servant left.

"Buckingham Palace?" Sean asked.

"Bit of a step up from Whitechapel, isn't it? Though no one there was as late on their bills. How can we help you, Mr O'Malley?"

"There were more victims attributed to the Ripper."

"Ah, that. You better come through to the back."

Charlie headed straight for the smoke-less fire. He waved his hand, and the flames vanished. "Like magic, innit? This one, I think," Charlie said, taking out one of the leather valises. He opened

174

it, nodded, and handed it to Sean. "That's everything we gathered on the later murders. Police reports, newspaper articles, and a few stories. Her ladyship is certain that it's the work of more than one killer, and that these were done by a person. I mean, not one of the star-folk."

Sean flicked through the file. "There are no suspects?"

"No, and there ain't been no more murders for years."

"What's in the other document cases?"

"That'd be telling, and her ladyship said we was only to tell you what you asked for when you asked for it, but you can ask for anything."

"Then I need a little privacy so I can communicate with my friends."

Charlie walked over to the wood-panelled wall. With another wave of his hand, it vanished.

Inside was outside, or so it appeared. Where there should have been another room in the shop, instead there was a stone-flagged courtyard where vines curled around stone pillars beneath a clear blue sky. Beyond the courtyard were rolling hills. It had to be an illusion since the sky was far too clear for it to be London.

"How does this work?" he asked.

"Beats me," Charlie said. "When you're done, wave your hand in front of the door and it'll open."

With that, he left. The doorway disappeared, becoming more rolling hills, but with a faint rectangular outline marking where it was.

Sean sat on a stone bench, enjoying a moment of calm in what was becoming an increasingly confusing day, before calling Hakon. She answered immediately, with an image of her appearing to stand just in front of him, next to Davir. Sean recapped his conversations with Sir John and with the three former urchins.

"I assumed Celeste would have destroyed all non-Earthly evidence," Hakon said.

"This is a delicate situation," Davir said. "We should return the Ripper's craft, and any personal possessions, to Regent Volmar. If they remain on Earth, their retrieval would give the Voytay a reason to visit."

"Let me travel to Hornchurch with Sir John. I'll assess what repairs the ship will need. What do we do then?"

"We can send for a transport ship, and have it taken to the borderlands," Davir said.

"But what about Sir John?" Sean asked. "What about the planet?"

"That is up to you," Davir said. "Sir John has links to those in power, does he not?"

"He does. I think we could get a meeting with the prime minister within the hour."

"And you're a member of the same empire?"

"Not by choice. I don't wish to arm any empire. I certainly don't wish to arm them all, but even if we make it clear to all that the Valley will have no part in terrestrial affairs, war is still likely."

"Then we will find another way," Davir said. "We must keep going forwards, but we must also be patient."

"And didn't you say you were good at being patient?" Hakon said.

"I asked for that, didn't I?" Sean said.

Sean ended the call and leaned back, watching imaginary clouds drift across the illusory sky. When he had thought of life after his return, it was with Hakon, walking the hills of his homeland. But his home wasn't free. He could buy its freedom with a single starship, but that would leave the British Empire ascendant. He could gift ships to every empire and nation, but how would that prevent war? Or he could have Davir land in Ireland, and declare it independent. But if independence was guaranteed by an army, how free would his relatives be? Whatever path he took, it seemed to lead to war. After seven years of conflict, he'd more than had his fill. A time when he and his beloved could walk beside each other under the sun now seemed a very long way off.

Reluctantly, he walked back through the door and into the shop, and found Charlie waiting for him.

"All well, sir?"

"It will be, eventually. Can you find me a book?"

"Any book in particular, or do you prefer to select your reading material by weight?"

"It's a story by a fella called Wells. *The Time Machine*."

"That's a corker."

"You've read it?"

"Of course. It's got the whole capital talking. It was serialised. The ending has only just come out. Her ladyship made sure we'd keep copies for her to read when she came back."

"Celeste has an interest in him? Do you know much about him?"

"He was a teacher, now he's a journalist, writing these funny short pieces. He did write a book on biology, but this is his first long bit of fiction."

"Biology? I think I know why Celeste is interested in him, and I think it's for the same reason as me."

"Oh?"

"I might commission a novel based on life in the Valley. Something that would make everyone believe that visitors from another world are friendly before they see them in the flesh."

"Nice idea. Do you still want a copy of *The Time Machine*?"

"Yes, but later. I've got to finish with Sir John first."

Chapter 20 - A Ship on a Dry Lake

"Ah, O'Malley. What news?" Sir John asked as Sean was let into the house.

"We're going to return the ship, and any personal effects, to the family of the Ripper."

"We are not!" Sir John said.

"His family are at the head of the enemy empire. We don't want to give them an excuse to send soldiers here to take them."

"Ah, no, agreed. Not until we've got a star-fleet of our own. I take it we're heading to Hornchurch?"

"We are. I'll assess what repairs the ship will need before it can be flown away from here."

"Flown? I'm tempted to ask if I could fly with it, though not if it were to mean I'd be away for seven years. I'll wire ahead, and tell Parker to expect us."

"I thought he was here in London."

"The son is here, learning the trade. The father oversees Hornchurch. I didn't want to hire too many new staff."

The parish of Hornchurch was on the north bank of the Thames, twenty miles east of Mayfair, and so far beyond London's borders. They took Sir John's carriage, with young Parker as their driver.

"After the other murders, I hunted the slums for signs of an otherworldly visitor. I found nothing," Sir John said. "If it is as you say, that this later killer, or killers, was a human seeking to conceal their identity, it is unsurprising. But it did lead me to wonder how our Ripper reached Whitechapel."

"By river, I suspect," Sean said, raising his voice above the rattle of the wheels and the noise of the capital, not to mention the noise of young Parker, cursing other drivers on London's traffic-packed streets. The young man clearly had inherited a measure of his father's impatient disdain.

"Do these other-worlders have horses?" Sir John asked.

"Not as such. There are quadrupeds on some worlds, but they aren't used for transportation. For that, they use horseless carriages."

"Ah. I've one of those. I bought a motorcar from Gottlieb Daimler, and keep it in Hornchurch. It's a good reason to have a workshop there. I'd much prefer we were driving that, but these damned Locomotive Acts make it illegal to drive one on a road. I'm lobbying the government for a change in the law."

"I imagine a lot of laws will have to change," Sean said.

It was a long and uncomfortable ride, made worse by the traffic. Even when they escaped the sprawling city's boundaries, the parlous condition of the roads ensured discomfort kept them company. It was a relief to finally arrive at the farm, where a recently built wall towered above their carriage's roof. The gate was just as tall. Parker had to climb down to ring a bell.

The gate was eventually opened by a shotgun-wielding gamekeeper. They drove through, passing a small cottage, as new as the wall. Beyond were a regiment of pine trees, planted in uniform lines. They were only as tall as Sean; clearly, a recently planted screen to hide what work went on inside. Beyond the trees, the track branched north and south, and bore distinct ruts Sean guessed were from the motorcar, but just as many hoof-prints from the mounted gamekeeper who was watching their approach. They turned left, heading downhill towards the drained lake, now become a flower-dotted grassland except where a large wooden barn, big enough to house a train, had been built. Another gamekeeper, carrying a rifle, stood outside.

Young Parker stopped the carriage outside a cluster of farm buildings built on what had once been the lake's shore.

"Stable the horses, Parker, but be sure not to scratch my motorcar," Sir John said as he climbed out. "We use that old barn as a workshop, not that there's been much to work on."

Sir John nodded to the guard, and the two men entered the wooden barn.

The ship was cylindrical, red, and about the length of two train carriages, with a diameter of about ten feet. Before the lake had been drained, the top would have been recklessly close to the surface. But everything about the killer was reckless. When landing, the skids had been deployed, but the rear-most had sunk into the lakebed, leaving the craft at a slight angle. Surrounding it now were wooden walkways, ladders, and platforms, allowing an up-close inspection of the sides and top. On a walkway at the rear, a man and woman had been taking measurements until Sir John and Sean had come in.

"That is Mr and Mrs Cooper. I hired his wife to be his assistant so as to keep fewer people in the know."

As far as Sean could tell, it was the wife who was taking measurements, and the husband who was writing them down.

"Cooper! Come down!" Sir John called. "This is Sean O'Malley. He's going to open the ship!"

The name clearly meant something to the pair, as they nearly jumped down the ladders.

"You're O'Malley?" Mr Cooper asked.

"*General* O'Malley," Sir John said.

"Mr O'Malley is fine with me," Sean said. "And yes, I am."

"How does it work?" Mrs Cooper asked.

"All in good time," Sean said. "Let me inspect the exterior, then we'll take a look inside."

"Where's young Parker? Such an event deserves a toast." As Sir John went to find someone to fetch refreshments, Sean began an inspection of the ship. Six and a half years of hammering, chiselling, and cutting had broken a good many tools, but done little damage to what he could see of the hull. Wooden box-like benches on the walkways obscured some parts of the ship, but otherwise the vessel appeared in reasonable shape. The only scars, on the port side, had come from the aerial battle with Hakon before she'd been shot down near Queenstown.

"That wasn't us," Sir John said, having returned from his hunt.

"No, this was from the battle that saw the ship crash off Queenstown," Sean said. "When inside a planet's atmosphere, wings can

180

be deployed, but this ship was designed for racing through an asteroid belt."

"Is that a sport?"

"Only among the very wealthy, and very foolhardy," Sean said.
"So, yes, it was quite popular before the war."

"I've sent young Parker to find a bottle so we can toast the success. I assume there will be something to toast?"

"Let me see if we can get inside," Sean said.

Sean climbed the ladder. The airlock was on the top, and near the
front.

While the lock-panel still had power, it required a voice command to open.

With a wave of his fingers, he contacted Hakon.

"Impressive machine," she said. "They haven't been able to enter?"

"No. The lock is encrypted to the Ripper's voice," he said, speaking softly so as not to be overheard.

"It probably requires a code phrase, too," she said. "Give me a
moment."

"Can you open it?" Sir John called.

"I'm working on it," Sean said.

"I've sent you a decryption programme," Hakon said.

Sean placed his thumb on the lock panel so his ring was touching
the mechanism, and then ran the encryption programme through it
and so through the lock. The hatch slid open.

"Keep your hand there," Hakon said. "I'm running the ship's di-
agnostics. Yes, it's as we thought, the faster-than-light systems were
damaged in the dogfight over Queenstown."

"What about the sub-light engines?"

"Those appear intact. We'll have to conduct a complete inspection, but I think it could reach orbit. Don't go inside yet. I'll send
down a team of engineers to conduct a thorough test, and they can
check for traps."

Sean removed his hand. "No. Davir has to be the first to set foot
on the planet, and he shouldn't do it here. He's right when he says

181

ritual is important. He should conduct the ceremony in the Neander Valley, from where the name of our new federation comes."

"We can arrange that for tonight, and send the technicians a few hours later."

"Sir John isn't going to wait. I'll check the ship out. I know what to look for."

"You promised to be careful."

"And I will be." He walked back along the scaffolding to the nearest ladder and climbed down.

"Is it open?" Sir John asked.

"It is."

"You did it. By Jove, I knew you could!" Sir John exclaimed. "Ah, Parker, where's the drinks? O'Malley's opened the ship!"

The older Parker, butler to Sir John, had just entered, with only a horsewhip in his hands. Behind him were four rifle-carrying game-keepers, and his son, looking cowed and scared.

"The ship is open?" the older Parker asked.

"It is," Sean said. "Good to see you again."

"Now," Parker said. It wasn't a reply to Sean, but a signal to the gamekeepers. They raised their rifles, while Parker drew a revolver, levelling it at Sir John's head. To Sean's right, the two scientists had also drawn pistols.

"What the deuce is the meaning of this?" Sir John demanded, taking a step towards the armed men. Parker fired a shot in the air.

"The meaning of it will become clear," Parker said.

"You're dismissed," Sir John said. "The lot of you. Leave now, or I'll be pressing charges."

As if the words were floating in mid-air, a message from his wife appeared on Sean's glasses. "Strike team is ready to deploy."

Keeping his hand by his side, Sean moved his fingers, slowly typing out a reply. "No. Leave this to me. Ritual is important."

Chapter 21 - The Many Faces of Jack the Ripper

"Sit here," Parker said. "I wouldn't want either of you to miss the show."

After they'd sat down, Mrs Cooper used rope to secure Sean's hands, while her husband tied up Sir John.

"This is an outrage," Sir John said.

"An outrage is a cripple like you becoming one of the most powerful people in the land," Parker said. "Do you know what the Spartans would have done to one such as you? After you were born, you would have been left on the mountainside to die. Instead, you are invited to dine with lords as if you are their equal. You make me serve you, as if you are *my* equal. I don't know who's worse, you or that deformity that calls himself the Kaiser. Under my rule, we shall sweep away the inadequate, the undeserving, the inferior who are mere pollutants of our race's stock."

"You're a fiend," Sir John said.

"The earl has a revolver under his coat and a Derringer in his pocket," Parker said. "And search O'Malley. I doubt he is unarmed."

Sean hadn't come to Earth expecting a fight, but he knew trouble had a habit of finding the unwary, so he had brought a knife, a knuckle duster, and a standard-issue towani sidearm. Those were placed on a wooden table, along with Sir John's revolver and Derringer.

"You'll hang for this," Sir John said.

"For this? No," Parker said. "It is you who have committed treason by concealing this vessel from your masters."

"I've always acted with the best interests of the empire in mind," Sir John said.

Parker flexed the horsewhip. With perfect aim, he sent its tip to slice across Sir John's cheek. "Quiet," Parker said. He picked up the towani firearm. "I know what you said to Sir John today, and I heard what you told him seven years ago." He pointed the gun at Sir John.

Sean's fingers moved frantically as he remotely accessed the gun's firing controls, confirming the safety was on just before Parker pressed the firing button. Thankfully, nothing happened.

"Yes, I heard what you said, as did my son earlier today," Parker continued. "It seems there is a great prize here. A prize far greater than this starship. There are two empires at war. As the Ripper was the nephew of the old emperor, we will be well rewarded for handing over his murderer. O'Malley, you will pilot this craft for us."

"You want me to fly you off into Voytay territory in the hope that Volmar gives you a reward?"

"I shall negotiate a treaty for the entire planet," Parker said. "We shall bring an end to the disease sweeping through our cities. Cooper, inspect the ship's interior."

"There might be traps," Sean said.

"Send him," Cooper said.

"Not until we've ensured there are no weapons he could take," Parker said. "Boy, you go."

"Me?" his son asked, his voice trembling.

The father raised the whip. "Do I need to ask twice?"

The boy sprinted to the nearest ladder.

A message appeared on Sean's lenses. "Can I intervene?"

Sean watched the child hesitate at the hatch's edge. He wanted to say yes, but there were bigger stakes than even a child's life. "Not yet," he wrote in reply.

"What kind of man are you?" Sir John asked, a question aimed at Parker but which Sean was asking of himself.

"The kind prepared to do what must be done," Parker said. "You should have informed the government. You didn't, so I will now claim the reward. One day, I shall be emperor. Cooper, see if the boy is dead."

The scientist couple climbed the scaffolding.

"Boy!" Mrs Cooper called. "Are you alive?"

"Yes, madam," the boy called back in timid reply.

"Cooper, search the ship for weapons," Parker said.

Another message from Hakon appeared. "Tell me when."

"Not yet," Sean wrote in reply. "Ritual is critical."

"Why should you be emperor rather than any of your fellows?" Sir John asked.

"You think you can drive a wedge between us so easily?" Parker replied. He laughed. "We are joined by knowledge, by belief, and by blood. Indeed, that same blood joins us to that ship's former owner. That is why the Voytay emperor will welcome us. We *understand*."

"Well, I don't," Sean said.

"It was evident after you departed that to learn the secrets of this technology would be the work of a lifetime," Parker said. "I was not prepared to wait so long. Since O'Malley's companions had been summoned here by the Ripper's murders, more murders should have summoned more other-worlders. We each took a turn replicating the crime. But it soon became clear that your friends have no interest in helping the slatterns in the slums."

"You? *You're* the imitation Ripper who murdered six innocent women?" Sean asked, scarcely believing it. Yet the man had always had a vicious streak, an inflated sense of his own position, and disdain for everyone below it.

"There were far more than six, and none were innocent. They are a disease, and must be destroyed."

Young Parker reappeared at the top of the hatch holding two axes with long curved blades, but short handles. "There are lots of weapons down there, sir."

"Be careful with those," Parker said. "I don't want them damaged. Bring them to me."

Awkwardly, the boy slowly descended the ladders, bringing the blades to his father.

"Those axes used to belong to the emperors," Sean said. "They're replicas of weapons said to belong to the towani prophet. Of course, the emperors said they were the originals."

"Then they are another prize for which I shall be rewarded. Boy, go to the house and inform the cook we'll need provisions for the voyage. How much will we need, O'Malley?"

185

"A week should do it," Sean said. In truth, it would take months, but he'd already decided on a plan. "In orbit," he wrote and sent to Hakon. No sooner than he'd sent it, he spotted a black and yellow fist-sized drone bobbing among the rafters near the doorway. He zoomed in.

"Celeste's drone," Hakon wrote.

Sean nodded his head and zoomed out. If the drone was here, Celeste couldn't be far off. He seemed to have his supposition confirmed when a distant explosion caused the shed to rattle.

Parker ran to the door. "I see smoke. Was that you, O'Malley?"

"I'm right here. How could it be me?"

"You two with me," Parker said, using the axe to point at two of the gamekeepers. With an axe in one hand and a revolver in the other, he ran outside.

"Was it you?" Sir John whispered.

"Quiet!" the taller of the two remaining keepers said. He seemed the more nervous of their guards. His hands shook as he switched aim between the two captives. "And stop moving!" he yelled at Sir John, whose attempts to free himself hadn't been surreptitious enough.

The Coopers were still inside the ship, making the numbers even, but as long as his hands were tied, the keepers had the advantage. He looked up at the black and yellow drone, and gave a slight nod, but the machine didn't move.

"We'll need a bag," Mrs Cooper announced just before her head appeared in the spaceship's hatch. "There are enough swords, knives, and axes to arm a Viking raiding party."

"Get her a bag, Henry," said the less nervous of the two gamekeepers.

As the keeper turned his back, Sean looked up. The drone was gone. Even as he wondered to where, he felt something brush against his tied hands. Before he'd properly had a chance to register the smell of burning hemp, his hands came free.

The shorter gamekeeper began to sniff the air, looking around for whatever was burning. "Do you smell that, Henry?"

186

Sean reared up, running forward, straight at him. He'd underestimated the man's concentration. The gamekeeper spun around, levelling his rifle, and fired. The bullet smacked into Sean's chest, just below his waistcoat's top button. The kinetic-resistant fabric easily deflected the slow-moving projectile, while the force of its impact was dissipated by interlocking layers of micro-mesh. Sean didn't even miss a step as he closed the gap between himself and his enemy.

The drone flew at the keeper's face, causing him to buck before he could load a second bullet into his rifle's breech. Sean grabbed the rifle's barrel, twisting it to his left as he swept out his right foot, knocking the keeper to the floor.

The other keeper fired and missed. Sean, now holding the rifle, hurled it at the second keeper before diving at the table. He grabbed his sidearm. The safety automatically disengaged. He fired, shooting the still-armed keeper first, and then the man struggling to stand. He grabbed his knife, but Sir John stood, the drone buzzing away from him.

"Where did you learn to fight like that?" Sir John asked, picking up his revolver.

"There was no place for spectators during the war," Sean said.

Mrs Cooper reared up through the ship's hatch, holding a towani breaching rifle. It didn't fire. Sir John's revolver did, clipping off the top of her head.

"Deal with Cooper. Just keep him inside," Sean said. "I'll go after Parker."

Outside, smoke rose from behind the farmhouse.

"There are five in the building, one approaching from the gate," Hakon said.

"Where's the boy?"

"The rear of the house," Hakon said as the front door opened. A gamekeeper stepped out and saw Sean. Before he could level his rifle, Sean fired, his shot guided to target by the display on his glasses. A downstairs window broke as a bullet was fired through it. The lead shot slammed into Sean's side, but failed to penetrate the fabric.

"At least *try* not to get shot," Hakon said.

"I am," Sean said, returning fire. His bullet tore through the bricks and into the shooter's head.

"Three people have moved to the stable," she said.

From inside the stable came an unfamiliar stuttering putter that grew in tempo and volume, nearly as loud as the neighs of distress from the horses. The stable doors were thrown open by young Parker. The boy stared at Sean, his face a painting of terror and hope that changed to confusion as he was pulled aboard a motorcar.

The cartwheel-sized tyres sprayed mud as the overloaded two-seater carriage accelerated. The young Parker clung to the back while the passenger sprayed shot from his gun. Sean dove into a shrubbery, out of the way of the horseless vehicle travelling nearly as fast as he could run.

As the car sped on, Sean headed for the stable. Three horses were saddled. It was a long time since he'd ridden, but he thought he remembered the principles.

"Yah! On," he called, even before his right foot had found the stirrup. Still settling himself in the saddle, the horse lumbered out of the stable.

It quickly became apparent that he'd overestimated how fast the horse was willing to run, but he'd also overestimated human ingenuity over the last few years. The motorcar was lumbering forward at no more than ten miles an hour.

"Oh, come on, Dobbin," he called, but his nervous horse was reluctant to get near.

The motorcar squeezed another mile per hour out of its engine. Sean tried to lock onto the driver or his passenger, but the horse was jolting him too violently. The car's passenger turned around in the seat and fired the shotgun.

Sean's horse reared.

"Would you calm down? Just get us alongside, and I'll do the rest."

Hakon's voice came clear through the arms of his glasses. "Let them go."

"We'd only have to track them down."

"I *am* tracking them," she said.

He didn't want to give up. The car was now a hundred yards ahead, and at the estate's closed gate.

The horse found a little more speed, but the gamekeeper fired. His horse reared again and came to a stop. The boy had opened the gate. The car shot through, leaving the boy behind.

"Take them now," Sean said, jumping from the horse. He sprinted for the gate where young Parker stood frozen, wearing an expression that was a mix of terror and hope until the explosion made him flinch. The missile, fired from orbit, turned the car to scrap, its passengers to meat, and did no favours to the roadway beneath.

"I think you overdid it," Sean said.

The boy looked at the wreck, and then sprinted off, disappearing into the farm's open fields. Sean breathed out, but his relief was short-lived. A constable atop a bicycle had come to investigate the earlier explosion and now stared agape at the crater.

"They were attempting to steal the earl's motorcar," Sean said. "It must have overheated. Dangerous machines, those."

"Indeed they evidently are," the constable said. "And who might you be?"

Before he had to come up with a lie, the earl, atop a horse of his own, reached the gate.

"What happened to my car?" Sir John exclaimed.

"And you are?"

"The Earl of Lenham. This is my land."

"We came here so I could see his motorcar," Sean said. "I'm only just back in the country after some time overseas. The butler stole it. We think he was attempting to steal a lot more."

"And who are you, sir?"

"He's General O'Malley," Sir John said.

That appeared to be the final straw for the constable. "I'll need to inform my superiors." With a shaky salute, he got back on his bike and began a wobbly ride in search of someone who was paid enough to deal with earls, generals, and exploding motorcars.

"Did you do that to my car?"

"My wife, aboard the starship. I'm sorry, but I'll get you a new one."

Sir John looked up, squinting into the darkening sky. "From up there?" he asked with martial wonder. "The possibilities, just imagine them."

Chapter 22 - The Fundamental Difference Between a Sapiens and a Towani

"Can you deal with whatever authorities arrive?" Sean asked.

"Of course," Sir John said. "Where are you going?"

"To fetch some rope and chains so we can drag that wreckage back inside the gates. Stick to the story. Tell no one about the ship, or the other bodies. Not yet."

"Agreed. We'll want to speak with the cabinet first."

As he headed back to the stable, Sean wondered what to do next. "What a nightmare."

"Are you in danger of being arrested?" Hakon asked.

"I don't think so."

"If it looks as if you are, we'll land."

"Let me see if I can tidy this mess up first."

By the time he'd fetched rope and chain, a small crowd of local farmers had gathered, and the story of the motorcar theft seemed well-established. The local magistrate had even arranged for the un-recognisable bodies to be removed. Seeing a supposed general carrying the ropes, the magistrate ordered the curious farmworkers to take over.

By dusk, those parts of the corpses that could be found had been removed, and the larger remains of the car had been dragged into the estate. With nothing to see, the crowd dispersed, and as the earl went hunting for a drink, Sean closed the gate.

The investigation, such as it was, had taken minutes. The earl's account had been believed without question. While that was certainly better than if the starship had been discovered, it was very different to Sean's previous experience with terrestrial policing. The earl lived in a different world, and one not too dissimilar to that of the regents. Where did that leave him? Where would it leave Maeve and her children if his next stop was Buckingham Palace?

191

Sean walked his skittish horse back to the stables. After he'd removed the saddle, he called Hakon. "I'm going to slow Sir John down," he said.

"Shall we bring him aboard the warship?"

"That'll only give him ideas. I think you should meet him. The three of us can have dinner."

"That won't slow him for long."

"We need to prepare the planet. Get people thinking about the possibilities in the stars. We could have Sir John's magazines publish stories."

"That will take some time," Hakon said.

"Better to take our time than start a war," he said, stepping back outside. Twilight was fading, replaced with the true darkness of a cloudy night. But ahead, there was a light, moving towards the wooden shed.

"Sir John's going to the ship. I'd better make sure he doesn't accidentally take off."

"I think it unlikely he'd manage that. Davir wants to complete the ritual tonight."

"Of course. So do I."

"I'll come and pick you up."

"I'll warn Sir John, and lock up the ship."

When he entered the shed, he saw it wasn't Sir John who had just entered the barn. Young Parker stood at the bottom of the ladder leading up to the wooden platforms, holding an oil lamp.

"There are much bigger ships than this one," Sean said.

The boy jumped, startled, and held his lantern up. Sean walked forward, into its dim beam.

"It's me, Sean O'Malley. I'm sorry about your father. Why don't you come back to the house, get something to eat."

The boy shook his head.

"Why did you come back here?" Sean asked.

"He said I should."

"Who?"

"My father."

"He's dead. I'm sorry."

The boy shook his head.

"What did he say you should do?" Sean asked.

The boy's entire body was shaking now. He turned and held up one end of a long thin piece of string.

"What is it?" Sean asked, stepping closer. "Is that a fuse?"

"He said I must."

"He's dead. What he says doesn't matter," Sean said.

"He's not dead," the boy said.

"I saw—" Sean began, but he hadn't seen the driver. The explosion had dismembered the corpse, leaving the pieces unrecognisable. Sean took another step forward. The movement startled the boy. Whether by intent or reflex, he thrust the fuse into the lamp's flame.

Sean reached for the fuse, but it had already disappeared beneath the wooden gantry. He grabbed the boy's arm, and pushed him towards the doors. "Run!" But when he got to the doors, he found them locked.

He pulled off his coat, wrapping it around the boy, even as he called Hakon.

"Take out a wall, I need a—"

Before he could finish, the fuse reached the explosives. The ship's hard armour reflected the blast outwards, turning the scaffolding to splinters, and demolishing the shed.

Hakon had already begun her descent before Sean called her. When her sensors alerted her to an explosion, she turned a graceful drop into a plunge.

"Sean? Sean?"

He didn't answer.

The moment the ship set down, she bounded from the pilot's seat, running to the airlock. The remains of the wooden barn had become burning scrap scattered across the landscape. An arrow on her helmet's visor told her which heap was her beloved.

Sean's shirt, waistcoat, and trousers had reduced the damage, but there'd been nothing to protect his hands and head. Blood dripped from the splinters piercing his skin.

"Oh, Sean."

She laid her hand on his neck, letting the sensors in her glove check his vital signs. His heart had stopped beating, and his brain was already dying.

"No, no, no!"

There was only one chance, and it was long and slender. She turned back to her ship and saw the chance already approaching. Celeste, wearing riding clothes in every shade of blue, had retrieved the stabiliser from the ship and was pushing it towards her.

"Why didn't you stop this?" Hakon asked.

"I'm not omniscient," Celeste said. She reached down, lifting Sean's body as if it was as light as a feather. With blood dripping from his wounds, she placed him atop the floating stretcher. Hakon turned it on. The lid seemed to melt, folding around the body, shrouding it in grey.

"What of the other one?" Celeste asked.

"The other?" Hakon turned back to the still-smoking debris. Sean's coat seemed to be concealing a lump, which began to move. Shedding the jacket, the boy slowly stood up.

"Are you okay? Let me see you," Hakon said.

The boy stared up at the blue-armoured, and helmeted, figure, and ran into the darkness.

"He appears fine. Sir Sean must have shielded him from the blast," Celeste said.

"O'Malley? O'Malley?" Sir John had come running from the house. When he saw Celeste and Hakon, he stopped. "By Jove. You're one of them."

Hakon retracted the opaque visor so Sir John could see her face. "I am Hakon. I wish we were not meeting under such circumstances."

"O'Malley, is he alive?"

"He's dying. I need to take him to our ship. I will return. Until then, let no one into this property."

Celeste pushed the stretcher onto the ship.

"Did you know that the butler was the imitation Ripper?" Hakon asked as she piloted the ship back towards space.

"I did not," Celeste said.

"But you knew that Sir John had kept that ship?"

"I did."

"Why did you let him keep it?"

"Because I have known many beings like Sir John. They are constant searchers, so I left him with a reason to stop looking."

"Why didn't you come to Sean's aid earlier?" Hakon asked.

"I was not here. I tasked my drones to watch him ever since he reached London, and came here as fast as I could."

As soon as she'd docked with the warship, Hakon ran to the airlock, waiting for the chamber outside to pressurise. She had the stretcher halfway down the ramp before two medics took it from her. She followed them through the corridors to the medical bay, where a doctor stopped her from entering.

"If it is his time, we will let you in. If it is not, we need to work," said the doctor, a young paxley who'd dyed the fur on his chin black. "Excuse me."

Hakon pulled off her helmet, hurling it at the wall. She turned to Celeste, who had followed her from the ship.

"He can't die! Not here. Not like this. Not after six years of street fighting and ship-taking, of capture and rescue, of battles in atmosphere and zero-g. He barely got more than a few broken bones. Now he dies, like this? Why?"

"We all die," Celeste said. "Even I will one day perish. But he isn't dead yet."

Davir and his assistant hurried along the corridor from the other direction.

"What happened?" Davir asked.

"I'm not sure. There was an explosion in a wooden barn that was concealing the ship."

"Did the ship explode?" Davir asked.

"The explosives were terrestrial in nature," Celeste said. "I would suggest it was some type of trap set by the butler."

"You know about the murderer?" Davir asked.

"When I learned Sir Sean had returned, I sent a drone to keep watch on him. It heard the butler's confession before assisting in Sir Sean's escape."

"I thought the danger was over!" Hakon said. "I thought it was over with the end of the war."

"Danger is always with us," Davir said. "Does this change things?" he added, addressing Celeste. "We agreed to bring him home, but never intended this."

"Of course not," Celeste said. "My contacts elsewhere in the galaxy kept me informed of the revolution, and the war. I told Mr O'Malley that, if he went with you, he would change the galaxy. He has, but his work has only just begun."

"Why don't we wait for news in my chambers," Davir said.

"I want to stay as close to him as I can," Hakon said.

"Then we shall wait together," Davir said.

An hour later, the paxley doctor came out of the medical bay. "He is alive. Remarkably, the stabiliser appears to have worked. The artificial cells restarted his heart, sealed the wounds, and began breaking down the foreign objects."

"The doctors on Towan always said it wouldn't work, that he was too genetically different from a towani," Hakon said.

"They were wrong," the doctor said. "But not entirely. If those cells had been injected into me, nothing would have happened. In him, they are rebuilding the damage. It was extensive. Now that he's stabilised, we can begin surgery."

"What is the prognosis?" Davir asked.

"When he was put into the stabiliser, you selected the species. That coded the cells as to what their role was. They think the sapiens part of him is a disease. His body is now battling itself. It is impossible to know what the long-term consequences will be."

"But you can just flush the cells out, can't you?" Hakon asked.

"Not until after surgery," the doctor said. "And perhaps not even then."

"Do what you must," Davir said. "I have faith in you."

The doctor nodded and returned to the operating room.

Hakon shivered, and then sighed. "If he dies—" she began.

"Have faith," Davir said.

"If he dies, how do we approach first contact?" Hakon asked.

"What did Sean say to you?" Davir asked.

"That if we arm an empire, or all empires, we will begin a war. He didn't want that."

"We should retrieve the Ripper's ship," Davir said. "What of Sir John?"

"I will speak with him," Celeste said. "He will do nothing until Sir Sean recovers."

"What about the ritual?" Hakon asked. "I suppose I've already ruined it."

"Ritual is important, but it isn't everything," Davir said.

Part 6
Disrupting a Funeral

Church Island, Area 51, and RAF Benson
20th - 22nd October

Chapter 23 - Remembering the Dead

"What happened next, Da?" Serene asked as Sean's pause turned into a halt.

"Hang on, I've just got an update from Greta."

"Has there been another killing?" Tempest asked.

"No, but they've got traffic camera footage of a car towing a fixed-rib inflatable towards the lake yesterday evening. She thinks that was the killers, and is about to cross-reference the vehicle with our satellite footage so we can find out where they came from and where they went. We'll catch Clee's murderers soon enough."

"What did happen after you were injured?" Serene asked.

"A hundred and thirty years of history," Sean said. "A team of mechanics set down in that farm and retrieved that ship. The explosion hadn't gone unnoticed, but no one came to investigate until dawn. Having met a squad of alien mechanics, Sir John was in heaven, and happy to follow Celeste's suggestion that first contact should wait until after I had recovered."

"And when was that?" Serene asked.

"I was back on my feet in a few months."

"That long? Oh, Dad."

"It's fine. And it wasn't the last time I ended up injured."

"Dr Griffin told us the stabilisers wouldn't work for us," Tempest said.

"They don't. Not properly. Recovering from that took much longer than the blast, and I'm still taking... let's call them supplements."

"You never said," Serene said.

"What would be the point of worrying you? Now that first contact has occurred, Dr Griffin can recruit test subjects to map out the workings of a sapiens body. Until now, he's only had the two of you and one of me. With that, the treatment can be properly adapted.

Until then, I have to have an injection every so often. It's no bother. Really."

"Why did the boy set off the explosives?" Harold asked.

"Ah. Because of his father. The butler, the sadist, the Ripper, hadn't been driving the motorcar. He'd hidden. After his first plan had failed, Parker thought that, if the ship was discovered, Sir John would be ruined. He thought the motorcar would bring the police to the farm because driving on roads was illegal back then. He sent the boy in to blow up the ship for the same reason, expecting the explosion would bring people to investigate. Fortunately, by the time they did, the Ripper's ship was aboard the warship. When Parker saw me enter the shed, he'd locked the door, even though his son was also in there. That says all you need to know about him."

"Tell me Parker died in the blast," Serene said.

"He fled before the technicians arrived. They did a thorough scan of the area, and maintained it while they worked in case anyone did turn up."

"But Parker, what happened to him?"

"The son was… cared for by Sir John. I won't say he was adopted. He was a servant, but well treated. He even received some schooling. The father went to ground. To avoid discovery, he stopped leaving his victims with their organs displayed. I got him in the end, but that's a different story."

"The book I had on Lenham House said the last earl was a Nazi sympathiser," Harold said.

"He was more than just a sympathiser," Sean said.

"But the way you tell it, the earl didn't seem such a bad guy."

"He was an imperialist, but no, for the time, he wasn't so bad."

"So what changed?"

"It's a long story, and a different one, not connected to the murder of Clee."

"What about H.G. Wells?" Harold asked. "You can't have commissioned *War of the Worlds*."

"Honestly, I forgot about him until that book came out. It definitely did not help the cause. The key detail as far as Clee's murder is concerned is that the story of Jack the Ripper, and of the copycat murders, was passed down from one Parker to the next until it reached the ears of the man currently incarcerated at Area-51."

"And you think he told his wife, and she organised Clee's murder?" Serene asked.

"I think she's running the gang now, yes," Sean said. "It's possible she's always been running it. Clee's murder must have been ordered by the Voytay, and before that old battle-station squashed Oxfordshire. I imagine it was payment."

"So why now? Why not a month ago?" Harold asked.

"Good question. So is the identity of whomever Dr Masadi is working with, and what she thinks will happen next. If the murder had occurred before the Oxfordshire incident, suspicion would soon have fallen on Parker. I treated him differently from the other UNCA employees. I confided in him. Only Greta, Johann, and I knew Clee was on this island, but I told Parker she was on Earth. He could have tracked me here when I came on a supply run."

"Why wait two months?" Tempest asked.

"Exactly. And why not wait a few months more? I think it might be linked to us finding that sooval deserter. Perhaps it's not a deserter after all. The next step is waiting on the autopsy. We've got other technicians up on the peace platform checking whether we missed a signal sent or received in the last few days. And we've got a net drawing in on the killers who came here. Their plot is unravelling. Within a few days, we'll have them arrested."

"Dr Masadi spent a long time with the towani smuggler in that tunnel beneath Iraq," Serene said. "Maybe long enough to learn the language. Didn't you say she killed the towani smuggler?"

"She did."

"I bet that was to cover their tracks," Serene said. "Then she hooked up with Parker because she knew he'd have a direct line to the embassy and so to a spy or smuggler when they arrived."

"Possibly," Sean said. "It's too soon to say probably, but only because her and Parker's involvement is still being investigated."

"What's all of this for, though?" Tempest asked. "Why kill Clee in that fashion?"

"It's a message, to me, and to the Voytay, and to the Valley," Sean said.

"A message saying what?" Tempest asked.

"That will depend on whether there are more murders. Celeste and Jess are collecting all the non-terrestrials she invited, or forced, to remain on Earth, and that she thinks might be in danger. Unlike Clee, they have communication equipment. We also need to answer what else Mr and Mrs Parker have been up to for the last twenty years."

"Didn't he tell Harry that it was all about the data-core from Mum's student?" Tempest said.

"Yes and no," Harold said. "He told me it was about ensuring Earth's independence from the Voytay and the Valley."

"Or, to put it another way, it was about power," Sean said. "The same power his ancestor wanted, and not too different from what Sir John was after. But what is it his wife wants?"

"He told us he was willing to talk if we transferred him to a prison near his wife," Harold said.

"And I'm starting to think that was the signal," Sean said. "I informed the local police we would be visiting the wife. I made contact with the Home Office asking for their opinion on whether a transfer would be agreeable. A few hours later, she fled."

"How would she have known?" Serene asked.

"Parker ran the UNCA in Britain. He'll have made contacts in the security service and government, and he had plenty of time to recruit at least one."

"Could Parker be expecting a rescue?" Harold asked.

"It'd be impossible from Area-51," Sean said. "If a ship appears overhead, it'll be detected. It would take half an hour to blast your way into the prison, assuming you wanted to do it without killing everyone inside, but less than five minutes for reinforcements to reach it from the peace platform. If you try to take any weapon through the scanner by the elevator, the place would lock down. Besides, why expend such an effort? No, this gang was used to operating with the assistance of the British UNCA. They've lost that, and, of course, Ireland isn't Britain. We'll find Clee's killers, but it's approaching midnight, and tomorrow will be a long day. I've got some sleeping bags."

"Are we sleeping outside?" Harold asked.

"It's either that or in a crime scene," Sean said.

"It'll be just like when we were kids," Serene said.

"I didn't think you'd been camping except in the van," Harold said.

"We slept outside a lot," Serene said. "Most of the Valley citizens couldn't leave the embassy during the daytime, so they became semi-nocturnal. Because we could go out in daylight, and did, we'd often go up with Gramps when he was stargazing, and sometimes fall asleep."

"You *always* fell asleep," Sean said.

Harold slept fitfully, until the unwelcome cold shower of a four a.m. Atlantic squall. It didn't even wake Serene. He retreated to the pop-up shelter, made some tea, and read until dawn.

"Sleep well?" Sean asked as the sun splashed across the lake.

"Not even close. That's two strikes for camping," Harold said, handing Sean a mug.

"The rule is you've got to try everything three times before you can truly know you'd hate it. My brother Liam used to say that. I used to say that once was enough, until somewhere around my hundredth birthday when I realised that life is too long to rule anything out forever."

Harold rubbed a crick in his neck that seemed to run all the way down to his knees. "Deal. I'll wait until I'm a hundred and twenty before I try camping again."

As the others woke, Tempest went to greet the dawn with prayer. Serene went looking for privacy; since it was still a crime scene, Clee's bathroom was off-limits. Harold made breakfast: porridge, pancakes, and more tea.

"Dr Griffin has finished the autopsy," Sean announced just as they were finishing. "We'll inter Clee tonight, and you three can head straight to the hotel."

"Is the conference continuing?" Serene asked.

"It has to. If the Voytay attack, we need to be able to protect ourselves. For that, we need to get the ball moving on membership of the Valley."

"This delegation to Towan III is mostly ceremonial, isn't it?" Harold said. "So why not send the flag carriers from the last Olympics? I'd prefer we sent artists, but athletes are better than politicians."

"It's an idea, and not a bad one at that," Sean said. "I'll put it to Mr O'Connell when he arrives for the funeral."

"Are all the delegates coming?" Tempest asked.

"No, just O'Connell, the Irish president, and whoever they bring. We'll keep the event quite small. I have a few things I want to check on below, but mind your head. Greta will be arriving soon."

She did, with Dorn-Tru, two acolytes, and twenty folding chairs. While Greta went to inspect the crime scene one last time, and Dorn-Tru and the acolytes went to bless the burial chamber, Harold, Serene, and Tempest set up the chairs.

The arrival of another spaceship hadn't gone unnoticed. Before they'd finished, the local police sergeant arrived aboard Brian Finnegan's tour boat.

"Is the president here?" the sergeant asked.

"Um... no," Serene said.

"I was told there was to be a funeral, and he'd be in attendance. Extra officers are being called in to deal with the crowd."

"What crowd?" Tempest asked.

"Your spaceships have been noticed. Word's already spread about who lived here."

"I think you better speak to our father," Tempest said.

Ashore, and on the small island, things began to get busy. A few locals who owned boats took to the lake, many with a reporter aboard, until the police chased them away. The reporters returned in a helicopter that nearly collided with the flying saucer bringing Mr O'Connell, the Irish president, and a small entourage. Ashore, a press conference was hastily organised in the hope it might prevent an accident.

Keeping out of the way of the towani security detail that had arrived with the saucer, Harold retreated to the ancient cemetery.

"I bring lunch. Or dinner," Serene said. "It might look like a sandwich, but really it's a work of art. Padraig made it."

"Your cousin. Is he here?"

"No, he's preparing Earth dishes for a wake to be held on the peace platform."

"Oh, is that a tradition among the towani?"

"No, but Gramps likes the idea, and Clee did live in Ireland for sixty years. Or beneath it. Don't you want the sandwich?"

"Are you allowed to eat in a cemetery? I don't go to them often. The last time was to visit my mother's grave."

"Did you go to her funeral?"

"No. I wasn't allowed. She's buried next to her parents. I went there when I was seventeen, about a week after I got out of detention, but it was too soon. Afterwards, I didn't leave the shop for a month. I went again just before the pandemic. I suppose I was hoping the visit would bring understanding."

"Did it?"

"Kinda. I mean, I came to understand that some things can't be understood, and some things don't need to be."

"Yep. I suppose Tempest and me went through our trauma so young that we don't remember it."

"What happened to the other babies who were with you on that ship, the ones who died?"

"They were buried in Ethiopia," she said. "Genetic tests said it was where we most likely came from."

"Ah. I don't know where my step-siblings are buried. Their maternal families claimed their remains. Sometimes I wonder if I should make contact and ask, but it's probably unfair to re-open old wounds."

"Okay, I'm calling it. You're being way too maudlin. Let's go to the shore and taunt the seagulls as we eat our lunch."

An hour before sunset, another spaceship arrived. The first to descend the ramp was a solemn-faced Johann tol Davir. Behind, an honour guard of armoured towani carried a sealed coffin to the small altar set up outside the ruined church. Johann spoke briefly with Dorn-Tru and the Archbishop of Dublin, then moved through the crowd, greeting each person in turn: the Irish president and his wife; Tadgh O'Connell and his husband; the local MP and her husband; the boatman and his two daughters; Sergeant Plunkett and her septuagenarian mother; Tempest, and then Serene, before giving Harold a warm handshake, and then the splayed-hand greeting of the towani.

"Welcome, everyone," he said, taking his place in front of the coffin. "Clee wrote her own funeral service, and requested she was interred in a chamber below ground which would then be sealed for five hundred years. In this way, she will rest as her spiritual ancestors did."

Harold politely stood, and as he did, he noticed that Sean and Greta were nowhere to be seen. As he looked around for them, a yellow warning flashed across his glasses. He followed the pointing arrow until he was looking at the lake. The glasses automatically zoomed in, showing six drones, rising from the waters, and flying towards the island.

Harold was about to ask Serene if they were part of the service, but from how the honour guard suddenly moved to protect Johann and the sapiens dignitaries, he guessed the answer was no.

"Stay calm, everyone," Johann said, a task made impossible when the drones opened fire.

Harold wanted to run, and doubted he was the only one. From the shore a hundred small discs had taken to the air. These discs intercepted the incoming bolts, creating a terrifying, but brief, fireworks display that continued over the lake as missiles launched from the saucer destroyed the enemy drones. The warning lights didn't stop. A new arrow appeared. There was a seventh drone, but it was heading for the people ashore.

Sean, feeling distinctly underdressed in jeans, a wax jacket, and a flat cap, was just another face in the crowd. He knew that, because he was methodically scanning every other face he saw. Up on the peace platform, those faces were checked against the UNCA employment records, and the British and Irish criminal databases. So far, there'd been no hits, but Parker had had plenty of time to erase any records of his co-conspirators. Sean didn't mind. He'd grown up in an age without technology, and though it was as helpful as often as it was frustrating, he'd learned to trust his eyes as much as any sensors.

Everyone, except him, had a phone in their hands. Some were taking pictures of the lake, and others were taking photos of the crowd. A few were recording, or streaming, video. A handful of the older onlookers were even making phone calls. He ignored them all, concentrating on the people who were looking at their screens. The teen in the green beanie was surely too young; his target would be at least in their mid-twenties. The woman with the uneven braids had too old a phone; his target would have money. The woman with the tan? Perhaps she'd just come back from holiday.

His lenses flashed a warning. Six drones had been tagged coming out of the lake, aiming for the island. He dismissed the alert. That wasn't his problem. A shout went up from the crowd, and they began pointing at the drones, but even when that was followed by the sound of distant explosions, the woman with the tan didn't look up from her screen.

He began making his way towards her, but his progress was hampered by some in the crowd, now running. His target did the same. When she started running, Sean did, too. She ran to the road and jumped into the back of a car in which the driver had been waiting.

Sean was only ten feet away when the car began accelerating, and only thirty feet away when the seventh drone smashed through the car's roof and exploded.

Chapter 24 - Gathering Evidence

Harold gulped his coffee. Tea just wouldn't cut it today. Did two consecutive nights spent outside count as two separate incidents of camping? In which case, he'd given it three tries and would be more than happy if it was *two* hundred years before he had to experience it again. His coffee finished, he returned to the task he'd begun last night, searching the island's shore for more scrap from the fallen drones.

As had been explained to him last night, the drone attack had been anticipated, if not entirely expected, by Greta and Sean. To assassinate the ambassador would require knowing where he would be at a specific time. Since first contact, the prophet had relocated to the peace platform. He *had* visited Earth, but on no fixed schedule, and with no prior announcement. One day might see him in a South African township, the next at a Brazilian favela, perhaps via a quick stop in Chicago for pizza. As Clee's plans to be interred on the island were well known in the embassy, the funeral of the spy had been the perfect opportunity to strike. But to have a funeral, you must first have a death. Clee's murder was a victory in its own right to the Voytay, but the death of the last prophet, killed by a sapiens so soon after first contact, would have raised doubts over Johann *being* the last prophet.

This time, they'd been prepared, but it wouldn't be long before Earth began receiving unrestricted visitors from off-world, any of whom could bring something far worse than drones. Who would be responsible for security checks at the atmospheric border? If it was Sean, then was it also him?

He spotted something grey and shiny, but it was just a rock. Most of the wreckage had fallen into the lake. The rest had filled a crate. After he'd completed a second sweep of the shoreline, he returned to the pier, where Dorn-Tru was also awaiting a boat.

"Are you heading to shore?" Harold asked.

"I am awaiting the arrival of a beekeeper. Unless perhaps you know how to herd the insects?"

"All I know is to avoid them when they're in large groups."

"Ah. Well, as the boat isn't here, check the shore once more," Dorn-Tru said.

"Of course."

Harold's childhood beliefs had faded as he became aware of the extent of his father's lies. The full spectrum of preachers had visited the detention centre, but Harold had kept his distance, a habit he'd maintained since moving into the bookshop. Perhaps that was why he found the cleric off-putting, but he'd much rather walk the shore than attempt small talk.

The third sweep turned up no more debris than the second, but when he returned to the jetty, the boat had arrived. While Dorn-Tru nervously watched the beekeeper tend the hives, Harold borrowed the boat, and took the crate to the mainland.

News of the attempted assassination had brought out scores of journalists, a good many curious locals, and nearly as many local politicians who were giving interviews on camera. The police cordon had been pushed backwards, corralling the bystanders on a nearby grassy hillside. The boatyard's car park had filled as it became a hub for the local police operation. While officers in uniform and high-viz jackets scurried about, Serene and Tempest were waiting by their SUV.

"Finished?" Serene asked, as Tempest came to help with the crate.

"I think so. You?"

"Absolutely," Serene said. "Da said we were to call him when we were ready, but let's call from inside the car. I'm getting tired of the pointed looks and piercing questions from the police."

"I get why," Tempest said. "They don't like how they weren't warned an assassination attempt was likely."

"Nor were we," Serene said. "They just don't think we belong here."

Inside the SUV, they placed the call. Sean appeared as a small 3D hologram projected on the dash. "I'll be with you in a moment."

"Cool hologram," Harold said, the terror of the recent attack momentarily forgotten.

"I borrowed the projector from the embassy," Serene said. "We should be able to use the windshield as a screen, but the software is super-glitchy."

"Hi, gang. All well?" Sean asked, his hologram turning back to face them.

"Yep," Serene said. "We've collected the scrap from the drones except for the bits that would require scuba gear."

"We'll leave that for the professionals. They should be in-system before the end of next week."

"How's Gramps?" Serene asked.

"Absolutely fine."

"You should have told us you expected an attack," Tempest said.

"I didn't want you to worry," Sean said. "This wasn't the first attempt on his life."

"It wasn't? Well, now I am worrying," Serene said.

"You don't have to, because I'm actually calling with good news. The attack seems to have focused political minds. The conference had a vote this morning and agreed to send the Olympic flag carriers to Towan III. That's one group of people we know can't be part of any plot. I'm going to add a few extras. First will be Padraig O'Keefe, and a ton of flour and other ingredients, to challenge some of the higher-profile towani chef-programmers to a bake-off. Cooking and cooking shows are genuinely alien concepts on Towan III. Everyone will be intrigued. We'll have some members of the ruling council as judges. It'll be great for public relations."

"Padraig's a great chef," Serene said. "He's abysmal at conversation."

"Which is why I'm also sending Niamh to soften his edges. She'll be the official representative of Earth as a whole, and the Pakistani film crew who've been making a documentary aboard the platform will make another about the ceremony, and another about the cooking contest. Let's be honest, out of the two we know which show people on Earth will most want to see. Besides, there'll be plenty of Valley press, but Earth should have a recording of our own."

"It sounds like you don't really need the flag carriers," Harold said.

"I don't, but Earth does. It might not be the decision I was hoping for, but the nations of the Earth did reach an almost unanimous decision. The next set of problems will be much harder. How do we share out the natural resources in the solar system? Where will we host the retraining facilities for astronauts, engineers, and teachers? We can't have them everywhere. How do we establish an exchange rate?"

"How do we fund a border and customs force?" Harold added.

"And whose customs are they?" Tempest said.

"And we can't open the border until we have an answer," Sean said. "It'll take time, but I'm feeling optimistic we'll get there."

"When does the delegation leave?" Serene asked.

"As soon as the ship arrives. This is a lot more delegates than we'd planned for, so we've sent for a ferry."

"How's the investigation going?" Harold asked.

"There's more good news there. We found the safe-house near to Parker's home where the rescue of his wife was planned and staged."

"Did you find her?" Tempest asked.

"No, the house was empty. A sapiens forensic team is searching it now. The Gardaí forensic team found a driving licence in the car's wreckage. It's a fake, but a very good one. We think it was made in the embassy. Whoever piloted that drone into the car must have worked in the embassy, or on the platform. We've identified five people who would have had access to comms equipment, and who would have been able to cover their tracks. Greta's interviewing them."

"The drone we found with the stray sooval had been reprogrammed," Harold said. "I bet this is linked."

"Very possibly," Sean said. "I'm at RAF Benson, and I'm going to question the mercenary in a few minutes."

"Cool, so what do we do now?" Serene asked.

"Put your feet up," Sean said. "I thought you should spend some time with Celeste before you leave."

"Leave for where?" Tempest asked.

"Towan III," Sean said. "Obviously you're travelling with the delegation."

Serene eagerly leaned forward. "We are?"

"Yes, but not as part of the delegation. Abi tol Demener has selected the new staff to work at the embassy. You can give them a briefing on what to expect here on Earth before returning home and taking up liaison positions at the embassy."

"Oh, no," Serene said.

"What's wrong?"

"Well, Abi set me homework, and I've fallen way behind," Serene said.

"Then you've got a few weeks to catch up," Sean said. "The Gardaí will give you an escort to the airport. The cargo plane from Benson will land, and pick you and those crates up. You'll be flown to Area-51 where Celeste will meet you. She wants to have a word with Parker."

"Ooh, I'll enjoy watching that," Serene said.

"And then you, and Jess, can hang out with Celeste. Stay on the base until she arrives. Ah, I've got to go."

"We're going to Towan III!" Serene said, nearly in a squeal.

"With all those athletes," Tempest said. "Imagine getting to train with the very best."

"What's wrong, Harold, don't you want to see the capital of the galaxy?"

"Honestly, I'm not sure. It's just… I know your dad started by saying it was good news, but it doesn't feel like it. He must not think the embassy or the peace platform are safe, or he'd have sent us there."

Chapter 25 - A Shining Beacon on a Runway

Ever since his children had come into his life, Sean had asked himself whether they were safe. Now, as then, the answer was no. A ping alerted him to a call from Greta.

"Tell me there's some good news," he said.

"There's been an arrest," Greta said. "A stolen car was spotted just outside the hotel in Cork. Inside were sapiens explosives and a remote detonator. The signal was jammed, and the driver was traced to the crowd of anti-towani demonstrators. He's been detained."

"Who is he?"

"According to his driving licence, Jack Smith from London. He hasn't said much, but his accent is South African, and his tattoos are military. He's probably a mercenary now, but trained with the South African Army. Records have been requested. It would be a lot quicker if this *wasn't* going through official channels, but Johann insists we let the sapiens handle it."

"How much explosives were in the car?"

"Enough to bring down a house, but the vehicle was in a car park. The only casualties would be anyone unlucky enough to be nearby, and that would mostly be protesters."

"How do we know this is linked to Clee's murder?"

"The car had been stolen from Rosslare. The owners were murdered. They also owned a fixed-rib inflatable that's missing from their driveway. Using traffic cameras, and security footage, we were able to count four suspects in the car when it drove west, towing the boat."

"Was Dr Masadi among them?"

"It's impossible to tell because their features were obscured by camo-hoods."

"Were they now? When Serene did her stock-take during the first lockdown, she found some of those had gone missing. This, or something like it, has been in the works for some time. The hoods wouldn't make them look like someone else, but they would make them unrecognisable, even to each other."

"If they can't recognise each other, they can't identify each other when caught," Greta said. "Not far from the lough, they were joined by a second car. That was the vehicle destroyed by the drone. Inside were two people."

"So we've at least six in this conspiracy, two dead, and one in custody. Any idea where the other three went?"

"Tracking the footage backwards, the four who killed the family in Rosslare arrived on a fishing boat. It's registered to an address in Rosslare. An identical boat, but with a different name, is registered to an address in Holyhead on the other side of the Irish Sea. That's where the boat currently is. We have footage of two suspects leaving the harbour. That's when they vanish, entering an area where the cameras had been disabled. We're only a few hours behind them."

"Only two of them? What of the third?"

"We don't know."

"So they could still be in Ireland."

"I've a new theory," Greta said. "The interviews with the staff on the peace platform and at the embassy turned up nothing. They all have alibis, and a lack of motive. I think the missing suspect is the killer who was controlling the drone that destroyed the car. I think they were at the lake. They killed those two to give us some suspects. But the suspects are mercenaries hired for a job and who don't know what their employer looks like. Jack Smith, or whomever he really is, would probably also have been killed after the explosion."

"Sounds plausible. It reduces the number of loose ends. But if the two who sailed back to Wales were expendable, they would have died in Ireland. Leaving bodies behind is a distraction, too. This isn't over."

"No, it's not. The car would have been discovered within a few hours. I'm sure the explosion was supposed to take place soon. Certainly within twenty-four hours, but probably a lot sooner than that."

215

"We're missing something," Sean said. "Serene and Tempest were attacked by a drone in Lincolnshire not long after she found those camo-hoods were missing. So, let's assume this is all linked, and the drones arrived on Earth before or during the pandemic. They can't have been intended for this."

"We'll know more as we dig into the past of the suspect now in custody, but I'm more concerned with what the bomb was to be a distraction for. I think they're planning something imminent. Something in Britain, otherwise those two wouldn't have sailed back to Wales. It must be at RAF Benson."

Sean looked up at the screens showing the sleeping prisoner. "You think there'll be an escape attempt?"

"Three of the captured sooval are pilots, and there are two spaceships at the base."

"They wouldn't know how to pilot the flying wing," Sean said.

"Are you sure?"

"I'm sure they couldn't unlock it," Sean said.

"It can be unlocked remotely from the platform," Greta said. "We know someone from the Valley was working with them at one stage, so perhaps they still do."

"I'll change the codes," Sean said. "But if I were planning a rescue, I'd bring my own ship. A car bomb in Ireland would have seen us deploy resources there to evacuate the dignitaries. The sapiens killers could set off a bomb in town, causing us to deploy resources away from the base before their ship skips in above the airfield."

"That would only be possible if there's a beacon," Greta said.

"I better look for it."

Sean watched the screen showing the larneth, seemingly unconscious on the bed. Was it really plausible that it had survived for two months undiscovered in a county where tourists were tripping over each other?

Pausing only to collect his weapons, Sean hurried from the prison, heading to the hangar where the scrap from the Oxfordshire wreck was stored.

"Trouble, sir?" Sergeant Linton asked.

"Possibly. A car bomb was discovered at the hotel in Cork. We've linked it to the attempted assassination of the ambassador, but we think it was to be a distraction. We would have deployed a large swathe of forces to Ireland, leaving fewer here to stop a rescue attempt."

"With a spaceship?"

"That's the concern."

Linton looked up. "Can they just appear anywhere?"

"Yes and no. You need coordinates. Since the Earth is rotating at 1,670 kilometres per hour, and spinning around the sun at thirty kilometres a second, you'd have to use a beacon or you're as likely to end up inside the moon. We've been scanning for them ever since the newly arrived prisoner told us that a rescue was part of the contract. None have been detected. If there is one, it's powered down, waiting to be switched on."

"Maybe it's in a nearby house with one of these terrorists, ready to be turned on."

"Possibly, but the enemy pilot will never have flown to Earth before. If they're too far away, they might not know in which direction to head. Their ship will have to skip into our star system, then skip again to reach their target. But the moment a ship appears anywhere near Earth, we'll know. They'll have minutes to complete the rescue, and they know it. The only possible way it could work is if they have a beacon nearby. What happened to the wreckage of that drone that came in with the new prisoner? Was it sent to Area-51?"

"It shouldn't have been. It's down as evidence in the murder of a dog. The air marshal's neighbour wants to press charges."

"Let's take a look at it," Sean said.

The diamond-shaped object lay on a trolley in the back of the hangar. When Sean scanned it, he picked up a faint power signature. After returning to his ship to fetch a cutting tool, he removed the outer panel. He frowned. The interior configuration was entirely wrong. There was too much circuitry, wiring, and an extra power pack, but it didn't feed into the machine's engine. Slowly, he smiled.

"Did you find it?" Linton asked.

"The entire drone is a beacon," Sean said. "Rather, they built a beacon to look like a drone. To ensure it could still operate as a drone, they had to strip out a lot of functionality. There is no way it's been active for two months. That small power cell wouldn't last more than a week."

"Can you disable it?"

"It won't work. When I shot it down, the signal amplifier was destroyed. But don't worry, I can replicate the signal using my ship."

"Why do you want to do that?"

"We don't know if there's a secondary beacon, or some other backup plan. The device still has power, and it's on standby. When it's turned on, it'll only be active for half an hour, maybe less. It would have to be switched on remotely, and I know by whom. First, I need to speak to the air marshal."

"You're out of luck. She's gone to meet the new prime minister."

"There's another new one already? Never mind. Find Major Owen and tell him I want his twenty best shots at my ship in five minutes."

Four minutes later, Sean carried the first crate out of the flying wing to find twenty soldiers, plus the SAS major, two junior officers, and the ever-curious Sergeant Linton on the tarmac outside.

"We're to expect an attack," Sean said. "A car bomb was just discovered at the hotel in Ireland where the international conference was taking place. The culprit is in custody, but he was one of six assassins who killed the hermit, and who attacked the funeral. Two others were tracked to Holyhead, but managed to vanish before they left Anglesey. The drone that arrived with the larneth contained a navigation beacon. We must assume they will attempt a rescue. I have a plan that should reduce the risk of an aerial battle, and the collateral damage it would bring. In case it doesn't work, the Valley soldiers will guard the prison. You'll guard the airbase. Assume mortars, car bombs, and every trick every insurgent has ever used."

"We can handle that," the major said.

218

"But you can't handle alien tech with the weapons you've got." Sean opened the crate. "This is the X-11 battle rifle."

"It looks like an M4-carbine," the major said.

"No, the carbine looks like an X-11. This was designed first. It works much the same. They're supposed to be used with an augmented reality display, but we don't have time to set it up, so I'll decouple them. There are sixty rounds of armour-piercing ammunition in the magazine, and one spare magazine per rifle. When I say armour, I mean like the kind you'll find on a drone. Expect a diversionary attack on the perimeter. If sooval mercenaries are part of the attack, engage from a distance. Anyone without one of these rifles should use explosives, because it would take a very lucky shot from an SA80 to pierce their armour."

"And air cover?"

"Leave that to me," Sean said. "I'll deploy a squadron overhead."

"When will the attack occur?"

"I don't know, but we're assuming within twenty-four hours," Sean said.

Leaving the major to prepare the base, Sean returned to the prison, and went straight to the hospital.

"You have come to give me sanctuary?" the larneth asked.

"Two months is a long time for you to have survived unnoticed."

"I am easy to ignore."

"And you turned up not far from the air marshal's house, where your drone was spotted by the air marshal's daughter? It can't be a coincidence. We found the beacon inside your drone. The question is, how were you going to turn it on?"

"You speak a strange tale."

"Do I now?" Sean said. He reached down, and took the medal from around the sooval's neck. "You won this for being a larneth?"

"I did."

"You won this for singing?" Sean said. "Go on then, sing."

Chapter 26 - No Weapons in a Prison

The cargo plane shook as it entered a patch of turbulence. Harold took that as a sign to end the call with his aunt, and to do up the buckle of his seatbelt. "You'll never guess where Jess is," he said.

"Earth," Serene said, looking up from the paperback biography of St Fionán Cam she'd borrowed from the boatman at Lough Currane.

"Yes, but I'm going to need something more precise."

"Mali?" Tempest said. "She loves Timbuktu."

"Closer. She's on a cruise ship in the Mediterranean. She's had helicopters pick up dozens of non-sapiens who were hiding in Egypt. She says they'll fly over to Area-51 tomorrow morning."

"So we'll be stuck in the base for twenty-four hours?" Tempest said. "What's there to do there?"

"The museum is pretty cool, and I would like some time to examine it properly," Harold said.

Each of their lenses flashed yellow, notifying them of an urgent incoming call.

"Hey, Da, what's up?" Serene asked as Sean appeared before their eyes.

"The larneth couldn't sing," Sean said.

"Is that the start of a joke?" Serene asked.

"I found a beacon hidden in the remains of the drone we shot down near the air marshal's house. The sooval prisoner, who claimed to be a larneth, had a remote trigger built into its medal. In fact, I'd say the trigger was built to look like a medal, and the beacon was built to look like a drone. Do you still have the portable scanners?"

"In my bag," Harold said.

"Check the crates, and the other crates that were put on the plane in Benson," Sean said. "Look for a power signature. This one was on standby."

The hold was pressurised, and accessible from the cabin, but as they entered, the plane rocked as it experienced another bout of turbulence. Holding onto the netting keeping the crates in place, they moved from one to the next, checking each in turn, but found nothing.

"You're sure?" Sean asked when they called him back.

"Positive," Serene said.

"If it was on standby, how would the sooval know when to turn it on?" Tempest asked.

"There'll be a signal, and figuring out what that is will be my next job," Sean said.

"What if we missed something?" Harold asked. "Shouldn't we set the plane down somewhere remote just in case?"

"If you think you missed something, check the crates again," Sean said. "When you get to Area-51, I want you to check all the crates that came from Benson. It's possible a beacon was slipped into an earlier shipment, but I think it's doubtful."

"If the Voytay are going to rescue the sooval, why not rescue Parker, too?" Serene asked.

"Why would they want to? What could he possibly tell them? The UNCA has been disbanded, but if the Voytay wanted any of the organisation's records, they had plenty of time to ask for them. The assassins were in Ireland, and now some are in Britain, and it was the British branch of the UNCA that was compromised. In case I'm wrong, we're deploying a fighter wing to defend the base. When you get there, go inside and stay inside until Celeste arrives."

"Maybe that's what this is all about," Harold said. "Maybe all of this is a distraction. Would the Voytay really want to assassinate the prophet? It would enrage the Valley, and start a war."

"Not if a sapiens is blamed," Tempest said.

"Even then, wouldn't people ask where the drones came from?" Harold asked. "No, what I mean is that everything that's happened so far has had the net result of Valley fighter craft, and soldiers, being deployed all over the planet. The intelligence officers on the platform and at the embassy are looking down on Earth, not watching for an attack on the platform itself. This is the perfect time to attack."

"And Gunther is still away," Serene said.

"I don't know if they could have predicted that," Sean said. "Or perhaps they could. Who else would we send to threaten the Voytay after the crash? Yes. Possibly. In which case, *do* expect an attack on Area-51. I'll warn Agent Burton, and send him some better weapons."

The flight was long and uncomfortable, and made even more tense when a towani fighter squadron took up position on their port wing. As they neared the United States, they gained a USAF escort to starboard. With each passing second that an attack on RAF Benson didn't come, Harold's imagination conjured scenes of destruction far worse than Oxfordshire. Woking, London, every city in the world, he pictured each being destroyed in turn. Unable to relax, he scanned the crates again. Twice. Tempest, by contrast, became increasingly convinced the attack had already failed, and the danger had now passed. Serene busied herself checking the notes on the embassy smuggling ring, trying to find a link between it and Dr Masadi.

Special Agent Burton was waiting when they arrived, and was the first aboard the plane, accompanied by a USAF sentry carrying a Valley rifle.

"Mr O'Malley said some kind of radio beacon was found in a waste-crate in RAF Benson," Burton said. "Did you check these crates?"

"Absolutely. They're clean," Serene said. "Well, they're filthy, but none have a power signature."

"Is that what you look for?" Burton asked.

"The beacon Da found was on standby, waiting to be turned on remotely," Serene said.

"We need to check every crate that's come from Oxfordshire. Can you three do that?"

"Sure," Harold said.

"Good. Follow me."

Their Valley fighter-escort had set down, but there were five more ships hovering ominously above the base. Other than the ground crew, now hurrying to unload the plane, everyone Harold could see was wearing body-armour and carrying a Valley rifle. Burton drove them from the aircraft to the hangar with the elevator-entrance to the bunker hidden below. Sergeant Washington was on duty, though now with two corporals.

"Weapons go into the tray," the sergeant said.

Burton removed his sidearm, and walked through. Serene followed, but the scanner pinged.

"What's on your arm?" Washington asked.

Serene rolled back her sleeve, revealing the dock to which her drones were attached. "It's not a weapon."

"It set off the scanner, so it has to be left behind," Washington said.

"Seriously?" Serene asked.

"Those are the rules," Burton said.

When Tempest walked through the scanner, it trilled a symphony.

"It must be broken," Tempest said.

"Don't tell a fish she can't swim," Burton said, tapping the scanner's display. "I worked with your father. I know what towani weapons look like. I'm not going to ask under which law you have a right to carry them, but you don't have a right to carry them down here."

"If we're about to be attacked, wouldn't it be better if I was armed?" Tempest said.

"There's another scanner built into the elevator," Washington said. "It'll shut down if you try to take those inside."

With obvious reluctance, Tempest removed a small arsenal.

"Dare I ask what's in your bag, Harold?"

"Just some portable scanners, a few books, and a change of clothes." Harold walked through without the alarm sounding.

"Sergeant, can you come with us?" Burton said, and then led them into the elevator, down to the underground bunker, and to a chamber the same size as the museum, but filled with towering racks of identical crates, stretching twenty feet into the air.

"Which ones are from Oxfordshire?" Harold asked.

"All of them," Burton said. "Do you need anything?"

"Dinner would be nice," Tempest said.

"I'll have some sent to you. Sergeant Washington will remain here. If you find anything, he'll raise the alarm."

Washington lingered by the door. Harold opened his bag, and took out the scanner.

"I can't believe you tried to smuggle weapons into a prison," Serene said.

"As an acolyte, they're cultural," Tempest said. "And what about the sisters?"

"What about them? They wouldn't help anyone escape."

Harold began running the portable scanner over the nearest crate. "It's clean."

"How are we going to reach the ones at the top?" Tempest asked.

"If I had the sisters, we could fly."

"I could climb," Tempest said.

"Or you could use those moveable steps down at the end of the aisle," Harold said.

It was dull and tedious work, and took nearly three hours after Harold insisted they check the crates twice.

"Nothing," Harold said.

"Which makes sense, since all the other attacks have been in Ireland or Britain," Serene said.

"What do we do now?" Tempest asked.

"Tell the sergeant. Where is he?" Serene said.

"He must have popped outside," Harold said, and opened the door. "Nope. He's gone."

"Why don't we go to the museum?" Serene said. "Didn't you say there was an exhibit on the tunnel in Iraq? If that's when Parker and his wife first met, it's got to be the key to everything."

"You've had an idea, haven't you?" Tempest asked.

"Sort of. The only Valley people implicated in the smuggling ring managed to slip away before they were arrested. Someone warned them, which… well, perhaps it's Abi tol Demener."

"No. You can't suspect them," Tempest said. "Besides, they're back on Towan III."

"Now, yes, but they were the senior archaeologist here for years, in charge of recruiting other specialists, and they spent an age re-searching that tunnel. Maybe I've got it wrong, so let's take a look."

The museum was just as Harold remembered, but his interest was waning. The long flight, tedious but tense work, and the stress of the assassination attempt had left him drained, while the lack of a good night's sleep hadn't left him with much in the tank to begin with.

"See anything?" Tempest asked, as they stood in front of the pho-tographs of the tunnel.

"No. Maybe. I'm not sure," Serene said.

Harold yawned. "I think I'm going to find somewhere to lie down."

The lights went out, but emergency lights then came on.

"What—" Harold managed before a wall of air slammed into him, throwing him across the chamber, head-first into the side of the Iraqi-found spaceship.

Chapter 27 - What a Difference Twenty Metres Makes

Sean read through the report, skipping over the apology. They'd been so intent on watching for ships *entering* the system, it had taken ten minutes before anyone noticed a hop drive had activated on Earth. The signature was too small to be a ship, so it was probably just a message-pod. As the location of departure was on the outskirts of Wrexham, it was likely to be Dr Masadi, or one of her assassins. Greta had flown there to begin an aerial search for the fugitives, while the local police were mobilised. That was three hours ago. So far, the search had turned up nothing. The progress of the interrogation in Ireland wasn't helping his mood. The suspect still refused to talk. Considering what had happened to the two in the car, it wasn't surprising.

Greta had put in a request to interview the suspect, but that had to go through official channels, and they were tortuously slow to navigate. Not for the first time, Sean wondered what he could have done differently, and what he should do differently next. There was no denying that first contact was not panning out like he'd hoped. In some respects, the very opposite of what he'd wanted had happened now that he'd had to hand out modern weapons to the British, the Americans, and the German soldiers maintaining a cordon outside the embassy, and to the Gardaí protecting the conference and Church Island. If he didn't ask for them back, there would soon be demands from other nations for equal treatment.

He'd pushed the idea of sending the flag-carriers to Towan III, because he knew none of them could be working for Dr Masadi. The last thing they needed was an assassin attempting to sabotage the ferry mid-journey. It didn't solve the real problem of the disparate nations finding an equitable way of making decisions on behalf of the entire planet. Handing out weapons to some would certainly make it more difficult.

His glasses flashed yellow. Contact. A ship had just skipped into existence above the Bristol Channel. He began to place a call to Greta, but was interrupted by a trio of explosions outside. He ran to the window. Smoke was rising from the runway. That had to be the signal to the sooval. He switched on the beacon.

"This is it. Linton, tell the major what I'm sure he knows. The arrival is imminent and everyone should stay away from the runway."

Even as the sergeant raised her radio, the hangar shuddered. The roof rippled. A fist-sized lump of concrete punched a hole through the wall, while a chunk of black-top smashed through the window. As sirens blared, Sean's glasses flashed yellow again, but this time he dismissed the message. He knew what it was going to say.

Outside, chunks of concrete, cement, and runway pattered to the ground. A fog of dust and smoke shrouded the airbase, but amid the haze was a hint of flame. He switched his glasses to low-light, and then to thermal. A transporter ship had attempted to materialise *above* the runway. Instead, and because Sean had used his ship to spoof the beacon's signal, it had reappeared just beneath the surface, causing a volcanic displacement of asphalt and of the soil beneath. Only a small section of the forward control deck was visible, and it was spouting flame. No one could have survived, but there was a very real chance of an explosion.

His glasses flashed yellow again. This time, he read the message, but it told him what he'd just seen. He stepped back into the hangar, waiting for the dust to settle. He placed a call to his wife. "Greta, the transporter that appeared here is mostly buried. I assume everyone inside is dead. I'm concerned the engines might explode. We need to evacuate the sooval prisoners."

"Forget about them, what about Area-51?" she asked, an unaccustomed edge of panic in her voice.

"What about it?"

"Didn't you get the alert? A ship appeared *inside* the facility."

Sean ran. As he did, he brought up the message he'd dismissed without reading. It said just what his wife had told him. He tried calling Tempest, Serene, and then Harold. They didn't answer. By the time he'd reached his ship, he'd been unable to reach Burton, either.

He'd barely buckled himself in before he took off. He sent a message to the captain of the Valley detachment guarding the prison to organise an evacuation of the mercenaries, one to the peace platform to send down a repair team to make the wrecked ship safe, then contacted the head of the towani fighter wing he'd deployed at Area-51.

"What's happening?" Sean asked.

"A ship appeared inside the museum," Captain Melissa tol Farrat said. "It— It just departed."

"They had help. Don't trust anyone, but find my kids."

He ended the call, breathed out, and called Greta.

"Greta, I can't reach the kids. I'm on my way to America. Where are you?"

"The Bristol Channel. I got here too late. That ship has gone, but they left a boat behind. The passengers must have been waiting aboard with a beacon."

"They must have had a beacon in Area-51, too. Someone helped them."

"Burton?"

"I hope not," he said.

The ship began to shudder as it punched through the atmosphere. The pain of g-force was replaced with the balm of zero-g, but fear and worry wouldn't allow him to enjoy it.

An update came from the towani captain. "Sir. I am sorry. Your children have been taken."

"Taken? Can you be more precise?"

"Abducted. They were taken aboard the transporter before it skipped. This was an escape. Of the fifty-six sapiens prisoners, forty-one are unaccounted for."

"Keep investigating," Sean said.

He called Greta, relaying the news.

"That's madness," she said.

"So is going to all this trouble just to rescue Parker," Sean said. "I better tell Celeste."

"I'll tell her," Greta said. "They are her children, too. It's an act of war, Sean. Not just against the Valley, but also against her."

Not having fully discharged all forward momentum, his flying wing skidded on the runway as he set down. As soon as he'd silenced the alarms, they sounded again, warning of a burst of small impacts as a nervous USAF sentry opened fire with a machine gun.

Burton and Melissa tol Farrat came to meet him, along with General Chung, the USAF commander of the above-ground part of the base.

"It was Washington," Burton said in lieu of a greeting. "He was the insider."

"Washington? Captain Farrat, get airborne. General, warn your people that there might be a follow-up attack. The ambassador has informed the world leaders."

"You think they'd attack now?" Burton asked.

"The murder of Clee, the attempted assassination of the prophet and the Irish president, and now this prison break and kidnapping of my children, this is an act of war. It makes no sense, but if they are going to attack, they'll do it now. My wife will arrive soon with the children's mother. Tell your sentries not to shoot at their ship when it lands. Burton, tell me what happened?"

"Their ship appeared in the museum. Your kids, and Harold, they were there at the time. They've gone. We think they were knocked out by the displacement of air when the ship appeared. Washington somehow cut power to the base. He killed the guards at the entrance to the prison, set the prisoners free, and led them to the museum. There were alien soldiers aboard. They killed at least four guards, but we're still counting bodies and tending to the injured. There are a few who won't make it. When they left, they took your kids with them. Five prisoners are dead. The rest remained in their cells. We're questioning them. So far, they say they knew nothing about this in advance."

"Where were you when this happened?"

"Above ground with General Chung, waiting for an attack. How was this possible?"

"That's what I want to know."

By the time Greta arrived with Celeste and Jess, he had most of the answers, while a technician had found one more.

"Where's Harry?" Jess asked, stepping around the wreckage now littering the museum chamber.

"I don't know," Sean said.

"Is he even alive?"

"I think so."

"They won't be harmed," Greta said. "It would be madness. It was madness to take them."

"But we will get them back?" Jess said.

"Of course," Sean said. "I want to interrogate that suspect in Ireland first, but then we'll set out for Voytay space."

"Do you know what happened?" Greta asked.

"The beacon was hidden in the holographic projector at the centre of the chamber. The projector could show the story of each ship that crashed on Earth."

"How long had the projector been here?" Jess asked as they all turned to look at the debris of the device, crushed under the weight of the ship.

"Three years," Sean said. "The sapiens insider was a former Marine named Washington. He was in Iraq on Parker's first mission with me. So was Agent Burton, who had just been transferred to oversee this base, and oversee the disestablishment of the prison. Washington has been working here for nearly twenty years, and mostly as a security guard. While he had plenty of time to try to circumvent the security measures, I don't think he was able. I think the beacon was hidden inside the projector before it arrived. The hack that knocked out the lights and opened the doors was achieved with a device disguised as a lump of shrapnel. It must have come in with one of the crates of junk."

"It must have been custom-built," Greta asked.

"Washington killed at least four guards himself. These were people he'd worked alongside for years. We know Olawayo killed at least two more. When the Voytay joined the fight, it became a massacre. One of the survivors reports a squad of five leaving the ship. She was the one who saw our kids being picked up and carried aboard."

"I'd like to speak to her," Jess said.

"You can't. She succumbed to her wounds."

"Without the beacon you wouldn't be able to skip into that underground hangar, even if you were parked right above it," Greta said. "This had been planned for years."

"Parker knew he was going to be caught after Oxfordshire," Sean said. "This must have been his solution."

"So we'll assume his wife was collected from the Bristol Channel," Greta said. "It's a lot of effort for just those two."

"Who are the other prisoners?" Jess asked.

"Killers and murderers," Sean said. "Other than that Parker arrested some, I don't know of any link between them and him. The only other point of note is that the items recovered from the tunnel beneath Nineveh were also taken. Most of the photographs and recordings were in the embassy database. The only unique physical objects were the broken flight recorder, and a few of the tiles that once covered the tunnel."

"What flight recorder?" Jess asked.

"It belonged to a collector who would sometimes visit my student," Celeste said. "Two thousand and six hundred years ago, their ship crashed. It was never clear why. The data on the flight recorder was corrupted. All that remained was a record of a previous trip to visit my student."

"But the Voytay might not know that," Sean said. "They might think it holds the secret to how your student was killed."

"Where's your spaceship?" Jess asked Celeste.

"Safe," Celeste said.

"Can you fetch it? I assume we're going to use that, and threaten to blow up a planet if they don't give our kids back."

"They won't harm the children," Greta said.

"You can't know that," Jess said.

"Their abduction was a crime of opportunity because they know who the children are," Greta said. "They might try to ransom them, or use them as leverage, but they won't be harmed."

"Don't you want to look for them?"

"Of course," Greta said. "First, we'll ask nicely. If that doesn't work, we'll find out where they're being held and rescue them."

"I will return to Iraq," Celeste said. "It is possible there is something the archaeologist found that I overlooked."

"We'll head back to Ireland," Sean said. "I want to interview the bomber we captured. Then we'll go to Benson, interview the sooval prisoners, and then we'll head to the borderlands, and meet up with Gunther before we have words with the Voytay."

Part 7
In Our Galaxy, but Still Far, Far Away

Deep Space
October 2022 - January 2023

Chapter 28 - Imperial Justice

"Urgh," Harold said. He'd tried to ask *where am I*, but his mouth was as dry as sandpaper, and just as coarse on his tongue. His head was pounding, and the beat grew louder as he sat up. A wave of nausea swept over him. He leaned forward, putting his head between his knees, and breathed slow and deep. The pounding began to subside. He rubbed his eyes and realised his glasses were gone. With the jolt of a quintuple espresso, he realised his clothes were missing, too.

Blinking, heart pounding nearly as loudly as his brain had been, he looked about. He was sitting on a bed in a chamber a little longer than the bunk, and about twice as wide. The walls were grey and windowless. What was probably a door was outlined in a pale red light. More light, this time white, radiated from a panel in the ceiling.

The last thing he remembered was being in the museum room at Area-51. This wasn't a USAF hospital. On the floor was a stack of clothes. The trousers, tunic, and semi-rigid socks were of a style similar to those worn beneath a Valley spacesuit, except these were patterned in red and grey. Seeing no reason not to, he pulled them on. As he did, a story of Sean's came to him, of how he'd woken up on Johann and Greta's spaceship. Why he, Harold, would be in space, he had no idea, but the answer wasn't going to be found inside the room.

When he'd finished dressing, he crossed to the door. Waving his hand in front of it did nothing. Pushing did even less. He tried pressing his palms against it to see if it would slide back into the wall. It wouldn't. He sat back on the bunk, now certain he knew where he was. He was in a cell.

When the door opened, there were three red-armoured people on the other side. Two were dressed in the standard combat armour, complete with opaque helmets, but the third wore two strips of red cloth on each shoulder, hanging down to her waist where they clipped onto a belt. She wasn't wearing a helmet, so he could tell she had the grey face of a towani, but without his glasses, her features were a blur.

"*Kal*," Harold said, and made the splayed-hand gesture of greeting. "Where am I?"

The reply came in Mid-Tow, but after a few words, an English translation began playing from a speaker on the towani's chest. "Aboard a warship. You are a prisoner."

"You're Voytay, aren't you?"

"If you comply, you won't be harmed. Your friends are waiting. You are to follow."

As they walked along the corridor, Harold squinted at walls and doors, but even if he'd had his glasses, there was little to see.

He was led to a large chamber, filled with tables that had five bolted-down stools, but only on one side. Two armoured guards stood in the middle of the room, back-to-back. One watched a large group of maybe forty people all dressed in white. The other guard watched a smaller group, perhaps a tenth the size, dressed, like him, in red. As best he could tell, neither group had grey skin.

"Harold! Hi!" Serene called out. A blur among the smaller group waved.

"Go. Sit. Eat," his jailor said, so Harold did, making his way over to Serene.

As he got nearer, he saw the trays in front of the four people, sitting in a row with a fifth tray at the end. This chamber must be a mess-hall, and it must be a meal-time. Sitting with Serene and Tempest were a man and a woman. Even close up, he didn't recognise the woman, but the man grew increasingly familiar until, when he reached the table, he realised who it was.

"Parker!"

"Hello, Harold."

"Sit down," Serene said. "Eat something. Are you okay?"

"Not really. What's going on?"

"We're prisoners," Tempest said. "All of us."

"Including Parker," Serene said.

Harold sat at the place with the unclaimed tray. "This is food?" He bent down, peering closer, but it didn't improve the appearance of the beige slab in a beige sauce.

"Standard military rations," Tempest said. "It's not great, but it's edible."

Harold sipped at the water, then glugged down the whole mug.

Tempest pushed their mug over to Harold. "You've been out for eight hours longer than us," they said.

"My stomach feels it," Harold said, taking a bite of the beige slab. The sauce tasted like a mix of tomato and vanilla. The slab was virtually tasteless, but had the texture of a sand-filled sock. "What's going on?"

"A ship skipped into the museum. Actually inside it," Serene said. "A beacon had been hidden in there ages ago. One of the American soldiers was working with them."

"Washington," Parker said.

"That name's familiar," Harold said.

"He was with us in Iraq after the invasion," Parker said.

"He loaded a virus into the prison's computer system," Serene said. "It knocked out the lights, he opened the doors, and killed some of the guards. Most of the prisoners came with him."

Harold turned to look at the neighbouring group. "Is that them?"

"Yep. We'd been knocked out by the shockwave when the ship appeared. Olawayo decided to bring us."

"Olawayo?"

"He's the traitor," Parker said. "Him and Afiz."

"Yeah, but you are still a *bit* of a traitor," Serene said.

"What about the other two, Penn and Ricard?" Harold asked.

"They died during the prison-break," Parker said.

"The ship skipped," Serene said. "It arrived at a rendezvous where it was picked up by this warship along with another ship that had gone to England to pick up Awat. There was supposed to be a third ship, but it didn't arrive at the rendezvous."

236

"Awat? Awat Masadi?" Harold asked, squinting at the woman. "Sorry. They took my glasses."

"Ours, too," Serene said.

"Hello, Harold," Awat said.

"So you weren't behind cutting Clee up like Jack the Ripper?" Even without his glasses, he could see she was confused. "Sorry, that's what we assumed, that you were co-ordinating everything on behalf of your husband."

"What's this about Jack the Ripper?" Parker asked.

"Yeah, we haven't got to that yet," Serene said, and quickly explained.

"That must have been the men who arrived... yesterday, I think," Awat said. "It's so difficult keeping track of time with no watch, and no windows."

"Arrived where?" Harold asked.

"The people who took me waited until after my son had gone to school, after I'd taken the police officers coffee. They shot them both and took me. I don't know to where, but we drove for about six hours. They were soldiers. Mercenaries, I think. I never saw who their leader was. They would always go outside to call him. I think he was off-site."

"Your son's safe," Harold said. "He's being watched by towani soldiers, as well as by local police. Of course, that's because they think you're the mastermind behind this crime."

"Are we sure they're not?" Tempest asked.

"If I were, I'd not have kidnapped you three," Parker said.

"You did once before," Serene said.

"I wasn't going to harm you," Parker said.

"No, you'd have left it to the Voytay," Serene said.

"And they haven't harmed you yet," Parker said. "Look, if I were behind this, I'd be in the control room, not sitting here."

"Why didn't they take your son?" Harold asked.

"I don't know," Awat said, her voice wistful and sad.

"Children make for complicated hostages," Parker said. "Our previous encounter in Lenham House is a case in point. But they can still threaten him, and they have. As Olawayo said, they broke into Area-51. They can go anywhere."

"Sure, but a rescue is dangerous and expensive," Harold said. "Didn't you say there's a third ship that's missing? So why go to all this trouble to kidnap you both?"

"It's all about Mum and her student," Serene said.

"I spent a year imprisoned in that tunnel beneath Nineveh, and three months examining it afterwards. In the years since, I returned there twice with the Valley's chief archaeologist, Abi tol Demener."

"Who you think might be part of the conspiracy, Serene?" Harold said.

"Not anymore. I'm worried Abi might be another target for kidnapping."

"Not much we can do about that," Tempest said.

"I suppose not," Harold said. "But I still don't understand why they kidnapped you."

"These aliens have found something," Parker said. "They haven't said what. They want our opinion on it."

"I'm an expert on the tunnel beneath Nineveh, and Alan is an expert on the chamber beneath Lenham House. Both of which were dug by one of these near-immortal chroniclers. I think they found another tunnel, and not on Earth. That's all we know, but we've only been conscious for a few hours longer than you."

Harold took a bite of what looked like a black bread roll. It was both as sweet and as chewy as toffee. "And why did they bring us?"

"Olawayo thought we'd make great hostages," Tempest said. "The red-robe is furious about it."

"The red-robe? The towani with the red strips of cloth on her armour?"

"That's her," Tempest said.

"Clee was a red-robe. I thought they were disbanded after Clee revealed herself to be a spy."

"It looks like they're back," Serene said.

"Why's she furious about capturing you two? I'm guessing I'm just extra cargo."

"You were the first sapiens to break bread with the prophet after first contact, and you gave permission for it to happen," Serene said. "You're part of the prophecy, and part of our tribe. We made sure the red-robe knows. You're safe."

"Thanks. Why's she furious?"

"Because it wasn't part of the plan," Parker said. "The deal was that Olawayo and Afiz would get rescued, and I would be abducted. No one else was supposed to be brought along. Olawayo obviously overestimated his position, and value. But I think there was something even more important. An object of some kind that was in the museum. That's all Olawayo said before the red-robe broke his nose. It was very satisfying to watch."

"Abducting us is a massive escalation," Serene said. "It could lead to war. Or worse."

"What's worse than war?" Awat asked.

"Mum. We're safe. The ex-convicts? I'm not so sure." She pointed at the other group of sapiens. "Do you see they're still wearing their old prison garb?"

Harold peered again at the prisoners. Serene nudged his arm, and pointed in the other direction. The red-robe had returned, this time with six armoured guards. She came straight to their table, and began speaking in Mid-Tow, with the words relayed in a flat English translation.

"You five may share the same room. You will be well treated if you follow instructions. If you do not, you will be sedated until we arrive. Follow him."

One of the guards led them out of the mess-hall and down another wide corridor. This time, Harold gave up trying to make out any details, and instead counted the doors. He'd reached ten when they came to their cell.

When they had stepped inside, the door closed behind them.

"How big is this spaceship?" Harold asked.

"Massive," Serene said.

"And old," Tempest said. "This is the old imperial style of bunk-room."

239

Harold slowly made his way around the room. There were five sets of bunk beds with an upper and lower bunk, each of which had a retractable privacy screen. To either side was an empty locker, while in front of each bunk was a table with a single bench, facing the door. On the left of the room was a small washroom. On the right were larger lockers that, like the others, were empty.

"Weapons and armour would be stored in here," Tempest said, pointing at the bigger lockers.

"Why do the tables only have benches on one side?" Awat asked.

"Towani think it's weird watching people eat," Serene said.

"Compared to the other cells I've been in, this isn't so bad," Harold said.

"Agreed," Awat said. "How long will this voyage take?"

"If we're going to Ellowin, the capital planet of the Voytay, months," Serene said.

"I bet we're not," Tempest said.

"Wherever we're going, it'll still take ages, and that will give you lots of time to explain everything you know, Parker."

"We're going to be here a while. Call me Alan."

"Not until I've decided I don't completely distrust you," Serene said.

"What do you want me to say? I wanted to set Earth up as a planet independent of both the Voytay and the Valley. We'd be open to visiting pilgrims, but we'd continue on just as before."

"That doesn't sound very appealing."

"How's your father's plan working out? Have all the nations of Earth come together to harmoniously sing the praises of Nowan?"

"Well, no," Serene said. "But give it time."

"Let's not fight with each other," Awat said.

"No, if we're going to fight anyone, let's start with Olawayo," Parker said. "At one time, he was based out of Addis Ababa, but he ran the team that worked the African countries where saying you were with the U.N. made you a target. After twenty years of that, he could have taken a lump sum pay-out, and retired anywhere in the world. Instead, he requested a transfer to Britain. That was about ten

240

years ago. He introduced me to Afiz, and eventually suggested we offer her a job. Nadia's a genius with technology. She'd often fly overseas to consult with other local teams. I think it was on one of those trips where she and Olawayo began to scheme."

"When did you tell Olawayo about your plan to cut a deal with the Voytay?" Harold asked.

"The Voytay *and* the Valley," Parker said. "And I first mentioned it... I don't know, but soon after he joined the British team."

"What, at the same time you offered him a job?"

"No. I said the UNCA wasn't working. There had to be another way. He agreed. I won't say we bonded over that, but we began to discuss options."

"Are you going to say sending a visiting card to the Voytay was all his idea?" Serene asked.

"No, but it was as much his as mine."

"But you joined the U.N. so you could learn more about the vault beneath Lenham House," Harold said.

"Sure. It was the cause of my father's death. I wanted answers. At first, I thought I would get them from the Valley, especially after what we found in Iraq, but excavations there were halted. The Valley, like the old empire, takes its sweet time over everything."

"And what was your plan for if things had gone as you'd wanted?" Tempest asked.

"Yes, I'd like to know that, too," Awat said.

"I'd have had a deal to respect our independence with the Voytay. The Valley would have followed suit. I thought I'd be detained, but because I'd ushered in the new era, there was no way I could be charged with a crime."

"That's naive, Alan," Awat said.

"Did you know any of this?" Serene asked Awat.

"Not exactly. I knew Alan wanted Earth to be free and independent, but not that he was trying to bargain with this alien empire."

"I didn't tell her."

"If you had, I'd have stopped you," Awat said.

"Who was your contact at the embassy?" Tempest asked. "Who's the spy?"

"It's Olawayo's contact, not mine," Parker said. "It was when he said he had a contact that an idle hope became a real possibility, or so I thought."

"Oh, Alan, it sounds as if he played you from the beginning," Awat said.

"The Voytay wanted something from the museum in Area-51," Harold said. "Washington could have stolen it at any time."

"No, because if he could have, he would have done," Parker said.

"Don't forget they wanted Clee dead, too, but she was only going to leave her hermitage after first contact," Serene said.

"No, we're missing something, because the original plan was to collect the data-core from beneath Lenham House," Harold said.

"We're missing a lot," Tempest said. "Instead of speculating, let's talk about escape."

"We can't while we're jumped," Serene said.

"We could skip," Tempest said. "If we can get to the hangar deck, we could board one of the transport ships they used to bring us here, activate the skip drive, and be free."

"Or be dead," Parker said.

"On the plus side, it would probably destroy this ship, too," Tempest said.

"That is not much of a consolation," Awat said. She sat on a bunk, and raised her hands to her face. "Ever since Alan was arrested, all that's kept Yūnus going is the idea he might one day travel aboard a spaceship. I said we'd go together, all three of us. I'm glad he's not here, but I do miss him so much."

"Did he know about the Valley and the Voytay?"

"Of course not," Awat said. "It wouldn't be fair to expect someone so young to keep such a big secret, but we did encourage him to read and watch science fiction." She smiled. "And during lockdown, he did watch a lot more than he read."

While she'd been talking, Tempest had been pacing the room, running their hands over the seams in the wall panels, and the door. "Could any of the other prisoners help us?"

"That lot?" Parker asked. "They're murderers and killers. Take Pierre Duval, he decided the existence of aliens was a personal message from God that he should start bombing synagogues. Or there's Lee Han, an archaeologist who actively hunted the towani. He knew their leading historians came to Neanderthal burial sites at night. He lay in wait, and killed two. Nearly killed your grandfather."

"I never knew that," Tempest said.

"Our job wasn't all bribes and weather balloons," Parker said. "The convicts are not nice people. Right now, our captors are treating us well. Attempting to escape would change that, and it would only be an attempt. Until we know more, like where the transporter ships are, how to get there, and how many guards we might meet on the way, we should bide our time."

Harold picked a bunk of his own. The material lining the base was too thin to be called a mattress, and the pillow was nearly as hard as the bulkhead. No books. No glasses. It was going to be a long incarceration. He *hoped* it would be a long one, because escape, rescue, or release all seemed unlikely.

His head was still pounding, with white dots and black spots swooping across his field of view. He climbed onto the bunk, but had barely closed his eyes before the door ominously opened. Outside were two armoured and helmeted soldiers. One spoke, but in Mid-Tow. The translation came a moment later.

"You are to follow."

In a line, with Tempest at the front and Parker at the back, they walked through the ship. Harold counted nine doors before a left turning, ten before a right, and another three before he realised just how vast this vessel must be. They were taken to a room in which the red-robe was waiting, and which had a window that overlooked a much larger chamber currently full of white-clad prisoners. Harold counted thirty-four.

"Is Olawayo in there?" he asked.

"No," Parker said. "Some of them are missing. Where are the others?"

"Watch," the red-robe said. When she continued, her translation had an echo as it was broadcast into the room next door. "You are murderers, found guilty by a Valley military tribunal. You chose to leave that prison and come here. Now you are subject to imperial justice. You have been re-sentenced in accordance with imperial guidelines."

With that, some of the convicts roared, pushing and shoving at each other as they tried to reach the door. As some tried to open it, one convict tried to break the glass, but other than a dull thud, his blows had no effect. He called to the others, and two joined him. At first they punched and shouldered the glass in a panicked frenzy, but then began to hit it with synchronicity.

"What does that mean?" Awat asked. "What are imperial guidelines?"

"You're going to kill them, aren't you?" Tempest said.

The red-robe didn't reply. Harold was sure the floor was going to drop away, hurling the convicts into space. It didn't. In fact, nothing at all seemed to happen. Slowly, some of the convicts began to calm down. A few sat. The three beating against the window seemed to tire. The one in front of Harold dropped to a knee, wheezing. The man in the middle weakly slapped his hand against the window one last time before he collapsed to the floor. The last pressed his hands against the glass, making eye contact with Parker.

"Stop this," Awat said. "You have no right."

Of all those in the room, the man in front of Parker was now the last one standing. His mouth opened as he gasped for breath. His eyelids flickered. Finally, he fell down. Of the others, some still twitched, but most were already still.

The red-robe finally broke her silence. "That is justice."

Chapter 29 - Arrival

There were no more executions, at least none that Harold was witness to. There were questions for Awat about Nineveh, and for Parker about Lenham House. Serene and Tempest were questioned about Celeste, but only briefly. The red-robes already knew that the siblings didn't have the answers they sought, presumably thanks to the spy in the embassy. Harold wasn't questioned at all.

Imprisonment had been the defining feature of Harold's childhood. First, living in the cult, moving from ruin to squat, where his every move was controlled by his father. Then in the deprogramming centre where he'd spent more time alone than with the other inmates. He knew how to cope. The trick was to keep track of time, but not to focus on how much of it lay ahead.

Three times a day, meals were delivered. Once every other day, they were taken, individually, to a shower. After the first time, and with execution ever uppermost in his mind, it became routine. Every fifth day they were given fresh clothing.

They filled their days with talking and teaching. Parker knew what each of the convicts had done, and so they debated the rights and wrongs of their execution, but it was too grim a topic to dwell on for long. As long as their movements were so proscribed, escape was impossible, and was soon dropped from their list of conversational topics.

Serene taught them Mid-Tow, and Tempest taught them the exhausting training regime of an acolyte. When Parker and Awat were taken for questioning, they would report back what had been asked. Awat told them all she knew of Nineveh, and the Library of Alexandria, but they could only make increasingly outlandish guesses as to why the Voytay would want a sapiens archaeologist. Harold contributed every story he'd ever read, and so the days ticked by.

Forty days had elapsed when their routine finally changed. After breakfast, Awat began a lecture on the religious significance of the tunnel.

"Of the twelve minor prophets of Judaism, Jonah, or Yūnus, is the only one mentioned in the Quran," Awat said, but got no further as there was a sudden sensation of weightlessness that was almost instantly replaced with the feeling of the universe pushing down. As swiftly as it arrived, it was gone, leaving nothing but a memory.

"I think we're back in normal space," Tempest said.

The mix of trepidation and boredom Harold had been feeling before was instantly replaced with unbridled fear. Nervously, his heart rate rising with the tension, he watched the door.

When it opened, the red-robe was on the other side, along with the usual two guards.

"You are to follow," she said. She led them to an elevator, and ultimately to an airlock.

Heart-stopping ideas of being flushed into space were quelled when the guards joined them.

Now was their chance, Harold thought, and from how Tempest had stiffened into a fighting stance, they thought the same. But when they went through the door at the other end, they found themselves in a transporter already packed with a mix of the remaining sapiens convicts and armoured Voytay. There were ten seats back-to-back in the centre of the chamber, with ten more against each of the two walls. All but five were full. Harold was pushed into a seat between two towani soldiers. After struggling with the straps, one of the neighbouring guards leaned over and buckled him in.

Harold didn't entirely relax, but it seemed that the threat of mortal danger had receded from imminent back to looming. He squinted, trying to make out some of his new surroundings, and realised Nadia Afiz was sitting opposite.

"Hello, Harold," she said, and might even have smiled. "You should never have left your bookshop."

"We saw them execute the other convicts," Harold replied, and got a sharp rebuke from the towani on his left. He said no more.

246

The ship seemed to drop, and keep on dropping. Gravity vanished. From the sapiens ex-cons there came cries of surprise, and a few of fear. *Please, no one throw up*, Harold thought. The lack of gravity was soon replaced with pressure, as they entered atmosphere. The sensation of dropping grew worse. Were they in free-fall? As best he could tell, Afiz was enjoying it far less than him, but that frisson of schadenfreude was jolted out of him when the engines came on. The drop became a hover, and with a bump, a landing.

The door at the rear of the transporter clanged downward to form a ramp. A frigid wind swirled inward, spraying ice crystals about the cabin. The towani soldiers were already out of their seats, hustling the ex-convicts into the ice-storm. Harold pressed, squeezed, and tugged at his harness's lock, but it didn't budge. An armoured towani loomed over him.

"Blurred features never look intimidating," Harold said calmly. Always be calm. He'd learned that as a survival tactic around his father, and had it reinforced in the detention centre.

His harness was remotely unlocked. The towani stepped back, and Harold stood. The hand at his back wasn't gentle, and from the angry tone of Tempest's "Hey, watch it!", they were all getting the same treatment.

He clomped down the ramp, and into a freezing cloud of ice and snow. He could see nothing ahead, and when he looked behind, he made out Serene and Tempest, but not Parker and Awat. The ramp began to close.

"Where are you taking them?" Harold asked, raising his voice above the wind, but the towani didn't reply, merely shoved Harold onward. "Where are you taking us?" he said, before putting his head down and trudging into the storm.

They didn't walk for long, only fifty paces, even so, his fingers, nose, and eyelids were numb by the time they reached a door. It slid into the wall, and they were pushed inside, into a corridor that ran alongside a room with a transparent wall. Inside there, he could make out tables, but little else. At the end of the corridor was another door, this one much thicker, and which led to a long room filled with free-standing cages.

A red-robe was waiting for them. Unlike the one on the ship, she had four strips of cloth hanging between each shoulder and her waist. "You are of the prophet's clan?" she asked, and in English.

"Yes. All three of us," Serene said quickly.

"You should not be here," the red-robe said. "If you follow instructions, you may roam around this room. If you do not, you will be locked in one of these cages. Do you understand?"

"Yes," Harold said.

The red-robe, and the escort, left them alone.

Harold walked between the cages, scattered around the room as if they'd been dumped. They were free-standing, cube-shaped, about two metres long on each side, and made of metal that was covered in deep gouges and abrasions. On one side of the room was a large loading-bay door, wide and tall enough that a cage could easily be pushed through. After orientating himself, he realised the door led in the opposite direction to that of the door they had entered the building by. In the wall next to the loading-bay door was a window, about as long and tall as his arm. But outside was a blizzard of snow and ice.

"Those red-robes really freak me out," Serene said.

"She spoke English," Harold said.

"She's a spy, and the Voytay have known about Earth for just as long as the Valley," Serene said.

"Sure. But it takes time to learn a language. Years. That's how long they've been planning this."

"Okay, but what is that plan?" Serene said. "It must involve Alan and Awat, or they'd be here, too."

"I don't know what *their* plan is, but ours should be to escape," Tempest said. "If we fail, we'll only be locked up in the cages. This might be our last best chance before we're taken to the heart of their empire."

"I'm not sure," Serene said. "It does seem like they recognise bringing us along was a mistake. Maybe we can just wait for a prisoner swap or something."

"That's one vote each way," Tempest said. "Harold, you've got the deciding vote."

"Escape if we can. I really don't like that the red-robe can speak English. Something about it is really troubling."

"Escape it is," Serene said. "How?"

"The saucer," Tempest said.

"What saucer?" Harold asked.

"There were two drop-ships parked out there, plus one saucer, and what looked like a freighter," Tempest said. "A drop-ship is like the vessel we arrived on. It can't travel faster than light. The saucer's a Type-8. Those are ancient. The designs are pre-revolution. The ship probably isn't that old, and it got here, so it must work. It's pre-skip, but it has a jump engine."

"You can fly one?" Harold asked.

"Absolutely," Tempest said.

"You haven't flown one before," Serene said.

"Well, no. Not exactly, but the controls aren't all that different from newer models. It's our best option, because I don't recognise that type of freighter at all. We'll take off, and jump from inside the atmosphere to the first set of coordinates we can select. Then we'll jump again, this time to Valley-space."

"How do we get to the ship?" Harold asked.

"I'm not sure, but we've only got to get through two doors," Tempest said. They went to try the door. It didn't open.

"What if there are guards aboard the ship?" Serene asked.

"We'll need weapons," Tempest said.

"No," Serene said. "If we kill any of them, things could turn seriously bad for us. Let's try something non-lethal. The sapiens ex-convicts didn't look happy. When they were tried on Earth, their sentences were cut by a fifth to reflect a sapiens' shorter life span. Maybe they were told they've now got to serve a full century before they're released."

"It'd be hard labour, too," Tempest said. "Are you thinking they might be able to help?"

"Maybe, or tricked into creating a diversion. But we need Parker to tell us whether any of them can be trusted."

"I wonder where he's gone," Harold said. "For that matter, where are we? Any ideas?"

"It's an old hunting lodge," Tempest said. "That writing up there is directions on feeding the hounds. After the Red Plague wiped out the imperial family, and billions of others, there was a population boom that kept on booming. People began to fret about resource scarcity, because that's what doomed the second empire. A huge geo-engineering plan was put into place. It had been done before to improve the habitability of worlds, but their new idea was to create a thousand liveable planets."

"They really wanted a thousand new worlds?"

"It was an exaggeration, but it's an eye-catching number. The quick way, using technology, was expensive. Instead, they did it slowly, just nudging things along by blocking the sun, melting an ice cap, or seeding the oceans with algae, that kind of thing. It would take centuries, but it was cheap and there'd be an unlimited amount of room for this new empire run by the regents."

"How does that tie in with hunting?"

"As soon as a planet had a breathable atmosphere, but before it was properly habitable, the regents and their cronies would bring in wild animals to hunt. In theory, with scarce food resources, any animals that weren't killed would die off. Sometimes they did, but not always. No one wanted to leave even the most cramped apartment on Towan III for a cabin on a desert world filled with apex predators. That's when the regents began shipping dissidents and troublemakers, like Gramps, Greta, and Gunther, to worlds like this."

"So there could be settlers here?" Harold asked.

"Possibly," Tempest said.

"If there are, they'll be Voytay," Serene said. "They won't help us."

"Were these cages used to bring in the predators?" Harold asked, looking at the claw marks on the bars.

"No, those are for the hounds," Tempest said.

Harold returned to the loading-bay door. "Could we get this door open, and then go around the side?"

"Maybe," Serene said, coming over to join him. "I'd need to get this panel open first."

"Hunting lodges were always built as a hollow square," Tempest said. "The landing zone is in the middle, with the buildings around the outside."

Harold returned to the window. Outside, the storm seemed to be dying, but otherwise, all he could see was ice.

"Could there be any apex predators out there?"

"Could be," Tempest said.

"So we might get eaten before we freeze to death. I think we'll need a different plan."

Minutes ticked into hours, but as the shadows lengthened outside, Parker and Awat were brought into the room. With them came food.

"You're alive," Awat said.

"Glad to see the same is true of you," Serene said.

"We were brought straight here," Harold said. "What happened to you?"

"Ninety-three seconds flight away, there's a long tunnel that begins in a natural cave," Parker said.

"It's similar to Nineveh," Awat said. "The wall has the same style of inscription, using the same alphabet. I couldn't understand it, but the characters are similar to the towani's machine code."

"How old is the tunnel?" Serene asked.

"It's impossible to tell merely by looking," Awat said. "The tunnel in Nineveh was never properly excavated. The tiles were dated to just before the destruction of the city, but the tunnel itself could be much, much older."

"So maybe this tunnel was dug by a different chronicler, or by Mum's student before he went to Earth," Serene said.

"Perhaps," Awat said. "The tunnel has become home to a pack of vicious beasts that come out at night."

"Hounds," Tempest said. "They were bred for hunting, and bred to hate the light so they could be scared away by a lamp."

"The entrance was littered with bones," Parker said. "So I've got to ask, what were they eating?"

"They said we're going to spend five days here before we have to leave," Awat said. "I got the impression there are other tunnels, or places with those inscriptions, that they want us to look at."

"Don't they have archaeologists of their own?" Harold asked.

"They do, including that two-stripe red-robe from the warship. But they wanted our specific interpretation. Don't ask me why. Only one of them spoke with us. She had four strips of cloth hanging from her shoulders."

"We met her. She must be the boss," Serene said.

"She can speak English," Awat said.

"That's significant, right?" Harold said. "The other one used a translator, but this one doesn't only want to communicate, she wants to understand."

"We saw Olawayo, Afiz, and the other ex-cons," Parker said, with a measure of glee. "They've been put to work tidying up. It's not a fraction of what they deserve, but I'll take it as a start."

Harold walked back to the window by the door. Outside, the storm had ceased, and night had arrived. The ice field was illuminated by the reflected light from two small moons and a thousand stars. "Did you ever study constellations, Tempi— wait. What's that?"

Outside, the ice was moving. A clawed paw slammed into the other side of the window. Harold jumped back. Beyond the window, a sabre-toothed mouth greedily opened. The quadruped was as big as a lion, but with blue-white fur.

"That's a hound," Tempest said.

"Yeah, I don't think we can escape that way," Serene said.

Chapter 30 - Short Days, Shorter Nights

The new day arrived sooner than expected, and came with the delivery of new clothes, brought by an unexpected courier.

"You are to change," Olawayo said, dumping the clothing on the floor. Behind him, a guard stayed by the door, watching the confrontation with curiosity.

"How are you enjoying your new position?" Parker said.

"It's better than yours," Olawayo said.

The towani guard growled. It wasn't even a word. Olawayo turned his back and left.

"These aren't bad," Serene said, examining the clothes. "They're high-end, civilian, and designed for the weather, but it's definitely Voytay fashion. These epaulette things on the jacket's arms hark back to the official imperial uniform."

Awat picked up a white coat patterned with jagged pink lines. "It's not too dissimilar to what I might buy to go skiing. I suppose, since we have a similar physiology, with similar parts needing similar protection from harsh weather, it's not surprising our clothing is similar, too."

"Twenty-seven species have a very similar genetic code," Serene said as they sorted through the clothes to find those that would best fit. "There's a theory we're all descended from the same common ancestor. It could be that the ancestral towani weren't the first to be abducted from Earth."

"There is so much to study," Awat said.

"I wonder which of the Voytay donated these clothes," Tempest said.

Harold ended up with a long-sleeved T-shirt and jacket that were too big, trousers that were too tight, but boots that moulded themselves to his feet. The gloves and hat were too large, but that was true for everyone's.

"Not bad," he said, as he buckled a belt almost wide enough to be a cummerbund. "I was thinking, if Afiz and the other convicts were put to work tidying up, there can't have been many people here before we arrived."

"Probably none," Tempest said. "And you're meant to tuck the jacket into the trousers to keep out the draft. The belt goes over the top."

"They barely fit as it is. This will have to do. Anyway, the tunnel predates geo-engineering, so it was built before there was an atmosphere."

"Possibly, but that wouldn't bother a chronicler," Serene said.

"But the tunnel is close to this compound, so the regents would have known it was there. Maybe the presence of the tunnel is why they picked this planet to geo-engineer. Maybe it's why they picked the others. You said that the Valley doesn't want to look too closely at anything linked to the librarian's death, for fear it hints they're after such a weapon. The same must be true for the Voytay, so if they did want to undertake such research, who better than the creepy clerics that everyone thought had been disbanded?"

"It's a theory," Serene said.

"But not much use to us right now," Parker said.

An hour later, two red-armoured towani came to collect Parker and Awat.

"You three wait," the soldier said, speaking in Mid-Tow.

Harold lost track of time, but he was getting hungry when another pair of guards came to fetch them.

"Where are we going?" Serene asked, and then repeated the question in Mid-Tow, but neither answered.

They were led out to the landing pad at the centre of the compound, and taken aboard one of the drop-ships. After a very brief flight, they set down. When the ramp was lowered, Harold saw a cave in a snow-shrouded mountain. The cave's entrance was a jagged pyramid, at least a hundred metres wide, and nearly as tall.

Harold walked down the ramp, and nearly lost his footing on the ground outside. The surface was littered with icy stones. Some were flat and black. Others were jagged and grey-white. As he lowered his gaze, trying to mind his footing, he saw a yellow flower atop a broad green stalk. Perhaps it was a sign of spring, but he took it as a reminder that not all hope was lost. That flare of optimism was doused by the realisation that the jagged grey-white stones were actually crushed and split bones.

A camp had been established at the tunnel mouth, around a trio of portable heaters. Three towani red-robes stood in front of an array of screens displaying what was probably a drones-eye view of the tunnel. A fourth was directing them, pointing at sections of particular interest. Behind them were four cages, two of which contained spare equipment. Next to them, and not quite close enough to enjoy the heater's warmth, Olawayo and two other ex-convicts shivered as they waited for an order to fetch and carry.

"Bring them lights," the red-robe said.

With indignation and anger in every step, Olawayo collected three small hand lamps from one of the cages and brought them over to Harold, Tempest, and Serene.

"Back to your place," the red-robe said. Olawayo stiffened, but said nothing. With a shake of his head, he returned to his station next to the other two escaped convicts.

"Come and see what we have found," the four-stripe red-robe said equably.

Five drones preceded them into the cave, shining lights towards the beginning of the tunnel. The red-robe and her two guards had lights on their armour, but they only made it easier to see the deep shadows.

The red-robe stopped a few metres into the tunnel. "Your adopted grandmother is one of the chroniclers," she said.

"Yep, and she'd be nearly as miffed at you calling her our grandmother as she will be at you keeping us hostage," Serene said.

"I know, and I apologise. Your abduction was not part of the plan. Yet you are here now, so we must make the best of the situation."

"Where did you learn English?" Tempest asked.

"Long ago," the red-robe said. "Is there anything about the tunnel you can share?"

"Not really."

"Take a look. Take your time. But don't stray far from the light. The grall-tors have made a den of this tunnel."

"Grall-tors?" Harold asked.

"The hounds," Serene said. "If you want to look on the bright side, it means there's nothing bigger living down here."

"Ah, optimism worthy of the Holy Nowan," the red-robe said, and headed back up the tunnel. Her two guards followed.

Harold walked to the side of the tunnel, shining his light on the frozen stone. A frosty sheen was spreading across the surface, but peering close, he could make out a neat line of characters. He rubbed the ice away with his gloved hand. Despite the tunnel's curve, the lines of writing were ruler straight. Most of the characters were no bigger than his thumbnail, but occasionally there was a larger one, about the length of his thumb. Those taller characters almost touched the bottom of the line above. These appeared as often in the middle or end of a word as at the beginning, assuming that the narrow gaps between some clusters of characters did denote a different word.

"Some of these letters do look like machine code," Serene said. "They're more angular, but I suppose that's because they're a carving. But there are others, like that backward 'r', I've never seen before."

"Does it continue like this all the way along the ceiling and down to the other side?" Harold asked.

"Row upon row," Serene said.

Harold leaned forward again, but the characters were already being obscured by the returning frost. "How cold do you think it gets at night?"

"It's freezing now, so I'd say a lot lower," Serene said.

"Too cold for someone to stand outside on guard?" Harold asked.

"Probably, but any guard would be ripped apart by the hounds long before you froze."

"If we can open that loading-bay door, and then climb up to the roof, we can run across the rooftop until we're close to the ship. If we can smash the lights, the hounds could get into the cage-room. They'll make enough noise to be a diversion while we get aboard the ship."

"I don't think we should escape. You heard what the red-robe said. She apologised. I don't think she'll harm us."

"The red-robes are religious zealots. Trust me, we're not safe, because we're not part of the plan. Nor were the convicts she executed. I don't want the same fate for me."

"Trying to escape might buy us that fate. I'll speak with Tempi, but if we're going to be here another four days, we might have time to develop a better plan."

Harold headed further down the tunnel, stumbling on bone and ice until he reached Awat and Parker. He was holding a heat-lamp close to the wall, melting the ice. Using what looked a lot like a tablet and stylus, Awat was annotating a 3D rendering of that section of wall, projected just above the screen.

"They said they were going to bring you here," Parker said. "Everything okay?"

"I have an idea how we can escape," Harold said. Keeping his voice low, he explained his idea.

"No," Parker said. "I say we do nothing to antagonise them."

"It's all or none of us," Harold said.

"Yes," Parker said. "And in this group, if they want to make an example of one of us, it'll be either you or me."

"I'm okay with that," Harold said.

"I'm not. On either account," Parker said. "This is what I was fighting against, or I thought I was. People like you and me, and Awat, even those two kids, we get caught up in the mad schemes of

257

people like O'Malley and Celeste, or Saddam, or even the ambassador. Now we're caught up in this cleric's shot at glory."

"Yes, and at some point, we'll be of no use at all. By then, it'll be too late to escape," Harold said.

"He's right," Awat said. "Our captor is a fanatic. We don't know why we're here, or what our value is, but it won't be infinite." She pointed at the wall, and at one of the upper-case characters. "In the towani machine code, a capital letter is used like a programming command. On the writing from the tunnel under Nineveh, Abi and I hypothesised that the capital letters were emphasis, or some other form of punctuation. In that tunnel, there were too few places where the writing was visible to draw a firm conclusion. With this tunnel, there's nearly too much. I'm not sure of the towani units of measurement, but it stretches for at least a kilometre before you reach a section those hounds use as a den. Beyond, it is flooded, and frozen over. On a previous visit, they used drones to record the writing on these walls. They could have shown us the recording when we were on the ship, or even while we were still on Earth. Instead, they brought us all the way here, at great risk and cost of life. That troubles me."

"Me, too," Harold said. "Do you have any idea what the writing means?"

"No. Most of the characters are similar to machine code, though not identical and there are at least five additional letters. It's a related language. The towani machine code had millennia to evolve before the first surviving written record, but it must have originated on the very earliest of spaceships, and probably from whatever language their captors used. This could be that proto-language, or it could be another descendant language, having evolved differently from that used by the towani. To translate it, we'll need a bridging language."

"Like with how the Rosetta Stone was used to translate hieroglyphs?" Harold said.

"Exactly."

"We think they've got one," Parker said. "They're only interested in the section of tunnel from the entrance to down there where those two drones are. That must be a sign they think they've found something."

Harold looked at the wall where the creeping ice was already beginning to return. "When you worked with Abi tol Demener, didn't you say you wrote a few papers that were published in the Valley?"

"I was a co-author of three," Awat said. "It was a kindness on Abi's part rather than a reflection of how much I contributed, but that could have been why these clerics decided I might be of use. Those papers were published before Olawayo went to work with Alan. If this tunnel was discovered during the days of the regents, then something about the discovery in Iraq made them certain they were close to solving this mystery."

"Whether they do or not, they've gone to a lot of trouble to keep us alive, Harold," Parker said. "All five of us, so no more talk of escape. Not unless our situation changes."

"Well, it was all of us or none of us," Harold said. "So I guess that decides it."

He peered again at the wall, but as fascinating as it was, he could make no sense of it, so he went back outside. Olawayo and the two ex-convicts were taking some equipment back to the drop-ship, while bringing different equipment off.

The red-robe had joined her subordinates by the screens, and seemed to be intently focused on one line of writing. On a closed crate, and inside a transparent box, was the brick-like flight recorder.

"Excuse me, can I ask a question?" Harold asked.

"It is how we seek enlightenment," the red-robe replied.

"If the tunnel was dug by a chronicler, could the writing have been created by them, too?"

"I believe it was, but what does it say?"

"I've never seen anything like it," Harold said. "It's hard to see anything without my glasses. I don't suppose I could have them back."

"No."

"Then can I help the convicts with the fetching and carrying?"

"No, that is their punishment. You want to work?" she added, approvingly. "That is good. And there is a task you must perform for me, but not yet. No, you are too valuable to merely be a porter."

Harold, nodded, smiled, and walked over to the heater furthest from the towani. The red-robe's words had sounded polite, but there was an ominous undertone he remembered from his childhood. She had the civility of the zealot who has yet to attempt to convert an unbeliever. Perhaps that was what they had in store next. Hoping Serene and Parker were right, he breathed deep, trying to lose himself in the moment. He was standing on an alien world. How many people could say they'd ever done that? It was just a pity that he was standing atop so many broken bones.

The day was as short as the night. As the dim sun slunk towards the horizon, Olawayo and the other two convicts were ordered to begin packing the gear into the cage. Tempest, Serene, Awat, and Parker returned from the cave's frigid depths.

"Have you learned anything new?" the red-robe asked.

"I'm beginning to see a pattern," Awat said. "I'll need more time, but I think I can decode it."

"You will have half a day tomorrow before we must depart," the red-robe said. "The abduction of these children has caused considerable difficulties. But you will have time to examine the recordings while aboard the ship."

"Does that mean Mum's blown up a few Voytay planets?" Serene asked.

"That would be in keeping with her kind," the red-robe said. "Your lamps, please."

They handed them over.

"Did either of you recognise anything familiar?" the red-robe asked, addressing Serene and Tempest.

"Nothing," Tempest said.

"Do you swear it in the Holy Nowan's name? I know you are a believer."

Tempest hesitated, but only briefly. "I so swear."

"It is further confirmation of my theory. When combined with the rumours and legends gathered by my order for centuries, it confirms what we long suspected. The writing was invented by the chronicler you know as the Librarian of Alexandria while he was an exile on this barren world. He then took it to Earth."

"How do you know he was exiled?" Serene said.

"As I say, some in my order have been conducting this research for long before the regents' fall."

"Was Clee one of them?" Awat asked.

"No. She was merely a traitor and heretic. You and your husband should return to the ship. I wish to speak to the children alone."

"Why?" Parker asked.

The red-robe raised a hand. Two of the towani guards aimed their weapons at Awat and Parker.

"It's fine," Serene said.

The couple were led away.

"Step inside the cage," the red-robe said.

"Why?" Tempest asked.

"The sun will set soon," the red-robe said. "It would be wise if we were not standing here when the hounds emerge."

"I always hate it when towani call us children," Serene said, but with no alternative, she, like Harold and Tempest, followed the zealot's instruction.

As soon as they were inside the cage, the door was closed behind them.

"Your abduction was a mistake, and a crime," the red-robe said. Her two remaining guards each raised their rifles and fired a shot, one each, killing the two escaped convicts. As their bodies crumpled to the ground, Olawayo spun around. But neither fight, nor flight, was an option as the guards levelled their rifles at him.

"You said they would be the foundation of my new army," Olawayo said.

"It is a poor general who thinks a murderer is the same as a soldier," the red-robe said. "Tell them who you are."

261

Olawayo clenched his fists, his head darting this way and that. "Why?"

"Why keep it a secret? Of what are you afraid?"

With apparent reluctance, Olawayo turned to the three in the cage. "I arranged for your birth," he said. "All three of you."

"Ours?" Serene asked.

"You sold babies to the Voytay? Why?" Tempest asked, slightly quicker on the uptake.

"To live longer," Olawayo said. "That was our deal. I would get to live as long as a—" But whatever else he might have said was lost to eternity as the red-robe fired. The bolt from the handgun shattered his skull, and he fell next to his two former prison-mates, spilling blood onto the ice-flecked stones.

"We are not monsters," the red-robe said. "We asked for orphans. We didn't ask that they be created."

"You wanted to buy sapiens babies? Why?" Serene asked.

"We wished to study the differences, and the similarities. The Valley's embargo on visiting the planet was, and is, absurd. There is so much to be learned."

"You mean experiments?" Harold asked.

"You would have felt no pain," the red-robe said.

"Experimenting on children is evil," Tempest said. "How is it any different to what the demons did to the enslaved ancestors?"

"The red-robes were formed to commit necessary sins so that other souls could remain pure. It is our sacred burden, but your people are no different. Do you not have many cultures living under the doctrine of the greater good?"

"What kind of experiments?" Harold asked.

"Earth is our homeworld, too," the red-robe said. "Olawayo should have been punished for his failure twenty years ago, but he was still of use to us. His actions during the escape, bringing along those killers, showed what I should have realised long ago. His soul could not be redeemed. Now he is dead. You have had your revenge. Take comfort in that."

"I'd have liked to take it more personally," Tempest said.

262

"But then your spirit would have been stained with sin." The cleric raised their gun again. This time, it was aimed at her bodyguards. They didn't raise their weapons, but merely closed their eyes. She spoke briefly in Mid-Tow, and then fired, killing them both.

"Why did you do that?" Harold asked.

"Night will come soon. The hounds will emerge. They will feast on the corpses. Depending on how long it is before you're found, there may be little evidence left, but it will appear as if there was a fight. You were left trapped in the cage where you froze to death. You will be safe from the beasts."

"But you're still killing us?" Serene said.

"Letting you die. Yes."

"But that's mad," Serene said. "It'll mean war. If Celeste joins in, the Voytay will be wiped out."

"The war is almost upon us. Because of that man's rash actions, it cannot be avoided. But the chroniclers are not immortal. They threaten, they cajole, but no one living has seen them perform their mythical acts of wrath. Perhaps she will destroy a planet or two, but the Voytay will retaliate. If they cannot destroy her, the secrets we have almost unwrapped will."

"Is that what this is about? You want to kill Mum?" Tempest asked.

"We want to rid the galaxy of the chroniclers. They could have revealed the location of Earth to the empire centuries ago. Instead, they hid the truth from us. The one you call the librarian was exiled from his kind for suggesting they cease meddling in the affairs of other sentient species. They created the demons who abducted our ancestors."

"You can't possibly think that," Tempest said. "It would invalidate all your beliefs."

"What is it on Earth you call the one who creates demons, the Devil, yes? That is the truth of who they are. I am certain the tunnel's inscription is a confession, and the secret to their destruction. Once they are gone we will finally be able to bring peace to the galaxy by reuniting the old empire. For that, there must be real peace, which can only be achieved after a real victory in war. Your mother destroying an entire planet will certainly assist in our goal."

"I don't get it. You'll lose," Serene said.

"No matter which side is victorious, we shall win. As it was prophesied, the discovery of the ancestral homeworld will end the war. What we have now is not an end, but a pause. No, one side or the other must triumph so that prophecy is fulfilled."

"You're not Voytay, are you?" Harold said.

"We are the holders of the light, the keepers of tradition. After the civil war, after the betrayal by the one known as Clee, we went into hiding. We didn't disappear. Take comfort that our return will be aided by your deaths."

She turned around and trudged off towards her ship.

Chapter 31 - The Best Teeth for Fishing

"Well, this is *blah*," Serene said. "Does anyone have anything we can write with? I want to leave a note so Mum knows exactly who to hunt down."

"Tell her yourself, because we're not going to die here," Tempest said.

"And how exactly are we going to prevent it?"

Tempest pushed at the cage's door. "It's stuck fast."

"It was designed to hold hounds," Harold said. In the distance, the drop-ship took off. The sound of its engines was soon lost to hearing. But nearer, from the cave, came the sound of claws on frozen stone.

"Do you think she was telling the truth about Mum?" Tempest asked.

"I doubt it. They haven't decoded the tunnel," Serene said. "That's why we've got to get out of here." She bent down, stretching her arm between the tunnel's bars, trying to reach Olawayo's corpse. "Urgh, it's too far away."

"What do you want it for?" Harold asked, even as he tested the bars on the roof.

"Maybe he's got a gun on him."

"If he had a gun, he'd have drawn it," Tempest said. "Maybe we can pick the lock. The mechanism is mechanical."

"What with?" Harold said. "The floor's been swept clean. Could we melt some of this ice, and put the water inside the lock? When it re-freezes, it might break the mechanism."

Tempest stretched their hand through the bars, reaching around the thick metal plate surrounding the lock. "It's out of reach. I can't even see it. I think that means we can't pick it, either."

"Harold, pass me your belt," Serene said. "You, too, Tempi."

"Why?" Harold asked.

"To make a lasso to pull Olawayo's body closer. We'll use his clothes to make a longer lasso, and use that to hook one of those guards' guns."

"Tell me one time you've ever lassoed anything in your life," Tempest said. "Anyway, my belt's sewn into my clothing."

"Then give me your trousers," Serene said.

"I'll get hypothermia," Tempest said.

"How about fishing," Harold said. He bent down and reached out, grabbing some of the gnawed bones littering the ground on which the cages had been placed. He held out the fragments. "Which is the sharpest? We'll use it as a hook."

"I think I can do one better," Tempest said, reaching out and picking up a broken piece of skull from which jutted a razor-sharp tooth.

"Perfect," Serene said as Harold pulled off his belt. "But I don't think this is going to be long enough." Her gloved hands fumbled as she tried to knot the belt to the bone, so she pulled them off. "Hold these. Oh, it's freezing!"

"And you wanted me to take off my trousers," Tempest said.

"Not now," she said. As she attempted to tie a knot, the tooth stabbed through the belt's thick fabric, easily cutting through the cloth. "Well, that worked."

A low growl came from the cave, rising in volume and pitch into a howl.

"I think you should hurry," Harold said.

Serene threaded the belt through the bars, and stretched out her arm. She made a tentative flick. The tooth stabbed into the ice a hand's width short of Olawayo's boot. "Almost," she said, shifting position before tugging on the belt. Instead of coming free, the fabric around the tooth tore, ripping like paper before the belt came free, leaving the tooth embedded in the ground. Her shoulders sagged with disappointment as she stood up. "Can you see any other teeth lying around?"

"Not within reach," Tempest said.

"Here," Serene said, and handed Harold his belt back. "Any other ideas?"

"If the cages were designed to stop the hounds from getting out, why don't we try pulling on the door," Harold said. They each took grip of a bar, and leaned back, putting their entire weight on the metal, but it did nothing. After a minute, with the cold seeping through his gloves, Harold let go. The others followed suit.

"How long do we have until we freeze?" Serene asked.

"Depends how cold it gets, and how quickly," Harold said. "Most of the books I've read about surviving in Arctic conditions generally have a happy ending, so the hero usually finds a forgotten cabin to shelter in. I'd guess at a few hours, but the red-robe seemed to think we'd freeze to death by morning, and she's coming back to check."

"I refuse to die here," Tempest said.

"I don't think we're going to get a say," Harold said.

"Well, come on, don't either of you have any ideas?" Serene asked.

"We could pray," Tempest said. "Wait, look over there."

The setting sun glinted off a small object rising from the mountainside, just above the cave entrance.

"Is that a drone?" Tempest said.

"It's not just a drone," Serene said as the black and blue dome came to a hovering halt on the other side of the cage. "It's Nemain!"

"You're kidding," Harold said. "Can you see your dad, or Greta, or Celeste, or anyone?"

"No," Tempest said, looking around.

"Nemain, where's the rest of the rescue party?" Serene asked.

The drone bobbed from side to side.

"Is that a no? Do you mean to say you're here alone?" Serene asked.

The drone bobbed up and down.

"I think that's a yes," Serene said.

"How did you get here?" Tempest asked.

The drone flew in a circle.

"Did you come here on the same ship as us?" Tempest asked.

Nemain bobbed up and down.

"Well, why didn't you help before? Why wait until now?" Serene asked.

The drone bobbed from side to side.

"No? No what? What does that mean," Serene said.

The other two drones detached themselves from the mountain and came to hover sheepishly next to their sister.

"Well, don't just float there. Open the cage," Serene said.

Nemain landed on the lock. The door began to vibrate before the stressed metal groaned under this unexpected strain. The entire cage juddered forward before, with a bang, the door swung outwards. The drone flew towards Serene's arm.

"Don't you dare! I'm furious at you. Anyway, I don't have the docking station."

Tempest made a beeline for the dead towani soldiers, removing their holstered handguns. "Harold, do you want a rifle or a handgun?"

"Without my glasses, it's fifty-fifty I'd be able to hit the ground."

Tempest unslung a longer-barrelled weapon from the dead fanatic's back. "You should take this, then. It's a bit like a grenade launcher."

"Oh. Thanks. That's much safer," Harold said weakly. "Will this work without my glasses?"

"Oh, definitely. These are old weapons. They don't have advanced targeting systems, or modern safety devices."

"It gets better and better," Harold said.

Tempest turned to the drones. "Why didn't you help us before?"

The sisters danced back and forth in a complex, but incomprehensible, pattern.

"They do that when they don't want to answer," Serene said. She turned to the drones. "Sisters, do you have a plan to get us out of here?"

They bobbed from side to side, almost in unison.

"I'm pretty sure that's a no," Serene said.

"Do you know of any settlement on this rock?" Harold asked.

Again, the sisters bobbed from side to side.

From inside the tunnel came another spine-chilling howl. Harold raised the grenade launcher, aiming the barrel towards the forbidding dark void.

"Don't waste a round," Tempest said. "There's no point staying here. Even if we set up one of those heaters inside that cage, the red-robes will be back at dawn. Either we hunt for another settlement, or we return to the compound, and steal a ship."

"If there was anyone nearby who might be inclined to help us, the red-robes wouldn't have left us out here," Serene said. "We should use Harry's plan, see if we can take out the lights, and use the hounds to distract the red-robes while we take the ship. Besides, we've got to rescue Alan and Awat."

"We can try," Tempest said, "but the priority has to be getting in contact with the Valley before the war begins."

"Speaking of which, can your drones open up the cage with all the screens?" Harold asked.

"What for?" Serene asked.

"Aren't they attached to a computer or something? We want the hard-drive, with all their research. The only way to disprove the theory about your mum and her student being responsible for the ancestral towani's abduction is to get the data independently translated by the Valley, and the Voytay, too. We just better hope the red-robe is wrong."

"Ladies, you heard him," Serene said.

The drones hovered close together, almost as if they were huddled in conference before Nemain wearily bobbed over to the cage. She settled on the lock plate. The metal began to creak, then snapped with a loud crack. From the cave came a chorus of howls.

"Hurry, sis."

"Just watch the cave," she said, and hurried into the cage.

The blurry darkness was growing thicker as the sun's inexorable decline continued. They had minutes, if that, and at least two of them went by before Serene declared, "Got it. Let's go. Sisters,

269

you're to fly us close to the compound. We'll take out the lights, rescue Awat and Alan, and then steal the ship."

The three drones flew low, one towards each of them.

"Wait, there's one last thing," Tempest said. They crossed to Olawayo's corpse. "Does anyone see any of those teeth?"

"What for?" Serene asked.

"I want to cut off a bit of cloth with his blood on it."

"Why?"

"You heard what the red-robe said, he didn't want us *made*. I want a sample of his DNA."

"No, you don't," Serene said. "I know *I* don't. Besides, I'm sure a DNA sample was taken when he was recruited to the UNCA. Dad would have checked."

Tempest bent down and picked up a razor-sharp tooth. With that, they cut away a short piece of Olawayo's blood-stained collar. "I need to know," they said, putting the rag into their pocket.

"We can discuss it later," Harold said. "The shadows inside the cave are moving."

"Okay, sisters, time to redeem yourselves. Brace yourselves, peeps, this is going to be cold."

A drone settled on Harold's belt. As the first of the ravenous hounds padded out of the tunnel, claws clicking on the frozen stones, all three of them were flung into the air.

An icy wind smashed into Harold's face, forcing his eyes closed as he was hurled through the air. When his feet touched ice, he skittered and slid, and slammed into a curving stalagmite, at least three metres tall. As he blinked the ice from his eyebrows, he saw a dozen more, with a dozen others opposite, curving towards him. "Is this a rib cage?" he asked, stepping back.

"It must be from whatever the hounds were brought here to hunt."

"Do you know what kind of animal it is?" Harold asked.

"No, so let's get out of here before we find out," Tempest said.

Two curving leaps later, they landed on a frozen ridge, beyond which they could see the compound. The sun had lost the battle with

270

the darkness, but the building was brightly lit. Searchlights slowly roamed left and right from each corner, with even more shining inward, illuminating the landing zone.

Harold shoved his hands under his armpits in the vain hope they might defrost.

"Do you see the dark spot in the middle of the wall?" Serene said. "I think that's the cage room."

"The lights will still be a problem," Tempest said.

Just as Harold was wondering whether the compound might have motion sensors, two of the searchlights swung their beams towards the ridge.

"Down here," Tempest said, and skidded down the frozen slope's far side. Kicking up a spray of ice crystals, Harold and Serene followed, landing in a drift of snow covering a thin layer of gnawed bones.

"We must have set off a motion sensor," Serene said.

"It's not us!" Tempest said as a hound bounded up the other side of the ridge. "Sisters, move us away."

This last flight was less a jump, and far more a horizontal fling, ending at an outcrop of snow-flecked grey stone, some fifty metres from the compound.

Tempest pulled the slung rifle around, aiming it back the way they'd come. "Clear. We should have brought some lights with us."

"Definitely not, look," Serene said.

A drop-ship rose from inside the compound, and began flying slowly towards the ridge where they'd just been standing. Lights from beneath the cockpit briefly illuminated a dozen hounds before they scattered into the darkness. The drop-ship slowly continued on, heading in the direction of the cave.

"I think it's going to check we're actually dead," Serene said.

"Another ship has just taken off!" Tempest said. "It's heading for the ridge, too."

"And the searchlights are all aimed away from the loading-bay. There must be another pack of hounds out here. It really is now or never."

271

Skidding and slipping on the ice, they ran across the frozen ground through the narrow cone of shadows the searchlights didn't reach. Even though his concentration was focused on not falling over, he couldn't ignore the growing number of howls from nearby. There were dozens, coming from every direction, as if many different packs were now heading towards them.

Tempest reached the loading-bay doors first, and knocked on the transparent window. "I can see them. They're both there. They've seen me. How do we get inside?"

Harold turned around, his back to the wall, aiming the grenade launcher into the darkness.

"The locking mechanism should be behind this panel, but it's frozen solid," Serene said.

"I could shoot it," Harold said.

"No," Tempest said. "From the direction of those searchlight beams, they haven't noticed us yet."

Again, it was Nemain who came to their aid, landing on the panel. With a groan of metal, then a snap, the cover fell off. Inside, there wasn't a lock, only three wide pipes.

"The wires must be hidden inside the pipes," Serene said.

The drone attached itself to the centre-most pipe. A rattle of stressed metal was followed by a brief spark. The door didn't open, but the lights went out.

"Brilliant! Now open the door," Serene said.

Nemain seemed to hesitate.

Distant shouts of consternation came from within the compound, but any enjoyment they could take from their enemy's fear was swiftly extinguished by a hungry growl from the darkness behind them.

"Nemain, what are you waiting for?" Serene asked.

"How does it do that?" Harold asked as the sound of creaking metal returned.

"I think it's nanobots and magnets, though that's my answer to most things about them I don't understand."

The door finally slid sideways, jamming halfway.

"You're alive!" Awat said and seemed genuinely happy.

Parker looked puzzled. "What happened to you?"

"They left us to freeze to death. We escaped. The rest of the explanation can wait. We're going to escape now. The sisters will fly us to the roof. From there, we'll go to the saucer."

"Hound!" Tempest said, and fired into the shadows.

"They're here!" Awat said as their prison's inner door opened.

"Serene, give me that gun!" Parker said.

Harold could only make out a red blur in the far corner of the room, but it was a clear enough target for an explosive. He fired. The explosion knocked him and Awat off their feet.

"You could have warned us you were going to do that," Serene said, pulling him upwards.

"Sorry," Harold said. Before he could check how much damage had been done, he felt pressure at his waist, and he was hurled upwards. Tempest and Serene came next.

"Go get Awat and Alan!" Serene said. With what might almost be called reluctance, two of the sisters did.

From inside the compound came shouts of confusion and yelled orders. Some of the shouting was in English, but Harold ignored it as he followed Tempest and Serene across the rooftop to take shelter behind a now-dark searchlight. Awat and Parker landed nearby.

"The drop-ship is heading back," Tempest said, pulling the two handguns from his pockets and handing them to Awat and Parker. "Press the button to fire."

As she reached out to take one, the roof shook from the reverberation of a trio of small explosions from inside the building, and Awat nearly dropped the gun.

"What are they shooting at?" Awat asked.

"Hounds, I hope," Serene said. "I think that grenade took out the inner door."

"Now, we need to get to the ship."

No sooner had they said it than Harold, Serene, and Tempest were launched into the air, landing hard on the frozen landing ground just outside the flying saucer.

"Nemain, get it open," Serene said. "Macha, Badb, get Awat and Alan. Go on, what are you waiting for? go!"

Harold turned to face the corner from where the gunfire was coming. No one seemed to have noticed them yet, but the drop-ship had returned and was now shining its lights on the roof above the cage-room.

As Awat and Alan set down, a light from the ship tracked across the compound, settling on the five of them. Acting on instinct, Harold fired, and completely missed. The explosive round detonated on the interior wall of the compound, near the entrance to the cage-room. Screams rose with the smoke, while another light from the drop-ship joined the first, spearing down to illuminate the fugitives.

"Give me that," Parker said, and took the grenade launcher from Harold. His first shot was wide, and detonated outside. The second hit the drop-ship. The craft veered away.

"You shot it down!" Awat said.

"No, it's just getting out of range," Parker said.

"We're in," Tempest said as the ramp began to descend

"Cover us while we get the ship operational," Serene said.

Parker handed Harold his handgun. "Awat, cover the right, Harold the left," he said, before firing a grenade into the darkness.

Harold fired blindly into the chaos of lights, shadows, and screams. Even if he'd been able to see properly, it would still have been a scene of utter confusion. A bolt ricocheted off the saucer, but most of the fighting appeared to be focused inside the building, near the cage room.

A shout of "No, please!" in English came from inside the smoking building, but was then drowned out by a scream.

Parker fired again at the drop-ship, which moved further away.

"I'm out!" Parker said as he turned around. "Awat! Behind you!"

Harold spun again. A hound had found its way inside, and was charging at Awat. Parker dived, pushing his wife out of the beast's path. The hound's front claws ripped through Parker's coat, shredding skin and muscle, before its head bucked down and then up, tossing Parker aside.

Harold screamed, levelled the gun, and fired over and over again. Each shot caused the beast to stagger, but it didn't fall. Lights came on from inside the saucer, and the hound slunk back into the darkness.

"Alan? Alan!" Awat bent over her husband. "Oh, Alan."

"Is he dead?" Harold said.

"Not yet," Awat said.

"We're ready to—" Serene began from the top of the ramp. "What happened?"

"Can we fly?" Harold asked.

"We can. Bring him inside."

Between the three of them, they carried the nearly dead weight up into the ship.

"Is there a medical bay?" Awat asked. The ship began to rise even as the door closed.

This might be an old design of ship, but some features hadn't changed. Harold hauled the stabiliser from its alcove.

"How does this work?" he asked, speaking to himself. Serene reached over and pressed the power button. She pressed another, and the lid slid off and under Parker, before retracting, dragging him into the box.

"Put the mask over his mouth," Serene said. "And take his shoes off. And… oh, this will have to do." She pressed another button, and the lid seemed to melt, flowing up and over Parker until he was utterly shrouded in dull grey.

"What's happening? Will he live?" Awat asked.

"Probably," Serene said. "We've done as much as we can for now. We'll do more after we're safe." She pushed the stretcher against the wall where it locked into place. "We need to go to the control room."

"I'm not leaving him," Awat said.

Serene opened a jump seat. "Sit down, and strap in. We'll come for you when it's safe."

Harold followed Serene to the control room where Tempest, now wearing a blue-patterned helmet, was sitting in the pilot's seat.

"You took your time," they said.

"Alan's injured. It's serious," Serene said, picking up another helmet. "We had to put him in a stabiliser. Here, Harold, put this on." She held out the helmet.

"What's happening?" Harold said. The helmet was tight at the sides, but loose at the front. The discomfort was forgotten as the visor automatically corrected for his prescription, and Serene's face changed from an indistinct blur to frantic worry.

"I want you in that seat behind me, Harry," Tempest said. "You'll run the firing controls. Do you remember how?"

"Serene should do it. I only did the VR thing once," Harold said.

"I've got to fix the navigation system," she said. "It's worse than fried. It's like it's not even there. Do you see the screen in front of you? The dots are ships."

"How do I know which are hostile?"

"They're *all* hostile," she said. "Select a target by touching it. Fire with this button, here on the left. Anything moving really fast is a missile, so try to hit those. I'm going to the engine room to see if I can initiate a jump from there." She hurried from the control room, leaving Harold frantically trying to remember the VR tutorial they'd played as a game a few days after first contact. With the memory of the aerial battle above Oxfordshire still raw, it had been too real for him to want to play it more than once.

"Why haven't we left the atmosphere?" he asked, watching the dots representing the two drop-ships pursuing them, but from a distance.

"Without a navigation system, we can't jump unless we manually input our coordinates," Tempest said. "I'm keeping us inside the atmosphere in the hope we might see a settlement, but I'm not picking up any signals."

"The drop-ships are keeping their distance," Harold said.

"They're not armed," Tempest said.

"Ah. Cool. We actually escaped. I didn't think we would." The frenzied panic of the battle began to dissipate. "Thinking back, they didn't really try to stop us. The drop-ships are pulling back. Is there anything ahead?"

"Not yet. It's still just ice down there. We'll go higher and leave the atmosphere, and then we can more quickly scan the surface of the planet."

The pressure of acceleration was soon replaced with weightlessness.

"Doesn't this ship have artificial gravity?" Harold asked.

"That system is recharged as a by-product of the jump drive," Tempest said. "I think that means they haven't used the engines in a while. They must have brought the ship here in the hold of something bigger."

"Do we even know if the jump engine will work?"

"Honestly, no," Tempest said.

"Sometimes it's okay not to be honest. Oh. I'm picking up something."

Harold pressed the dot. The image changed, becoming a three-dimensional rendering of a ship. The display brought up a summary, all in Mid-Tow. Most of the words were too technical for his meagre vocabulary, but he recognised the words for length and mass, and this ship was huge.

"We've got company. Do you know what it is?"

"It looks like an old imperial battleship," Tempest said. "That must be the vessel that brought us to the planet. It must have been in orbit all this time."

"Do I fire?"

"Our weapons wouldn't do any damage. Not against that. I'm going to steer us away."

Even as their craft began to accelerate, smaller objects began to detach themselves from the battleship. "They've fired missiles."

"No. Those are fighters, and they'll fire the missiles. When they do, you try to hit them, and I'll try to dodge."

"Can we outrace them?"

"Do you want me to be honest?" Tempest said. "This is a really old ship. They've got new fighters."

"This is why they let us take the ship," Harold said. "They must have known we couldn't jump. They'll board us, so they can take us alive, and make sure we freeze to death down on that planet."

"Or maybe they do need Awat for the next part of their plan," Tempest said. "Watch for missiles. I'll... I'll try to think of something."

The basic controls were barely more complicated than point and click, but he was under no illusion that the approaching fighters would be able to neutralise his weapons.

"C'mon, sis," Tempest said. "Hey! What are you—?"

Before Harold could ask what was happening, the ship jumped.

"Serene did it!" Harold said, raising his hands in triumph. As gravity returned, his arms sank back down.

"It wasn't Serene," Tempest said. "It was one of her drones."

Chapter 32 - Monochrome Meals and Missing Medicine

When Serene entered the control room, she found Harold and Tempest watching the drone, now lying on the floor, its carapace fluttering.

"How did you activate the jump engines?" Serene asked.

"It wasn't me," Tempest said. "It was Nemain. She latched herself onto the control panel, and entered some coordinates."

"We'd have died if she hadn't," Harold said. "The warship that brought us to that ice planet was still in orbit. They'd launched fighters."

"Then I'll do a quick woo-hoo to celebrate not being turned into debris, but where are we heading?"

"Don't know," Tempest said. "The navigation interface is still down."

"Nemain, do you know where we're going?" Serene asked.

The drone's carapace rippled weakly, its colour shimmering from black to blue.

"What does that mean?" Harold asked.

"I've no clue. If I had the docking station, she could send me an answer by text. Not that she always does. But I don't have it. I don't even know if the sisters can recharge without it."

"Nemain, are we going back to Earth?" Harold asked.

The drone stuttered into the air, managing a jerky up and then down, before clunking back to the deck.

"I think that's a yes," Serene said as the other two drones flew into the control room, settling atop their companion. They attached themselves to their sister before all three rose up and flew back through the door, disappearing into the ship.

"Earth," Harold said. He removed the helmet and wiped the sweat from his brow, and then the back of his neck. "Forty days, and we'll be home."

"A bit longer than forty days," Tempest said. "The transporters took us from Earth to a rendezvous with that battleship. Our priority now must be a stock-take to see if we can survive that long. I'll stay here and run a diagnostic check on the life support systems. You should check on food and other stores."

"And find the medical bay for Alan," Serene said.

As they stepped back out into the corridor, and the door closed behind them, Harold stopped and closed his eyes.

"Are you okay?"

"My brain's just caught up, and decided now's a good time for my life to flash in front of my eyes." He took a deep breath. "At least there's oxygen."

"But is there enough that the recyclers can keep up with our consumption?" Serene said. "The same goes for water. Then there's food and power. I want to celebrate our escape, but we've still got work to do."

He pulled the helmet back on. The corridor was wide enough for three to walk abreast, and curved, in both directions, following the shape of the hull. The floor and walls were a pale grey, trimmed with blue and illuminated by soft white light from panels in the ceiling. "What kind of ship is this?" he asked as they began walking clockwise, passing one closed door after another.

"A cheap one. The Type-8 was supposed to be a flexible, all-purpose ship that could be quickly modified for lots of different tasks. It was a financial failure, and one of the last new designs before the collapse of the regency. We had to study it in business class."

"In the embassy?"

"We were doing remote learning long before the pandemic made it cool. All Valley children have to study the economic conditions at the time of the collapse of the old empire. This style of ship was too big to be a fighter, and too small to transport much freight, but because the contract had gone to a firm owned by Regent Kudon, they kept building them. Some were used as prisoner transporters, others for long-range science missions, or search and rescue, but most just ended up in storage. The centre of the ship contains the core services, like the control room, the galley, the medical bay, the washroom, the gym, and the garden. Then you have this corridor, and then the outer cabins which can be adapted to run as science labs, or accommodation, or jail cells. And the airlock, of course. Below are the engines and a small cargo hold you can access through the airlock."

Harold turned his head from one door to the next. There were no signs, on either side of the corridor, as to what lay inside the rooms. Frustratingly, nor did his helmet's visor display any description. "How do you turn on the helmet's AR? It's not telling me what's in which room."

"The helmet's functionality is run through the ship's systems. From what I saw in the engine room, those were majorly stripped down."

Awat was still in the airlock, slumped in her seat, one hand on the hovering stretcher. "Are we safe?" she asked, without looking up.

"I think so," Serene said. "Maybe. Probably. Safer than we were. The navigation system has been stripped out, but one of my drones inputted some coordinates. We're heading back to Earth."

"We're going home, Alan," she whispered.

"Let's move Alan to the medical bay," Serene said, detaching the stabiliser from the wall.

"What did that machine do to him?" Awat asked as Harold pushed the stretcher to the door.

"It's easiest to think of it as injecting him with millions of organic nano-bots that are pre-programmed to repair the body. It won't heal him, but it will seal the wounds, repair the organs, that kind of thing. There's a catch. You have to specify the species before you turn it on. Sapiens aren't in the medical database, so it thinks he's a sick towani."

"It'll turn him into a grey Neanderthal?" Awat asked, as they returned to the circular corridor.

"No. But it'll see the sapiens bits as being diseases to cure. He'll be in a lot of pain when he wakes up. Now, we've just got to find the med-bay." Serene swiped her hand across the access panel next to the door opposite the airlock. The cabin was completely empty. Every instrument, tool, and piece of furniture had been removed.

"Where's the medical equipment?" Awat asked.

"Usually the med-bay is opposite the airlock, but not always," Serene said, but the doubt in her voice was evident. "We'll just try each door until we find it.

They continued along the corridor to the next door. Again, Serene opened it with a swipe of her hand. As the door opened, a bolt flew through it, hitting the stretcher before ricocheting off into the ceiling. Before them, his twin-barrelled handgun raised, stood a towani wearing the blue and black armour of the Valley, though he had no helmet to cover his ragged beard or emaciated face. With a scream that was as much surprise as fear, Harold shoved the floating stretcher through the door, straight into the shooter. The blow knocked the gun from the towani's hand. The weapon skittered across the floor.

"It's us! We're friendly," Harold said, trying to remember how to say it in Mid-Tow. "We're from Earth!"

The towani clearly didn't understand as he drew an ornate knife, and pushed the stretcher aside. Harold raised his fists, backing up a step. The blade danced through the air until a bolt slammed into the soldier's armour. The zealot backed up a step. So did Harold, glancing sideways at Serene, now holding the gun.

"Stop it!" Serene said, before speaking quickly in Mid-Tow.

The towani smiled, before raising the blade to his own neck.

"No!" Harold said, but it was too late. The smile never left the towani's face as he slit his own throat.

Before the body had hit the ground, Awat was by her husband's side. "Is this machine still working?"

"Let me check," Serene said. "Yes. It's fine. He's fine. It didn't do any damage. These are built to be used on a battlefield."

"He's a Valley soldier. He must have been a prisoner, too," Harold said.

"No," Serene said. "I told him we'd escaped and were going back to Earth. He's dressed as a Valley soldier, but since he slit his own throat rather than be captured, I think he's a red-robe."

The three drones flew into the chamber. Nemain was trailing behind the other two, but otherwise seemed to have recovered from the earlier exertion. Macha and Badb flew over the corpse, while Nemain settled onto Alan's stabiliser. Serene crossed to a panel in the room's wall. "Tempi? We're in the galley. There was a red-robe here. Seal the control room."

"Done." Tempest's voice was broadcast through a speaker in the wall above the door. Built into the far wall, and the wall to the left, was an L-shaped bench before which was a row of small tables. The other wall contained the food printer, whose lights were ominously off.

"Tempi, are you still armed?"

"Of course."

"Good. We're going to search the rest of the ship. You stay there."

"I'll bring the internal cameras back online," Tempest said. "Be careful."

"Harold, where's your gun?"

He patted his pockets. "I must have dropped it when we were carrying Alan aboard."

"Mine is in the airlock," Awat said.

"And I left my rifle down in the engine room," Serene said. "Nemain, stay with Alan. Macha, take the lead, and Badb, watch our backs. We'll check the inner doors first until we find the armoury."

The gun raised, Serene took the lead, with the drone flying above and just ahead of her. At the next door, Harold waved his hand over the panel. The cabin beyond was as bare as the room opposite the airlock.

"Next one," Serene whispered, and they moved on.

The next door led into what was more like a closet, barely wider than the door, with closed cabinet doors on each of the other three walls.

"Bingo, the armoury," Serene said, opening the doors to the left, revealing neat rows of racks, containing tools, scanners, portable lights, but more gaps than devices. She opened the cabinet opposite the door. "That's weird. Those are restraints, body armour, and electrical stun batons. Ah, bingo." The third cabinet contained five handguns and a lot of empty spaces. Serene picked up a gun, then put it back. "It's loaded with explosive rounds. Ah, this one." She held one out to Awat. "Are you okay with firearms?"

"After what I saw in Iraq, I made sure to learn," she said, taking the twin-barrelled handgun.

"I'd be happier with one of those batons," Harold said.

She handed him one. "Awat, watch the rear. Harold, open the doors. We'll check the inner corridor first."

The next chamber was empty. The one after contained the washroom. Wishing there was time to test whether the toilets worked, they continued on to the control room where Tempest opened the door. "The internal scanners don't work, but I've got the cameras operational. Serene, if you take over monitoring the feed, I'll finish searching the ship."

"No, because if someone else is aboard, this is where they'll come. Have you sealed the engine room?"

"I have, and I've got images from there, and from the cargo hold. Both are empty. It's only the cabins where I don't have a feed."

"Then keep watching," she said, and closed the door.

Harold's heart thumping loud enough to start an avalanche, they continued on. Other than a small supply room, whose cabinets were as bare as the armoury, they found nothing but one empty room after another until they returned to the airlock. Awat retrieved the handgun she'd left on the floor, while Serene called Tempest.

"Seen anything?" she asked.

"Nothing yet," Tempest said.

"The inner rooms are empty, and most are stripped bare. We're going to check the outer ring now."

The cabin clockwise of the airlock was filled with three-tier bunks, each bed having barely enough to lie down. Between each row, there was just enough room for two people to stand facing one another, as long as they didn't mind their noses touching. There were no mattresses, just a rigid base on which to sleep, with restraints attached to the frame at both head and feet.

"It must be a prisoner transport," Serene said as Badb flew beneath the bottom bunks.

"Sixty bunks," Harold said. "But this would be crowded if there were ten people. It's smaller than our cell on that warship."

"It looks clean and unused," Awat said.

"Let's try the next," Serene said.

Like the first, the room was a cell, as were the next three. In the next, though it was the same size as the others, there was a single bed, built into a fitted unit against the left-hand wall. Harold opened the tall closet at the head of the bed. Inside was a blue-patterned armoured spacesuit and helmet of a style and design used by the Valley, and identical to that of the towani they had just killed.

"Where did you find these helmets?" Harold asked, tapping the one on his head.

"In the emergency locker in the control room," Serene said. "There are some flight suits in this closet, but no personal effects. No table, no chairs, nothing but a bed."

"We should finish the search before curiosity completely replaces caution," Awat said.

Room-by-room, they finished searching the outer ring. By the time they had checked them all, they'd found ten prison cells, and ten single-occupancy cabins. Of the cabins, nine contained two sets of the close-fitting flight suits and an armoured spacesuit. One, undoubtedly belonging to the dead red-robe, only contained one Valley flight suit and a helmet.

They returned to the galley, where the corpse lay on a completely dry floor.

"Where's all the blood?" Harold asked.

"There's a micro-mesh built into the floors, and the walls. It filters water into the recycler," Serene said.

"So we'll be drinking him?" Harold asked.

"The best way to think about it is that every atom in the universe was once part of something else, and will one day be part of something different."

Awat went to check on Alan. Seemingly, so did Macha and Badb, settling next to Nemain at Alan's feet.

"What are they doing?" Awat asked.

"They won't hurt him," Serene said. "They might even help." She crossed to the communicator built into the wall. "Hey, Tempi. We've finished. We didn't see anyone."

"Nor me."

"I want to recheck the engine room, but this is a weird ship."

"Come tell me in person, and bring some food if you can."

Harold walked over to the food printer. It was an older model than the one Johann had given to RAF Benson, but the controls were much the same. He turned the power on, and nervously watched as one light, and then the next, turned yellow. "We've got power. But do we have food?" He brought up the status panel, but this was very different to the one he was used to. "Serene, can you translate?"

"The good news is we've got food," she said. "The cartridges should last between five and six months, depending on when Alan wakes. Check the cupboards for more."

As Harold opened the cupboards, Serene began scrolling through the menu.

"There are ten bowls and sealed cups with straws," Harold said, "and there are spoons and those weird forks, but no spare cartridges."

"Is there a sanitiser to clean the bowls?"

"There is, and it came on when I powered up the printer."

"The best way to test it is to dirty up some bowls, so stick four in, and select number four. If I remember correctly, that's the most edible." She left the screen, and returned to the corpse, examining his armour.

"What are you looking for?" Awat asked.

"His *jeed*, the personal computer that would link to the ship's systems and his helmet's AR functionality. He doesn't have one."

Nemain rose from Alan's stretcher, and flew over to the body, tapping the armour on the left-hand side, just above the waist.

"Is there something there?" Serene asked. Nemain tapped against the armour again, before flying back to the stabiliser. Serene examined the armour panel, before disconnecting it. Beneath, from the pocket of the corpse's flight suit, she removed a small black case, only a centimetre deep, and five wide.

"What is it?" Awat asked, as Serene opened the case.

"A data chip, I think. Have you got the food, Harold?"

"I've four bowls, but I don't know what of," he said, handing a bowl of jet-black cubes in a snow-white sauce to Awat, and another to Serene.

"What is it?" Awat asked.

"A genuine rarity," Serene said. "Come on, let's take these to Tempest. The sisters will watch Alan."

Tempest opened the control room door with the battle rifle in his hands. When he saw their lunch, his brow furrowed in surprise. "Is this what I think it is?"

"One hundred percent," Serene said.

Tempest leaned their rifle against the door and took a bowl from Harold. "Wow. I'd never imagined I'd get to try any of this."

"Is it expensive?" Awat asked, taking a seat at one of the workstations. Harold took the chair next to her.

"Expensive? I suppose it is, in a way," Tempest said. "Monochrome meals were a fad from about fifty or sixty years ago. Everything is about bright colours now."

"It was another famous economic failure, like the design of this ship, that we had to study," Serene said.

"That I studied," Tempest said. "I know you copied my coursework. This menu was so unsuccessful, it bankrupted the firm that made it. The idea was to have colourless food, simple shapes, and one overwhelming flavour. Everyone hated it. They couldn't even give the stuff away. The fate of the unused cartridges has entered legend. Some say they dumped it on an uninhabited world where it's slowly evolving into a new life form, but others say it was reserved for prisoners until the courts ruled it as a cruel and unusual punishment."

"But if you bought some different recipe codes—" Harold began.

"The sauce code," Serene said.

"Only you call it that," Tempest said.

"If you bought the different recipes, wouldn't you still be able to use old cartridges?" Harold asked.

"Oh, the innocence of youth," Serene said. "That's not how capitalism works. The cartridges have to match the recipes, otherwise you'll end up with sludge. It would be digestible, but it'd taste disgusting. The question is whether it'll taste better than this."

Harold looked down at the unappetising bowl, but it had been a long time since he'd eaten. He spooned up a cube. As the gelatinous square touched his tongue, his eyes widened in shock as his mouth filled with a peppery taste so intense, he thought he was about to choke. The flavour dissipated almost instantly, leaving only a soft and slightly slimy black cube on his tongue. As he bit down, the fiery sensation returned, but was gone just as quickly. He swallowed.

"I can see why the chef went bankrupt," Harold said. The sauce was just as intense, but with a citrusy tang whose flavour vanished just as quickly.

"I've tasted worse," Awat said, as she methodically devoured her bowl.

"I've had less," Harold said, trying another spoonful. "Is this really the best dish on the menu?"

"I'd describe it as being the least bad," Serene said. "Tempi, you know how you said there's a myth they gave this stuff to prisoners?"

"That's just a legend," Tempest said.

"Well we found ten cabins set up as prisoner transport, with chains on the bunks."

"Why would the Voytay want a Valley prisoner transport ship on that ice-world?" Awat asked.

"Oh, you don't know, do you? They're separatists," Serene said, and then explained what the red-robe had told them while they had been confined in the cage.

"If the red-robes had agents among the Voytay, they must have them among the Valley, too," Harold said. "In fact, thinking about it, if the red-robes were behind Oxfordshire, then it's their agents working in the embassy, not the Voytay."

"Probably to the last part," Serene said. "But the Valley doesn't have prison transports like this. That's how the old empire transported people like Greta, Gunther, and Johann off to settle a new world. After the civil war, there were sweeping reforms to the penal code. Tempi, do you recognise this? I found it on the red-robe." She took out the small data-chip.

"That's cool. It's another antique. Gunther told me about them. It's a data storage device, but it dissolves in water. Spies used to use them, because if you swallow it, it'll be destroyed."

"Ooh, I wonder what's on it?" Serene said, and swung around to plug it into the workstation.

"Figuring it out can be our entertainment for the next forty days," Tempest said. "There's no media database on the ship."

"But we are going back to Earth?" Awat said.

"Yes, so it'll take about forty days. How much food do we have?"

"Just what was in the cartridges," Serene said, "but that will last us five or six months, assuming we don't snack too much."

"I don't think that'll be a problem," Harold said. "What about water?"

"The tank is low," Tempest said. "But there should be enough as long as we stagger when we shower."

"Is there a laundry aboard?" Awat asked.

"No, and there are no clothing printers," Serene said. "Ah, the chip's encrypted, but it's a simple encryption. I think I can get into it."

"There's no medical equipment aboard," Harold said.

"Is there a garden?" Tempest asked.

"No, and no gym or entertainment room," Serene said.

"The navigation database is missing," Tempest said. "That's like a star map. There's no navigation interface, either, so you can't set a direction and time, and fly to uncharted space. To jump, you'd have to do what Nemain did, and enter the coordinates as machine code." They turned to their console, tapped in a few commands, and brought up a page of incomprehensible characters. They slowly scrolled down, through line after line. "You'd need to be an expert in quantum mathematics to write any of this. There's one message-pod, loaded and ready for launch, but it doesn't have a navigation system either. There's no flight recorder, and the camera systems were turned off when we arrived. Basically, there's no record of where the ship has been."

"But we're safe?" Awat asked.

"Safer than we were," Tempest said. "I want to check the engine room to see what spare parts we have, but if we have to do anything more than basic maintenance, we'll have to drop out of jump space and hope we've arrived in an inhabited system." They put their bowl aside. "I'll do that now."

"I'll go and sit with Alan," Awat said. "I don't like the idea of him being alone."

"I'll move the body," Harold said. "Any ideas where we could put him?"

"He's a bit big to fit into the waste recycling system, at least in one piece," Serene said.

"I'll seal him in one of the empty cabins."

Chapter 33 - Waste Not, Want Not

Harold woke disorientated and confused. As he sat up, the lights automatically came on, but it took him a moment longer to remember where he was. When was impossible to guess, but since he didn't feel tired, he decided it was morning. The helmet was beside the bed, but he didn't put it on; there was nothing to see in this cavernous room with its solitary bed. Why was so much space on this ship wasted? If the jail cells were full, the food wouldn't have lasted long, and the water even less.

Last night, if it was night, after dragging the body to a cell, and then watching the trail of blood slowly vanish, he'd had a brief shower, and gone to bed. He'd thought sleep might bring clarity, but he'd woken with a head full of questions, not just about the ship, but about their escape, and about Celeste.

He stood up, and found every muscle stiff and sore. Hopefully that was just from the exertions of the escape, and not something more serious. With no medical equipment, there was nothing to do but ignore the pain. The sudden awareness of the precariousness of their situation did the work of a cold shower. Shivering, he selected one of the clean, close-fitting flight suits from the closet, packing away his Voytay cold weather gear in its place.

He picked up the helmet, but didn't put it on. His first stop was the washroom. He'd not noticed before, but there were no mirrors. That was probably a good thing. His second stop was the galley, where the only occupants were Parker, and the drones.

"Morning, Alan," he said. The lights on the side of the stabiliser were still yellow, not wake-me-up blue. "Having a lie-in? Sorry, that's bad taste. Speaking of which..."

He crossed to the printer, glared at the menu, and decided to chance his luck. He selected a dish at random, and was given an oily black soup.

"I think I've found coffee," he said. He hadn't. The taste was intense and floral, almost like liquid lavender, but it was warm. It was on the want-not end of the waste-not spectrum, but the same could be said for the meal he'd had last night.

A beep from his helmet was followed by Tempest's voice. "Morning, Harry. Can you bring me a snack?"

"Only if you tell me what you want, because it's definitely not what I'm eating."

"I'll take *frolli suf cane*, that's what we had last night."

Harold printed a dish of the black cubes. "See you later, Alan." He picked up his bowl and Tempest's, and made his way to the control room.

"Whoosh," Harold said as he entered.

"Whoosh?" Tempest said.

"Even after all that time on the red-robes' warship, I can't rid my head of the idea that doors on spaceships should have sound effects. Is it morning?"

"It is somewhere," Tempest said, taking the bowl from Harold. "But it's five hours since you went to sleep."

"Is that all? I thought it was longer. Hang on, what clock are we using?"

"The old imperial interstellar standard, the same as on the red-robes' warship."

"So that's one hundred seconds to a minute, fifty minutes to an hour, and twenty hours in a day?"

"That's it. Are you really going to eat that?"

"I don't like wasting food," Harold said, taking another sip, but knowing what to expect didn't improve the flavour. He took the seat at the same workstation he'd sat at the night before. While his screen and control console were dark, Serene's screen displayed lines of text written in Mid-Tow, while Awat's showed an image of the tunnel wall from the ice-world.

"What's on the screens?" Harold asked.

"Serene opened that data-chip, and Awat was looking at the data storage device we took from the cage on the ice-world."

"Ah. Have they gone to sleep?"

"About an hour ago," Tempest said, before yawning widely.

"You should get some rest, too."

"Standard protocol is for a pilot to always be present. If we drop out of jump-space unexpectedly, we might reappear in an asteroid field, shipping lane, or heading towards some other obstacle."

"Is that likely?"

"It happens occasionally, particularly with older ships. What's more likely is that a critical system fails."

"What do we do then?"

"It depends on which system and where, but there aren't many spare parts. We can do basic maintenance, but if it's anything more serious, we'd have to drop out of jump space and hope we arrive somewhere inhabited."

"So show me how what to watch, and how to shut down the jump engines, and then get some rest."

"There's no VR training modules."

"You can't stay here for forty days. If something goes wrong, it won't take you more than a few minutes to get up here."

With obvious reluctance, Tempest stood up. "Take a seat."

"This is comfy," Harold said as he sat down. "Captain's log, stardate… Halloween, give or take. So how do I drop out of jump-space?"

"This button, then this one, and this one. Lots of alarms will sound. Ignore them."

"Great. And how do I know when to do that?"

"Do you see all these graphs, dials, and numbers on the console?" Tempest pointed at a multi-coloured array of lines and numbers, all in Mid-Tow. Some fluctuated wildly, while others remained static. As Harold looked at each in turn, his helmet's visor displayed a scrolling library of annotation in the centre of his field of view.

"You got the AR working," Harold said.

"Only for the controls. It's been stripped from everything else."

"So what does it all mean?"

"Hull integrity, life support, and artificial gravity are at the top. The engines are below. The smaller numerical readouts are for the sub-systems. Press any to get a more detailed breakdown, but it'll take a few days to teach you how to read it all. For now, if any of the top two rows flash yellow, wake me up. If any turn solid yellow, bring us out of jump."

"Yellow. Right. And if we drop out of jump-space, how do I steer?"

"That'll take longer to teach. The thrusters are these sliding controls on the right, but it's not just about powering them up. Once you begin to turn, there's no friction to slow you down, so you have to fire a burst in the opposite direction, or you'll end up in a circle or a spin."

"I'll stick with waking you up and hoping we don't end up in an asteroid belt. And what are the odds of that? As the book says, space is big."

"Hopefully," Tempest said, and picked up their bowl.

Harold turned the chair to look at Serene's screen. "What did you find on the red-robe? It looks like a letter."

"It is," Tempest said. "It says that there were ten escaped Voytay prisoners aboard this ship who had been held at a secret Valley prison. Some of the guards were sooval. The blade with which he killed himself is a sooval weapon. It's more of an heirloom, handed down within a family but given to someone when they go to war. Afterwards, the conflict is acknowledged with etching, or other decoration. Do you remember at Lenham House, the ceremonial war-axe that one of the mercenaries was carrying?"

"Vividly."

"I started researching their weapons after we found that axe. It belonged to a former general who'd retired to a farm on a planet in the borderlands. When the mercenaries raided the monastery, the general went to their defence. It was killed, and the axe was taken."

"Which army was it a general in?"

"The imperial army, and then with the Valley during the revolution. The knife we found would be easily identifiable, and would link its former owner, supposedly a prison guard, with a specific sooval family."

"Who were these prisoners?"

"If you believe what it says there, they were captured during the civil war and have been held captive ever since. The document says they stole this transport, and escaped, but were pursued. It says they hope they won't be recaptured, and request help. Right at the end, it says it includes the coordinates of where they crashed, but that part's been left blank."

"That's a pity."

"Not exactly. The only other thing on that data-chip were two sets of coordinates written in machine code. One must be for where the ship was due to crash and to be written on the letter, the other for the message-pod, which would have contained that plea for help. I can't tell which is which."

"So this ship was supposed to crash with ten people aboard?"

"No, I think there was only ever supposed to be that one red-robe aboard. He would have killed himself after he crashed, or he expected to die in the crash itself. When the rescue party arrived, they were to assume that the other nine had been recaptured. It's why there's no flight recorder or navigational system, or any other clue as to where this ship came from. It was probably bought from a junk-yard, and kitted out with as much authentic Valley gear as the red-robes could get their hands on. Those food cartridges must have been stored in a warehouse, or a museum. They predate a law that stated the cartridges must include a code that says where and when it was purchased. They probably decided, for a suicide mission, it wasn't worth finding gym or medical equipment that matched the ship's age."

"In Oxfordshire, none of the towani soldiers let themselves be taken prisoner," Harold said. "One definitely committed suicide. We thought they were Voytay, but they were red-robes like that guy we found aboard. He must have had the same orders as them, not to be taken alive."

"I think so. He probably thought that we'd jumped blind, and with no navigational system would starve before we reached the sanctuary of an inhabited world. Like you said, space is big."

"Really big. So the Voytay would think the Valley had secret prisons where they'd held people for over a century. The Valley would think that the Voytay had attacked Earth, and they'd think some sapiens had tried to assassinate the ambassador."

"Some sapiens *did* try to assassinate the ambassador," Tempest said.

"But they were working for the red-robes, not the Voytay. What I'm trying to work out is whether this is enough to start a war. That was what the zealot said she wanted."

"It's probably not enough in itself. There'd have been some more steps, but they don't matter now. Gunther was already in the borderlands, threatening the Voytay after Oxfordshire. When he hears we've been taken, I don't think even Gramps could stop him from launching an attack. You've only ever met Uncle Gunther. You've not seen General Dannan. He can be terrifying. Some of the things he did during the war *are* terrifying. And then there's Gramps, Da, and Greta. They won't sit back. Nor will the faithful, not when they hear the grandchildren of the prophet have been abducted. They will demand action, or maybe even take it themselves. And then there's Mum."

"Celeste, yes," Harold said, glancing at the screen showing the image of the tunnel wall. "Could the Voytay kill her?"

"I'm not entirely sure. I had one theory. It's about how the red-robe wanted us for experiments. She didn't say it, but I think she meant biological warfare to make all sapiens extinct. Covid was similar to the Red Plague. Different, but similar. Take Ebola, or AIDS, or any of the other terrible diseases that appeared last century."

"None of which wiped us out, and I don't think any had any realistic chance of doing so."

"Which is why she wanted test subjects after her early attempts failed. She wanted to return to the days of the empire, and sapiens had no place in that. Even if she's not perfected a virus, one more pandemic will turn Earth into chaos. The Valley would get the blame for not preventing it. Because of our relation to all towani, there are many among the Voytay who would be angered by that, or at least use it as an excuse to be angry at the Valley. Since Earth is their ancestral home, too, and with no sapiens left alive to say what they wanted, control of Earth could easily become the flashpoint to start a war."

"Then I'm glad we *were* abducted," Harold said. "But how does getting rid of Celeste fit into this?"

"It might be that's how the red-robes think they can end the war. Once billions have died, and one group is ascendant, they can reveal that the chroniclers were behind the ancestral towani's abduction, and have been manipulating events ever since. That could turn collective anger towards Celeste. By then, maybe the red-robes will have figured out how to kill her, or maybe they think they can just ask her to leave."

"That's... awful."

"It's just a theory, but I don't think it's far off." Tempest yawned again.

"Get some sleep. Maybe I'll even have finished my soup by the time you wake."

"Sure. Thanks."

Harold pulled his helmet back on, and moved his gaze from one dial to the next, but the volume of unintelligible data was overwhelming. Instead, he stood, walked over to the workstation where he'd left his bowl, and picked it up. A bowl was something he understood. As with clothing, a similar physiology had led to the development of similar eating implements. That was logical. It was understandable. The zealot's beliefs were, like with those of any of the religious fundamentalists he'd known as a child, a tangled knot of rhetoric that twisted all good aspects of the faith they were based on.

He'd wanted to ask Tempest how he felt about Olawayo. What he really wanted was for someone to tell him how *he* should feel. He'd not had a chance to properly process what the red-robe had told them, though her actions spoke volumes. Having locked them in the cage, she'd then forced Olawayo to confess, but killed him before they could ask any questions. With the worst horror of their childhood once again fresh in their minds, she had left them to freeze to death. That was who she was. Whether he knew who he was working for or not, that was who Olawayo had been. Parker truly was different.

Since he couldn't clear his mind, he removed his helmet and sipped at the floral-flavoured soup, trying to overwhelm his senses. He'd just finished when Awat entered the control room.

"Can't sleep?" Harold asked.

"Not really. Where's Tempest?"

"Resting. I said I'd watch the controls for a while. As long as nothing flashes yellow, we're fine."

She took a seat at her workstation and looked up at the screen showing the writing on the tunnel wall.

"Have you been able to decipher it?" Harold asked.

"Not really," she said. "But I haven't really begun trying. I'm still going through the annotations that the red-robes made." She looked down at the controls. "This one, I think."

Notes appeared over the image. Sometimes one word, sometimes a phrase.

"This is as far as they got. They've deciphered, or think they had, about a quarter of the words. Here, it probably does say *exile*, but words change their meaning over time. There's a sentence here they've translated as *This is how my brother died*. I think this is the basis of their assumption that the inscription includes the secret to killing the chroniclers. Do you know if they have siblings?"

"I'm not sure. But brother doesn't always mean a blood relation."

"No, exactly."

"How were they translating any of it?" Harold asked. "Don't you need something to bridge the two languages?"

"Yes, hang on, let me find it." She stared at the controls, her hand hovering over a button and then another before she remembered which she needed. "Here."

The image changed, becoming a photograph of a section of writing exposed among a row of terracotta tiles. Next to it, in Mid-Tow, was a page of text.

"Is that from Nineveh?"

"It must be. I think this came from the flight recorder. This section of writing was not exposed when I examined the tunnel, and do you see how vivid the colours are? I think this image was taken while the tiles were being installed."

"And the page of text?"

"Is a translation. It's similar, very similar, to what you'd find in the Book of Genesis. It's different from the earliest Hebrew versions, but that would be expected, and not only because we're translating from Mid-Tow into English."

"Do you mean that the chronicler made up the Biblical story of creation?"

"I don't think so. It's a common practice, across all faiths and times, for a preacher to adapt scripture to the life experiences of an audience. Had a preacher heard the chronicler's tale and then incorporated parts of it into his scripture, and was it that the chronicler wrote into those walls? We really are only at the beginning of discovery's long journey. All I can say, with near certainty, is that this was the language the chronicler used at that time. And if he really did go to Earth to study our species' development, it would be natural for him to write things down."

"I'd have thought he'd have used a computer. He is supposed to have one."

"I have a computer, but I still use a notebook," she said. "I think that's what he was doing here, writing down what a human told him, probably on the request of that human who didn't know how to write."

"If it's his language, he wouldn't have learned it after he came to Earth. And by the time those tiles went up, the towani empire was using Mid-Tow, right?" Harold asked.

"Yes. So maybe he did live on that ice-world, back when it was a lifeless rock. Or one of his species did. It's dangerous to leap to conclusions, even if I've just done it with this translation, but sometimes we have to make that leap of faith, even if it's only to be proved wrong later. I haven't been through all the data yet, but there's one more piece you should see. Like that biblical tale, it must have come from the flight recorder."

She brought up an image showing the tunnel's large, square chamber in which, many centuries later, a spaceship would be dragged. From the angle, the image had been taken from the top of the stone stairs. Bright lamps dangled from the ceiling, illuminating vivid wall hangings, and elaborately carved screens that divided the floor of the chamber into rooms. Wooden tables, and what looked to be a proto-bookshelf, were stacked with scrolls and clay tablets. At the bottom of the stairs, just in front of two towering pot plants, stood a sapiens of Middle Eastern descent, wearing a belted robe. Above his head were three black specks.

"We think that's the librarian," Awat said. She tapped the controls, and the image began to change, becoming a short movie. The perspective remained the same, but showed a green-faced, long-limbed jajan, wearing what was unmistakably a flight suit, descending the stairs. Before it was halfway down the stairs, the jajan's body began to change. The limbs became shorter, the head more rounded, and its clothing adjusted to fit, until she appeared to be a brown-skinned Neanderthal. The librarian raised his arms in greeting, and the three drones, circling above his head swooped towards the visitor, and the camera. Two more drones moved into view, these white rather than black. As one of the black drones, now rippling with blue, flew so close to the camera that it filled half the picture, the movie froze.

"That's all there is," Awat said.

"The visitor, the jajan that became a Neanderthal, is that another chronicler?"

"We think so. We think one of its drones recorded this meeting, and it was stored on the flight recorder."

300

"No. I know all the chroniclers were supposed to have a data-core to record everything they saw, but if that was the flight recorder, there is no way Celeste would have let it languish in Area-51."

"From what Serene and Tempest have told me of her, I agree. The visitor's ship was supposed to have crashed. If the legend of the indestructibility of the chroniclers' ships is real, it must have been travelling on a different vessel. But are those myths true? Neither Serene nor Tempest can recall any incident in living memory where their mother gave a demonstration of her powers. The more pertinent question is whether the red-robes believe those myths."

"You mean if that jajan-Neanderthal died in a ship crash, then there is little to be feared by drawing Celeste into a fight? But yes, it doesn't matter whether it's true or not, just whether the red-robes believe it. Why does she look like a Neanderthal, not a sapiens?"

"This is now straying into anthropology rather than archaeology, but the most likely explanation is that it's the form she always uses when meeting the librarian."

"And this is only two and a half thousand years ago, but she's not grey, so it is a Neanderthal's form, not a towani."

"Exactly."

"But what does it mean?"

"There isn't enough here to draw a conclusion. There are many more records to go through, and we only have what the red-robes were able to recover."

"There's no sound?"

"Not with this file."

Harold stared at the drone on the screen. "It kinda looks like one of Serene's drones."

"She thinks it's Nemain, and that her drones once belonged to the librarian."

"Did you ask the drones?"

"We tried, but they won't leave Alan's stretcher."

"Let me get this straight. The red-robes hate the chroniclers because they ensured the overthrow of the regency, and that Earth wasn't discovered by a loyalist, which would have reinvigorated the regency's grip on power. They think that orange flight recorder is a data-core, and that the chronicler's ship crashed, so it isn't indestructible. And they see this and think there's a link between the chroniclers and the Neanderthals, and so with the ancestral towani's abduction."

"Yes, but is any of it true?"

Chapter 34 - On the Thirty-Ninth Day...

"That's it, I've had enough," Harold said on the thirty-ninth day. He pushed his breakfast bowl of black cubes aside. "I'm going to get the knife."

"Are you sure?" Serene asked.

"I just can't take it anymore," Harold said, running his hand over the patchy hair on his neck. "Enough is enough. I've reached my limit. No. I've just got to shave. Of all the things missing on this ship, I'd never have thought a razor would be near the top of my want-list."

"For me, it's a comb," Awat said, running her fingers through her tangled hair. "At least there are no mirrors in the bathroom."

"In the Valley, you would use your ocular implants, or glasses, coupled with a bathroom camera to see what you look like," Serene said. "Those are usually sponsored by cosmetics, accessories, or clothing companies. They can show you what you'd look like if you'd been using their product, and always have a buy-now feature."

"They have cameras in their bathrooms. Now, that's alien," Harold said.

"An ocular implant is essentially a camera," Serene said. "That's one way the regents were able to keep such rigid control over the last empire."

"But there's make-up in the Valley?" Awat asked.

"Sure, though it goes in and out of favour. Before the revolution, and then in a big way afterwards, there was a trend for tattoos, similar to Nowan's swirling red lines. But after a few decades, questions arose as to whether Nowan's facial markings were tattoos, paint, or even just blood. That tied in with growing interest in the development of societies on Earth, and a comment Da made about woad during an interview. People started painting their faces. Red or blue at first, and then other colours. These days, more minimalist make-up is favoured, but I'm sure a new trend will be along soon. That's mostly among the towani. Paxley favour dyeing their fur. Sooval paint the tips of their scales. Jajan are more into garlands of dried and colourful kelp. I can't think of any world that favours beards like that, Harry, so you're making the right choice."

There was only one knife on the ship, the ornate blade taken from the dead red-robe. The only other cutting tools would also remove his head since they were designed to cut through a ship's deck plating. As Tempest kept the blade wickedly sharp, Harold had eschewed shaving after his first attempt made his face look like he'd gone ten rounds with an irate badger.

He collected the blade from the armoury, and went to the washroom. The lack of mirrors presented a problem. So did his lack of glasses, since he could hardly shave with the helmet on. He propped it on a shelf, tentatively raised the knife, uncertain whether to ask one of the others for help, and nearly sliced off his nose when the gravity suddenly dropped.

"We've left jump space," Tempest said when Harold reached the control room just behind Awat and Serene.

"It's only the thirty-ninth day. What went wrong?" Harold asked.

"Nothing," Tempest said. "We've reached the destination Nemain plugged in, but it's not Earth. We're in a system with a single star, and at least five planets. I'm still running scans, so we'll get more data as we go, but four of the planets are gas giants, closer to the size of Saturn than Jupiter. There are at least three asteroid belts. I guess those are planets that didn't form because they were too close to a gas giant."

"What about the fifth planet, Tempi?" Serene asked.

"It's solid. It's got an atmosphere. Two moons. One small, one about the size of Luna. The planet's about a quarter again as big as Earth."

"Is it inhabited?" Awat asked.

"Let me check comms," Serene said, slipping into the co-pilot's seat.

"I'll bring up a 3D rendering of the planet," Tempest said.

A green and blue planet, dotted with clouds, appeared in front of the pilot's chair. For a brief moment, Harold thought Tempest was wrong, and this *was* Earth, but a thick bank of clouds moved, revealing the landmass below was actually a pair of neighbouring island continents.

"There are no ships in the system," Serene said. "No beacons, and no satellites."

"The planet's atmosphere is breathable," Tempest said. "It has a little more nitrogen and a lot less carbon dioxide, but there's oxygen, too. I think there are plants, but there's no indication of technology."

Harold stepped out into the corridor. "Nemain, Badb, Macha?"

The three drones arrived so swiftly that they must have been waiting outside. They buzzed into the control room, narrowly missing Harold's head.

"You said we were going to Earth," Harold said.

"Yeah, but you know what we didn't ask?" Tempest asked. "Whether we were going there immediately."

"Is this where Celeste wants us to be?" Harold asked.

Nemain bobbed up and down immediately. At first, the other two didn't move, before each gave a curt nod.

"What do you mean by that question?" Serene asked.

"Think back to when we were on Earth," Harold said. "Your mum gave you the drones to keep you safe. In Area-51, they could have flown the three of us to safety. Instead, they let us get captured, and then hid away on the red-robe's ship until we were in imminent danger of becoming icicles. They were clearly watching us the whole time. When we escaped, Nemain could have sent us to Earth, or any Valley planet. Instead, we're here because this is exactly where Celeste wants us to be."

"She can't have planned for us to get abducted," Tempest said.

"Whose idea was it for us to meet her at Area-51, your father's or hers? She was in the Mediterranean, wasn't she? Why didn't we fly there?"

"You're implying she knew about the prison escape before it happened," Serene said.

"The trouble with conspiracies is that when you get caught up in one, you start to think everything is connected. But maybe, somehow, she did know. She sent me to Lenham House."

"When?" Serene asked.

"When we first met. I picked Lenham House to go camping because of a book. That book had been returned in a box we'd loaned out as a video-conferencing backdrop. On the page for Lenham House was a handwritten note saying it was a great place to camp for free. It was written by your mum. The handwriting matched a note she sent, with a guide to North Rhine-Westphalia, after the Oxfordshire crash."

"Why didn't you say?" Tempest asked.

"Because it made me question a lot of other things I wasn't sure I wanted to know the answer to, like how Jess was tipped off as to where I was back when I was a kid."

"You think it was Mum?" Tempest asked.

"Jess and I always thought it was *my* mum, but how would she have ever known where Jess was? How did Two-Halves Mick land the job with Oxford F.C.? A job which started the same day I needed a ride up to Oxfordshire. Why did she set up that puzzle beneath Lenham House to be solved by three people, when there's only two of you?"

"That's a point," Tempest said. "Three drones and three of us."

"You can't be saying you agree with him?" Serene asked.

"I don't know. It's worth thinking about."

"Think about what, exactly?" Serene said. "Mum can't have known that we'd have been in the museum room when the ship arrived."

"She can't foretell the future, but she does try to rig it," Harold said. "She certainly did with your father. Okay, yes, maybe you're right about the abduction. Wait." He turned to the drones. "Is this planet the default location you were to bring us if we ever ended up on a ship we barely understood?"

306

Again, Nemain frantically bobbed up and down. The other two, with reluctance, did the same.

"There you go," Harold said. "Back in Lenham House, she had set up a treasure hunt to be solved by three people. The three of us. Except when we solved it, Tempest was in space, and Jess took their place. If Tempi had been there, I think we'd have found ourselves teleported to this planet."

"Teleportation doesn't exist," Serene said.

"Transported, then," Harold said. "Because this is where she wanted us to be."

"Why?" Awat said, and turned to the drones. "Why are we here?"

"Hang on," Serene said. On the workstation screen to the right of the door, she brought the alphabet. "Spell out the answer."

The drones didn't move.

"I've got it," Tempest said. "This is a puzzle. When Da told us the story of his return to Earth, he said those spice merchants working for Mum would give him the information he asked for, but not until *after* he had asked for it. This is the same sort of thing."

Nemain began to bob up and down until Badb knocked into it. Nemain sheepishly flew towards the door, the other two drones on either side.

"If Mum wanted us to come here, there must be some kind of communication system here," Serene said. "Maybe this is where she hid the librarian's ship. I'm going to scan the system again."

"We need to get Alan to a hospital," Awat said.

"As long as he's in the stabiliser, he's fine," Tempest said.

"How long can it keep working?"

"I think seven years was the record," Tempest said. "A medical transport ship was raided by pirates. The crew were killed, but the patients were ignored. The ship wasn't found for seven years. One of the patients was successfully revived."

"How many weren't?" Awat asked.

"Twenty-three," Tempest said. "Okay, yes, maybe that's a bad example, but looking at it the other way, we have just over four months of food left. We're in greater peril than Alan."

"I don't think any of us are in danger," Harold said. "Have you noticed how the drones often sit on Alan's stretcher? I think they're helping. The drones clearly won't let us get harmed."

"They let us get captured," Serene said. "What you mean is that they won't let us die, but it might not be up to them. I can't find any signal of any kind in this system. There's no one here, and no hints as to where we should go next."

"The planet," Harold said. "We should land. If we solve the puzzle, the drones will take us home, or it's as you say, and we'll be able to fly there in the librarian's ship."

"Harold's right," Awat said. "We need to get back in contact with the Valley before a war begins, and we need to get Alan to the hospital. Let's solve the puzzle."

"Everyone sit down and buckle in," Tempest said. "I'll take us closer to the planet so that we can get a more detailed scan of the surface."

The ship accelerated towards the planet.

"There are still no signals," Serene said. "Spectroscopy tells me the planet has a lot less carbon dioxide and a smidge more nitrogen, but it's breathable. But there's also no indication of industrialisation. I'll bring up a view of the planet's surface onto your workstations. See if you spot any buildings."

Tempest set a course that took them into orbit, and then travelled against the planet's rotation. After one complete orbit, they travelled from pole to pole, and then obliquely.

After three orbits, and lunch, there were still gaps in their three-dimensional map of the planet, but it was increasingly clear there was no technological life on the surface.

"Let's land," Harold said. "We can get some fresh air, top up the water tanks, and ask the sisters for the next part of the puzzle. You've noticed they're hiding again?"

"Where should we land?" Awat asked. "If this is a puzzle, there should be clues, but where do we even begin to look for them?"

"I suppose one place is as good as another," Harold said. "Maybe the sisters will tell us when we set down. Here, on the largest continent, there's a plain surrounded by a forest, and there's a river in the south which runs into the sea, not that far away."

"The south?" Serene said.

"It makes things simpler," Harold said. "Those trees don't look so dense. Maybe the forest grew up around the ruins of an old city."

"I'll take us down."

Chapter 35 - To Boldly Go

The ship shuddered and shook as it made re-entry, but then settled into a slow descent, and a very tentative landing.

"We're down," Tempest said, even as the craft dipped to aft.

"Is this a swamp?" Serene asked.

"No, we're fine," Tempest said as the ship's movement ceased. "The ground's just soft, that's all. Everyone get suited up, gloves and helmets, and weapons, too. When we leave the ship, assume everything is lethal until proven otherwise. That includes the plants."

"And the animals," Awat said. "This is a plain surrounded by forest. Something grazes here. Where there are grazing animals, there are usually predators."

Tempest checked that their suits were sealed before opening the outer airlock door. "Cameras are clear," they said. "I'm lowering the ramp."

Harold walked to the edge of the ramp as it slowly descended, digging deep into a carpet of green. Slowly, gun reluctantly raised, he walked to the ramp's end. The ground cover appeared to be broad-leafed plants, with a solitary and leafless stem rising in the centre, topped with a blue flower.

"Here goes nothing," Harold said, stepping off the ramp's end. When his boot touched the green plants, they didn't try to eat him, nor did his foot begin to dissolve. He took a tentative second step. "Cool, I'm still alive."

Awat laughed. "At least that will look good on a t-shirt."

"You've lost me," Serene said.

"This is a historic moment. Unless Sean O'Malley ever came here, you are the first sapiens to set foot on this planet. Possibly the first ever person. We may not have built the ship, but this is the first entirely sapiens-crewed expedition to an alien world. Your words will go down next to Armstrong's."

"I wish you'd told me that before," Harold said. He bounced on his feet. "Go on then, your turn."

"This is one giant leap for a sapiens," Serene said, stepping off the ramp. Then she jumped, but not very far. "But a disappointingly small leap for humankind."

"Gravity's higher here," Tempest said. "About eleven point five against Earth's nine point eight."

"Where we've been is never as important as where we're going," Awat said as she left the craft.

"As the Holy Prophet said, always go forward," Tempest said as they set foot on the alien world.

"Ooh, sneaky," Serene said. "You absolutely know that's what the Valley clerics will claim were the first words."

"I'm happy if mine are forgotten," Harold said, taking a few more steps from the ship. "Can we remove our helmets?"

"All the readings say yes," Tempest said.

Harold released the seal on his helmet, and breathed deeply. "It smells sweet."

"I'm going to inspect the ship," Tempest said.

"I'll go with you," Serene said. "Can you two watch the ramp, and make sure no bug-eyed monsters sneak onto the ship while we're not looking?"

The sisters flew out of the ship, and began flying a figure of eight overhead. Harold watched them, wondering if they'd give a hint as to what they were supposed to do next, but they kept flying back and forth, seemingly enjoying the wide-open space.

The ground cover stretched for half a mile ahead before it was replaced with a forest.

"That's south, isn't it?" he asked.

"The direction of the river, yes," Awat said.

He turned around, and looked north. The plain wasn't entirely flat, and rose and dipped until replaced by more forest at least five miles away. The forest created a green band on the horizon, above which poked a towering mountain range whose slopes were dotted

311

with snow, but whose peaks were lost to the clouds. He removed his helmet, relishing the soft brush of a cool breeze against his face.

"It feels like spring," he said. "Or is it autumn?"

"It could be a day before the monsoon," Awat said. She bent down to examine the flower. "This is interesting. A flower would suggest there are pollinators on this planet, but the flower hangs down, and is almost concealed from above by a collar at the top of the stem."

Harold opened the optical controls of his helmet's visor, and zoomed in on the trees to the south. The trunks were stout while the branches were thin, and both trunk and branches were covered in green needles.

"Photosynthesis must be a universal law," he said. "The trees aren't very bushy, and the trunks look to be wide rather than tall. I wonder if this place gets lots of strong winds."

As Awat turned to look at the forest, Harold caught a flash of green soar up and then back down into the safety of the branches. "A bird!" he said. "Another. They have green birds in the trees."

"They won't be birds, but bird-like animals," Awat said, as she turned to look at the swooping pack of avians. "And I don't think they're very like birds at all. They're gliding, not flying, but birds is as good a name as any, until the biologists can argue a new one into existence. What do you want to call them? If this is an uninhabited planet, never previously lived on, who else should have naming rights?"

"A name? I'll have to give that some thought." Harold took off his helmet, letting the warm breeze caress his skin. The extra gravity, and the weight of the armoured spacesuit, was already making him sweat.

"All's well," Tempest called out. Harold turned to see the siblings returning, but Serene was holding a long yellow root.

"Is the ship okay?" Awat asked.

"There's only some superficial damage, probably from before we took off. The ship looks fine."

"What's that, Serene?" Harold asked.

"The root of those plants. This one was exposed by the weight of the landing gear. I want to test whether it's toxic. If it's not, we might call it lunch."

"How do we test it?" Awat asked.

"With the food printer, I hope," Serene said. "Having an input-testing feature has been a required feature of the machines for millennia."

Harold looked up at the sisters, still flying back and forth overhead. "If this is where we're supposed to be, what do we do next?"

The sisters didn't respond.

"We need to top up the water tanks," Tempest said.

"I'll fetch a sample," Harold said.

"I'll go with you," Awat said. "No one should go anywhere alone until we know a lot more about this planet."

"The helmet's comms system is switched on, so call if there's trouble," Tempest said.

Reluctantly, Harold put his helmet back on.

"There's a worm," Awat said, pointing at a yellow and red creature crawling towards one of the blue flowers. "Ah, no, it's more like a centipede."

Harold bent down, holding out his hand to get a better sense of its size. Before he could, the centipede burrowed down, vanishing beneath the close-packed ground cover.

"Were you trying to add some protein to our diet?" Awat asked.

"Even after a month of monochrome meals, I'm not ready to eat insects yet."

"Since they aren't insects, as we understand the word, but insect-like creatures, you could call them fish if it helps."

"I'm not sure it does." He stood and looked upwards as they continued towards the treeline.

"What is it?"

"Nothing," Harold said. "The centipede fled as soon as my hand came near it. It's used to something trying to eat it, but there's nothing up in the sky at all."

The plain came to a sudden end at the beginning of the treeline. Looking left and right, there was a clear delineation between the two biomes. The trees themselves were perhaps thirty metres tall, and with a diameter just bigger than his outstretched arms. The trunks were covered in pointed needles that angled downward. Long pole-like boughs stuck out horizontally from the trunk in every direction, but those boughs had no branches. Like the trunks, the boughs were covered in fine needles, these angled towards the trunk. Where the needles joined the bough were small seed clusters. If the needles on the trunk and boughs were an evolutionary attempt to deter animals from getting to the seeds, it had failed.

"They're not birds," Awat whispered, pointing to a four-legged lizard-like creature, about the length of his hand, whose limbs were covered in green feathers. The creature was crawling along a nearby bough, using a small hooked claw on its forelimbs to move the needles aside before tugging the seed-cluster free. Holding it, squirrel-like, in its two front paws, it nibbled and chewed before dropping the casing to the forest floor, and continuing on. When it reached the trunk, it leaped up and out, towards the bough of a neighbouring tree. Its limbs straightened as its short feathers extended. When it landed, the feathers seemed to fold inward as the reptile began munching its way through more seeds.

"Cool," Harold whispered. At which, the creature took fright, leaping from one branch to the next until it was out of sight.

"A feathered squirrel," Awat said.

"Or a lizard-squirrel," Harold said. "Or maybe a squirrelizard. No, there's got to be a better name than that."

"We should test the needles to see if they're poisonous," Awat said as they threaded their way between the stout boughs.

"And the feathers on those gliding lizards," Harold said, looking at the ground to see if he could spot one.

As the trees had no canopies, plenty of light reached the forest floor. In addition to clusters of the blue-flowered, broad-leafed plants they had seen on the plain, were long stems topped with a puffball head, about the size of his fist, and made up of hundreds of thin green hairs. Where a tree had fallen, a sprawling vine had taken root, curling around the fallen trunk and under its patchwork bark.

"There's a feather," Awat said. "Except it's brown, not green."

"And large," Harold said, bending down to examine it. "About the length of my arm. Is it a feather? It's almost fluffy. I wonder how big those reptiles grow."

"Alan would love this," Awat said. "He always wanted to visit an alien world."

Harold stood up, the joy of discovery replaced with the reminder of how precarious their situation was.

From the images taken while in orbit, the river hadn't seemed far from the plain, but the interlocking, and overlapping, boughs created an almost impenetrable wall. Even after the river came into view, it took another quarter of an hour to reach it.

The river was five metres wide, and dotted with rocky outcrops around which the water languidly foamed white, while the shore blazed yellow with flowering moss. On the other bank, the trees were just as dense. An occasional bough jutted over the water, providing a platform for the feathered lizards to reach the mid-river rocks on which some were sunning themselves.

"I think the centipedes are the pollinators," Awat said, following one along the shore.

Harold walked onto an ironing board-shaped rock that jutted into the river. "There are fish with legs down there," he said. "Although, if they have legs, maybe they're amphibians."

"I've found a... well, a crab with no claws. It's yellow, like the moss, and I think its mouth is underneath. It's eating the centipedes."

"Oh, that's not—" he began, but stopped as the forest rustled with the sound of approaching feet. A squat, four-legged, brown-feathered beast meandered out of the treeline. About the size of a pig, it had a barrel body, short legs, and an almost flat face, and seemed nearly as startled as Harold. Its furry-brown feathers plumed outwards, making it seem three times the size.

"Shoo! Go on! Get!" Harold said.

"Shoot it!" Awat called from further down the riverbank.

Harold reached for his holstered gun, but the feathered quadruped took the initiative and charged.

Harold tried to jump obliquely back to the shore, but his footing was poor. He slipped, and fell into the shallow river. Since he'd unsealed the helmet, water began seeping in. Splashing to his feet, he tugged the helmet off, letting the water out.

On the slab of rock, the feathered beast gave a caw of triumph that abruptly ended when Awat shot it.

"Are you okay?" she asked.

"I think so," Harold said, dripping his way to dry land.

"At least we know that *is* water, not acid, and it's not instantly fatal."

Harold shivered, thinking of all the liquids it might have been. "I'll get a sample, and I think I'll head back with less sightseeing."

"And we should get the knife," Awat said.

"What for?"

"To gut and skin this animal. If it's edible, it would be a shame to waste it."

As the sun set, they gathered around a crackling fire, over which they were roasting the long tubers and slivers of flesh from the brown-feathered animal, speared on some of the forest's thinner branches.

Harold stretched, trying to ease the ache of an afternoon spent gathering firewood. He'd removed the armoured space suit. At least the day was warm enough that he and his clothes had quickly dried out.

"Those trees are a bit like a monkey puzzle tree," Harold said. "So I think they should be called a squirrelizard puzzle tree."

"That's too long a name," Serene said.

"Call it tree-one because it's the first tree we've identified," Tempest said.

"That's too boring," Serene said.

316

"Our dinner had a few organs I couldn't identify," Awat said. "But there were a heart and lungs. Like the tree, it's not dissimilar to what might be found on Earth."

"When you think about it, nor were the hounds on that ice-world," Harold said.

"Humanoids aren't the only similar species across the galaxy," Tempest said. "Maybe this was one of the worlds geo-engineered during the regency."

"It's too nice for them not to occupy it," Harold said. "You wouldn't need to force people to live here, either. Serene, are you sure this meat will be safe to eat? Serene?"

"Hang on, I'm just watching the footage from your helmet-cam again."

"Why, do you recognise that quadruped?"

"No, I'm watching it because it's hilarious." She removed her helmet. "Sorry, what did you ask?"

"Is it really safe to eat this root and that meat? If we get sick, there's nothing we can do about it."

"Nothing I tested came back as deadly, except for those green puffball plants," Serene said. "It should be edible, but it's up to you."

"Did you do a lot of hunting, Awat?" Tempest asked.

"Never. Alan and I went fishing a few times, but he's always been too restless to enjoy it. I grew up with goats."

"How do you know when it's cooked?" Tempest asked.

"Don't you do much cooking?" Awat asked.

"Not in the embassy," Tempest said. "All our food was printed, or bought. Besides, I'm vegan."

"Vegan-ish," Serene said. "There's an exception for pizza, obviously. And the occasional burger. And we never look too closely at the ingredients."

"Give it another five minutes, I think," Awat said.

"Which gives us just enough time to figure out what we're supposed to do next. Want to give us any hints, ladies?" Serene added, raising her voice and addressing the drones now perched on the saucer's hull. They didn't move.

"My drenching aside, this place seems like a hunter-gatherer's paradise," Harold said.

"Until we break a leg, cut our hands on a rock, or get attacked by an animal further up the food chain," Awat said. "We shouldn't fool ourselves. Our situation is perilous."

"I think we should top up on water, and then fly over the coastline in search of the ruins of a city," Tempest said.

"I've reviewed the footage we recorded as we landed," Serene said. "I didn't see anything that looked as if it were built."

"And we didn't see anything among the trees," Awat said.

"Right, so what do we do if we don't find any ruins, and how long do we search?" Serene asked.

"Until the sisters get bored and tell us what to do next," Harold said.

"What if they won't, or don't, or can't?" Awat asked.

Serene turned to the drones, sitting on the edge of the saucer. "Can we go back to Earth now, please?" she asked. The sisters were unresponsive. "It was worth a try."

"Unless or until they help us, I think there are four options," Tempest said. "Whichever one we pick, we can always send the message-pod off to one of the sets of coordinates we found on that red-robe. One of the locations must be a Voytay world or outpost, so we have an even chance of picking the right one."

"And what are the four options?" Awat asked.

"The first is to stay here," Tempest said. "By the look of it, we'll have enough food and water. The message-pod was supposed to be sent to somewhere in Voytay space. If we can guess the right set of coordinates, and tell them about the red-robes' plan for war, they might send someone to rescue us."

"Or they might not," Serene said.

"Then we have the other three options, which involve us travelling back to the ice-world, or to one of the two sets of coordinates held by the red-robe."

318

"And we think one is an uninhabited system, the other is run by the Voytay," Harold said.

"And we don't know how long it would take to get to any of them, or from one to the other," Tempest said. "We could run out of food, or fuel for the sub-light engines."

"What would we gain from heading back to the ice-world?" Awat asked.

"The red-robes were planning to leave," Tempest said. "By now, they might have gone. Perhaps they left a ship behind, or there's a navigation database in the hunting lodge, or on the personal device of a corpse."

"How likely is that?" Harold asked. "Isn't it more likely they obliterated the hunting lodge from orbit?"

"Possibly. Look, I know. None of them are good choices," Tempest said.

"I don't suppose you ladies want to give us a better one," Serene said, addressing the drones. They still didn't move. "Thought not."

"We don't have to decide tonight," Tempest said. "Though I think, wherever we go, we should send the message-pod somewhere else."

"There's one other option," Harold said. "We've got four months of food in that printer, yes? But it'll last four times as long if you go alone, Tempi. The three of us can remain here. You'll surely have enough food to visit all three sets of coordinates, and if there's nothing good at any of them, you can jump at random and hope you get lucky."

"We'd have no shelter, no food, no clothes, no medicine," Awat said.

"We can strip out some of the cabins for materials to build a shelter," Harold said. "Hunting seems easy enough, and we have guns. I don't know what we do about clothes, and there's nothing at all we can do about medicine. Look, I know it's a terrible plan, but unless we can solve this puzzle, it might be our best one."

Chapter 36 - The Doors Beneath Our Feet

As soon as Harold woke, he reached for the helmet. The clock, set to the old imperial standard, told him it was morning, but the external cameras said it was still the middle of the night. He removed the helmet, got dressed, and decided attempting to do some laundry was a must now that they had access to a river.

"Morning, Alan," he said as he entered the otherwise empty mess. "Not that it is morning outside."

He checked the lights on Parker's stretcher, but they still hadn't turned blue. Harold made himself a bowl of the black cubes that experience had proven really *were* the least inedible option available on the menu, and took them over to the corner where he'd be close to the stretcher. To distract himself from the food, he brought up the footage recorded as they'd fled the ice-world.

"Last night was nearly perfect," he said, speaking, as he often did, to the unconscious Parker. "It was camping like I thought it should be, especially since we got to sleep inside. I know that doesn't bode well for my idea of staying behind when Tempest leaves, but I'm sure we came here for a reason."

He began flipping through the footage recorded as they left the ice-world, pausing and zooming in on star-lit shadows, but there just wasn't enough light to make out any details. He closed them down, and brought up the footage of this planet they'd recorded from orbit. There were no lights on the night-time side of the planet, and no hints of canals or roads on the part that had been illuminated by the sun.

"All this talk of prophecies and visions has crept under my skin. I never used to believe in some guiding hand of destiny, or grand conspiracies. Okay, yes, there *was* a grand conspiracy, but the only guiding hand was an accidental shove from Sean, Celeste, or Johann. Looking back at the history of the twentieth century, Sean didn't have a plan so much as a series of mistakes that were each designed to fix an earlier blunder. Celeste acts on a whim. Johann's the Last Prophet because he led the revolution, and he led the revolution because he's the Last Prophet. The more I go over it, the more I think you were right. We got caught up in the big schemes of other people. If they had just left Earth alone, and if the Valley and the Voytay would just leave us alone, we'd... well, we'd still muck up the planet, but at least we'd have no one to blame but ourselves."

He shut the videos down, removed the helmet, and realised Awat was standing in the doorway.

"Can't sleep?" she asked.

"I can't adjust to the clock."

"You talk to Alan a lot."

"I suppose," Harold said. "If I don't speak my thoughts aloud, they pinwheel around my brain on repeat, and it's easier talking to someone. I think he can hear me, even if he can't reply."

Awat smiled. She walked over to her husband and laid a hand on his shrouded chest. "As a consequence of your childhood, you want control, or at least to feel that no one has control over you. When I was held captive by Saddam, I realised that our lives are never truly our own. The actions of others influence our path. Some have a bigger, or longer-lasting, influence than others, but it doesn't diminish our own effect on those around us, and on the future."

"Does that mean you don't believe in destiny, or you do?"

"I believe in hope," she said. "So do you, I think."

"I suppose so." He stood and crossed to the cupboard in which the sealable water bottles were kept. He began taking them out, and stacking them on the table. "We've been over every inch of the ship. There are no barrels or buckets. We'll have to collect water with these."

"That'll take a long time," Awat said.

"Not if we can draft the drones to help with the carrying," Harold said. "I'm going to see if I can make a net."

With there being little to do during their thirty-nine days in jump-space, they'd examined every inch of the ship. There were no nets, let alone bags, but in the lockers which had stored the armoured space suits were webbing for carrying tools or weapons when in zero-g. He took three, weaving the straps around each other until he had a net big enough to hold ten bottles.

The lockers were adjacent to the airlock. Through the window, a splash of daylight was washing over the plain. He returned to the mess, and found it empty, except for Alan. He loaded ten empty bottles, took a gun from the armoury, and returned to the airlock. Thinking it would be easier to navigate through the forest without wearing one of the armoured space suits, he didn't don one.

Outside, the flowers were beginning to droop, but it appeared they had been pointing upwards during the night.

"Nocturnal pollination?" he asked the plants. They appeared to nod as the rising sun caused them to droop a little more.

He trudged across the plain, with the net in one hand, and the gun in the other. Of that, he was glad when he neared the treeline. Three feathered quadrupeds had been rooting among the leaf litter. When they saw him, they extended their feathers.

"Just go somewhere else, or I'll call you breakfast," he said, raising the gun.

The animals, unfamiliar with people and their weapons, charged. Harold fired. The helmet didn't provide targeting assistance, or a warning that this particular gun had been loaded with explosive rounds. Three bolts flew from the barrel before the first blast sent him flying backwards. Dirt, leaves, flowers, and tubers fountained upwards, before raining down with varying degrees of force. Harold slowly picked himself up. Of the feathered quadrupeds there was no sign. He picked up the handgun, and looked for a physical safety catch. There didn't seem to be one. His shots had created three small craters. At the edge of each, the long tubers were exposed. The forest ahead looked forbiddingly dense. Perhaps it had been unwise to come out alone. He'd gather some of the now-disturbed roots, take them back to the ship, and return with Awat, and a different weapon. As he approached the nearest crater, the ground gave way.

He only fell for a few seconds, but he hit the ground hard, softening the landing of the soil and plants that tumbled down after him. As the hole above grew bigger, the soil, root, and plant waterfall moved further away, and he was able to take in his new surroundings. He was in a shallow cave. Above was a crevice about five metres wide and one deep, covered in a mat of soil held together by the overlapping roots of the ground-cover plants. A sinkhole, then? He switched on the helmet's light, stood, looked down, and froze. He was on the lip of a much deeper crevasse that stretched down into darkness far deeper than his light could penetrate.

Slowly, he inched backwards before turning around. In front of him was a perfectly circular tunnel.

He opened his helmet's comms, and called Awat.

"Hey, where did you disappear to?" she asked.

"Funny you should ask that. I've fallen into a hole. The ground at the edge of the plain fell away. I'm fine, but there's a deeper cave beneath this ledge, and a perfectly circular tunnel behind me."

"Like on the ice-world?"

"Could be. It's a lot smaller. Maybe three metres in diameter."

"I'll wake Serene and Tempest. Don't move."

"That won't be a problem."

For safety's sake, he took a few steps into the tunnel, before stopping with the thought that it might be home to more hounds, or something worse. There were no bones beneath his feet, only soil, and not much of it. The tunnel's walls were utterly devoid of writing. He ran his hand along the wall. It wasn't as smooth as he'd first thought, and felt more like metal than stone. He began walking down the tunnel. The soil thinned. After only a few paces more, his helmet's light shone on something utterly unlike the tunnel on the ice-world: a wall. In the wall was a solid, but recessed circle with a radius a forearm's-width shorter than the tunnel. He knocked with his knuckles, and got a dull clang in reply. There were no windows, but on the left, and halfway up, was a recess with a rod descending from the top, which ended in a hollow triangle. Was it a handle? There was no letterbox, keyhole, or bell, but maybe this was a door.

Wisdom advised caution, and this time, he was inclined to agree. He walked back to the tunnel entrance.

"Harry? Harry?" Serene's desperate voice came through on his helmet's speaker.

"Guess what I found," he said.

"You weren't answering. Are you okay?"

"I was just checking out the tunnel. It leads to a door."

"Well, stop exploring until we get there."

"Okay, but be careful around the hole. The ground is very thin."

He waited at the edge of the circular tunnel, running through the possible explanations for what lay behind the door.

"Hi, Harry. We can see the hole," Serene said. "How easy would it be to climb up?"

"Impossible without a rope."

"What about us climbing down?" Tempest asked.

"That could prove deadly. The tunnel entrance has a ledge. Below is a much deeper hole."

"Okay. Hold on. The sisters are being difficult."

"Then I'll take another look at the door while you figure it out."

He'd only taken a few steps when lights behind him made him turn around. Serene was gently lowered into the tunnel by one of her drones. The drone detached, and flew back to the surface.

"Which one is that?"

"Nemain. The other two are being stroppy."

"Really? Interesting."

"Weird tunnel," she said. "What happened?"

"Three of those feathered hogs charged at me. I fired, not realising this gun had explosive rounds. The ground gave way."

"Feathered hogs? Is that what we're calling them?"

"It did taste like pork," he said.

Nemain flew down with Awat. After depositing her on the edge of the tunnel, it flew back up through the hole.

"Weird find, Harry," Tempest said as they landed.

"I don't see any markings on the wall," Awat said. "And the material doesn't appear to be stone. This is nothing like Nineveh or the ice-world."

"I think this structure spreads out beneath the entire plain," Harold said. "The ceiling isn't far from the surface. I think that's why there are no trees on the grassland."

"That would make it massive," Tempest said. "Maybe it's a hunting lodge, buried by time."

"I thought hunting lodges were built as hollow squares," Awat said.

"True," Tempest said. "But it could still be a building."

"If it is, they built it in a canyon," Harold said. "Have you seen how deep that hole is?"

"It's probably not bottomless," Tempest said, before picking up a pebble and dropping it over the edge. A minute passed with no sound of an impact. "Or perhaps it is."

"Or it landed on all the soft dirt that just fell through the hole," Serene said. "Shall we try the door, then?"

As they moved down the short tunnel, Macha and Badb finally joined them, adding their lights to Nemain's and to the lights on their helmets. Even under the combined glare, they saw no identifiable features, markings, or symbols on the tunnel's walls before they reached the door.

"I think the triangle is either the doorbell or the locking mechanism," Harold said.

"In case there is a monstrous beast inside, Harold, you'll offer yourself to be eaten so we can escape," Serene said.

"Why me?"

"Because of the ancient saying, he who makes the hole, takes the most dangerous role." Serene reached out and pulled on the triangle.

Nothing happened, nor when she pressed, or tried to tug it forward. But when she pushed it upward, it moved. A clank came from inside, followed by a nerve-scratching creak. The door rolled aside. A breeze became a hurricane as the air around them was sucked into an airless chamber. Harold fell to his knees, holding onto the edge of the doorway so he didn't join the dirt-storm being dragged into the chamber.

When the inflow of air began to subside, Harold slowly stood up. "What was that?"

"A vacuum," Tempest said, stepping through the door into a rectangular chamber with another door at the far end.

"Could this be a spaceship's airlock?" Harold asked.

"It must be," Serene said.

"I think this is the librarian's spaceship," Harold said. This must be where your mum stashed it."

Serene turned to the sisters. "Is it?"

The drones didn't move.

"It was Nemain who inputted the navigational data," Tempest said. "And *only* Nemain who brought us down to the tunnel. The other two didn't seem to want to."

"Which is something I'll be discussing with them later," Serene said. "I assume we're agreed we just have to find out what's inside?"

"Yes, but we'll need oxygen," Tempest said.

Chapter 37 - The First Prophet's Last Prophecy

An hour later, now wearing the armoured spacesuits, they returned to the hole. This time, Macha and Badb seemed to have decided whether they helped or not, the humans wouldn't be stopped, so they assisted in flying them down to the tunnel.

"Do we have to close the outer door before we can open the inner one?" Awat asked.

"Probably," Serene said, examining the inner door, but as she pushed against the metal surface, it began to roll back into the wall without the handle being pushed upward. Loose soil began to swirl, though not as powerfully as when they'd opened the outer door.

"I think the door's broken," Harold said.

"That should be impossible," Tempest said.

The airlock led into a square corridor, about two metres wide. To the left of the airlock, ceiling and wall panels had fallen, creating a jagged obstacle course and revealing rows of otherwise hidden pipes.

"Let's go the other way," Serene said, and led them down the corridor, stopping at the first door. Next to the door, a narrow passageway branched inward.

"Any guess as to how the door opens?" Tempest asked.

"Try sliding it," Serene said.

"You try."

"Look, here, is this a panel?" Awat asked, pointing at a rectangle, just larger than her hand. When she touched it, the panel fell away, clanging to the floor. Inside was another triangular handle at the bottom of a long bar.

"So much for the chroniclers' ships being indestructible," Harold said.

"Maybe these ships are only everlasting if they're maintained," Tempest said.

"The mechanical handles are interesting," Serene said even as she reached over and pushed it up.

The doors slid ajar. A sucking draft pulled them all forward, and Serene from her feet. Harold grabbed her hand as she fell into the empty shaft that lay beyond the door. Harold fell, too, dangling over the shaft, Serene hanging from his hand. Below her, the shaft stretched down, down, down, into darkness. The pain in his shoulder was replaced by one in his shins as Tempest and Awat grabbed his legs.

"Don't let go!" Serene said.

Nemain buzzed past Harold, flew down and attached itself to Serene's back, and then lifted her upwards.

"Now you can let go," Serene added. Harold released her hand. Tempest tugged him backwards.

"Let's be a bit more careful from now on, shall we?" Tempest said as Serene brushed herself down.

Harold, still sitting, watched the newly arrived dirt billow towards the shaft. "Is it an elevator?"

"Or the shaft," Tempest said.

"Come and see this," Awat said. She'd ventured into the passageway to the side of the elevator. Serene and Tempest joined her. Harold crawled for another metre before he decided it was safe to stand.

In the floor, and next to the door, was a rectangular hatch, about one metre by two. It was closed, but had a rectangular panel in the centre identical to the one for the elevator door. Built into the wall was a ladder that almost went up to the ceiling.

"If we open the hatch, I think we'll find a ladder descending to the next level," Awat said.

"Let's not open it," Serene said. "Not until enough air's crept into this ship that we won't get sucked to a pancake death."

"If the librarian's form was a projection, why would he need a ladder?" Awat asked.

"Why would he need such a large ship?" Harold asked.

"We won't find the answers here," Tempest said.

They returned to the main corridor. At the next door, the panel concealing the handle wouldn't open.

"It's jammed," Tempest said.

"So we keep going," Serene said. "I'm starting to think this ship still has power, or the doors do. They can't be entirely mechanical. Oh, the door ahead is open."

The door led into a cabin that had been someone's bedroom before it had become a tomb. In the centre of the room lay a rectangular open box made of grey metal, half a metre wider than the skeleton lying inside it.

"Is that a coffin?" Harold asked.

"A bed," Awat said, stepping closer. "Can one of the drones shine a light here? I think this is a towani."

"It's not," Tempest said in a hoarse whisper. "No one touch anything. Harold, help me with this cupboard door."

Harold finally noticed the paintings covering the walls, except where one rectangular floor-to-ceiling panel had fallen down. That panel looked to be a cupboard door. Inside the cupboard was a small armoury containing neatly arrayed axes and blades.

"Very carefully," Tempest said as Harold bent down to lift the other side of the fallen door.

The panel was far heavier than it looked, but together, they lifted it up and leaned it next to its neighbour. While most of the chamber was covered with paintings and an occasional annotation, these two panels had a message.

"Is that machine code?"

"It's ancient and archaic," Tempest said. "But I can read it."

"Don't let us die of suspense," Serene said.

"It says: *Here sleeps Jallin, the last of those who wandered the stars. Now I am returned to the soil.*"

"Jallin? It says that? Where?" Serene said.

Tempest wordlessly pointed at the door.

"You've lost me," Harold said.

"Jallin was the first high priest," Serene said. "She was Nowan's acolyte."

"This is the Holy Prophet's ship," Tempest whispered. "Four ships crashed on Towan. One set out in search of Earth. We're standing inside it."

"It's got to be a common name," Harold said. "And there's a tradition of changing names, isn't there? So perhaps, knowing she was dying, she adopted that name for spiritual reasons."

"Then explain the axes," Tempest said. "They're identical to the one she carried in the recording."

"There's a story painted on the wall," Awat said. "There are lots of planets, and next to each are figures fighting. Sometimes fighting each other. Sometimes they're fighting animals. Here, there's a figure fighting something with tentacles."

"It's definitely no whale," Harold said.

"This is her story," Awat said, "but do you see how she's never at the centre? The centre of each picture is this figure from whom light is radiating."

"The Holy Nowan," Tempest said.

"Maybe," Serene said.

Tempest began trembling.

"Maybe we should step outside," Serene said.

"We should seal this chamber, and this ship, and not disturb anything more," Tempest said.

"She left the door open. She expected to be discovered," Awat said. "She must have pumped the air from the ship first."

"That would have killed her," Harold said.

"Perhaps she was dying," Awat said. "Or perhaps she set the air to be removed after her death. But she made sure that everything inside would be preserved."

"Exactly. It would be sacrilege to disturb it," Tempest said.

"The forest is the same elevation as the plain, near enough," Harold said. "They wouldn't construct a building in a canyon."

"I'm ninety-nine percent positive this is a ship," Serene said.

"I'm just thinking aloud. The only alternative was a building. But if this was a ship, it must have crashed, creating a crater. Over time, it filled in, and those plants grew up over it."

"Probably. Why do you think it matters?" Awat asked.

"She expected to be found. It's the second door, not counting the elevator." Harold walked back up the corridor to the door they hadn't been able to open. "This would be the first door, the room closest to the entrance. That was a tomb, not a bedroom, yes?"

"Probably," Awat said. "There were no furnishings apart from the death bed, and the closet only contained weapons."

"The mural would have taken some time to create," Harold said. "She chose that room, but not this one. Why?" He thumped the door panel.

"Don't do that!" Tempest said.

"We were brought here for a reason," Harold said, hitting the panel again. This time, it shuddered downward into the frame before sticking halfway. "You should open it, Tempi."

Tempest shook their head.

"What do you think's inside?" Awat asked.

"Open it, Tempest," Harold said.

Their hand trembling, Tempest pushed the handle upwards. With a hiss of inrushing air, the door slid open.

"Go on," Harold said, gently pushing Tempest inside before following.

This cabin had also been turned into a tomb, and had a deathbed in the centre, occupied by a single skeleton. Here, the walls had been covered with words.

Tempest turned a slow circle before the light from their helmet settled on the words above the bed. They fell to their knees. "Do you see what it says?" they whispered. *"This is Nowan who led us to freedom."*

"What does the rest of the writing say?" Harold asked. "Is it the story of what happened next?"

"No, it's the prophecy, and it's in a different hand to the annotation naming the Holy Prophet. Jallin must have added that posthumously. That section is the first of the prophecies, predicting the people would win their freedom. But it's odd. The first line, and every alternate line after it, are in machine code. It's archaic, and some

331

of the letters are different, but it's readable. The line beneath, I don't know what that says. I don't recognise the language."

"I do," Awat said. "It's the same language as the inscription in the tunnel on the ice-world and in Iraq. This is our primer. This is how we translate those carvings."

Tempest slowly stood up, pointing their hand at the wall as they silently read the scripture. "This part lists the prophecies concerning how they will make new homes on many worlds and meet many new peoples. It's often seen to be predicting the rise of the empire. These final paragraphs speak of new prophets and a last prophet who will bring in an era of peace. But this section on the wall with the door, this I don't know."

"It's more prophecies?" Harold asked.

"I think so. The first matches something Clee once said. Members of the last prophet's clan will determine whether all shall live in peace, or that all shall die, after they discover this tomb."

"Is that us?" Serene asked.

"It is," Tempest whispered in utter wonderment.

Epilogue - Chance, Destiny, or a Meticulously Orchestrated Plan

After ensuring they had made a recording of the walls of both tombs, they sealed Nowan's burial chamber and returned to the ship. While Tempest went to their cabin to pray, Awat and Serene went to the control room, and Harold went to the galley. He sat next to the stretcher, trying to collect his thoughts, but each time he thought he had a grip on them, they scattered and split, birthing more questions and doubts.

He wasn't sure how long he sat there, though he was growing hungry when Serene broadcast a ship-wide announcement. "Everyone to the control room, please."

Harold met Tempest just outside the door.

"How are you holding up?" Harold asked. Tempest merely shook their head.

"There you are," Serene said as they entered. She sat in the pilot's chair. Awat was at her usual workstation, where she'd brought up an image of the prophecy written on the walls of Nowan's tomb, and the carvings from the ice-world's tunnel, complete with the red-robe's annotation.

"I have so many questions," Harold said.

"I bet I have more," Serene said. "Like what happened to the rest of the ship's crew, and why didn't Nowan go with them? Was this the first planet they came to after Towan I, or were there others? And if this is one of the five ships, and if they were commanded by tentacled aliens, why is there a ladder? Why are the corridors the right height for humanoids?"

"Why didn't Mum ever tell us?" Tempest said.

The group grew silent.

"She knew about it long before we came onto the scene," Harold said. "She could have told Johann after he brought your dad back to Earth."

"Exactly," Tempest said.

"No, I mean that he wasn't the right person, and that wasn't the right time. You said one of the new prophecies is about the ship, and tomb, being discovered by members of the last prophet's clan. It doesn't say the last prophet discovered it. So until you two came along, that was only Gunther and Greta."

"And Dad," Serene said. "And now it includes you, Harry, though I suppose you've always been part of the clan even before we knew it. And it now includes Awat, and by extension, Alan and Yūnus."

"Why?" Awat asked, briefly turning away from her screens.

"Well, you can't go through what we've been through and not form a bond," Serene said. "But mostly because the prophecy said the prophet's clan would discover the ship. You helped discover the ship, so you must be part of the clan."

"Or the prophecy is invalid," Tempest said.

"Why?" Serene asked.

"Because the drones brought us here. We didn't discover the ship; Mum did. She knew what the prophecy was and so engineered that it would be fulfilled."

"No, the sisters brought us to the system," Serene said, "but Harold picked the landing site, and blew a hole in the ground."

"But if he hadn't, maybe the sisters would have brought us here eventually," Tempest said.

"That's irrelevant because Harold did pick a spot he thought was best, and look what we found," Serene said. "How is that not the guiding hand of destiny?"

Harold found himself looking at his hands with newfound suspicion. "Nemain brought us here," he said. "The other two were reluctant to take us down into the hole. I don't think they were unanimous in their decision that we should come here. Remember how they were reluctant to bring Alan and Awat with us back on the ice-world? I think it was supposed to be just us three."

"Well, we're all here now," Serene said.

"But why did Mum keep this a secret?" Tempest asked.

"For the same reason she didn't tell the towani emperors where Earth was," Harold said. "By which I mean she's got a reason, but until she explains it to us, there's not much point guessing."

"I think I have something," Awat said. "We don't know the date of the carvings, and we don't know precisely who wrote the words on the tunnel on the ice-world. But if you look at the words used to describe the ancestral towani's abduction, you can see the similarities with the beginning of the tunnel's inscription. If we say it was by the librarian, and the first few lines are a preamble, it says he *chose* exile after failing to stop other enslavements. If I'm right, this next section speaks of battles and fighting. Then this line doesn't talk about how his brother chose to die, but how he chose to live."

"What does that mean?" Harold asked.

"I think it means that a chronicler went with the Neanderthals when they were abducted from Earth. Why wouldn't they? It's what they do, observing other species. Thousands of years later, she returned to Earth, taking the form of a jajan and then the Neanderthal we saw in the footage."

"And the librarian chose exile on the ice-world, until Mum sent him to Earth as a sort of replacement," Serene said.

"Perhaps going to Earth was seen as exile," Awat said. "Each answer creates more questions, and it will take time before we can answer even a fraction, but I think we can be certain that the red-robe's translation is inaccurate."

"Of course it is," Harold said. "Celeste isn't going to leave instructions on how to kill her, or something as explosive as a confession to being behind the abduction, lying around. They're observers, Tempi. They watch but don't interfere."

"The librarian tried to *prevent* more abductions, and Mum sent us here. How is that not interfering?"

"That's a theological question best answered by decoding the rest of the inscription," Awat said. She leaned back in her chair. "This is astonishing. It's the greatest archaeological find in fifty thousand years and across all the planets in the galaxy."

"It can't be a find because it wasn't lost," Tempest said. "Not really. Not if Mum knew where it was."

"We can, and will, be debating that for years," Serene said. "What do we do now?"

"Tempi, would it be sacrilege if we were to search Nowan's ship for something we can use to carry water?" Harold asked.

"What?"

"As important as this discovery is, we're still facing the same problem as last night," Harold said. "We need more water, and then we need to get back in contact with the rest of the galaxy."

"Could that ship have a navigation database?" Awat asked.

"I... no," Tempest said, shaking their head. "The Holy Nowan didn't know where Earth was. If there is a map, it definitely won't show our home. Any systems they have will be so antiquated, they won't be compatible with ours, assuming they haven't been corrupted by time."

"We should look," Serene said. "Respectfully, of course."

"I suppose so," Tempest said.

"And could we borrow a barrel?" Harold asked.

"If we can find one, and as long as we return it," Tempest said. "If it's in aid of bringing this new truth to the faithful, despite what that might do to the faith, then I think it would be allowed."

"Great," Harold said. "We should get something to eat and then return to the prophet's ship. Tonight, we can discuss what we do next."

"I'll stay here and work on the translation," Awat said.

"I'll see you in the galley in a few minutes," Harold said. "I want to get the soil out of my boots."

He left the control room and headed back to his cabin. In truth, he wanted a few minutes to think.

Had it been chance that he'd selected this plain as their landing site? If the sisters could operate the jump engine, surely they could manipulate the map the ship's cameras had generated so the plain was centred on his screen when it came time to pick a spot to land. Could they have lured the three feathered-hogs to that part of the forest? And could they have moved the weapons in the armoury around so it was inevitable that he take a gun loaded with explosive rounds? The answer to all had to be yes, it was possible. But had they done it?

He had an idea why Celeste wanted the ship to be found by the three of them. Nowan had never returned to Earth, and so there was no way that the people of Terra were descended from that lost tribe. Thus, having the missing ship discovered by sapiens would ensure Earth retained a central role in the faith, strengthening the bond with the towani. That was good for sapiens, but why was it good for Celeste? To that, he had no answer.

Celeste had told Sean that departing Earth with Johann would change the galaxy forever. She hadn't said it would bring peace, though Harold's reading of Earth's history told him that whenever peace arrived, it never stayed for long. Maybe this discovery would bring peace between the Voytay and the Valley, *true* peace, at least for a time. First, they had to spread the news. And the first step to achieving that was to follow the prophet's words and to keep going forward.

To be continued…

Printed in Great Britain
by Amazon